D0849082

THE
STARS
COMPEL

Tor Books by Michaela Roessner

Vanishing Point
The Stars Dispose
The Stars Compel

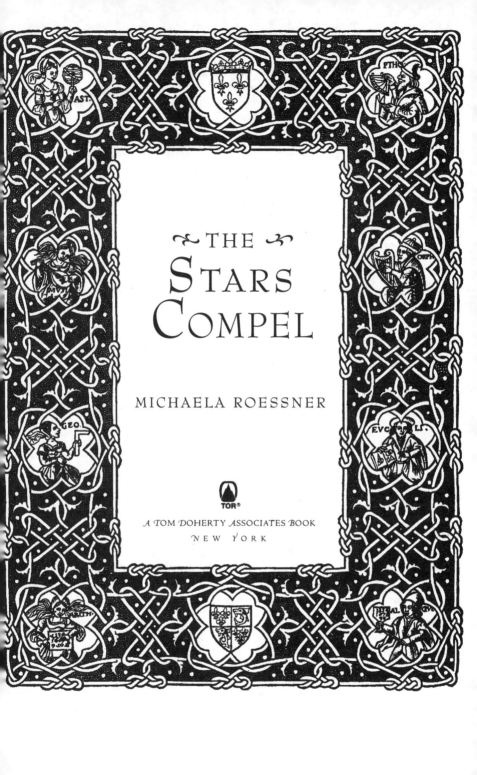

❧ THE ❧
STARS
COMPEL

MICHAELA ROESSNER

TOR®

A TOM DOHERTY ASSOCIATES BOOK
NEW YORK

THE STARS COMPEL

This book is printed on acid-free paper.

Edited by Beth Meacham

A Tor Book
Published by Tom Doherty Associates, LLC
175 Fifth Avenue
New York, NY 10010

www.tor.com

Tor® is a registered trademark of Tom Doherty Associates, LLC

Library of Congress Cataloging-in-Publication Data

Roessner, Michaela.
    The stars compel / Michaela Roessner. — 1st ed.
      p.   cm.
    "A Tom Doherty Associates book."
    Sequel to: The stars dispose.
    ISBN 0-312-85755-1 (alk. paper)
    1. Catherine de Médicis, Queen, consort of Henry II, King of France, 1519–1589 Fiction. 2. Florence (Italy)—History—1421–1737 Fiction. 3. Rome (Italy)—History—1420–1798 Fiction.   I. Title
PS3568.O3675S72 1999
813'.54—dc21   99-36368
                                                            CIP

First Edition: October 1999

Printed in the United States of America

0 9 8 7 6 5 4 3 2 1

This book is dedicated to

my father, Donald Stirling Roessner,
and
Faraway, my muse and best beloved

CONTENTS

I

Rome

1

October 12, 1530

An artist can't see his work until he steps back far enough away from it to see it as a whole. At that point he views its composition, examines its balance in terms of lights and darks, the different hues of color. In some fashion he'll liken it to all the art he's seen or made up to that point in his life.

In a similar fashion, the young cook Tommaso Arista only truly began to understand his native city of Florence on the day he arrived in Rome as a member of *Duchessina* Caterina de' Medici's entourage. Like a peasant, he gaped at the city that would be his new home, and felt the first pangs of homesickness for Florence.

Florence's buildings were the pride of generations of skilled architects. Each structure was unique, yet compatible with its neighbors. They sat tidily next to each other like individual but responsible citizens in a civilized, well-organized state.

In contrast, Rome epitomized chaos. Where Florence was self-contained, Rome sprawled. The ancient emperors' vast palaces lay in giant-bone mounds of broken white pillars and tumbled walls and cornices on Palatine Hill. Sheep the same shade of white as those sad remains drank from rain puddles and grazed in thatches of dark green rosemary crawling over the shattered masonry. Goats leapt and played on toppled arches.

Below the Palatine, graceless buildings from Rome's dark post-Empire centuries crawled through the ruins like mold, gaining a foothold wherever they could in the decay. Some palazzis were burnt out, remnants of the savagery of the *reiters* during the sack of Rome three years earlier. Scattered here and there, new or still under construction, edifices in the reinvented classical style stood tall, springing from the remnants that had inspired them, their very substance bought at the past's expense: Huge ox-driven wagons laden with marble blocks plundered from ancient sites unloaded their booty before half-built villas, their task impeded by the pools and muck remaining from the torrential storm that had flooded Rome several days before.

Tommaso was both fascinated and appalled.

Michelangelo Buonarotti rode up beside the cart that Tommaso shared with Michelangelo's apprentice Ascancio. "If only I had some paper, charcoal and a more stable seat for a drawing board than this mare! I would love to capture the expression on your face at this moment. What does that gaze mean, Tommaso?"

Tommaso looked up at the sculptor he loved as much as he did his native city.

"It's so different here, so fragmented. Florence is so *whole*. So complete, like a person, with a character one can grasp." He shook his head at his failure to convey his thoughts. "You know words aren't my greatest strength."

Michelangelo grinned. "Your modesty does you disservice. You express yourself well. But it *would* be easier to sketch both places and set the drawings side by side, letting the images speak by way of contrast more clearly than our voices can."

Tommaso looked at Michelangelo gratefully. The sculptor understood. As always.

Michelangelo's mare danced with impatience at being held back with the draft horses. She fidgeted to return to the head of the entourage and the companionship of the Strozzi brothers' lively mounts. "Rome is old and rawly new at the same time," the sculptor said. "It lacks the noble soundness of our estimable Florence, but in compensation offers opportunities by way of its very deficiencies. Those with talent, such as yourself, Tommaso, do well here."

Ascancio had said nothing, but after Michelangelo rode off Tommaso looked at the apprentice sharply. "What are you smiling so slyly about?"

"My handsome, auburn-haired friend, I smile with nothing but the pleasure of witnessing pleasant, well-considered discourse," Ascancio protested. Then he coughed. "And of course, at the enjoyment of the good humor your presence always puts my master in." He ducked as Tommaso swatted at him.

Pope Clement had decided that his cousin, the little *Duchessina* Caterina, would for the duration of her stay in Rome live with another de' Medici relative, Lucrezia Salviati. Madonna Salviati was one of Lorenzo il Magnífico's daughters and Caterina's great-aunt.

As the entourage approached its destination Tommaso saw that the Salviati mansion was far grander than the home of the physician and occultist Ruggiero, where Tommaso had been raised, yet a little more modest than either the de' Medici palace or the foreboding Palazzo Salviati in Florence.

Tommaso now understood the wisdom of the choices of Caterina's escort. It would have been difficult to absorb her entire retinue into that building. But once she was safely delivered to her great-aunt, her cousins Piero and Leone Strozzi and their men-at-arms would retire to a Roman palazzo maintained by their own family. Michelangelo had traveled more lightly than the Strozzi brothers, bringing only three carts, his assistant Pietro Urbino de Pistoia, his apprentice Ascancio Condivi and two servants. The sculptor would also constitute no burden for the Salviatis: He, too, had a studio with living quarters in Rome.

At this moment the street was having difficulty absorbing Caterina's entourage. The Salviati mansion sat squarely in one of the newly built-up sections of Rome. Not only did the convoy of carts, carriages and horsemen block the route's regular traffic as it maneuvered around deep puddles, but it had attracted a crowd of curious onlookers. It took several minutes for Caterina's carriage to deploy its way to the steps before the great front doors.

Then, as if on cue, the portals flung open. Servants and elegantly dressed Salviati family members swarmed out. They met the crush of the Strozzi youths and their retinue like the front lines of two armies engaging, but with cries of delight and good cheer instead of battle shouts. A corridor opened up in the phalanx of people before Caterina's carriage. Tommaso could barely see the top of Caterina's head as she left the carriage, her golden hair elaborately coiffed high. She made her way to the mansion's steps and the gray-haired matronly woman who waited there with outstretched arms. Two ladies-in-waiting followed closely behind the *Duchessina*. The crowd surged in to fill the gap behind them. Tommaso stood up in the cart and strained to see, but the young girl he'd chosen to follow all this long way was gone.

"She's inside already," Ascancio said. "They wouldn't leave her out in public view for long."

Tommaso looked at the apprentice, knowing what Ascancio implied. Since the sack of Rome, Pope Clement suffered the least esteem of any pontiff within memory. It wouldn't be wise to leave a young relative of the Pope's exposed for long to the Roman populace at large. There were too many who'd lost everything to the *reiters* during the sack, thanks to Clement's incompetent diplomacy. Caterina was a pawn too valuable not to attract the attention of those desiring revenge.

Tommaso gazed over the crowd with anxious eyes. Did he see bitterness in some of those faces? The emptiness of grief and loss, leavened only by hatred? Those thronging just in front of the mansion were Salviati, Strozzi and Medici retainers, many of them friends separated the past few years by Rome's sack and Florence's plague and siege. There he saw only gladness as old comrades embraced each other.

A flare of red near the steps caught Tommaso's attention. A cleric wearing a Cardinal's scarlet robes engaged Leone Strozzi in dialogue. Cardinal Passerini? The man's back was to Tommaso, but surely it couldn't be the former tyrant of Florence—Leone's face was too animated and amiable. Tommaso knew well how much the Strozzi heirs disliked Cardinal Passerini.

What about the Roman citizens milling about, trying to get around the edges of the entourage? Tommaso couldn't read their faces clearly. He hoped the resentment he glimpsed there was only that of ordinary tradespeople delayed in going about their business.

"I'll bid leave of you for now, good Ascancio," Tommaso said, leaping from the cart.

Ascancio reached down to clasp Tommaso's hand. "When you have settled into your new abode and duties, remember that Master Buonarotti gave you good directions to the *bottega*," he said. "I expect to see you soon. In this new place, know that I'll be anxious to lay eyes on a familiar, friendly Florentine face."

"As will I," Tommaso replied. He joined in at the end of the line of Caterina's servants and baggage carts progressing the long way around to the back entrance to the mansion. He rounded the ornate back gatepost with the last of the procession, and stopped to help the house steward swing the great gates closed and lock them at top and at bottom.

Looking up from this task Tommaso came face-to-face—only the ornate wrought iron of the gate stood between them—with a shabby youth near to his own age, wearing threadbare, once-elegant raiment.

At last Tommaso found the sort of visage he'd sought in the crowd out front: sour, envious, completely poisoned with rancor. Tommaso shivered, glad that the young man stood on the outside and he on the inside.

"You've refurbished this suite," Caterina said, looking around the rooms she'd been led to. "Before, tapestries hung from the walls. The bed was bigger, with a carved oak headboard."

Now intarsia paneled the walls of the salon, a sort of receiving room. The bed in the master bedroom was of a comfortable size, although much smaller than the predecessor that Caterina remembered. The new bed sported a *baldacchino* with a full canopy and *piumacci* cushions of amber-colored velvet. Rugs lined the floor, so soft and thick that walking on them felt like walking across the bed.

"They've been refurbished to suit an heiress of the house, and a descendant of Florence's leaders." Lucrezia Salviati gestured toward the intarsia. Paper-thin strips of glowing, exotic woods had been cut and assembled into a clever, puzzlelike picture of Florence. The Arno river wandered through the middle of the composition, all its beautiful bridges perfectly reproduced from highly polished slivers of wood.

"If anything displeases you, it can be rearranged to your taste. In earlier years these rooms quartered visitors. I'm amazed you remember. You were still a little girl when Giulio sent you off to Florence." Lucrezia Salviati might be one of the few people in the entire world who still referred to Pope Clement by his boyhood name. "Now look at you—a young lady of eleven. But for your hair and eyes I wouldn't have recognized you."

"My hair, my eyes and the fact I arrived in the most ornate, *palle*-encrusted carriage the de' Medici coach house had to offer. That should put Alessandro's nose nicely out of joint when he takes up residence and finds it gone."

Lucrezia Salviati tried to muster a stern look at Caterina's flippancy, but gave up and settled for a grimace of discomfort.

"The servants will unpack your baggage for you, my darling," Lucrezia admonished gently as Caterina unhooked the latch on the open-weave wicker basket she'd insisted on carrying into the palazzo herself.

"Indeed they shall," Caterina agreed, setting the basket down. "All but this piece. It would be discourteous to restrain my traveling companion a whit longer than necessary." She lifted the lid and a tortoiseshell cat, fluffy with indignation, hopped out onto the floor.

"Your small attendant is beautifully marked, like Joseph and his coat of many colors. Perhaps, after her long journey, she might wish to attend to her natural needs." Lucrezia motioned to one of the maids. "Valerina, take my grandniece's pet to the garden, that she might be acquainted with the proper place to relieve herself."

The servant picked up the cat and left the room. Lucrezia Salviati looked after her thoughtfully. "Your catling takes me back to my youth. I remember exactly such a creature stalking about the halls of our palazzo in Florence, in my father's day. I believe she belonged to the kitchen help, but one would have thought her the mistress of the manor, such queenly airs she gave herself."

Caterina smiled and said nothing.

2

Caterina did not send a maid to summon Tommaso to her suite until late, well after supper. She received him while seated behind a small ebony desk inlaid with a pattern of green malachite grapevines twining around ivory swans. One lady-in-waiting was acting as her secretary, sorting through several sheaves of paper. Now that Caterina's things had been taken care of, the other women of the entourage were unpacking and organizing their own clothing and toiletries. They were being helped by some Roman ladies whom Lucrezia Salviati had selected to join Caterina's entourage. A Salviati maid stood on a step stool filling then lighting the suite's hanging censers with a blend of dried sage and lavender. After an afternoon spent working in the meaty, oily steam of the kitchen, the scent refreshed Tommaso.

"Have you settled in, Tommaso? Have the staff here adequately accommodated you?" Caterina asked.

Tommaso bowed low. "Indeed, *Duchessina*, I've been received graciously, even eagerly." Little surprise there. Three years after the slaughter of the sack of Rome, the city still suffered a shortage of skilled domestics.

Yet for all their pleasure at gaining an extra pair of skilled hands, the Salviati chefs had seemed uncertain for a moment when he'd introduced himself. "Arista? From the House of Cavalieri? Why have you been sent here? . . . not that we're complaining."

Tommaso was equally bewildered. "Cavalieri? No, I just arrived from Florence with the *Duchessina* Caterina de' Medici. I'm her personal cook."

"Ah, ah, of course. Pardon the confusion. We expected the little *Duchessina* to arrive with her own chef. We hadn't been told your name. Arista? Imagine that. And we didn't expect someone so young."

Tommaso flushed and was glad that he'd grown tall quickly and looked at least a year or two older than fifteen.

Should he mention the mix-up to Caterina? No, it wouldn't be fitting to take up her time with such a trivial matter.

"A journeyman showed me the living quarters and helped me settle in. Then with kind, flattering words he petitioned me to aid them in preparing the evening's repast," Tommaso finished.

"I'm pleased you've been properly welcomed, but be wary of over-extending yourself," Caterina warned. "I intend you for my master chef, Tommaso. While it's true that it will benefit your culinary development to assist in the preparation of this manor's banquets, refrain from all but the largest and grandest occasions. Most of the time you'll be too busy cooking for me to volunteer for extra duty."

Tommaso glanced around at the bevy of maids and ladies-in-waiting adorning Caterina's apartment. He blanched.

Caterina understood his look. She smiled. "No, you'll not be responsible for cooking all the daily meals for me and my ladies. Those will be provided by the main kitchen. Instead, I need your able assistance with these." She spread her hands, indicating the sheets of paper covering her desk and the batch her "secretary" was sorting through.

"I've been here less than a day and am already besieged with requests—a visit here, an audience there." She riffled some of the pages. "I'm expected to entertain, and that will include refreshments. Not heavy meals, but the kind of light fare that predisposes goodwill."

"Of course, how could I have forgotten?" Tommaso said, bowing low again. "All your childhood comrades, from your earliest years here in Rome with your Aunt Clarice Strozzi—they must be anxious to renew their friendship."

Caterina waved her "secretary" away, instructing her to fetch more ink and writing paper from the house steward. Once the woman left the room Caterina said, "Yes, there are some of those here too." She dropped her voice low but continued in a conversational tone, rather than in an attention attracting whisper. "Those of my friends who survived the Sack, no thanks to my Holy cousin's cupidity. But most of these requests and queries, good Tommaso, are aristocratic horse traders, come to inspect the horse."

Tommaso knit his brow. He didn't have an inkling as to what she was talking about.

Caterina chuckled at his confusion, but there was a bitter undertone to her mirth. "Myself, my gossip. I am the horse to be traded. My cousin the Pope is receiving marriage bids for me. I'll be scrutinized closely for my abilities and virtues. Scrutinized almost as closely as Clement will scrutinize my prospective bridegrooms for political advantage and wealth."

Tommaso didn't know why he felt shocked. From the day he'd first met her he'd known this would be Caterina's fate. But there was a cold look in her eyes that told him she meant to have, in some way, a say in the proceedings.

She picked through the missives, then sorted out and passed a handful to him. "These are the first within the next few weeks. Set them into your schedule and then return them to me. We'll begin discussing appropriate menus the day after tomorrow. My relatives are freeing up some of my estate so I might practice management skills. I have a budget allocated for you. In the morning familiarize yourself with the Roman markets and what they have to offer."

Tommaso reached for the papers, but Caterina didn't relinquish them immediately.

"Most of these visitors will come calling from residences here in Rome, but others will be staying as guests of my Aunt Lucrezia in this very house. I'll require you to prepare and present small delicacies for these guests in their rooms from time to time, as a gesture of my esteem and regard for them."

Her voice dropped even lower. "Tommaso, my gossip, there are few I can trust here. Only you and two or three others. Besides toiling as my good cook, I need you to serve me as another set of eyes and ears— you can reach places unnoticed where I cannot go at all. I mean to act, Tommaso. But first I must know what Clement plans for me, and who are his friends, and who might become mine."

Tommaso nodded. She released the papers to him. His mouth was dry. He knew exactly what Caterina was asking of him.

Caterina smiled, more genuinely this time. Tommaso guessed that his fear amused her. "Take heart, Tommaso. Is this not what you were born to do? I have every confidence in you. Have you not already faced greater danger than the kitchen in my behalf?"

"With the *Duchessina*'s pardon, I believe all the dangers she refers to actually *did* take place in, or near, kitchens," Tommaso said. The kitchens of the Medici palazzo in Florence when it was stormed by the mob, and earlier on its steps when Caterina was threatened by her ostensible half brother Alessandro de' Medici. The kitchen of the convent of the Murate when Florence's *Signoria* came to spirit Caterina away to an early death.

Caterina laughed, sounding for the first time like an eleven-year-old girl. Her ladies-in-waiting and maids all looked up, attentive as a pack of hounds.

"By the Wise Three, you are right, Tommaso." She shuffled the remaining papers together, and her attendants lowered their heads.

"But that is not all, Tommaso. I wish you to continue some schooling in the classics and also in art. It's not decided with whom yet. Perhaps a fellow Florentine."

Tommaso's heart quickened. *With Michelangelo. With Michelangelo*, it thrummed. But Caterina wouldn't choose Michelangelo. Tommaso was sure she knew of his liaison with the great artist and that she wouldn't place either of them in such an indiscreet position.

"Benevenuto Cellini might do well," she mused. "Or perhaps not," she said, smiling at Tommaso's involuntary grimace. "Cellini *is* difficult to stomach at times.

"But there is one other I've heard of that I insist you train with: one Bartolommeo Scappi. He's a fashionable chef-for-hire of some renown. He's making his mark in that same integration of art and cuisine in which you've shown such talent. You'll be introduced to him at the end of the week." The finality of Caterina's tone indicated their audience was at an end. Tommaso bowed low and backed out of the room.

Still unfamiliar with the layout of the Salviati mansion, and with no maid to guide him back, Tommaso lost his way trying to return to the kitchen. The Salviatis were so wealthy that rugs carpeted even the hallways; if he'd only paid attention, he could have used their different patterns as a map to return him to the kitchen. He stopped to get his bearings, breathing slowly, thoughtfully; the slightest whiff of cooking food would guide him in the right direction.

While he was thus occupied a group of boisterous laughing young men turned down the hallway in his direction. Tommaso flattened himself against the wall to make way for them.

He'd never seen such a band of youths before in his life. Most sported dark-colored skin, in hues ranging from swarthy honey to cherry wood to dusty ebony. Their features were equally exotic. Tommaso easily recognized those with almond-shaped eyes and high cheekbones: Tartars were commonly used as slaves in Florence. The first and only maiden he'd ever been attracted to had been a half-Tartar slave in the kitchen of his family's employer, Ruggiero the Old.

And he knew the race of some of the others: he'd met dark brown Moors before. But there were those whose skin gleamed truly black, like obsidian, and whose startlingly full, finely etched lips could have been sculpted by Michelangelo himself.

Every single young blade, regardless of their various barbaric bloodlines, boasted the physique and grace of an accomplished athlete. The speech of all these young men, as they chattered merrily, bore a kind of resemblance to their garb: Italian, but barely recognizable, colorfully accented and gaudily foreign. In the middle of the crowd bloomed the brightest raiment of all, the deep scarlet reserved for cardinals. Tommaso remembered the cardinal's robes he'd glimpsed in the throng of Salviati householders. Tommaso frowned. He knew he was unreasonable, but since the day his family had run afoul of the dreadful, incompetent Cardinal Passerini, Tommaso mistrusted the upper echelons of the clergy.

. "Such an expression on such a beautiful face," exclaimed a fellow with mahogany red-brown skin and highly oiled wavy black hair. His accent was so thick that at first Tommaso didn't understand him. "Such fairness marred by—what? discontent? disapproval?—is in discord with the proper harmonious nature of the universe."

Tommaso mumbled an apology. As he edged past the man, his nose filled with the pungent reek of the fellow's hair oil—a blend of clove, mace and spices Tommaso couldn't identify. Tommaso's eyes were almost as blistered as his olfactory senses. The man wore an ensemble riotous with color: a saffron-and-gold jacket piped with crimson, hanging down over green-and-violet leggings. The colors combined in such an eye-jarring manner that Tommaso wondered what *would* constitute harmony in the fellow's personal universe.

"Tommaso, are you suddenly shy? Surely you don't mean to shun old friends."

Tommaso spun around. He'd know that voice anywhere, though he hadn't heard it in three years. "Ippolito?"

Ippolito de' Medici stepped out from the middle of the crowd. All Tommaso could do was gape.

The de' Medici heir appeared no different than what one might expect from three years of transition from youth to manhood. He now sported an elegant black beard and moustache and had grown a little taller. But his huge, dark de' Medici eyes (so like Caterina's) and his mellifluous voice were the same. He was still one of the handsomest human beings Tommaso could ever have imagined.

What shocked Tommaso were the red cardinal's robes Ippolito wore.

"Ah! I see by your expression that you hadn't heard of my, uh, change of status. Or, I'm sure, the circumstances leading up to it," Ippolito said with a rueful smile. "As an old friend, I must rectify that. I assume you're still well connected in the domain of the kitchen? Good. If you'd be willing to dull my own and my companions' appetites, I'll relate to you the events leading to my current strange situation."

Tommaso no longer had to worry about finding his way back to the kitchen—he just let himself be carried along by Ippolito's entourage.

In the kitchen, the staff mock-grimaced at the descending horde and jestingly grumbled, evidently accustomed to invasions by Ippolito's compatriots.

Tommaso set a large pot of oil to heat and directed two of Ippolito's comrades—a Tartar and a Moor—to slice several loaves of bread. Then, while Tommaso assembled olive oil, onions, lemon juice, spices and some leftover fish, Ippolito told his tale.

"After fleeing Florence, Passerini, Alessandro and I wandered about the countryside," Ippolito said, seating himself on a stool by a large worktable. "We couldn't return to Rome, of course, since the Imperial forces controlled the city and Clement was still a captive in Sant' Angel. So the three of us moved from family estate to family estate, Passerini terrified that agents of the Emperor, agents of the *Signoria*, even agents of the Pope, all searched to assassinate him."

"But Passerini *is* an agent of the Pope," Tommaso interjected.

Ippolito smiled. "Yes, and Passerini feared that my cousin, His Eminence, would punish him for the incompetence which resulted in our being driven out of Florence. And Clement *would* have imprisoned him, I'm sure, if He Himself hadn't been imprisoned in the ecclesiastical palace. By the time Clement escaped He'd had months to brood on the subject and was laying blame elsewhere."

"On Florence and the *Signoria*," Tommaso said, hefting a cleaver and chopping the onion with forceful blows.

"Exactly," said Ippolito. "In the meantime, Passerini came to wax quite self-congratulatory, for the plague descended first on Florence, then on nearby towns and villages, and eventually arrived here in Rome. Yet the three of us managed to evade it entirely.

"I, however, was near madness from Passerini and Alessandro's constant company. For Passerini I feel disgust and scorn, nothing more. He's scarce worth expending even those emotions on. But my feelings toward Alessandro, whom I'd only disliked before, blossomed into full-blown hatred, starting with his unacceptable behavior toward your siblings, Tommaso. What kind of man bullies children, then murders their little cat before their eyes?" Ippolito's handsome dark features twisted with anger.

Tommaso, mashing the tuna, onion, oil, spices and lemon juice together in a large mortar, was grateful to the raw onion fumes for the water welling up in his eyes. Ginevra, Beatrice, Pietro—his lost sisters and brother, tortured by the plague before it killed them, dying in a rat-infested farmhouse. Tommaso ground down as hard as he could on the pestle.

"Tommaso, I regret so many things: that I let myself be forced away from Florence; that I could not find a way to return; that I was not by Caterina's side during the plague. But I regret nothing so much as my belated arrival on the bridge that day," Ippolito said softly.

Tommaso could only nod through his tears.

"That was the beginning of my committed antipathy toward my cousin," Ippolito continued. "Once Clement left Orvieto and resumed power here, we also returned, Alessandro and I quarreling at every opportunity.

"The Pope commenced his intrigues to place Florence under siege and regain de' Medici control of the Florentine government. He seemed insensate to the danger he was placing Caterina, Aunt Clarice and her children, and all our old family friends and supporters in Florence in. Nothing mattered but the seething heat of his revenge."

The oil in the pot simmered. Tommaso sprinkled in a handful of fresh sage leaves to flavor it, then motioned one of Ippolito's friends, a fellow who looked as if he might also be Italian, to slide the bread slices in. They met the oil's surface with an angry sizzle.

"I debated at length with Clement, trying to alter His course," Ippolito said. "Alessandro of course argued against me. His eyes shining with greed for gold, my cousin spoke of the fortune to be made from the eventual confiscation of our enemies' estates."

Tommaso examined the *crostini*'s progress as they bobbed about, gilding in their oily scalding bath. Ippolito hadn't lowered his voice during his litany. Tommaso cast a sidelong glance at the rest of the kitchen crew. They continued their own chores with no show of reaction. Evidently they felt as little love for Alessandro as Ippolito did.

"My pleading came to nought. The Emperor's forces besieged Florence. From that time on I didn't expend precious breath in futile debate with His Eminence, though I still fought with Alessandro. I began to work clandestinely at cross-purposes to their plans, arranging for supplies to be smuggled into Florence, and bankrolling when I could Francesco Ferrucci's efforts, through lines of communication I'd already established to trusted friends in the city."

Tommaso knew who Ippolito spoke of: Tommaso's own family's employer, Ruggiero the physician and astrologer.

"That's how you were able to smuggle in the lion brooch for the *Duchessina* on the Epiphany before the siege began," Tommaso said.

"Exactly," Ippolito said.

Tommaso ladled the crisped bread out of the oil with a slotted spoon and laid the slices on a large platter. Before Tommaso could turn to ask him, the Italian-looking youth began spreading the fish-and-onion paste on the *crostini*.

"I don't think His Eminence ever knew for certain that I worked against Him, but I suspect He suspected. Once it became clear that the siege was coming to an end, the expatriate Florentine population here in Rome made noises to the effect that they preferred that I return to Florence to head the postsiege government instead of Alessandro. They knew the city would receive mercy from me." Ippolito shrugged. Everyone knew how that had turned out. Even now Alessandro was on his way back to Florence.

"If it were *only* that, at the very least you'd not be trapped in Cardinal's robes this day," the *crostini* spreader said, finishing his task. "Tell your young friend the whole tale."

Tommaso looked up. The young man was not only Italian, but his accent marked him as a fellow Tuscan.

"That's true, Pier Antonio," Ippolito said. "I fear I overplayed my hand. I'd taken to defying Clement openly, arranging to be unavailable when He wished to set me tasks, or openly refusing His commissions, such as taking a command in the forces besieging Florence. As His Eminence's plans for Alessandro to return to Florence as its Duke progressed and Caterina's arrival in Rome loomed imminent, I believe Clement feared I might slip away to Florence, prevent Caterina from leaving there, and with her compliance accomplish a takeover of the government."

"Which is exactly what you *were* thinking, and exactly what you should have done," Pier Antonio said, setting the *crostini*-covered platter down on the table with an emphatic thump.

Ippolito waved his hand wearily. "The siege ended when Florence ran out of ammunition and food. I heard of people starving in the streets. They couldn't have withstood a second assault by Clement and the Emperor. How could I visit further misery on my beloved city?"

"And why would the Pope have attacked again?" Pier Antonio argued. "He'd have gotten what He wanted, Medici family members in power in Florence again."

Ippolito shook his head. "Because it would have blocked His ambitions for Alessandro. You choose to ignore the great efforts He went to with the Emperor to have ducal status conferred on my cousin. If I had acted, in Clement's eyes I would have been the worst of traitors, betraying my own family. His retribution might have been even harsher than the siege. I couldn't do that to Florence or to Caterina."

Tommaso handed out clean napkins to Ippolito's party. Then he placed a particularly nice slice of *crostini* on an extra napkin and presented it to Ippolito. To his amazement, one of the Tartars reached over, snatched up the proffered piece, and bit into it. Tommaso was aghast. He knew foreigners practiced barbaric customs, but the Asian's actions went beyond all bounds of propriety.

Ippolito put out his hand toward his crude companion. "Domenico," he said in a quiet but firm voice, "that is unnecessary here. This is my family's house. Haven't you noticed how freely I speak here? If I had ought to fear, would I speak thus?"

Tommaso flushed red with horror and anger. The Tartar was a food tester. He'd thought Tommaso might poison Ippolito.

Ippolito understood the look on Tommaso's face. "Good Tommaso, don't take offense," he pleaded.

Pier Antonio leapt in. "We've learned to be careful everywhere. I'm sure Ippolito holds everyone in this household above reproach, yet who knows what merchant guest of the Salviatis' might have been bribed to slip a little poison into the olive oil, or diamond dust into the flour? Domenico here has never seen you before."

Tommaso felt the blood drain from his face. He picked up a *crostini* and, glaring at the Tartar, bit into it. The Tartar only shrugged.

The *crostini* was perfection itself. Still warm, it crunched briefly under Tommaso's teeth, then melted in his mouth, the flavors of fresh tuna, onion and golden bread marrying together in a perfect union. But once swallowed, it hit the bottom of Tommaso's stomach in a dull lump, spoiled by the atmosphere of suspicion.

With looks of embarrassment, Ippolito's cadre hastily grabbed *crostini* for themselves, Ippolito reaching for an untested slice.

"You haven't arrived at the high position of cardinal yet," Pier Antonio, anxious to get past the social gaffe, reminded Ippolito of his place in the tale.

Ippolito patted some crumbs from his moustache with his napkin. "It happened quickly. Shortly after the siege ended, I was woken early one morning by a group of stout guards from the ecclesiastical palace, sent by His Eminence to fetch me for an audience. When I arrived, I found to my distress the entire college of clerics assembled for my ordination as Cardinal." Ippolito shook his head. "Forewarned by my earlier responses to His edicts, Clement allowed me no chance to escape or prepare a resistance this time. It was accept or disappear into prison.

"But even as I knelt to receive the Cardinal's hat, it occurred to me that this was not entirely a bad thing. As Cardinal I would finally have access to power I'd been held in check from all my life. I might at last be in a position to help rather than injure Florence."

Brave words, but to Tommaso it sounded as though the de' Medici

heir was, typical of his generous, noble nature, making the best of an
unhappy bargain.

"And with Caterina now here in Rome under the same roof as
myself, I can help rather than jeopardize her future also."

Gattamelata covered up the hole she'd dug for her needs with distaste.
The dirt was still so wet from the rains that it was close to mud in
texture. Water dripped on her head and back from sodden bushes. She
shook it from her fur. But rather than return to the warmth and dryness
of the *palazzo*, she lingered for a while in the garden. In spite of the
dampness, she enjoyed the air and openness after her days of confinement
in the basket.

The centuries weighed heavily on her fine bones. She stretched, hind
end up, front legs neatly crossed and extended forward, pulling the kinks
from her sore shoulders. A little of the stiffness relieved, she padded
around the garden, exploring her new surroundings thoroughly. Now and
then her head and tail dropped in wariness. She knew she'd be uneasy
as long as she was separated from her native land. But other allies had
taken up her duties of guardianship in her absence, unbeknownst to the
enemy, who'd been lulled into thinking that they'd won. In the meantime,
she'd bide her time while she regained her strength in this foreign land,
and while Caterina grew into *her* legacy of power.

3

The Salviati household seemed to be one of the world's great hubs. Lucrezia's husband Jacopo Salviati, in addition to his traditional family holdings in Florence, owned estates and businesses in a number of Italian city-states and traveled frequently among them. In this manner he'd avoided being caught in Florence during any of its calamities. Subsequently, he'd never been forced to take sides openly, so he'd never been exiled or suffered confiscation of any property. Merchants, diplomats and scholars gravitated to his estates for advice, advantage and hospitality.

That was why the Salviati culinary staff accepted Tommaso into their ranks so easily. They were happy to accommodate anyone who possessed the training and inclination to help them with their work, which too often resembled the labors of Hercules. At the time of Caterina's arrival, Jacopo Salviati was away on business in Bologna, but in his absence Lucrezia hosted not only Salviati cousins and Ippolito and his entourage, but also the ambassador of Venice, a Florentine textile broker and three visiting Greek translators.

Until Caterina's assignments became more demanding Tommaso preferred to be kept busy. He felt shy surrounded by so many strangers and uneasy about walking the streets of an unfamiliar city alone. But in the kitchen he was among his own kind. He soon made himself at home.

The Salviati mansion boasted two master cooks—Marcus Gavius Spada and Bindo Ramerino.

Neither lived at the palazzo, but rather in small homes of their own nearby. They arrived early in the morning—first Bindo Ramerino and his wife and children, then Marcus Gavius Spada and *his* wife and children.

Ser Spada was a native Roman. He served as the Salviati's master carver and produced all the fleshy courses, whether they be fish, fowl, beef, lamb, kid or wild game. And whether they were roasted, braised, fried, stewed, poached or grilled.

Ser Ramerino had been brought from Bologna by the Salviatis years before and subsequently married a local girl. He acted as the factotum of flour, producing all the pastries, bread, pastas, and any dishes based on grain.

The two men conferred pleasantly with Madame Salviati on the weekly menu, then fought with each other on coordinating their efforts. Although *Ser* Ramerino relied on *Ser* Spada's feather-light concoctions of forcemeats to stuff his splendid pillows of ravioli, and *Ser* Spada needed slices of *Ser* Ramerino's fulsome bread to act as the base for his complex *crostini*, one might have thought the two were condottierri engaged in a series of skirmishes. They blustered about, each hurling invectives and complaining of the other man's shortcomings.

In contrast, the two wives worked well together, moving calmly about their tasks through kitchen air made thick by steam and fanciful insults. The women were responsible for all the food not claimed by their husbands: soups, salads, cooked vegetables, extraneous sauces, ices and beverages other than wine.

Tommaso guessed that underneath all their bluster *Ser* Spada and *Ser* Ramerino were unadmitted fast friends who would never come to blows, but that if the wives ever had occasion to fight it would be a serious matter indeed.

The scullery boys' and apprentices' room lay on the far side of the kitchen, away from the main door that led to the banquet room. The kitchen maids were quartered in the upper floors of the mansion with the other women servants, but they were expected to be the first ones up and about in the morning. It took Tommaso less than two days to discern that the oldest apprentice, Averardo, and one of the kitchen maids, Laudomia, longed for each other—a longing as yet unconsummated. To complicate matters, it was just as evident that *Ser* Ramerino's eldest daughter Alessa also found Averardo attractive, but she was barely pubescent and her interest in Averardo unrequited by that apprentice.

Tommaso spent the early part of one morning filleting scorpion fish and striped mullet while he watched the in-house *commedia*. Averardo worked close to the lovely Laudomia at every opportunity. Meanwhile Alessa contrived to be assigned to assist Laudomia with her chores, so the two sweethearts never got a moment's peace together.

Tommaso tried not to laugh out loud. He guessed Alessa's age at no more than twelve, if that, and she was not nearly as worldly or wise as eleven-year-old Caterina. But Alessa possessed a quicker wit than either Averardo or Laudomia. By placing herself in their way she prevented any growth in the affection she'd observed between them, and at the same time brought herself to Averardo's attention. Unfortunately, she wasn't mature enough yet to know how to parlay her charms to their best effect. She drove Averardo to distraction with her meddling.

At midmorning Tommaso was loath to leave to attend his first lesson with the culinary impresario Bartolommeo Scappi. It looked as though Averardo would soon explode with irritation. Tommaso hated to miss the fireworks.

But when Tommaso took off his apron to get ready to leave, Averardo leapt up from where he sat stuffing a large platter of larks with olive paste.

"I'm finished here," Averardo informed *Ser* Spada. "Since these must marinate before simmering"—he indicated the larks—"why don't I guide Tommaso to Maestro Scappi's? Our guest doesn't know Rome's streets well. I'd hate for him to be late or encounter any peril."

Marcus Gavius Spada raised rather bushy eyebrows and looked at Tommaso. "How about it, young Master Arista? Do you desire an escort to *Ser* Scappi's *bottega*?"

"I'd be grateful for a guide this first time, and someone to formally introduce me," Tommaso said. Although the real reason for Averardo's suggestion was transparent to Tommaso, he didn't relish making his solitary way through an unfamiliar city.

"Then by all means go," *Ser* Spada told Averardo. Tommaso noticed how Laudomia's and Alessa's faces fell. "But don't loiter on your way back."

Averardo quickly napped the larks with the marinade Laudomia and Alessa had been preparing beside him—a concoction of dried mushrooms rehydrated with red wine and fresh garlic pulp.

"If you're going to let our senior apprentice fly off, at least you could instruct him to bring back any secret techniques he might observe at Scappi's that could be used to our advantage," Bindo Ramerino scolded from the opposite side of the kitchen.

"Hah! Why should I do that?" Marcus Gavius Spada shouted back at his colleague. "Since Tommaso now resides here, I'm sure we'll enjoy ample opportunity to learn all of Scappi's tricks from Tommaso in the comfort of our own kitchen!"

Those were the last words Tommaso and Averardo heard as they hurried out the door.

"I've another year until I qualify for journeyman," Averardo said glumly as the gatekeeper let them out the back. "I think I'll go mad before then. It's agony working so closely to my beautiful Laudomia. I'm hardly allowed to speak to her, let alone woo her or touch her." He sighed. "But at least it's an exquisite agony.

"That bratling Alessa, on the other hand..." His look of yearning changed to a scowl. "I may yet strangle the little minx.

"Tommaso, all the other apprentices are so much younger and immature—all they do is snicker, joke and derive what amusement they can from my sad situation. You're more experienced and enjoy an outsider's view. What do you think I should do?"

Tommaso looked at his new friend. Averardo was probably about nineteen years of age and only a little taller than Tommaso, with a broad-shouldered muscular build that was enhanced by a will to work hard at all he did. He was of an age where his complexion was not at its best, undoubtedly not helped by continuous exposure to the greasy steam of the stews, fried *crostini* and spitted roasts Messer Spada made him work over all day long. But his skin would clear in the next year or so. His features were regular and chiseled, set off nicely by startling green eyes and glossy black hair. Tommaso understood why the two girls were so taken with Averardo. They recognized his potential as an attractive lover and responsible spouse.

Tommaso was flattered by the apprentice's confidence but guessed that it stemmed from a misperception. At fifteen, Tommaso was probably closer in age to Alessa than Averardo. The shortage of food during the siege of Florence had deprived Tommaso of bulk, but not prevented him from sprouting up in height. He knew that fact, plus the gravity of his position as head-chef-in-training to the *Duchessina*, led others to assign him more years than he possessed. Tommaso didn't disabuse them of the notion, though if asked he would have responded honestly. So he hesitated in answering the apprentice. He had some experience of love, but nothing like Averardo's situation.

"I indeed see your plight with an outsider's eyes," he agreed. "But my lack of familiarity is more likely to lead to unfortunate rather than beneficial advice. Allow me some time to observe. Then if I'm graced with any insights I'll help you in any way I can. Until then, anytime you need the relief of escape, volunteer to guide me again. At present I only know how to make my way to the *mercado* to shop and Maestro Buonarotti's *bottega* to visit my old friends there."

Averardo looked at Tommaso with awe. "You are elevated indeed, Tommaso, that you can visit as you please at the studio of the most revered artist in all Italy."

Tommaso flushed uncontrollably and hoped Averardo took that helpless response as an indication of modesty. It wouldn't do for the apprentice to guess at Tommaso's true relationship with Michelangelo.

"Don't render me esteem I haven't earned," he told Averardo. "You know that besides cooking I also apprenticed for several years in art. My master in Florence is a good friend of Maestro Buonarotti. The artists in Florence are a close-knit lot. Their apprentices therefore are often thrown together, so I count Ascancio Condivi as my comrade-in-exile here in Rome."

Something occurred to him that would ensure Averardo was thrown off the trail. "You must know of Maestro Buonarotti's reputation for high temper. Having observed him frequently, I can testify that this is unjustified calumny, *except* when he feels that his own or his apprentices' work time is imposed upon. As it so happens, Maestro Buonarotti has returned to Florence at the Pope's request for an undetermined length of time."

No sooner had Michelangelo arrived in Rome then Clement gave him new instructions for the Medici sacristy in Florence, and the assignment to paint the walls of the Sistine Chapel, since the ceiling Michelangelo had painted for Pope Julius had gained such acclaim. Michelangelo departed for Florence to delegate responsibility for his projects there to artists he trusted.

Averardo took Tommaso's intended meaning. "Aha! No wonder you can visit there on your afternoons off. When the cat is away, both mice and apprentices play."

"Exactly," Tommaso said firmly.

Tommaso had never before seen a kitchen like Bartolommeo Scappi's. Banks of ovens lined one wall. On the wall opposite, shelves were crowded with every kind of utensil imaginable. In front of these were freestanding stoves interspersed with kneading troughs and flour bins. Huge worktables marched down the center aisle. This place was as much a *bottega* as any art studio Tommaso had ever visited.

Tommaso glanced at Averardo beside him. The apprentice was just as gape-mouthed as himself.

"I'm surprised at your surprise, Averardo," Tommaso said. "I thought you knew both the place and the man."

"I've met Signor Scappi several times when I accompanied Master Spada to guild functions. And I've passed this place many times, knowing well who it belonged to. But this is the first time I've set foot within," Averardo confessed. "Look at it, Tommaso! No wonder that in spite of the esteem my masters Spada and Ramerino are held in by their peers, they're jealous to know the secrets of Scappi's success."

Just then an apprentice approached them and asked them their business.

"I am Averardo Fancelli, apprenticed to Maestros Spada and Ramerino, who are in the culinary employ of the estimable Salviati family," Averardo introduced himself. "I act as escort to this young man, Tommaso Arista, who is newly arrived in Rome from Florence. His employer, the *Duchessina* Caterina de' Medici, arranged for him to receive instruction from *Ser* Scappi, who should be expecting him."

The apprentice nodded and hurried past clusters of working journeymen and apprentices, to the back of the enormous kitchen. There he spoke deferentially to a man bent over a large mound of pastry dough. The man nodded in cadence to the boy's words, then his brow furrowed as if he were puzzled. At last he stood up straight, wiped his hands clean and followed the apprentice to where Averardo and Tommaso stood, giving Tommaso ample time to study him.

Bartolommeo Scappi appeared to be in his thirties, with a boyish, clean-shaven face. He was of the type that becomes heavier with age, but so far his physique remained trim, probably due to the hectic demands of his successful business.

He nodded perfunctorily at Averardo, whom he obviously recognized, then turned to Tommaso, a perplexed expression on his face. "An Arista? One of Galleoto's sons?"

It was Tommaso's turn to be confused. "I am the son of Gentile Arista, head cook and master carver to Ruggiero the Old, the most respected physician and occultist in Florence. I enjoy the employ of the *Duchessina* Caterina Romola de' Medici."

Scappi's face cleared. "Ah yes, the *Duchessina* de' Medici. Her agent didn't mention an appellation for you. So just now, when I heard your name . . . well, my mistake is understandable, wouldn't you agree? Arista is not a common name anywhere, let alone in our pragmatic yet rarefied field."

Tommaso nodded, though he was still mystified. This was the second time he'd been misidentified. He made a mental note to ask Averardo later who these other Aristas might be.

"You may go now." Scappi waved Averardo away. "Your service has been discharged. Give my regards to Messers Spada and Ramerino, of course."

The overawed Averardo backed out of the studio.

"I work on a very tight schedule," Bartolommeo Scappi said. "While I finish my task you may attend to me and apprise me of whatever training you've had."

The mound of dough Scappi was working on proved to be a roast suckling pig covered in a thick sheet of pastry. The back portion was shaped like the tail of a great fish. In the front, on the side Scappi had already sculpted, the fishy torso gave way to mammalian ribs and a horse's muscular leg and hoof.

"The Clerk of the Camera, Giovanni Gaddi, has commissioned a great banquet to celebrate the sparing of his properties during the recent flood," Scappi said as he began to work on the other leg and hoof. He didn't seem all that interested in querying Tommaso about his background.

Tommaso noticed that the limbs weren't purely made of dough. They'd been given a bonelike structure for support by wrapping the pastry around long hard sausages first.

"Therefore a headless hippocampus as the centerpiece for the feast?" Tommaso asked.

Scappi looked up with a frown, but when he saw Tommaso's gentle smile he realized Tommaso only jested.

"In fact, the first order of the presentation *may* be a ritual decapitation," Scappi said. "I haven't decided yet. Look over there." He gestured to another work table.

Three apprentices were carefully packing a finely ground forcemeat into an awkwardly shaped pastry vessel. Tommaso turned his head almost upside down and saw that it bore a rough resemblance to a horse's neck and head.

"We half baked it on a form beforehand so it would hold its shape," Scappi explained. "When I'm finished here we'll graft it to this." He patted the disguised suckling pig. "Then I'll add more pastry, sculpt it up, and finish baking it."

"Will you lacquer it after that?" Tommaso asked. For especially glorious occasions master cooks sometimes adorned showcase pieces in that fashion, or sprinkled their masterpieces with colored salts or sugars.

"Yes, I intend to silver it, to enhance the illusion of a rare creature caught fresh from the sea. You're familiar with the process of lacquering?" Only the grandest houses indulged in dishes of such ostentation.

"Not familiar in the sense I would attempt the task by myself. But yes, I assisted my grandfather with gilding various dishes in the Medici palazzo kitchen."

Scappi looked impressed, and Tommaso was grateful for the opportunities he'd enjoyed because of his Befanini relatives' position at the Medici mansion, before the plague had arrived and changed all their lives so drastically. He doubted that the plain fare he'd prepared for the artist Tribolino's apprentices, or even the excellent but unadorned cuisine at the Ruggieros', would have met with such favor in Scappi's eyes.

"Since you've had some experience, would you care to recommend any additions to this presentation?" Scappi's voice was amused, but he looked at Tommaso intently. Tommaso wondered if Scappi thought him impudent. Or was the question sincere, an attempt to measure his mettle?

Tommaso took a deep breath. "Just one small thing. Fish fresh from the sea, depending on their kind, of course, are not only silver in appearance, but their scales also shine with a lovely phosphorescence. As soon as this piece is well silvered, I would sprinkle it sparingly with violet-and-blue-colored salts, to hint at that glow."

Bartolommeo Scappi looked at the pastry with some surprise.

"You're right, young Master Arista. A very little effort, yet it would greatly enhance the effect." He looked at Tommaso appraisingly. "I believe that not only will you prove an apt pupil, but also a welcome addition to my studio. Sit yourself comfortably and tell me all about yourself. Then I can best ascertain how I can help you."

Tommaso pulled up a stool. Scappi would be pleasant to work for and learn from, but Tommaso could well finish Scappi's sentence in his own mind: "...and how you, Tommaso, can best help me."

4

Mid-November, 1530

Caterina was playing chess with one of her ladies-in-waiting when Tommaso responded to her summons one night after dinner.

"As you know, Tommaso, my estimable host and great uncle, *Ser* Jacopo Salviati, and my cousins his daughter Maria and her son Cosimo de' Medici, all arrived from Bologna this afternoon," she said. She glanced down at the board as her lady-in-waiting slyly moved a piece, hoping to take advantage of Caterina's lapse of attention. "My uncle raised some matters that you and I must address."

As she studied her opponent's move Tommaso thought swiftly.

"Your uncle and cousins will expect you to receive them. You require refreshments for these occasions," he ventured. "This food should be special, not leftover kitchen scraps. I understand Madonna Maria is fond of sweets. May I suggest some molded fresh cheeses flavored with fig liqueur and honey, accompanied by *pinolata*, and, to freshen the palate, either lemon or ginger sorbet?"

Caterina pushed a pawn forward a square and then looked up, amused. "Excellent, Tommaso, though I think it would be nice to have tiny portions of *both* the lemon and ginger ices, and apricot as well. What would you recommend for a luncheon with my Great-uncle Salviati?"

"I'd like to consult with *Ser* Scappi first on the exact dishes, but certainly several savories. Spinach dumplings in venison sauce; buckwheat polenta graced with late asparagus and *pancetta*; ravioli stuffed with a forcemeat of lark and chopped egg—these are all possibilities."

"Truly wonderful suggestions." Caterina was almost laughing openly. Tommaso couldn't guess what he'd said that was so amusing.

"I'll consider them all carefully. But Tommaso, these are matters I could have conferred with you on the morrow. I called you here for another reason this evening."

Tommaso blushed with embarrassment at his presumptiveness. At least Caterina seemed entertained by his unwitting performance.

"After dinner tonight my uncle announced that in a week he's taking Cosimo to the country for a hunt. The weather is finally splendid and the time of year right. I'm also invited, as are Ippolito and his friends, and the Venetian ambassador, who is bringing the Milanese ambassador. I'm to limit my entourage to just a handful of servants. I'd like you to be one of them. If the hunt is successful we'll be more in want of good cooks than wardrobe mistresses. I thought you should know as soon as possible so that a messenger might be sent to Messer Scappi in the morning to rearrange your program with him, and so we can reschedule several of our little salons."

Tommaso bowed, assuming his audience with her was over. But when he looked up he saw she had more in store for him.

"And I've decided who you shall continue to study art with. It will be Benevenuto Cellini after all. A difficult man, it is true, but a fellow Florentine and an artist of much merit. That is all, Tommaso."

Tommaso bowed again, lower this time, as much to hide his misery as to show his obeisance. The *Duchessina* must have reasons beyond his knowledge for assigning him to the jeweler, since she knew how he disliked Cellini. He turned to go.

"Oh, and one more small thing I just remembered. There will be another guest from outside the household invited on the hunt. A great friend of Ippolito's—Michelangelo Buonarotti. He returns to Rome tomorrow and I'm sure he'll accept the invitation. He's fond of hunting."

Caterina watched with pleasure as Tommaso transformed at her words. Though he struggled to eliminate all expression from his face, it glowed with the special loveliness that was Tommaso's alone. He fairly floated out of the room. Caterina turned back to her chess game.

Since leaving Florence, she'd begun to wear the masses of jewelry expected of one of her station. Hidden beneath the ropes of pearls and twining filigreed gold chains lay a simple silver strand that terminated against her breast with a medallion set with a single red cabochon. Warmth from this stone spread across her skin to chide her.

I know, thought Caterina in response. *But I'm not really being cruel. You know I would never hurt Tommaso. I only manipulate him so as to yield him greater delight in the end.*

Just as long as you never fail in that goal he shall always trust you, Ginevra's spirit replied. *Be warned that as he grows to be a man he'll come to know all your tricks, and his trust will be edged in wariness.*

Caterina put her hand to her bodice, pressing the stone against her chest. *In his life Tommaso will be required to participate in many acts whose final results will be so beyond his ken that it will be as if he were required to duel blindfolded. I would not wish him to be unwary, even of me.*

The stone acquiesced and fell silent.

"*Duchessina,* has my gambit proved so profound that it causes such reflection on your part?"

Caterina looked across the small table at her lady-in-waiting, who was trying diplomatically to draw her from her reverie. Caterina shifted her attention to the board.

The woman had slid her bishop far into Caterina's territory in an attempt to threaten Caterina's king in three moves. On the most elementary level it was a foolish action, for in two moves Caterina could move a pawn out of the way of a castle standing ready.

The woman realized her error and tried not to look nervously at the rook. Caterina's hand hovered deliciously over the board.

The woman sighed. "You'll be moving your pawn, I presume?"

"Not at all," said Caterina. She hesitated just long enough to see the woman's face brighten before she struck. "I think I'd rather move my true friend here, who can proceed and capture around corners he himself cannot see around." She picked up her knight from where he'd sat unplayed at the back and swept the woman's bishop from the board.

5

The Salviati family maintained a country manor near the hilltop town of Ostia for whenever they desired the diversion of hunting. As the master carver and meat chef, Marcus Gavius Spada was naturally the other cook assigned to the outing. On the journey he entertained Tommaso by describing the place.

It was situated not far from the sea, in an area where forest marched down from low hills to meet marshlands. In that manner a variety of game was guaranteed—at this time of year a plentitude of waterfowl in the marshes; deer, boar, pheasant, partridge, fox and hare in the woods and thickets; and *cabra*, the wild goats, up in the hills.

Besides the portrait in words Spada painted of the place, he explained in great detail how he prepared and cooked each kind of game according to Roman tradition. Tommaso paid close attention. This was the kind of information that expanded his cooking prowess.

The Salviati entourage arrived at the lodge early in the evening. A small group of servants who constituted the lodge's permanent caretakers greeted them. A calf was spit-roasting over a huge fire pit. Fresh loaves of bread graced a sideboard.

"The staff here contracts with local farmwives for baked goods for the duration of the Salviatis' visits," *Ser* Spada told Tommaso in an aside.

In the rough relaxed spirit of the hunt, several of Ippolito's companions volunteered to help the lodge staff serve supper. This left *Ser*

Spada, Tommaso and three younger apprentices who'd come with them free to unload cooking supplies and get organized.

Tommaso appreciated Caterina's wisdom in requiring him to accompany her. This matter of catering to a hunting party's needs was new to him. Back in Florence, Ruggiero the Old hadn't cared much for blood sports. On holidays to the Ruggiero farm property there had been forays, of course, but only as an adjunct activity to the pastoral respite. The two oldest sons, Cosimo and Lorenzo, found more opportunities to hunt with the sportsmen families of some of their friends than with their scholarly father.

So this would be different than tracking game with a well-stocked farmyard as a base. If the hunting party was successful, of course they'd desire to feast on whatever game they caught that didn't require aging. But what if they caught little or nothing? Woe betide the kitchen that didn't prepare for such a contingency.

Or blundered in a certain diplomacy in the provisioning. A party that failed to capture a fleet stag would not be pleased to find a haunch of braised venison waiting on their return, mocking their inadequacy. No, what was called for was comfortingly domestic product, like the waiting spit-roasted calf, or several dozen plump capons.

Ser Spada explained all of this as he rearranged the kitchen to his liking while the lodgeman's wife looked on with lips pressed thin and arms folded tight.

"Of course, you can't bring *everything* with you, as if you were Noah preparing for the flood. If the hunt goes well, then you're faced with hauling back everything you've brought with you in addition to all the new meat that wants hanging.

"You must rely on these good folk that comprise your resident experts. They know which local farmers' sows farrowed well in the spring, which goodwives bake the best local bread. They know which gardens produce fresh lively salad greens this late in the year. They gather this information in spite of the long hours they labor keeping this lodge ready for any of the Salviati family who may drop in at a moment's notice.

"So we must appreciate how the efforts of these fine people make our own task that much easier." With these last words *Ser* Spada rummaged at the purse hanging from his belt and drew forth a paper packet and a small pair of sewing scissors with handsomely embossed handles, which he presented to the lodgewife. The woman had already left off scowling during his flattering soliloquy. The packet, when she opened it, proved to contain a blue velvet hair ribbon. Now all smiles, she left to put her new treasures away.

Ser Spada rolled his eyes and grimaced. "Everything I said was true, but observe how a little diplomacy smooths the way for our sojourn."

"The lodgewife is not the only resident we'll inconvenience," Tommaso observed.

"My bag is not yet empty," *Ser* Spada said, patting his purse.

Tommaso guessed that in spite of the litany of chores *Ser* Spada credited the lodge staff with, they probably lived the easiest life it was possible for a servant to enjoy. Although they certainly did a fine job maintaining the manor, they didn't suffer the strain of employers in constant residence. He also guessed that during those hectic periods when the Salviati family *did* descent, the staff consoled themselves with under-the-table gratuities from farmers anxious to sell the extra provisions needed.

Michelangelo arrived late, at the end of the meal. Ascancio accompanied him as his single attendant. Since much had been cleared from the table already, *Ser* Spada sent Tommaso out to serve the two a hastily concocted supper.

"We thought you'd decided to arrive on the morrow," Jacopo Salviati was saying as Tommaso entered the rough-hewn dining hall bearing a tray laden with the impromptu main course: thick beef slices laved with a *dulceforte* sauce, surrounded by cardoon croquettes and eggs nestled in tender green nests of steamed borage and spinach.

Michelangelo shook his head and held up his hand, his mouth too full to answer. He and Ascancio were feasting on the light fare of *primi servizi di credenza* to dull the initial edge of their hunger. They'd made respectable inroads into a large platter of slices of celery heart *in pinzimonio*, fried eggplant, olive paste spread on toast rounds, and marinated St. Anna beans. Ascancio beamed as Tommaso set down his burden of more serious fare before them.

"I couldn't escape easily for a lighthearted jaunt so soon after my return to Rome without the risk of incurring papal wrath," Michelangelo said when he could speak again. "I had to be sure Urbino was well instructed on all my current projects, so he'd be prepared when the Pope's agents came to call. If Urbino displeases the Pontiff in my absence, I trust Ippolito here will use his ecclesiastical offices to help gain pardon for my humble *bottega*."

"Alas, I'm more likely to ask you for that favor," said Ippolito. "You stand in higher regard with His Holiness than I. My appointment to Cardinal is more a constraint than a reward, so I doubt it will afford you any consideration. I confess myself far more comfortable in this role than that of Cardinal." He spread his hands, indicating his huntsman's garb of russet jacket and bloused white shirt.

"These clothes suit you better than those red flapping cloaks," young Cosimo de' Medici said. "They made you look like some giant flopping tropical bird."

The entire company laughed at the image that conjured. Caterina sat directly across the long narrow table from Cosimo. She reached over to press his hand. "My cousin speaks plainly and honestly, as always. And to great effect, as usual."

"Perhaps," said Maria Salviati. "But if anyone can make the Cardinal's red look rakish and sportsmanlike, it's our Ippolito."

"A toast to the ladies," the Venetian ambassador said. "My heartfelt thanks for their gracious and civilizing presence on this outing, so that we shall not be tempted to descend into the boorishness too common to men gone a'hunting."

"My dear ambassador," Pier Antonio chuckled. "You may come to regret your gallantry. These particular ladies have not accompanied us to smooth our rough ways, but to best us in the hunt. I've attended several of these expeditions with Madonna Maria and know whereof I speak. I've not had the pleasure of chevying beside the *Duchessina* before, but Ippolito has, and he boasts of her prowess."

Tommaso cleared empty plates from the table. Though Maria, Caterina and their handful of attendants were the only women present in the large company of men, they seemed more than capable of holding their own.

Maria had gained weight since the time Tommaso had glimpsed her and her son Cosimo at the Murate. Her haunted eyes protruded more in her round face, but her skin still maintained its unusual morbid pallor. Her manners were hospitable and refined, but with a feeling of steel behind the silk.

Cosimo had grown taller than Tommaso would have expected. Cosimo and Caterina were the same age, but Cosimo could pass as years older. He kept his hair cut as short as it had been the first time Tommaso had seen him, and his expression was almost as severe, in spite of the relaxed atmosphere of the gathering. He was dressed in the rough garb of a trooper expecting to be called away on a campaign at a moment's notice. Tommaso had heard in the Salviati kitchen that this was the only kind of clothing Cosimo wore.

"Considering my father's hunting prowess"—Maria nodded with a smile at Jacopo Salviati—"it might surprise you that everything I know of the sport I learned from my mother. *Her* father, il Magnífico, started her riding to hounds as soon as she could hold her seat in the saddle. She's told me many a tale of how she and her sisters and brothers on their little ponies scrambled after their father on his stallion, coursing after game over the Tuscan countryside."

"Indeed, no one can match a Medici at the hunt," Jacopo said. "I think it was only because I could keep up with Lorenzo the Great that he consented to accept me as a son-in-law. To bring luck to our hunt, I toast the great spirit of Lorenzo il Magnífico."

Servants rushed forward with more wine. Everyone raised their glasses.

"To Lorenzo, my grandfather," said Maria.

"To Lorenzo, *my* grandfather," said Ippolito.

Caterina and Cosimo locked eyes. "To Lorenzo, our great-grandfather," they said in unison.

"To Lorenzo, my patron, friend and teacher." Michelangelo added his toast in a quiet, clear voice.

Then everybody drank.

"And to maintain that spirit and our luck," Jacopo said as he put his goblet down, "I hereby declare that the rules of this hunt shall be the same as those practiced during il Magnífico's time: Firearms are only to be used as starting guns and, if necessary, to flush out game."

"But I brought my best fowling piece," the Venetian ambassador protested.

"Then you may act as our starter," Jacopo said. "But weaponry will be limited to spear, crossbows, nets and, as is the case tomorrow on the marshes, falcons."

The company rose early the next morning, except for Michelangelo. Although he loved falconry, his devotion to his art left him little time for maintaining a mews, so he declined and slept in rather than hunt with someone else's raptor. A little while after the hunting party left, Ascancio wandered into the kitchen to join the servants for breakfast.

"My master requires that I groom our horses after I sup," Ascancio said as he heaped a *tondo* with bean tarts, cheese, Pisan biscuits and slices of Spanish melon. "He fears the hostler is so busy with the mounts for the hunt that our two might suffer some neglect. Tommaso, would you be so kind as to take him a tray? I'm sure he'd not be adverse to re-counting any news or gossip from his recent trip to Florence for your pleasure."

Tommaso's heart pounded as he set up a tray. The staff wouldn't find it surprising if Ascancio dawdled over his stable chores. What apprentice didn't seek a few quiet, easy moments, especially if he was indentured to a notorious taskmaster like Michelangelo?

Michelangelo was waiting impatiently just inside the door to his room when Tommaso knocked. He took the tray, set it aside on a small table, and turned to Tommaso with a hunger greater than that for food.

Later, when they lay contented and sated in each other's arms, Michelangelo apprised Tommaso of Florence's current trials and tribulations, and how the artists and apprentices who were friends to both of them fared.

"Francesco Guicciardini's reprisals have continued in their severity, but the politics of artists and artisans during the siege aren't being examined closely—the bombardment caused so much damage that even the Pope won't risk imprisoning badly needed skilled labor."

"So most of our companions are doing well?" Tommaso asked.

"Yes, all but Giorgio Vasari, who I fear is heading straight for disaster. Not that that would be his assessment, I'm sure. He's a journeyman now and just launching his career. Alas, he's chosen to court Alessandro de' Medici's patronage. Nothing but ill can come of that." Michelangelo rose, wrapped a robe about himself and turned his attention to the food Tommaso had brought.

"Although I spent most of my time in Florence arranging for Tasso, Tribolo and others to take over my affairs, I did manage to find time to drop in on other acquaintances as well. Make yourself decent Tommaso, then look in my surcoat. You'll find something for you there." Michelangelo pointed with his fork.

Tommaso drew on his clothing. From an inner pocket of his lover's surcoat he pulled several sheets of paper, folded up and held closed with a wax seal.

"I was visiting Ruggiero the Old one day," Michelangelo said. "When I took my leave, your father approached me in the hall. He'd obviously been waiting for me. He asked if I remembered him, and you, and reminded me that I witnessed your apprenticeship papers to Tribolo." Michelangelo smiled wryly. "I assured him that I did indeed remember you.

"He asked if I ever had occasion to frequent the Salviatis' palazzo in Rome. When I replied that of course I did, he begged me to see that that correspondence reached you."

Tommaso looked at the folded pages in his hand with dismay. He didn't know what to think.

"Didn't you tell me you gave him leave to write you?" Michelangelo asked.

"Yes," Tommaso admitted. "But now I discover I fear to find out what he has to say."

"Someday you'll return to Florence, and then you and your father will have to come to some kind of accord. Won't it be easier to begin the process at a distance, with well-considered letters replacing the sometimes rashly spoken words of a face-to-face encounter?" Michelangelo pointed out gently.

"That's true," said Tommaso, but he was still reluctant to break the seal on the papers.

"You don't have to read them this instant," Michelangelo said. "Wait for a quiet moment when you find that you desire to."

Tommaso looked at his lover gratefully and tucked the packet into his own vest.

By the time the hunting party returned in the early afternoon Michelangelo had been outside sketching with Ascancio for several hours. Tommaso had long before returned to the kitchen to help prepare the kind of fare suitable for a crowd whose appetites would demand immediate gratification. To that end, the staff had cooked chestnut soup, *crostini* topped with a cuttlefish forcemeat, fish pies made with seafood bought fresh that morning at the nearby port, and salads of late radicchio and lettuce.

When they heard the telltale cacophony of barking hounds and cheerful cries, *Ser* Spada, Tommaso and the apprentices ran out to relieve the hunters of their prey and take it away for plucking, skinning, gutting and any other necessary preparations.

The sportsmen had done well. The catch included various waterfowl from the marshes, and partridges, rabbit, ortolan and thrushes from the meadows. In spite of his complaint about the ban on firearms, the Venetian ambassador glowed with success, for he'd managed to spear a fat crested porcupine.

Tommaso held up a basket and Caterina's falconer dropped her catch into it: several small game birds bound together by their legs. Their gold, russet, carmine and madder feathers looked like a bouquet of autumn leaves.

Michelangelo and Ascancio ambled up, providing an audience for all the anecdotes of the day. Michelangelo couldn't keep his eyes from the mare Ippolito rode.

"'Lito, where did you get that enchanting creature?" he asked.

"Through the auspices of Domenico here." Ippolito tilted his head toward his Tartar companion. "I know of no finer judge of horseflesh, nor one better connected. This mare harkens from one of the finest bloodlines in Araby."

"She looks to be as agile as a cat," the sculptor said.

"Exactly how agile you shall see tomorrow," Ippolito replied. "We passed a farmer who says he knows of a thicket in the woods serving as the lair to wild boar. They've been rooting in his fields and he wants them gone. In the morning he leads us to them. Then this steed will prove her nimbleness."

6

When the kitchen's activity finally slowed to the last cleaning up by the junior apprentices, Tommaso took the time to sit by the fire and read his letter. Letters... when he broke the seal and glanced over the pages he found that both his mother and father had written.

His father's script was written in a sure hand—only the words themselves showed hesitation. Gentile wrote of those things which were important but not too close to the heart: how busily Florence was healing itself, gossip about their fellow cooks throughout the city, news of the Ruggiero family. It was the letter of a man making a first tentative attempt at contact. Tommaso would answer in kind, and perhaps bit by bit they could rekindle their affinity.

The closest Gentile came to personal tidings was in a description of Tommaso's little sister Luciana. *This child both amuses and bemuses me,* he wrote. *There is about her a calm unheard of in a three-year-old, yet the sense of it is not that of tranquillity. She is very close to your mother, but treats me as though I were a younger brother instead of her father. I may deserve this treatment, for I often play the fool with her to coax a rare smile out of her.*

Tommaso imagined the scene easily. Gentile, stricken with guilt at the loss, one way or the other, of his other four children, desperate to do well by the one remaining.

Piera wrote in the laboriously clear hand common to many of Florence's nonaristocratic women, who only attended public school for a scant three or four years. Her words, however, were surer and warmer than Gentile's.

She told Tommaso how much she missed him. That she had great confidence in his ability to meet new friends and make the most of his opportunities in Rome. *Please send me news of yourself, and also of the Duchessina, who you know is as a daughter to me,* she wrote. Like Gentile, she described Florence's efforts at recovery. Unlike her husband, she was not so optimistic. *Even when the sun shines, there's no light in the sky. A terrible cloud oppresses our land and will not leave. Eventually it will break and a foul black rain will descend upon us all.*

Tommaso shuddered at her analogy. He hated to imagine a life in Florence under Alessandro de' Medici's rule.

What was most curious about the letters was how each parent wrote about what the other could not.

From Gentile, this: *The talk of the town amongst those of our profession is news from your mother's family. Shortly after you left, your Great-grandmother Angelina Befanini made a singular recovery from the effects of old age. You can imagine the conjecture this generated, especially since the priests aren't anxious to claim this miracle as one of their own. You know how I deplore being disrespectful, whether of religion or of our master's profession, but it irritates me to see superstition assigned to the recovery of this lively woman's senses.*

Tommaso could well imagine thumbs entwined in fists in *mano en fica* to ward off witchcraft whenever his great-grandmother passed by, now that she was mobile and out amongst the populace again.

And from his mother, news his father would have never dared tell him: *We received a letter from your grandfather Arista, from the farm. Ottaviano proposed to Filomena and she accepted. The banns been have been posted.*

Tommaso put his head in his hands. That was the end of it, then. For Filomena, a happier ending than she ever could have hoped for. But did that absolve his family's guilt?

7

Tommaso, you *must* ride on this hunt. The game will be much bigger—we can't truss stags and boar up into neat little bonnets to hang from our saddles," Caterina said as she finished the last of the breakfast Tommaso had brought to her room. She and her cousin Maria Salviati shared one small table between them. Their ladies-in-waiting shared another.

Tommaso stood his ground, though he knew it was risky refusing Caterina openly.

He'd lain awake much of the night thinking about his parents' letters. Then the hunt began so early in the morning that he'd delivered Caterina, Maria Salviati and their lady attendants' breakfast at about the hour when he'd normally just be rising to prepare it. Through the window of Caterina's room the sky shone with that pallid color that precedes daybreak—a pale gray that Tommaso was sure matched the color of his own exhausted face.

"If you insist, I'll attend and lead the packhorses. But I'll ride in a cart with the packhorses tethered behind it," he said.

"You can't keep up with the hunt in a cart," Caterina protested. "And a cart can't negotiate its way through thickets and dense forest. You'll get stuck or even topple over. It's too dangerous."

"I'm more certain to fall behind or topple over if you put me astride a horse," Tommaso countered. "I'm a servant, a cook. And a *city* servant at that. I've helped drive carts my whole life, but on one hand I can count the times I've sat atop a horse. It's far more dangerous to expect me to ride. *Especially* on any of those creatures that can keep up on a hunt."

Tommaso felt comfortable with the thick, sturdy, gentle cart horses. The high-strung steeds the upper classes favored were such a different manner of animal that they might as well indeed be the cats that Michelangelo and Ippolito had compared 'Lito's mount to yesterday.

"The meadows and fields meander in and out of the forests all about here," Tommaso reasoned. "If the hunt enters dense growth I'll parallel its course. Then when the kill is accomplished, I'll lead the packhorses in. I'm not a brave individual, *Duchessina*. I'll lay down my life for you if I must, but please let it be for a more dignified or worthwhile cause than being thrown from a fine mount rightfully offended by my clumsy and uneducated efforts to stay astride it."

Caterina's cheeks pinked at Tommaso's quiet, reproachful words. "Forgive me, my gossip. You've been such a part and parcel of my childhood that I sometimes forget there are skills we do not share. We need your services, of course, but I wanted you to have some pleasure in the hunt. You're right. I acquiesce to your conditions. Go ready the cart."

Maria Salviati handed Tommaso her own finished plate. She'd sat by silently while Caterina and Tommaso resolved their differences. Now she tendered her own opinion. "A wise decision, Caterina. A cart will be more practical. Besides wanting it for carrying game back to the lodge, we require a conveyance for transporting the beverages and refreshments we'll need to recover from our efforts." She waved Tommaso away. "*Ser* Spada will see that you have everything you need," she told him.

In the kitchen Marcus Gavius Spada helped Tommaso select knives for eviscerating and jointing large game. Meanwhile the groomsmen harnessed a placid draft horse to one of the lodge's carts. By the time Tommaso led it around to the front to join the hunting party, Caterina had changed into a riding gown and was being helped onto her mount by Ippolito.

Tommaso looked at Caterina sitting on her sidesaddle, a small crossbow slung across her back, a spear and short sword set into her saddle gear. He was suddenly more concerned for her safety than his own.

Asymmetrically and precariously perched, she'd be galloping over hill and dale, through marshlands, meadows and thick forest. And not in pursuit of the delicate waterfowl and timid rabbits of the day before, but chasing after fierce wild boar and lethally horned stags.

This is madness, Tommaso thought. If women are the weaker, more fragile sex, why are they handicapped in this wise, put in such a disadvantageous position in a dangerous undertaking? If they must be included on a hunt, why not let them forgo modesty in exchange for safety, and let them sit straddling horses as men do?

Yet even as he thought it, Tommaso knew it to be a scandalous idea. He slouched on his cart seat in misery. Before the ouster of the Medici from Florence Caterina had gone out on several hunts. It had never occurred to him to worry about her then. He'd been tranquil in his ignorance. He wished he were ignorant still.

Crossbowmen and beaters had already left the lodge to track the boar to their lair. The hunting party made last-minute arrangements as it waited for word on the tracker's success. Domenico, the surly Tartar, rode up leading two packhorses. He tethered them to the back of Tommaso's cart without the barest word of greeting. Tommaso looked closely at Domenico's own mount. If the Tartar enjoyed a reputation for being an expert on horseflesh, his mount constituted poor proof. It was a stocky creature not much larger than a pony, thick-necked and broad-headed, its coat a drab, dusty brown.

Tommaso knew little of riding stock, but Domenico's mount seemed remarkably unprepossessing, even to his unlearned eye. The packhorses must belong to Domenico too. They appeared nearly identical to the Tartar's mount.

Tommaso glanced over at Ippolito and found further fuel to doubt Domenico's abilities. Tommaso admitted that Ippolito's horse was very pretty, with big eyes, a deerlike face, black mane and a gleaming coat that Tommaso, with his artist's background, would have called ocher, but which he'd heard the horsemen call dun. And unlike Domenico's own horse, it looked lively and intelligent. But so small, barely taller than the Tartar's horse. Even Caterina's chestnut palfrey stood higher. How could it keep up with Jacopo Salviati's and Cosimo's big chargers? Yet it was the same horse Ippolito had ridden hunting yesterday, and which Michelangelo so admired.

Just then a crossbowman rode up hard. "We found a place where stags bedded," he said. "But the dogs didn't follow the scent far. So we proceeded onward according to the farmer's directions. We found the pigs' spoor. The hounds tracked them to a huge patch of brambles they've claimed as their home. They're hiding in there now."

"You're sure of that?" Jacopo Salviati asked.

The man nodded. "One of the dogs plunged in before we could stop it. We heard it yelping and screaming as they trampled it."

Jacopo Salviati looked satisfied. "Messer Venier, will you honor us by starting the hunt?"

The Venetian ambassador pointed his ornate, ivory-inlaid fowling piece into the air and fired. At the sharp report the company set off, singing and cheering. The crossbowman led. Tommaso brought up the rear in his cart.

The party followed the rough country road as long as it could, then cut across fields and meadows. Now and then farmers turned from their work to smile and wave.

The hunters did make an entrancing sight. In keeping with Jacopo Salviati's mandate for an old-fashioned hunt, many sported the lavish accouterments that in former times embellished festive occasions of frenzy and blood: saddle blankets of gold brocade, gilded spurs and tack, velvet hunting jackets in scarlet or azure or emerald, stiff with embroidery.

Tommaso guessed that if the crops weren't already in and the fields turned under, the countryfolk wouldn't have been so cheerful at the sight of all these blithe equestrians, not to mention his cart, churning up their neatly plowed furrows.

The cart more or less kept up with the hunters; falling behind when it had to bump its way across pasturage, catching up when a country road intersected their route for a while. As the party climbed into the hills the fields fell away. The roads became mere trails. Tommaso's back and rump began to ache as the cart bumped along, straddling the narrow tracks.

Larger and larger patches of forest penetrated rolling meadows. Now the party only encountered a few goatherders. Tommaso fell farther behind. When a clangor of horns over a near rise heralded their destination and the crossbowman waved them on, the hunters surged ahead, passing a crude farm wagon that the beaters must have ridden up in.

When Tommaso finally caught up, the hunting party was arrayed around a huge expanse of brambles. Michelangelo rode up to him. "Stay off to the side, Tommaso, where you'll be out of danger," the sculptor warned.

The thicket grew along the boundary of woodland and meadow. It didn't penetrate deeply into the forest—the trees were tall with a thick canopy, allowing little light for underbrush. But the briars sprawled well out into the meadow. Thorny as it was, the thicket's foliage was ragged and chewed. Small black fruity pellets peppered the ground all about, evidence that herds of goats kept the thicket from completely taking over the swale.

Michelangelo explained the hunters' strategy to Tommaso. "The beaters will stand in the back, where the forest meets the thicket. Note how the hunters and hounds position themselves off to the sides, leaving the way to the meadow clear. The boar will naturally desire to escape by the clearest route. Once in the open, they're more easily chased."

This made sense to Tommaso and cheered him. If the boar ran away down the meadowy hillside, he'd have little trouble keeping the hunt in sight as he followed them. Taking Michelangelo's advice, he guided the cart off to one side, well behind the hunters and back closer to the forest. As he did so he noticed several tunneled entrances broken into the brambles. At least two were large enough to accommodate a crouching man, if that man were dressed in thick enough leather to repel the thorns.

When everyone was positioned, Jacopo Salviati gave the signal by raising his hand, then letting it fall. The beaters commenced banging away on old pots and battered shields they'd brought with them, at the same time screaming like demons. The hunt master and his assistants blew on their hunting horns. The Venetian ambassador and several others shot their fowling pieces up into the air. The hounds turned their noses to the sky and howled. The coursing dogs snarled and barked.

The thicket quivered as something deep within it flailed about at the noise. The coursing dogs strained at their leashes. Hunters and horses tensed in anticipation, waiting for the prey to burst from the bush.

Nothing happened. The commotion in the bush subsided to an ominous stillness. The hunting party renewed its noisy efforts, to no avail. One by one the beaters left off their commotion and looked to Jacopo Salviati for guidance.

"This is cunning quarry indeed," he marveled. "Let us try another approach." He positioned those with firearms more toward the back of the thicket. "When we recommence our clamor, shoot directly into the foliage. We must declare this slight exemption to the rules of the hunt, or there may be no hunt. Directly assaulted, our swine should flee in alarm."

He raised his hand again. It fell. The din was even greater than before. At its peak, the shooters fired into the brush. Their goal was only to route the prey, but one or more of the blind shots found a mark. A horrendous shrieking, squealing and thrashing rose from the center of the thicket. The hunters leaned forward again on their horses, eyes trained on the tunnels emerging on the meadow side of the brambles.

The visible rattling of the brush suddenly took on direction and speed. Tommaso, perched well back and taking in the whole scene rather than focusing on the expected course, was the first to see the danger.

He stood up on the seat of the cart and screamed, "Turn about! They're coming out the..." Before he could finish with his last word "back," the beaters saw the thrashing in the bush moving toward them like a fast-breaking wave and started scrambling away. Too late. The boar erupted out of the thicket right on top of them.

There were more swine than Tommaso expected, more than he could count in the ensuing chaos: sows and their numerous offspring, ranging in size from dainty babies to more than half-grown weanlings. The sows were enormous. Their short, coarse, dark fur bristled. Their small black eyes gleamed. They looked more bent on revenge than escape. They ran over several of the beaters. One poor man tried to dodge behind a thick tree. The sow pursuing him spun her huge bulk about as nimbly as a deer and, with a sideways toss of her head, threw him into the air. The beater briefly flew, then fell hard.

Tommaso hadn't been overly impressed by the Venetian ambassador before, but now he admired the way the man, white-faced with fear, managed to keep his seat as his horse danced and leapt to avoid the charging pigs.

The tracking hounds, held back once their work was done, broke loose. They were onto the swine before the coursing dogs could race around from the meadow side. One fastened its teeth on a piglet's hind leg. Hearing its young's frantic squeals, the mother and several other boar surged toward it and swarmed over the dog. The piglet broke free and raced away into the forest. Seconds later its rescuers followed it.

Tommaso could hardly discern the dead dog from the ground it had been trampled into.

The hunters on horseback rounded the thicket and chased after the boar scattering deep into the woods. Tommaso cursed. There was no way he could follow with the cart.

Their work done, the beaters gathered to assess their injuries. Because the boar hadn't tarried, most were only battered and bruised. Tommaso now noticed that every one of them was bulky with numerous layers of old clothing; padding against just such an eventuality as they'd endured.

One man suffered a broken or sprained ankle. The worst casualty was the fellow tossed by the huge sow. His collarbone and right arm were broken and he bled freely from a long gash on the outside of his thigh where the sow's tusk had slashed through layers of leggings. Although his face had turned the color of whey and he trembled with shock, Tommaso could tell from the silent looks the other beaters exchanged that he'd been lucky. If the sow had ripped through the inside of his leg to the artery he'd be dying at this moment. The beaters drew up their wagon, loaded the injured man into it and left, leaving Tommaso alone in the clearing.

Tommaso heard distant sounds of horns, hounds and shouting deep in the woods, off to his left. He sighed. His only recourse was to parallel the hunt as best he could along the boundary of meadowland. If he completely lost track of the party, he'd return here, this being the only place where they might think to come fetch him when he was needed. He turned the cart to the left.

With the hunt moved on, the meadows lay still and peaceful again. Considering the lateness of the year, the morning had turned surprisingly warm. The time for the furious hum of swarming summer insects was past. A few industrious bees droned about, taking advantage of the sunny reprieve from the rains of the last few months. Their buzzing and the calls of a few birds constituted the only distractions from Tommaso's strained attempts to track the sounds of the hunt as he drove the cart along. Sometimes he lost the distant din. At other times the noise converged so swiftly toward him that Tommaso pulled the cart up short, fearful that horses, hounds, hunters and boar would come bursting out of the forest on top of him.

And then something *did* crash through the woods—one of the nearly grown boar, a razor-tusked male near enough in size to the mother sows that Tommaso guessed him only scant months from being driven from the brood. Close behind the beast was Caterina on her lithe palfrey.

"Hold back, Tommaso!" she shouted when she saw him. "If your cart stands between him and the meadow he'll run back into the trees. If I run him into the open I can aim cleanly."

Tommaso blanched when he saw that Caterina had her spear out and aimed. Her slight frame didn't possess enough power to deliver a single killing thrust. And there was no one about to aid her in taking the boar down.

Tommaso hauled in on the cart reins and did as Caterina bid him. But as soon as she passed, riding still parallel through the thinner trees of the forest's edge, he slapped the reins with one hand, urging the cart horse forward again, bouncing along to keep Caterina in view. With his other hand he reached behind him and unlatched the box built into the back of the cart. He'd laid his bundled knives on top of the usual farm tools stored there. Between jolts he worked free his longest, sharpest, butchery blade.

The boar resisted Caterina's attempts to drive it into open pasture. Ducking, spinning, feinting, it tried to dodge past her into deeper forest. *Thrust now!* Tommaso thought hopefully, watching the way it took all Caterina's skill to weave her horse through the trees and counterfeint the pig. If she misthrust—or, better yet, lost her head and threw the spear and missed—the creature would seize the opportunity to escape. Even Caterina wouldn't pursue such prey with only her crossbow.

Thrust and miss, Tommaso prayed. He'd jointed, gutted and quartered many swine in his short life—but all of them already dead. If he had to act as Caterina's second in this duel he didn't know if he could save her from an enraged wounded boar.

But Caterina was too experienced a huntress to gamble away her single opportunity. She and the boar continued their impassed dance— she unable to culminate her attack, the beast unable to break free of her. Tommaso despaired. It could not end well.

Then, to the rear, at last the sound of more hoofbeats. Tommaso turned on the buckboard to look. Only one horseman was riding to Caterina's aid, but it was Ippolito. Tommaso begged God's forgiveness for his disparaging thoughts about Ippolito's steed: The small horse twisted through the trees like a fast, sure wind. Ippolito raced abreast of Tommaso, then passed him.

The pig heard Ippolito too. It redoubled its efforts to escape. Caterina urged her mount and stayed close on its heels. The boar, Caterina and Ippolito began to pull away from Tommaso.

The retreating perspective and the way the light and shadow of sun and trees flickered over the speeding hunters played tricks on Tommaso's straining eyes. Both Caterina and Ippolito looked paradoxically larger the farther away they drew. Tommaso felt dizzy. Seen in striped glimpses between the wavering trees, Ippolito looked like a different man, with a broader, duller face and hair leached in color from black to brown, hunting garb blanched from green and gold to black and silver. Caterina appeared years older, a full-figured woman.

The boar made a last desperate maneuver. With a breathtakingly beautiful movement, spinning its bulk impossibly fast on dainty feet, it lunged straight for Caterina's horse's belly. Like a cat, the horse gathered itself and jumped straight up. Caterina thrust her spear under the horse's extended legs and deep into the pig's neck as it passed underneath.

All this unfolded before Tommaso's eyes as slowly as a dream. She knew, he thought. She knew exactly what the boar would do, even before it did. She was ready for it.

The boar screamed. Mortally wounded but far from dead, it whirled, trying to dislodge the spear from its throat. Blood splattered everywhere. The spear's handle whacked against trees, bushes, tangled itself in the hooves of Caterina's mount as the horse leapt up a second time. The palfrey stumbled hard coming down, righted itself, then fled away riderless into the forest.

Miraculously Caterina hadn't been thrown against a tree. But she was down, scrambling to dodge the frantic boar. She looked once again as young and delicate as Tommaso knew her to be. Her hands were outstretched. Tommaso saw she meant to grab the spear handle sticking out of the boar and finish the thrust home. He shouted hoarsely. If the flailing spear struck her, the least it would do was break her bones.

Ippolito at last caught up. Pulling back hard on his reins, he dismounted before his horse fully stopped. He drew his sword as he ran and slashed the swine across its hind legs. Hamstrung, the boar dropped to its knees. The spear end thudded into the ground. Caterina grabbed the spear, twisted it upward, and bore down with all her weight. Blood gurgled from the pig's open mouth, but it still had strength enough to wrench its thick neck around, vaulting Caterina clear over its head. Ippolito shrieked. He plunged his sword between the boar's ribs. It rolled over to its side and lay still. Ippolito was already scrambling over its body to reach Caterina.

Tommaso jumped down from the cart, butcher knife in hand. Other riders at last rode into view: Ippolito's companions and Michelangelo.

Ippolito's face was pale as ice. His voice shook. "Are you all right? Are you injured?" He gently tried to draw Caterina to her feet. When she winced he knelt to pick her up.

She slapped his arm and glared at him. "It was *my* kill. It was already dying when you struck."

"Yes, yes, of course," Ippolito assured her, frantic to see if she was hurt. "My blows were to cripple it only. You'd already finished it."

Caterina looked somewhat mollified.

Looming over them on his horse, Pier Antonio coughed. Ippolito might be a cardinal and Caterina's cousin, but it was inappropriate for a man of his age to be touching a young girl so intimately, no matter how good his intentions. "Perhaps we should send for a physician," he said tactfully.

Now it was Ippolito's turn to glare. "There *is* none here. Caterina's life is dearer to me than my reputation."

"Let me offer my services," suggested Michelangelo. "Though not a professional leech, I've a certain reputation as an anatomist. Considering my age and the contingencies of the situation, I'm better qualified to ascertain the extent of the *Duchessina's* injuries than yourself, 'Lito."

Domenico rode up, leading Caterina's wayward palfrey. Caterina answered the concerns for her well-being by scrambling up and storming over to her horse, though she limped and moved stiffly. Tommaso guessed that by the next morning she'd be black-and-blue, but she obviously suffered no broken bones.

"This is the culprit!" she snarled. She unbuckled the girth of the sidesaddle, pulled the saddle off and flung it as hard as she could against a tree. "My lovely Marcella performed just as I asked her, and my aim was true. 'Twas this hideous contraption betrayed me. It catapulted me almost to my death. A thousand curses on the woman-hating man who invented this obscenity!"

Ippolito's companions openly grinned their amusement. Caterina turned on them. "You find this droll? I'd wager half the Medici fortune to see a single one of you ride to hunt strapped and bound off-balance to one side."

Pier Antonio put up a hand to stop and placate her. "That's not why we smile, *Duchessina*. I believe every man here would concede that the women we know who hunt are our superiors in equestrianship, forced as they are to ride under those difficult restrictions you just described." He turned to look at the other young athletes, struggling to smooth their faces to some degree of solemnity. He pointed down at the boar. "We smile because you rage like a warrior, even with your foe well-vanquished. You are one of us."

The other men hastily nodded.

Somewhat appeased, Caterina at last let Michelangelo examine her.

"No bones broken, no joints damaged," he verified. The sculptor peered into her eyes and cupped the back of her head gently in a gesture Tommaso remembered well. "I discern no concussion and no internal injuries," Michelangelo said. "Still, you must be closely monitored. It would be a grave matter should you start to bleed from the nose or mouth. We'll return you to the lodge immediately. The sooner you're poulticed the better. I'm afraid that even if you could be ministered to this very instant, you'd still find yourself facing some days of misery and discomfort."

He turned to Tommaso. "Load the swine as quickly as you can into the back of the cart. In the meantime we'll endeavor to make the *Duchessina* as comfortable as possible on the seat beside you."

Tommaso wrestled the pig's carcass onto the back of the cart with the help of several of Ippolito's companions.

"Since we're absconding with this conveyance," Ippolito said, "Domenico, you take the packhorses and search out the rest of the hunt. I'm sure they'll also have game to haul home. The rest of you go with Domenico."

Ippolito and several of the other young men piled their hunting jackets to make a softer seat for Caterina on the cart. Some unspoken interchange passed between Ippolito's friends, for when they rode off Pier Antonio stayed behind, reining his horse next to Michelangelo's. Ippolito looked irritated but said nothing.

Tommaso climbed up onto the seat next to Caterina. Her face was drawn. Braced up against her as he was, Tommaso felt how she held herself tight and still. She'd begun to feel the pain but refused to show it.

Pier Antonio tried to allay their anxiety on the journey back with light banter. When he'd exhausted his supply he turned to Michelangelo.

"*Ser* Buonarotti, since you've just returned, tell us how lovely Florence fares these days."

Michelangelo hesitated a moment before replying. "Florence demonstrates her strength by the resiliency with which she recovers," he said. He grudgingly told them some anecdotes about his friends among Florence's artists, some vignettes on the postsiege reconstruction efforts of Florence's leading citizenry. The sculptor's conversation was notable for the names not mentioned. Tommaso knew from his parents' letters of all the families banished from the city, their wealth confiscated to enrich de' Medici and papal coffers.

Even in the face of Michelangelo's obvious reluctance, Pier Antonio was determined to mine what optimism he could from Michelangelo's stories. "When you return from your next visit surely you'll have news of even further improvements," he said cheerfully.

Michelangelo looked at Pier Antonio with more than a little irritation. He gave up on humoring the irrepressible young man.

"There will be no further visits," he said sharply. "Alessandro de Medici had the *Vacca* lowered and smashed to pieces in the *piazza*, declaring the death of the Republic. I shall not return to my native land as long as he holds sway."

Tommaso felt a movement beside him. He turned to look at Caterina. She was white as alabaster and trembling with cold. The bravado with which she'd held herself together since her fall had vanished.

"Ippolito!" Tommaso called urgently. He jerked his head at Caterina when the Cardinal glanced around.

Ippolito took one look at his cousin and leapt from his horse, tossing the reins to Michelangelo. He clambered onto the cart and began chafing Caterina's hands and wrists to warm them. Michelangelo took off his own hunting coat and handed it to Ippolito to drape about her shoulders. Ippolito did so and then drew Caterina to him, warming her.

Pier Antonio produced a small flask of brandy. Ippolito held it to Caterina's lips until her cheeks showed some pink again. Tears streamed down her face.

"Oh 'Lito," she sobbed. "I treated you vilely, though I hold you in higher esteem than life itself. You saved me from great injury, yet I had not one word of gratitude to spare you. I'm unworthy of your attentions."

Ippolito laughed with relief and hugged her to him fiercely. "No, dearest. It's just that your valiant heart wouldn't acknowledge your distress. Like a good soldier you kept on battling. My men are right to call you one of us."

Finally Caterina's tears and trembling subsided. She looked embarrassed at her outburst.

"An expected reaction," Michelangelo assured her. "Such shivering is natural to the shock you suffered. I've seen worse. You should see how Benevenuto Cellini quivers with the feverish ague he suffers."

This caught Tommaso's interest. "Cellini is ill?"

Michelangelo nodded. "I stopped by to see him before I came here."

Ippolito laughed. "Ill this and every fall. He's famous in Rome for catching a seasonal sniffle, then 'curing' himself in the 'bracing, healthy, outdoor air' by hunting in foul autumnal weather, so that he defeats a small cold by turning it into pneumonia."

"*Every* hunting season he does this?" Tommaso asked.

Ippolito nodded.

Tommaso turned and stared at Caterina.

"Oh, did I forget to tell you?" she said, her composure and good humor restored. "I meant to. Until Cellini recovers, *Ser* Buonarotti here will tutor you."

By the time they intersected with Maria Salviati, who with the two ambassadors and several of the other hunters had come looking for them, Ippolito was back on his horse and all was decorum again. Caterina, though she admitted to feeling more sore and bruised every moment, sat sedately next to Tommaso, Michelangelo's jacket still wrapped around her.

Maria Salviati made a great commotion over Caterina. As soon as they returned to the lodge she whisked her young charge away to their sleeping quarters and placed her in a bed piled high with cushions.

Tommaso spent the next few days divided between cooking duties and preparing fresh batches of poultice for Caterina's bruises. The lodge had a decent supply of flaxseed, but he had to send servants searching for valerian and the other ingredients. No longer was there time for sweet stolen dalliances with Michelangelo.

Tommaso rejoiced the day they left the lodge. He hoped never to attend a hunt again. With the experience behind him, there was nothing but good to look forward to. Soon he'd be learning art again, this time by Michelangelo's side. He was eager to return to the Salviati kitchen in Rome and his cooking. After the events of the hunt, surely his life would be restful by comparison.

His expectations of any kind of a respite were dashed the moment the hunting party returned to the Salviati compound.

The entire household sizzled with anxiety, all of it centered around the *Duchessina*. How badly was she hurt? When would she be well? Or at least presentable?

"What is all this commotion about the *Duchessina*?" Tommaso asked Bindo Ramerino.

"Her uncle is arriving in Rome in just a few days. Mostly to meet with the Pope, but he's also requested an audience with the *Duchessina*. He'll want to have some say in the plans for her future," the baker said.

Tommaso thought. Caterina's father Lorenzo, Duke of Urbino, had no siblings other than Clarice Strozzi. Clarice's husband Fillipo Strozzi was Caterina's only uncle.

"Why such a fuss over Messer Strozzi?" he puzzled. "The Strozzis and Salviatis have been compatriots for generations."

"Not *that* uncle," said *Ser* Ramerino. "The other one."

Tommaso looked at the man blankly.

"The *French* one. One of the brothers of her mother. The Duke of Albany."

8

Tommaso wished his heart would stay where it belonged, in his chest. It insisted on leaping into his throat, then plunging down to his gut, then bouncing back up past his tonsils. I can't do this, he told himself as he shuffled through the papers in front of him with one trembling hand. His other hand held a linen-draped majolica plate.

The papers belonged to the room's occupant, one of the Salviati's houseguests, Gianmatteo Vitelli, a Florentine textile merchant.

I know nothing about spying. I'm a cook, Tommaso thought.

He sorted through bills for orders of watered silks and Persian taffeta from Venice's port, New World dyes from Spanish captains. Forms for sales of Florentine brocade, velvet slippers and silk-lined shoes to Germany and Hungary.

There's nothing of use here. Tommaso was relieved.

The bottommost sheet caught the attention of his hands rather than his eyes. Instead of the thin, brittle texture of sales papers, his fingers met the soft, thick surface of good vellum. Tommaso drew it out. It was a letter from Gianmatteo Vitelli to one Cardinal Salviati. It was unfinished and unsealed. Tommaso skimmed its contents.

He heard footsteps just as they reached the door, and cursed that the Salviatis were so wealthy that rugs lined and muffled all the hallways. A key turned, then turned again in the lock. Tommaso just had time to slip the letter back to the bottom of the pile.

"I wondered why my door wasn't locked. Who are you? What on

earth are you doing here?" Gianmatteo Vitelli stood in the doorway, angry at finding a stranger in his room. He was a thin, sedentary-looking man of average height, but his indignation swelled his presence.

Tommaso swung the covered plate he held in front of him when he saw the man's hand drop to the dirk hanging from his belt.

"I'm Tommaso Arista, the *Duchessina* Caterina de' Medici's chef," Tommaso said hastily. "This morning Her Grace awoke quite homesick. She entreated me to make her some of these." Tommaso thrust the plate at the man, whose hands rose up defensively at the motion, then automatically grabbed the plate as Tommaso started to let it go.

Once Vitelli safely held the platter, Tommaso whisked off the linen covering its contents. "*Brigidini,* her favorite sweet." He waved the towel gently, wafting the thin wafers' aniseed scent up to the merchant's nose. "The *Duchessina* took such succor from them that she commissioned me to prepare a batch for all expatriate Tuscans in the house." Tommaso had spent the better part of the day pressing the cookies, one by one, between heated flatirons.

"You were among those she insisted I mustn't fail to serve. Your manservant was supping in the kitchen as I finished baking these. Since he was in the middle of breaking his fast, he consented to lend me his key to the room, so I might deliver them. I was trying to place these somewhere where they wouldn't leave crumbs, yet you wouldn't fail to see them.

"And Her Grace wished this to accompany them..." Tommaso fished around in a pocket. He drew forth and handed the merchant a note secured with red wax stamped with Caterina's seal.

Mollified, the merchant gave the plate of sweets back to Tommaso. "Set these anywhere," he said as he opened the note. "I adore *brigidini.* I was just mentioning to Cardinal de' Medici the other day how much I miss them. There will be no crumbs to worry about."

Tommaso watched Vitelli read the note. The merchant's eyebrows rose in pleased surprise. He smiled to himself and nodded. Then he looked up. "What are you still doing here?" he asked, frowning.

"Your manservant's key," Tommaso said politely. "Since you've returned to your room, do you wish me to leave the key with you, or return it to him in the kitchen?"

"Oh, that." Vitelli waved his hand to dismiss the matter. His eyes had already dropped back to the note. "Give it to him there."

Tommaso bowed and left. I'm invisible, he marveled, dancing a little jig down the empty hallway. As I'm long as I'm seen as just a servant doing his business, I'm invisible.

Caterina was preparing to attend the theater with her Salviati relations when Tommaso reported to her. She sat very still as one of her maids dressed her hair. Tommaso could hear Caterina's ladies-in-waiting getting dressed in the wardrobe room. Caterina rolled her eyes toward him. "What did Messer Vitelli think of the contents of my note?" she asked.

"He said nothing," Tommaso replied. "But he looked both pleased and surprised."

Caterina started to nod. The woman working on her hair clicked her tongue and sighed.

Caterina grinned at Tommaso, but said contritely, "Forgive me, Nannina."

"*Please*, Your Grace. Only a moment more." Nannina gathered up several of Caterina's blonde braids and tied them with several flat gold chains.

Caterina obediently froze in place. "Messer Vitelli should look pleased," she said, barely moving her mouth to speak. "I wrote him that as a fellow Florentine and Tuscan, I hoped he'd like the treat I sent him. And that as a fellow Florentine and Tuscan, I felt—seeing how I need some fine brocade for myself and my ladies—that I should order from his business. I requested he come see me, bringing samples of his finest, most expensive cloth. I trust he liked the *brigidini?*"

Now it was Tommaso's turn to grin. Ippolito had told Caterina of Vitelli's weakness for the sweet as soon as the merchant told Ippolito. "I didn't stay to watch him eat, but I'm sure he did. How fortunate for him that Your Grace should have suffered such a nostalgic craving this morning."

"Indeed. Perhaps I will suffer similar cravings in the future. Speaking of food, shall we begin our new system?"

"Yes. I brought these, as you asked." Tommaso held up a slate and several pieces of chalk.

"There, my lady. I'm finished," Nannina said, handing Caterina a chased-silver mirror. Nannina held up a second one behind Caterina, so the *Duchessina* could see her hair from every angle.

Caterina turned her head to look. "Excellent. Next I need a damp-ened, clean rag. While you fetch it, Tommaso and I have menus to discuss."

When the woman left, Tommaso wrote down a quick summary of what he'd read in the unfinished letter in Vitelli's room, then handed it to Caterina.

"It's as I thought," Caterina said. "He writes to Cardinal Salviati—a cousin of Jacopo's and also the papal legate in Parma. Vitelli is spying on me for the cardinal, who is spying on me from afar for Clement. Now that he'll be supplying me with fabric, Vitelli will have greater opportunity to observe me."

"Is that wise?" Tommaso whispered.

Just then Nannina returned with the damp cloth. With a stroke, Caterina erased what Tommaso had written. "Would you please bring me the small carved ivory *cassone* from the wardrobe room? It contains the earrings I mean to wear tonight," she said to Nannina.

As Nannina entered the wardrobe, several of Caterina's resplendently dressed ladies-in-waiting came out of it. Caterina wrote something on the slate, then handed it to Tommaso, facedown. It said: *The more Vitelli observes me, the more he'll observe exactly what I wish him to, which he'll convey to Clement, by way of Salviati.*

Nodding, Tommaso reached for the damp cloth, then wiped the slate clean.

"I wanted to speak to you about one other thing, my gossip," she said. "I know that your tutor Bartolommeo Scappi often caters large banquets for Rome's most influential citizens. On evenings such as this, when my relatives and I are gone and the labor in the kitchen here lessens, let Messer Scappi know that I'd not be averse to your helping him out on occasion. Such experience can only improve your skills and knowl-edge."

Knowledge, especially, of anything I might overhear, Tommaso thought as he bowed and took his leave.

9

Tommaso set the tray laden with the *primi servizi de credenza* and a salad down on Venetian Ambassador Venier's desk. "The *Duchessina*, hearing that Your Excellency suffers from a depressed appetite, begs that you sample these humble morsels. She hopes they regenerate your health, so your wit and wisdom may once again be enjoyed in the banquet hall," Tommaso said. "There's enough here for yourself and your secretary."

Tommaso turned and gestured to Averardo to enter the ambassador's suite and unload *his* burden: a larger tray carrying a small tureen of pheasant broth, a dish of gnocchi napped with a sienna-colored sauce made from Caterina's wild boar, and a platter of squab stuffed with mushrooms and tiny onions.

Signor Venier lifted the napkin to peek at the appetizers on Tommaso's tray. For an instant he paled, lending credence to his pose of infirmity. But when he leaned forward with gleaming eyes to sniff at the *crostini*, the marinated prawns, and the *sedani in pinzimonio*, Tommaso wagered that if the Venetian were to faint at that moment it would be for pleasure.

Poor Signor Venier! Forced to hide away in his room for days, the main kitchen sending only the plainest of comestibles up to his suite. The cooking staff was taxed preparing grand meals for the most recent august visitors. Therefore, they weren't inclined to deliver anything but the simple invalid's food required by Signor Venier's supposed infirmity.

Signor Venier suffered in silence. What else could he do? If he complained and requested richer food, his hosts would presume his illness over and expect his presence in the banquet hall.

Which Signor Venier didn't dare. If he left his suite he risked running into one of the people he feared most in the world: Clarice Strozzi's old friend Isabella d'Este, the Marchessa of Mantua.

And well should he fear her, Tommaso thought. During the siege of Rome the marchessa had taken the ambassador into the protection of her palazzo, along with hundreds of others. In his case she even ransomed him from a Spanish nobleman who'd first sheltered him and then threatened to turn him over to the *reiters.* More than that, the marchessa included Venier in the small circle of her friends and servants who fled the city under her soldier son Ferrante's protection.

The ambassador repaid the marchessa's kindness poorly. He refused to compensate her for the funds she'd spent to ransom him. In fact, he denied the entire affair and pleaded diplomatic immunity. Since the marchessa had remained in Mantua after the siege, he'd been able to skirt the issue for several years.

But now she'd returned to Rome to shop for her eldest son's new bride. Even worse, the marchessa enjoyed free access throughout the Salviati mansion. Because of her familiarity with the French court, she enjoyed excellent rapport with the Duke of Albany. The Salviatis had asked her to coach Caterina and present the *Duchessina* to her uncle the Duke.

"How kind of the *Duchessina* to remember my humble self," Venier said. "It would be ungrateful not to at least try to avail myself of her suggested cure." The ambassador turned his attention to the *sedani in pinzimonio.* He dipped the end of a pure white stalk of celery into the bowl of newly pressed olive oil and took a small bite. "Ah, perfectly tender." He sighed.

"Grown wrapped away against the sun in one of the Salviati gardens in Tuscany." Tommaso smiled at the ambassador's pleasure. "Then, still wrapped, transported here swiftly in one of their messenger coaches, so that its freshness is not lost."

"After such care, I shall not act the accomplice to any detrimental aging on its part," Venier declared. "My secretary and I will attend to our preprandial ablutions this very instant. You may clear a space over there and set our supper up." He gestured toward a table covered with papers.

Tommaso smiled again. Venier could not have been more accommodating to Caterina's wishes than if he'd known them.

"Averardo, I'll clear the table and pile the ambassador's work, so if anything is out of order no blame will attach to you. You may arrange the plates and food," Tommaso said as soon as the ambassador and secretary retired to a room deeper in the suite to wash up.

Tommaso shuffled paperwork as he transferred it to the desk, ostensibly straightening it as he scanned documents and letters quickly. There were a few items he knew would interest Caterina, and one letter in particular caught his eye.

When Venier and his secretary returned, Tommaso and Averardo respectfully stood by to serve them and discreetly carry away the dishes. During the meal Venier gave away nothing useful in his idle chatter with his secretary. Tommaso had to content himself with the information he'd gleaned from the correspondence.

The next day Tommaso served a midmorning repast in Caterina's rooms for the *Duchessina*, Maria Salviati, Isabella d'Este, the Duke of Albany and a few of his menservants. All but two of the ladies-in-waiting had been dismissed from the intimate gathering. This made it easy for Caterina to draw Tommaso aside when he arrived.

"Please excuse me, Your Excellency, while I confer with my chef for a moment," she said to her French uncle.

The Duke of Albany bowed to her, then swept back his reddish-tinged hair from where it had fallen across his high, fair-skinned forehead.

Tommaso waved Laudomia and two of the kitchen apprentices to set up the buffet of veal sweetbread pastries, smoked mussels, a timbale of cod tripe, a salad of bitter greens garnished in the Tuscan style with olive oil and *caciocavallo* cheese, grilled squares of buckwheat polenta shot through and through with tender leeks, and that Milanese sweet, *panettone*.

Stepping aside with Caterina, in a few softly spoken words Tommaso summed up the information he'd gleaned the day before from Venier's desk. He felt the Duke of Albany's gaze on their backs. Each time Tommaso had seen him, the man was studying Caterina as if she were a medical specimen.

"It's always useful to avail oneself of whatever intelligence the Venetians share back and forth amongst themselves," Caterina said quietly. "Besides their Council of Ten's notorious hunger for knowledge pure and simple, for now, at least, they stand outside the arena of politics we find ourselves enmeshed in, and so may be our best source of nearly unbiased information."

Tommaso was impressed at her astuteness. Currently, the wily, canal-dwelling merchants governed the only major Italian state not burdened by the yoke of Emperor, Papacy or the French. Even Isabella d'Este, perhaps the wiliest diplomat in Italy, had tactfully accepted the Emperor's dominion, albeit at the same time negotiating Mantua's advancement from a simple state to a duchy. *She* might have married downward from her royal lineage of Ferrara to become only a marchessa in Mantua, but her eldest son Federico was Mantua's first duke, by decree of the Emperor.

"Tell me, Marquesa, more of your friendship with Signor Castiglione," Albany was saying to Isabella d'Este, though his gaze hadn't left Caterina. "His book is all the rage these days in the French court. Now that my king has decided that *The Courtier* is the text we should model our lives after, any true anecdote of its author that I can entertain His Majesty with on my return to France will strengthen my standing with him."

"François could have served as the model for *The Courtier,*" Isabella said. "I'll never forget the courtesies and favors His Most Christian Majesty lavished on my son during Federico's visit to the French court all those years ago. Federico left Mantua a callow youth and returned a polished gentleman."

Tommaso liked the marchessa. Even in plump middle age her face was pretty, her warm brown eyes bright with intelligence and wit. And she treated Caterina well.

"How astute of François to require his court to make a study of my beloved Baldessare's book," Isabella continued. "But I doubt, Albany, that *your* standing with your royal cousin needs any buttressing."

"Perhaps not with His Highness," the Duke admitted. In demeanor usually cool, almost cold, he now seemed somewhat discomfited. "But the rest of the court still japes me for what they see as my failure to retain the regency of Scotland. They quip that it's an irony that my uncouth blood and manners were the very impediments that turned those uncouth, exasperating people against me," he said. "The court pretends not to understand that I had no wish to return to the land of my northern ancestors. I only did so at my cousin the King's desire, and to protect my infant cousin the heir from the venal bumbling of his slow-witted English mother."

Albany recovered himself with a smile. "So I will best the court at its own game of manners by returning from Italy with the latest news on the most current fashions, a new air of Italian polish, and special insights on the author of the model on exemplary behavior from those who knew and loved him best."

Tommaso made a deliberately loud promise to Caterina to serve sea bream *poltettina fritte* when Albany next visited. Then he finished up the last-minute touches to the buffet. He was still adjusting to the information that Caterina was not actually the "half-French little Medici" all Florence referred to.

Caterina's grandfather the Duke of Albany—the father of *this* Duke of Albany, and also of Caterina's mother—had been brother to the king of Scotland and next in line to the Scottish throne. The Scottish king imprisoned Caterina's grandfather and another brother on no stronger a reason than a soothsayer's obscure prophecy. The other brother died while shut away, possibly murdered. Caterina's grandfather escaped by killing his guards and letting himself down the castle walls with a rope. From there he'd fled to France, where he married into the French royal family.

Tommaso had been appalled when, with great relish on her part, Caterina told him the story as if it were a grand adventure. But afterward he reflected on the strange fact that the least aristocratic blood in her veins was that of the Medicis.

Isabella d'Este wouldn't let Albany change the conversation gracefully. "When you say the French court japes you about your visits to Scotland, perhaps you're referring to the incident with the hat?" she said, with a slight smile.

"Incidents," Albany corrected her. "And the Scots' peculiar headgear is called a *bonnet*. The first time I went to that accursed land I must have thrown twelve *bonnets* in the fire over a two-year period, so in a rage did those people put me."

"What a harmless, if eccentric, manner of dealing with one's sub-ordinates," Caterina observed politely.

Albany might be a frosty and at times bad-tempered man, but he wasn't stupid. He looked at Caterina sharply. "It was that or execute the whole lot of them," he said. "As it was, I showed remarkable restraint in dispatching only a few members of the Hume family, those treacherous blackguards."

Caterina nodded disinterestedly, just barely acknowledging her uncle's point that he was not a man to be crossed.

Tommaso's reaction to the man wasn't as mild as Caterina's. He was furious. How dare Albany imply a threat to the *Duchessina*? Besides that, he'd been staring in the most rude manner at Caterina during the entire soirée, as if she were a horse he might buy. Tommaso half expected the Duke to march up to Caterina, pry open her mouth and inspect her teeth.

Caterina saw the seething look on Tommaso's face. "The buffet looks splendid, Tommaso," she said hastily. "You and your assistants may leave. Surely my uncle the Duke's gentlemen will be gallant enough to serve us."

Perhaps in France its king had to order the highest levels of aristocracy to read *The Courtier* to learn some manners. But here in Italy everyone of any learning studied its virtues, including Tommaso. Although, he admitted, in his case it was because both Caterina and Michelangelo insisted. Right now he was glad of that insistence. What was it Baldessare Castiglione had said of the French? Oh, yes, that was it:

> "And if you consider the court of France, which is today one of the noblest in Christendom, you will find that all those who there enjoy universal favor tend to be presumptuous, not only toward one another, but toward the king himself."

Indeed.

Domenico the Tartar stood waiting in the corridor just outside Caterina's suite. "The Cardinal wants to see you at once," he announced. Tommaso sighed and gave Laudomia and the apprentices leave to return to the kitchen. Because of the residue of feelings he bore Filomena, he wanted to like Domenico as a countryman of sorts to the slave girl. It was impossible. The fellow was too abrupt for Tommaso's taste.

Ippolito's manners, on the other hand, were the opposite of his Tartar comrade's.

"Tommaso, forgive me for calling you away from your duties so precipitously," Ippolito said. He was dressed almost as eccentrically as his companions, in a cordovan-colored velvet Hungarian hunting outfit. This surprised Tommaso. Since Albany's arrival in Rome, Ippolito had almost exclusively worn his cardinal's raiment. Tommaso was sure Ippolito hoped to persuade both the duke that he was merely Caterina's devoted cleric cousin, and the Pope that he at last accepted the fate Clement had chosen for him.

"Not at all. I am, as always, *your* humble servant," Tommaso replied, glancing pointedly past Ippolito at Domenico. The Tartar ignored him.

At Caterina's behest, everything Tommaso told her he also reported to Ippolito. He updated Ippolito on the discourse in Caterina's suite and the correspondence he'd spied out in the Venetian ambassador's rooms.

"What excuse do you have for me today?" Tommaso asked when he finished. When by himself, Tommaso could slip away and find Ippolito discreetly and unnoticed. Unfortunately, more and more Tommaso was accompanied by an entourage of apprentices or some of the two chefs' children to help with his service to Caterina. On those occasions Ippolito had to come up with a reason to request Tommaso.

"A very real errand. One I would have needed your assistance with in any case. One which no one will question. Come, my friend. I want you to deliver a gift of thanks to a fellow Florentine for the services he rendered our *Duchessina*."

Tommaso followed Ippolito, Domenico, and Beroaldo, the Bengalese diver who'd quipped with Tommaso in the hall when Tommaso first arrived at the mansion. They went through the mansion and out the back courtyard to the stables. In the stables, the aisle between the stalls was crowded with mules braying in protest as grooms loaded heavy sacks on their backs.

"You're giving someone all these mules?" Tommaso asked.

"No, just the provender they carry." Ippolito laughed. "Pier Antonio! Is she ready?"

Pier Antonio Pecci and a young groom emerged from a nearby stall with the deerlike horse Ippolito had ridden on the hunt.

"Tommaso, I hope you will do me the great favor of escorting Frisio here"—the young groom bowed—"and Aquila"—Ippolito indicated the mare—"to my good friend Michelangelo Buonarotti. Present them to him in my name, as thanks for his care of my cousin Caterina when she was so sorely injured. Tell *Ser* Buonarotti that Frisio's wages and board will be covered by my account for as long as he finds the lad's work acceptable. The mules carry enough fodder for Aquila to last her at least a little while."

Behind Ippolito, Domenico rolled his eyes at the understatement. It was the most emotion Tommaso had ever seen the Tartar express.

Patrons often courted Michelangelo with presents. A man of simple and austere wants who wished to resist undue influence when he could, the sculptor regularly refused almost all gifts. Tommaso guessed he would accept this one.

Ascancio answered when they knocked at the *bottega*'s door.

"Tommaso, what is all this?" he said, staring in bewilderment at the eleven animals milling about, filling the narrow street. The muleteer Ippolito had rented the pack animals from had his hands full making them behave.

Tommaso grinned at the apprentice. "Fetch your master, and say nothing to him other than that I wait at his door with a delivery."

Michelangelo came to the door looking as bewildered as Ascancio, yet pleased to see Tommaso. When the sculptor saw the little mare his eyes glowed.

"Maestro Buonarotti," Tommaso said formally, "please accept this steed, sent to you by His Excellency Cardinal Ippolito de' Medici as a small measure of the great esteem in which he holds you, and in thanks for the many services you've rendered his family. Including, most recently, attending to the injuries incurred by his cousin, the *Duchessina* Caterina Romola de' Medici, during the hunt near the Salviati family estates." Tommaso stopped to catch his breath.

Michelangelo inspected the mare with delight. "Tell His Excellency I gratefully accept this treasure," he said. "Ippolito is one of my few true friends in the world, who knows what truly pleases me. Tell him I'll be forever in his debt."

"So that you'll be in no way inconvenienced by his gift, he's also sent along provender in these sacks"—Tommaso waved his hands, indicating the mules and their burden—"and Messer Frisio here." He introduced the young groom, who bowed in awestruck silence. "Despite his youth, Frisio is most competent with horses. He can care not only for Aquila, but your other horses as well. His wages are covered by His Excellency's accounts for as long as you find his work acceptable."

Michelangelo left off murmuring to the mare long enough to acknowledge Frisio.

Few Romans possessed the wealth of the Salviatis and could boast their own stables. Michelangelo, preferring the sparse lifestyle of his studio, boarded his few steeds at a stable a short distance away. He sent Pietro de Urbino, Ascancio and his other apprentices to arrange for a stall for Aquila and board for Frisio there, and to help unload the grain sacks. Tommaso stayed behind while Michelangelo penned his gratitude to Ippolito, then lingered a while longer in Michelangelo's arms.

Michelangelo could not have been more tender. But Tommaso noticed, to his amusement, that while the gift of the mare put the sculptor in an even more sensuous mood than usual, until Tommaso could hardly bear the edges of ecstasy his lover brought him to, a part of Michelangelo was distracted. So, Tommaso thought, apparently there is one more mistress besides his art that I must compete with. Even while Michelangelo kissed him deeply, Tommaso could tell the sculptor was thinking about when he would be able to find time to ride the beautiful animal. Tommaso couldn't bring himself to resent the mare. She would bring Michelangelo such pleasure, and she didn't really compete with what he and the sculptor shared.

That night as Tommaso lay on his cot in the Salviati mansion he thought of the way Michelangelo touched things, looked at things—the stone he sculpted, Tommaso, the mare as he realized that she was his.

Michelangelo tried to comprehend and appreciate each object, being, or creature on its own terms. That was why his assessments were so clear and swift, often mistaken as brusque. That was why, when he chose to, he sculpted so quickly and cleanly.

In contrast, look at the way the Duke of Albany—who was certainly intelligent, and probably no better or worse than any other man—had stared at Caterina, appraising her with not even as much appreciation as Michelangelo's for the mare.

But then, no one seemed to truly see Caterina. The Milanese ambassador had stayed in the Salviati mansion for several days after the hunt. Tommaso spied on him for Caterina. Among other letters written in the ambassador's hand, Tommaso had read this:

> "I have seen her now twice on horseback. She seems to me rather large for her age, fairly good-looking without the help of any cosmetic, a blonde with a rather stout face. But she appears very young and I do not believe she can be called or considered a woman for a year and a half or longer. It is said that she has good feelings and a very acute and adroit mind for her age."

Then this very morning, in Venier's suite, Tommaso had read a report buried amongst discussions of Venetian policy:

> "The *Duchessina* is of a rather vivacious nature, but shows an amiable disposition. She was educated by the nuns of the Convent of the Murate in Florence and she has very good manners. She is small and thin. Her face is not refined and she has the big eyes characteristic of the Medici.
>
> "The Most Reverend Cardinal de' Medici is very envious of Duke Alessandro because it seems to him that the Pope did him a great injustice in putting the Duke instead of him at the head of the government of Florence. I have also heard it whispered by some that the Cardinal de' Medici wants to put off his ecclesiastical robes and to take as his wife the *Duchessina*, his third cousin, with whom he lives on the best possible terms and is also very much loved by her. Indeed, there is no other in whom she confides in so much or whose counsel she is apt to seek."

Tommaso hadn't told Caterina of these letters. What would be the point? To make her more conscious of the rumors she already knew too well?

But he couldn't understand why the ambassadors saw her so differently. True, they did perceive in common certain essentials of her nature, such as her intelligence and her lively good manners. But that they should observe her physical attributes so differently puzzled Tommaso. The Milanese ambassador saw her as a large girl with a stout face. Venier saw Caterina as small and thin. One would almost think that when they looked at her a different girl presented herself to each of them.

10

February, 1531

Although Clement wished Michelangelo to labor full time on the *Last Judgment*, the artist refused to let his life be taken over the way it had been when Pope Julius commanded him to paint the ceiling of the Sistine Chapel.

"One pope almost killed me decorating that building. I won't let another one finish the job," Michelangelo growled, centering a wax maquette in position on a spitlike arrangement set in a long trough. He rotated the handle attached to the outside of the trough. Gears meshed together and turned, lowering the maquette inside its container.

"Perfect," Michelangelo said. "Urbino, you may commence with your task."

Urbino nodded and reached for a bucket from Ascancio, who stood first in a row of apprentices bearing pails of water. Tommaso was third in the line, affording him an excellent view of the proceedings. Urbino poured the water along the sides of the trough, taking care not to disrupt the maquette's position on its spit. Bucket after bucket was emptied. Apprentices ran for more, until water filled the trough, covering the maquette. Meanwhile, Michelangelo arranged his chisels and hammers next to a huge block of creamy white marble placed on its side nearby.

"Now we're ready to address this technique," he said, turning again to the trough. "Notice that the water is smooth and level." The apprentices nodded. The water lay as flat as a mirror.

The sculptor turned the trough's handle in the opposite direction, raising the mechanism. A small portion of the maquette broke free above the water. Michelangelo stooped until he knelt eye level to the waterline and emerging model. He motioned that all the apprentices do likewise.

"Observe how in this manner the highest parts are revealed first and act as your guide."

The sculptor stood. Picking up his chisels and hammer, he started cutting away at the marble block, glancing over his shoulder frequently at the trough. The sections of the maquette that showed above the water looked like nothing more than a few shallow anonymous islands adrift in a rectangular sea. He finished a quick rough-out of those tiny sections in the marble, then raised the maquette a fraction more. "Little by little the lower sections come into view. If one goes slowly and with care, it's impossible to get ahead of oneself and sculpt in error on a piece," he said.

Michelangelo was *not* proceeding slowly. Chips of fine stone flew from the marble block. Urbino took over the task of turning the trough's handle when it was time to raise the model higher above the waterline.

Michelangelo also appeared not to take the care he recommended. He didn't spend time studying the placement of the chisel before he struck, yet the emerging, abstract, disconnected sections were perfect enlarged replicas of what showed of the model. Michelangelo might insist that nothing could go wrong with this method, but Tommaso observed that if one's eye didn't measure the distances between the "islands" correctly, one could end up with a piece where all the details were perfect but the various sections wouldn't connect together properly or in the right proportion.

Even a master like Michelangelo wasn't going to rough-cut an entire sculpture in a single demonstration. He set down his chisels at last and picked up some charcoal. As Urbino continued to raise the maquette, Michelangelo marked up sections of the marble with the charcoal, explaining how he'd proceed. Then he demonstrated how, by turning a second handle, the maquette could be turned in place, like a roast on a spit. Finally, he returned the wax model to its original position.

Tommaso paid attention as best he could. As the maquette emerged past the halfway mark above the water, however, he became distracted by its reflection in the pool that held it.

It appeared as though the growing model had budded a perfect twin in the water, which grew more complete and closer to separation with every turn of the raising-lowering handle. There could be a whole separate world in there, Tommaso thought. Like the identical but opposite world of the slave girl Filomena's people. Tommaso watched with fascination as the image of the lovely, substanceless second statue grew in the water.

I must remember this idea, he thought. Surely I can find a use for it someday.

11

March, 1531

"Vittoriano, be sure that any who aren't dancing don't go thirsty." Tommaso raised his voice to be heard over the musicians. The youngest apprentice nodded that he understood, then picked up a bottle of wine and made his way over to where a number of Ippolito's companions either lounged against the walls and pushed-back furniture of Caterina's reception room, or sat on the rolled-up carpets. Some watched the dancing lesson in progress, others talked and laughed about the tennis tournament Ippolito had hosted earlier in the afternoon.

The day of the dancing lesson was Tommaso's favorite of the entire week. His preparations precluded his doing any other work in the kitchen, but the fare was light and easy—plenty of beverages and an assortment of *primi servizi di credenza*. Today the table was spread with platters of clams sautéed in their shells, slices of various cured meats, *pane fritto*, and tender early-spring vegetables either pickled or served fresh to dip in newly pressed olive oil. Caterina's cat crouched under the table. She stalked out whenever anyone approached the clams, stretching out a paw to them in endearing, if arrogant, supplication. It made Tommaso laugh to see how often she succeeded with her entreaty.

He soon discharged his responsibilities, except for two: standing ready to respond to any requests and warning those of Ippolito's comrades who eschewed pork flesh away from certain dishes. Otherwise, Tommaso was free to enjoy the music and the spectacle of the dancers.

Caterina's dance master first demonstrated the footwork with precise, fastidious steps. Then Caterina, her ladies, Ippolito and those of his entourage who deigned to dance aped the master's choreography until they performed it to his satisfaction. At last he'd consent to let the musicians sweep them along through the whole dance with a tune.

One of the things Tommaso missed most about Florence was its music. Someone playing pipes on a street corner, the sound of a viol drifting down from the upper windows of a merchant's home, the glory of horns that accompanied every pageant, his mother and the other Ruggiero kitchen servants singing old Tuscan songs together as they worked—these were such an integral part of the weft of Florentine life that Tommaso had never taken notice of them until he suffered their lack here in Rome.

So these dance lessons lifted his spirits. The tunes set his toes and heart tapping. The bright-colored garb of Ippolito's companions and the gay dancing raiment of Caterina's ladies-in-waiting acted as songs for the eyes.

There was no man there so handsome as Ippolito. He always wore his Cardinal's robes to Caterina's apartment, an outward symbol that as a cleric his relationship with her was chaste and beyond reproach. But his brilliant clothing and the way it swirled about him as he danced set off his erect carriage, lean face, and black hair and beard, and pointed up the truth of his sardonic feelings toward his sacral duties.

Ippolito's splendor and flash was the perfect complement to Caterina's delicate coloring: her cheeks pinked from dancing, her golden hair left long to ripple as she moved, her gowns sewn in delicate harmonies of mauve, cream and rose.

And when they looked at each other, Tommaso caught his breath. He saw the growing romance and passion that the Venetian ambassador had noted, and something more: Their gazes shared the humor and knowledge of old friends. With only a glance one could reduce the other to helpless laughter. So perfectly attuned were they that with only a wink, one could goad the other to play a prank on one of the ladies- or men-in-waiting. With no more than a nod, they withdrew from the others for moments of quiet conversation.

This was how it was meant to be, Tommaso thought. If not for Passerini's and Alessandro's interference, we could be bearing witness to this love in Florence.

But there *had* been a Passerini. And Alessandro now ruled as duke in poor Florence. Tommaso shuddered, grateful he'd moved with Caterina to Rome. He relished his work, enjoyed his lessons with *Ser* Scappi, and knew love himself with Michelangelo. Could life be more perfect?

Of course, it hadn't always gone so smoothly here, especially at first. He'd made some embarrassing blunders in the kitchen, and gotten lost in Rome's streets more than once. Caterina had experienced a few difficulties in brokering a position of power for herself in the Salviati household. To Tommaso's surprise, her laconic cousin Cosimo had stepped forward as her advocate before he and his mother returned to Bologna. Things proceeded more smoothly after that.

There'd been the occasional disaster. One morning, not long after they'd arrived, young Alessa served Caterina breakfast in her rooms.

Caterina had eaten half of her food and was drinking some cinnamon water when she suddenly turned white and held perfectly still. She stared into her goblet, and then started shivering and moaning. She spat up the drink and doubled over in pain.

For a short while suspicion fell on Alessa; that she'd poisoned Caterina, or let a poisoner have access to the food. A terrified Alessa and the rest of the Ramerino family huddled in the kitchen under house guard until a doctor arrived.

Thankfully the doctor discovered that the *Duchessina* had simply begun her first menses and reacted badly to it, as some delicate, highly bred young girls are wont to do.

Caterina wasn't comforted by the doctor's report. She stayed in her room, weeping, refusing to speak to anyone, even Ippolito. A few days later the rest of the family had cause to feel as distraught as Caterina. They received the devastating tidings from Florence that Clarice Strozzi had died terribly from a sudden illness, curled up in agony and coughing blood.

Tommaso couldn't believe the news. It seemed impossible that that brave, indomitable woman was gone. The stunned look on the Salviati family members' faces told him that they felt the same way. Only Caterina, though she grieved, seemed unsurprised.

Weeks afterward rumors reached the Salviati servants' quarter from friends in Florence that Alessandro de' Medici had had Clarice poisoned.

Tommaso shook his head to clear the memory. Don't dwell on the sadness of the past when there is such joy in your present, he chided himself. For who knows what tomorrow will bring?

Who knew? He made a face. *He* did. The news bandying about Rome was that Benevenuto Cellini was healing rapidly. That meant an end soon to Tommaso's temporary apprenticeship with Michelangelo. Eat, drink, be merry, Tommaso thought as he helped himself to a glass of wine and a lump of *pane fritto*, for tomorrow you'll have to dance attendance on the most conceited goldsmith in the world.

12

May 14, 1531

Dear Tommaso, I've perpetuated some fond jests at your expense the last few months. I was tempted to play another such prank, but alas, the occasion is too important to indulge myself this time." Caterina shut the book she was studying and waved her tutor away, but not before Tommaso glimpsed pages covered with renderings of buildings. He recognized the *Ducchesina*'s new teacher as a guest from the banquet celebrating Caterina's birthday the night before. He was one of Rome's up-and-coming architects.

As was expected of him, Tommaso smiled politely at Caterina's coquettish words. The jests referred to were Caterina's habit of arranging menus with him for anonymous attendees of her soireés. Then, when he delivered the meals to her suite, he would unexpectedly find familiar faces from Florence waiting there. In this fashion he'd been surprised by Antonio Gondi and his wife one time, the sculptor Rafaello da Montelupo another, and, most recently, Leone Strozzi, back from one of his many visits to Florence. Caterina always clapped her hands with delight at his genuine surprise.

It *was* good to see friends from home, but Tommaso wished Caterina understood it was more important that he conduct himself professionally than be pleasantly startled.

On reflection, he thought, perhaps at this time in her life it was more important to *her* to tease him. How much longer would she be allowed to indulge in youthful high spirits? Newly twelve, how much longer could she retain *any* of her childhood?

Tommaso resolved to develop more confidence in his own abilities, to believe his cooking would not fail to please, even under less than perfect conditions. Still, his chef's heart mourned just a little that if he'd only been forewarned he could have prepared the artichoke fritters he knew Antonio Gondi adored, or the *arrosto morto* favored by Rafaello da Montelupo.

"So," he said, "this time you'll inform me of the names of our honorable guests in advance. And because I know them, I'll be able to use that knowledge to prepare them dishes they love."

Tommaso took care to speak in respectful tones, but the asperity of his meaning wasn't lost on Caterina.

"My gossip, I fear I've hurt you when I only meant to please and charm you with my little jests," she said so contritely that Tommaso instantly regretted his words. "But see, I mend my ways just in time not to irk you further, for I know you'd never forgive me if I failed to notify you of Cosimo Ruggiero's arrival in three weeks. We'll hold a special gala to celebrate his arrival."

Tommaso flushed with pleasure. He could think of no one he'd be happier to see from Florence than Cosimo Ruggiero.

Caterina beamed at him. "I believe we've found a compromise. I see I can still enjoy surprising you, but without discomfiting you in front of guests."

All the rest of that day and most of the next Tommaso racked his brains to come up with an idea for Cosimo's reception.

The menu itself was set. Caterina had expected Tommaso to propose cooking Cosimo's favorite fare from home.

"Not at all," Tommaso said. "My family spent years perfecting those dishes exactly to Cosimo's palette. The best I could hope for would be to cook as well as they the meals he eats there all the time. No, let me cook new courses I've learned here in Rome, ones that I believe will complement his taste."

Caterina agreed, but her next requirement for the affair proved more difficult to fulfill.

"I want to make greater use of your artistic training," she said. "Cosimo is one of those who will appreciate your progress in that field. Concoct for me an entremet of some sort—an *edible* entertainment of artistic merit, not the usual capering of buffoonish performers. And I want it to be a true *sotelty*: something elegant enough for the other guests, but containing special, subtle meaning for Cosimo."

Tommaso and Caterina talked at great length, but progressed no further in their planning, save for the notion that since the date for the event would fall well into the sign of Gemini, the entremet should honor Cosimo's training as an astrologer by somehow referring to that placement of the stars.

It wasn't until later in the week when Tommaso spent his day apprenticing at Cellini's that he thought of the perfect idea.

Besides teaching his apprentices about jewelry and sculpture, Cellini was responsible for his charges' development as the sort of educated, cultured men artists were expected to be. He'd taken a cue from Il Tribolino and often read to them while they labored on the tedious finish work that took up so much of a goldsmith's time.

> "If my rough hammer shapes human countenances
> Out of the hard rock, now this one, now that,
> It is held and guided by Divine Fiat
> Lending it motion, moving as He elects."

Like Tribolino, Cellini often recited poems by Michelangelo. Cellini gave the verse a heartfelt, creditable rendering, Tommaso grudgingly admitted.

> "But that Divinity, which in heaven dwells alive,
> By His own doing makes lovely others, Himself
>   even more;
> And since no hammer without another hammer
> Can be made, from that one Life all other lives
>   derive.
>
> "And since more power has the mallet-blow
> When it falls upon the forge from its highest
>   point

And this one has flown to the very heaven,
I unfinished am and all undone and riven
Unless the Divine Smith should deign to bless
Me and help me, alone here below."

Cellini then analyzed the piece. "See how even one as great as Maestro Buonarotti is aware that his genius springs from One even more divine than he. Keep this is mind as your own art grows more accomplished. Don't fall into the error of thinking yourselves self-engendered. Know that in the end your inspirations spring from the efforts of your teachers—such as me—and God himself."

The apprentices shared a grin at the idea of any advocacy of humility coming from the vainglorious goldsmith.

But later the poem spun Tommaso into a reverie of those too-brief months he'd spent in Michelangelo's *bottega*. The sculptor's lessons floated, unbidden, into his mind. Tommaso smiled. He would have his whole life to recall them, learn from them.

He thought back to the time Michelangelo demonstrated the technique of raising a maquette slowly from a trough of water. He saw again in his mind's eye the maquette's twin forming on the water's surface as the small sculpture was raised, and suddenly knew what he was going to create to honor both Cosimo Ruggiero and Caterina.

13

It took several days for Tommaso to fabricate sugar blocks of the right size and sufficient hardness for sculpting. If the figures were too small it would prove impossible to carve them to any degree of perfection. If he made them too large they'd lose the charm of miniaturization. He decided on a height of a little over a hand for each.

Long after everyone else in the kitchen retired to bed he stayed up nights sketching details for the pieces by the light of an oil lamp and the dying embers of the kitchen hearth. Caterina's cat often wandered down to the kitchen and kept him company, watching him with half-lidded eyes as his sticks of charcoal stormed across the paper. Every now and then she'd leap onto the middle of a page he was working on and pat his hands, saying as clearly as if she could speak, "Enough. You're done with this one. Now stop and pay attention to me." He'd pick her up, taking care not to smudge his work, put her on his lap and pat her a while before renewing his efforts. He smiled ruefully to himself, that a cat's assessment of a piece of art could be as good and sometimes better than a man's.

When both the sugar blocks and the drawings were finished he started to sculpt. Too likely to crumble if he employed chisels, the hardened sugar could only be worked with fine files and narrow rasps.

"You're paying homage to an ancient form," Marcus Gavius Spada said approvingly, looking over Tommaso's shoulder at a half-finished piece. "The ancient Romans also made pretty sugar pieces to grace their tables."

"Does your hubris know no bounds?" Bindo Ramerino chided *Ser* Spada from the other side of the kitchen. "The ancient Romans no more had sugar than they had those ugly, crepe-necked New World pheasants. Sugar didn't come to Italy until long after Rome fell. Leave the boy alone to make his own mark."

"What do you know, you ignorant Bolognese?" *Ser* Spada shouted back. "It was not for nothing my sainted father named me after Marcus Gavius Apicius, the greatest culinary artist not just of ancient Rome, but of all time. The entire history of cooking is as the flavor of his most sublime invention—fig-force-fed geese livers—upon my lips. In other words: true, complete and delicious! That's the trouble with Bolognese cooking—it's ignorant of history!"

"Flavor on your lips, eh? Then let that flavor not be the last that was on Marcus Gavius Apicius's lips. You know so much history? Surely you haven't forgotten how your namesake took poison after he'd mismanaged his affairs into irretrievable bankruptcy," Ramerino said with malice-spiked laughter.

The kitchen filled with the usual sounds of verbal battle, leaving Tommaso alone to work.

When he finished the figurines he took them to Bartolomeo Scappi to solicit that master's advice. Scappi didn't say much of use concerning the small sculptures, though he liked them and queried Tommaso on the tools he'd used and on Tommaso's specific techniques.

Scappi did make some astute suggestions on the arrangement of the presentation and offered to track down sources for some of the other supplies Tommaso needed. Since Tommaso was in the midst of final preparations—the rental of a large mirror, the purchase of fresh herbs and bags of fine, colored sugars—he appreciated the master cook's help and support.

Early in the afternoon of the gala, on June 12, Tommaso arranged his entremet in the ladies-in-waitings' dressing chamber. The women had graciously bedecked themselves earlier so he could work there in peace. The components of his creation consisted of too many delicate pieces

for Tommaso to transport assembled through the mansion. And this way
Caterina could examine the entremet at her leisure before the party. She
and her ladies passed the time while he completed his task by playing
card games with Ippolito and his companions.

Over the last week the weather had turned balmy. Spring was passing
its sultry ways over to summer. Tommaso found himself perspiring as
he organized his materials, but not just because of the day's warmth.
Although he'd gained approval from Caterina for his idea and kept her
apprised of his progress, this would be the first time she viewed the
completed piece. Since it was her first artistic commission from Tommaso it *must* impress her.

In spite of his nervousness, Tommaso worked surely, quickly. Only
so much time was allocated for this assemblage. The banquet's actual
food was only half-prepared back in the kitchen.

Cosimo Ruggiero had sent word yesterday that he'd arrived safely
in Rome. He'd eventually stay at the Salviatis', but until his rooms were
readied he was visiting at the Strozzi mansion. He expected to arrive
promptly for the celebration. All the other invitees had similarly responded. Tommaso wouldn't enjoy any leeway in his preparation time.

Averardo had helped Tommaso carry a large, rectangular mirror up
to the dressing room, wrapped in bedding so as not to mar its surface.
They carefully set it on a flat-topped chest. Tommaso wiped the mirror
clean with a cloth dipped in a vinegar-and-water solution.

Next he applied a baked pastry border to the mirror's edges, gluing
the strips in sections with a beaten-egg-white-and-sugar paste. Dabs of
the same paste anchored small glass vials and bowls densely along the
sides, leaving the middle of the mirror clear. Tommaso filled each small
vessel two-thirds full of water before setting it into place. Then he carefully poured colored sugars onto the mirror, between the small vessels.

The cat had followed him in. Tommaso feared she'd leap up on the
chest the mirror sat on in a search for food. But evidently she was simply
trying to escape Ippolito's boisterous companions—she picked another
chest to perch on and just sat there, overseeing his labors.

By the time Tommaso finished with his pouring, the sugar paste was
dry. Now he could safely place small bouquets of greens and fragrant
herbs in the bowls and vials. Clumps of parsley took on the form of
bushes. A thick line of *dragoncello* became a hedge. Cuttings of tall early
basil looked just like small trees.

Bit by bit, the mirror transformed into a miniature lake surrounded by a park. Colored sugar-sand paths meandered throughout, leading down to sugar-sand beaches. A marzipan boat lay moored to one side of the mirror lake. Set just far enough back so that only its dome reflected in the "water," a pavilion in the form of a small Greek Revival temple offered elegant shelter from nonexistent elements. Its columns and cornices were carved not from marble but from celeriac, soaked long hours in lemon water. Its golden cupola was fabricated from pastry glazed with egg yolk and honey.

Tommaso unwrapped the final, most important elements from the boxes he'd stored them in, swaddled as carefully as infants in soft clean rags. Each was a miniature sculpture, painstakingly filed and whittled from the blocks of crystallized sugar. Every maquette was classical, and every one referred to astrology: Orion, Cassiopeia, Sagittarius, Ursus Major, Aquarius and more.

They could not have been clearer in their portrayal, but a few figures alluded to the kind of multilayered symbolism that Caterina and her friends so enjoyed: the sort of insinuations that gave guests the opportunity to match wits as they puzzled out the hidden meanings. So the figure with the belt, club and pelt could be identified as Orion, but a closer examination revealed a border decorated with St. John's wort fringing the hunter's rough garb, and a small lamb peeked out from behind the hunter's legs—all attributes of Florence's patron saint John the Baptist. And the demure, simply gowned maiden crowned with stars: Was she merely Virgo, or also the Virgin Mary?

Tommaso placed the small sculptures on the mirror-lake in roughly the order they appeared in as constellations in the heavens. He adjusted their positions until the composition pleased him. A dab of sugar glue to the bottom of each, a little firm pressure as he set them in their final positions, and they were fixed in place.

He stood back to survey his creation. He'd sculpted all the major astrological characters, with one omission. There was no Gemini. No twins. And yet, in the mirror's reflection, *everything* was twinned. This was the riddle posed for Cosimo Ruggiero's perceptive eye. Since the stars at this moment lay under Gemini's sway, it was almost an affront that the twins weren't there. Yet they *were* present, implicit in every piece.

Tommaso had only one last chore: the placement of the final sculpture. He took this one from its box with great care. It was the moon,

Diana the Huntress, with her stag. It was also Caterina. De' Medici *palle* interspersed with the Magis' gifts decorated the figurine's cloak. At her feet lay a vanquished boar. Tommaso put the maquette in the center of the lake, with all the other pieces arrayed around her.

The effect was what he'd hoped for. Just as the moon commands the sky when it rises above the horizon, so the figure of Diana eclipsed the other statues.

Tommaso straightened and leaned back. His shoulders felt tight, pinched together from all the fine, careful work. His neck ached. He hadn't realized how greatly the last weeks of extra work had tired him.

He stretched and tried to take a deep breath. There was a strong, sweet scent in the air, like cloves and cinnamon. The room suddenly seemed too warm and close. Tommaso doubled over with dizziness, backing away so he wouldn't knock the entremet over. He went down on all fours. The cat peered at him from her perch. "Rrroowr?" she queried. Tommaso put his head all the way down. The air close to the floor was cooler, fresher. After a few moments he felt revived enough to rise back up to a kneeling position.

He stopped as his eyes came level with the edge of the mirror. From this vantage point he could imagine himself just within the boundaries of a park, looking through the foliage and across the breadth of a real lake graced with larger than life-size statues set on bases ingeniously anchored in the lake's bed. The illusion was so perfect Tommaso almost hoped to hear birds trilling in the distance; hoped to feel a soft, light wind blowing off the water, caressing his hot face. The water looked refreshing. He yearned to slide into it.

"Prrt?" Gattamelata's questioning purr made him remember himself. Tommaso continued to get up, slowly, taking in his creation with each change of angle.

Now he was high enough to see again the upside-down twins appearing to take root out of each sculpture's base. It looked so precisely like the reflections in a perfectly still pool that Tommaso fancied he saw fishes swimming beneath the surface. They drifted upward, becoming larger, paler, until Tommaso realized they resembled no fishes he'd ever seen, but women-shaped languid creatures with great, milky-blind eyes.

Then behind them something even paler, brighter, arose—so bright it leached the water-dwellers of all form. They faded away like wraiths, and Tommaso saw that what was filling the lake was the moon itself, centered just below the statue of Diana. The lustrous sphere looked as though it were going to rise and rise until it swallowed the statue of Diana's reflected twin, then continue upward to break through the surface of the mirror and engulf the statue itself, then perhaps continue to rise up into the sky.

Tommaso gasped.

At the sound the moon shrank instantaneously to a pinpoint. Then it disappeared. For the briefest instant a face appeared in its place, peering down into Tommaso's face as he peered down into it. Then it, too, was gone. Tomaso dropped to his knees again, hard, sweating with shock. The face he'd glimpsed was that of his mother, Piera.

He shuffled on his knees away from the table before getting to his feet again. Something possessed this mirror. Tommaso didn't know *what* he was going to do. He certainly couldn't present the centerpiece to Caterina and her company. He didn't even know how he was going to get the thing taken apart and out of the room.

He edged back to the table with small cautious steps, fearful of what he'd view next in the mirror's depths.

Nothing. No fish. No vast merwomen. No moon. No Piera. Tommaso stared hard into the mirror. There were no depths; just the mirror's shallow gleam reflecting the charming vignette he'd created.

Tommaso felt nauseous and suddenly very, very tired. The illusion must have been in his own mind, not in the entremet. It was safe to present to Caterina. But was he?

The question proved valid. When he emerged from the room, Caterina looked at him with a frown. "Are you all right, Tommaso? You look quite gray."

"I confess to some inclemency of disposition," Tommaso said wanly. Over Caterina's shoulder he saw Ippolito look up with concern.

One of Caterina's ladies-in-waiting stepped forward. "Allow me, Your Grace," she told Caterina. "I raised seven children to adulthood and successfully nursed them through all manner of illnesses."

Caterina nodded; Ippolito went back to dealing cards to his friends. The woman held her palm to Tommaso's damp forehead. Then she tugged downward gently on each of his lower eyelids and gazed there intently.

"He has no fever," she announced. "In fact, his skin is cool. *Too* cool. That and the kind of discoloration of his inner eye indicates not illness, but severe exhaustion."

"Tommaso, have you been doing regular duty in the kitchen, besides the schooling and cooking tasks I set you?" Caterina gently chided.

"When the household entertains extra guests," Tommaso admitted.

"But that's all the time," Caterina pointed out.

Tommaso felt relieved. His centerpiece wasn't enchanted. His overly tired eyes had played tricks on him. But if he was that depleted, could he be trusted to manage the celebration this evening?

The same doubt occurred to Caterina. "After tonight I'm going to arrange for you to take some rest, Tommaso. You'll make yourself ill if you continue in this fashion. I'll speak to Aunt Lucrezia and ask her to assign several of the household staff to serve us tonight. All you have to do is be sure the food and courses are ready to send up. Now come, show me what you've made of your commission."

Ippolito left his seat to open the door to the room for her. Caterina and the older lady-in-waiting swept through. Ippolito started to follow. Caterina pushed him back through the door with a laugh. "No, cousin. This is meant to be a surprise for you too. Since its presentation will include guessing games as to its hidden subtleties, I don't mean to let you have the advantage over my other guests by way of an early viewing." She let Tommaso slide past behind her before she closed the door on Ippolito.

Tommaso held his breath as Caterina circled the table, taking in all the details, looking for the hints and nuances they'd agreed should be included. Would the mirror play pranks on Caterina's eyes too?

Nothing happened.

Tommaso released his breath, free now to concern himself with other worries. Did she like it? Was she pleased? Was it adequate to present to her guests?

Silent, sober, Caterina finished her circumlocution. The cat jumped down from the chest where it had been grooming itself to follow her. When Caterina came full circle and reached Tommaso she looked up and favored him with a delighted smile. "It's wonderful, Tommaso. Almost *too* perfect. It makes me wish I could miraculously transform myself into a poppet so tiny that I could walk along the banks of your lake."

Tommaso felt his face glow at her praise.

"I especially enjoy your own embellishments," she said. "Like the way Sagittarius's face resembles Pier Antonio Pecci, and the allusion here to the sign of Taurus as the balance of both bestial and divine." She pointed to the bull's incorporation with a man's body, indicating the minotaur, and also its small, neatly folded wings, signifying St. Luke.

Ah, she'd noticed.

"But what about this? Diana with a swine at her feet?" Caterina pointed.

"That is your boar, *Duchessina*." Tommaso bowed. "And the analogy is to yourself as a huntress."

Caterina smiled and bent forward to examine the figure more closely. The smile faded from her face. "No," she whispered. "It cannot be."

Tommaso followed her gaze. Dark clouds boiled across the mirror, forming—as clouds are wont to do—shifting, recognizable images. Horrible, horrible images. Tommaso looked up and glanced quickly out the window. The sky was a perfect, cloudless blue.

Caterina began to tremble. "No, it shall not be."

"Your Grace, what is it?" The lady-in-waiting rushed up to support Caterina, who shook in earnest now.

Caterina threw her off. "Be quiet! Don't speak!" Her dark eyes were huge in her pale face. She stared intently into the mirror. Her hands fussed at all the jewelry twined about her neck. She clutched at something there. "I won't let it happen! You must aid me in this! You're mad if you think I'll be forced to go there!" she suddenly shouted, teeth chattering.

Caterina's face began to glow with a white light that spread down her chest, her arms. To Tommaso's horror, something within the mirror started to siphon that light toward the mirror's depths, where an oily blackness spread.

Caterina's eyes rolled up to show white. She tottered for a moment, then fell over backward. Tommaso and her attendant barely caught her. The terrified lady-in-waiting screamed. Tommaso felt a core of molten heat rage up his spine. It reached through him to Caterina, pulling her away from the vacuum drawing her toward the mirror. Then he, too, began to bend forward, in the grip of an uncanny gravity.

Ippolito and his men burst through the door. The cat dashed out, her fur bristling her to twice her size.

"Her Grace has had a fit," the woman cried, herself in a state of hysteria.

Ippolito seized Caterina, wrenching her from Tommaso and the lady-in-waiting. Tommaso felt the sucking force from the mirror snap and slide back through the silvered lake. Ippolito carried Caterina from the room and laid her on a settee.

"What happened?" he asked.

"The *Duchessina* started shivering and muttering nonsense. Then she fainted." The poor woman wept. "It was much like that one time before, when we feared her poisoned, but worse."

Ippolito rubbed Caterina's wrists and fisted hands, as he had when she'd fallen during the hunt. Her hands relaxed and a simple pendant of silver set with a dark red cabochon slid free to hang down her breast on its silver chain.

"I'll call for Maestro Rastilli, the Salviatis' physician," Pier Antonio Pecci said, leaving the suite at a run.

Caterina opened her eyes. She looked bewildered and struggled to sit up. Ippolito pressed her back down. "Lie still, dear cousin. Pier Antonio has gone to find the Salviati family doctor."

"Then send someone else to fetch me Cosimo Ruggiero," Caterina said in a weak voice. "He, too, is a physician, and far more familiar with my frail nature."

With Caterina indisposed, surely the soirée would be canceled. Tommaso wondered if he should return to the kitchen to salvage what he could of the half-prepared food for the event. At the very least he should dispose of his beautiful, dreadful centerpiece before it caused more harm.

He slid as unobtrusively as he could into the dressing room. Domenico the Tartar, who'd crashed in with Ippolito and the others, still stood there, examining the entremet. He turned as he heard Tommaso enter, then glared when he saw who it was.

"You people imagine yourselves so knowledgeable, with all your book learning and schools of philosophical and rational thought. You're nothing but ignorant philistines. Dangerously ignorant," the Tartar said flatly. "You don't know what you've done here, you stupid child."

He gestured to the mirror. "Can't you see? There it is. You've invoked the brother world, our opposite twin." His narrow eyes narrowed further. "You have no idea what I'm talking about, do you?"

Tommaso stood, frozen.

Domenico bared his teeth in an angry grin. "Then to you I only seem to speak the superstitious cant of an infidel Oriental." Scorn dripped from every word. "And you can't know any better."

But after Domenico left Tommaso felt shamed. He *did* know what the Tartar spoke of. The slave girl Filomena had told him about that opposite world. Could he, indeed, have known better?

14

Since Tommaso couldn't remove the entremet without carrying it out in pieces right in front of Caterina, he waited until he heard Dr. Rastilli arrive, then sidled out into the receiving room of the suite. Everyone still gathered around Caterina, so he drew aside one of her pretty, Florentine ladies-in-waiting and instructed the young woman to let no one into the room with the centerpiece—that he'd return later to take it away. As for the food for the evening, he'd salvage what he could and wait for word as to its dispersal. Then he returned to the kitchen.

A half hour later, the kitchen received word through the house staff that Cosimo Ruggiero had arrived to attend to the *Duchessina*. Less than an hour after that, the young lady-in-waiting Tommaso had spoken to appeared, out of breath from hurrying, to announce that the soirée would take place as planned.

Dr. Rastilli had decided Caterina suffered from one of those common maladies of unbalance suffered by young women, intensified by the warmth of the day and unhealthy vapors rising off the Tiber. Cosimo recommended a nostrum, Rastilli concurred, and they were able to concoct it by combining philters from the supplies each man had brought with him.

The *Duchessina*'s health immediately improved upon partaking of their cure. She declared herself well enough at least to preside over the celebration, while promising not to tax her strength by indulging in any strenuous activities, such as participating in the dancing planned for after dinner.

"Her Grace was adamant," the maid said with admiration. "She declared that since the principal guest had already arrived, and since it would take a great deal of effort to send word to disinvite the other expected visitors, and since all would be hungry anyway in a few hours, she saw no reason not to proceed."

Caterina also remembered what she'd said before her collapse about Tommaso's own exhaustion. Several men from the Salviati house staff arrived to fetch the food at the proper time. The kitchen help rushed to assemble the plates and cutlery needed for the service.

Tommaso was relieved he wouldn't have to return to Caterina's suite. But he was nervous about the centerpiece lurking in the wardrobe room like some great, malignant spider. He drew one of the serving staff aside and told the man to ask one of Caterina's ladies to throw a cloth over it, and that he'd come to remove it the next morning.

The man brightened. "Can I ask that pretty maid that just brought you the news? I believe her name is Reparata."

Tommaso rolled his eyes at the way men turn any calamity into an opportunity for a conquest, but agreed.

He relaxed a little when the first few courses were sent up and no news came back of any mishaps. As soon as this meal was finished he intended to crawl into his cot and sleep.

He was garnishing a plate of *papero alla en lancia* with its orange sauce when Alessa tugged at his sleeve. "Tommaso, this man seeks an audience with you."

Tommaso looked past her to where Beroaldo, the Bengalese diver, stood grinning at him. Tommaso never failed to marvel at the unnatural whiteness of the man's teeth, made more startling by its contrast with his red-brown skin.

"Your presence is requested, nay, *demanded* at Her Ladyship's banquet," Beroaldo said in his thick accent, taking Tommaso's arm and guiding him from the kitchen.

Tommaso gestured beseechingly back at the platter with its still half-naked roast duck.

"Surely one of your colleagues can finish that," the Bengalese said, propelling Tommaso forward.

Tommaso wondered if he should worry, but Beroaldo was so jovial that surely nothing had gone awry. Of course, Tommaso reflected, he'd never seen the Bengalese *not* in a jovial mood, even when Caterina's horse threw her during the hunt.

They reached Caterina's suite. Beroaldo pushed the doors open. The throng inside turned as one and burst into a pandemonium of clapping hands and shouted congratulations.

"Pure genius, Tommaso."

"We'll have to commence calling you Maestro."

"You've set a new standard, young Signor Arista."

Among the smiling faces were Antonio Gondi and his wife, Jacopo and Lucrezia Salviati, Isabella d'Este, Ippolito and even Cellini. Tommaso felt mortified with embarrassment. At least Michelangelo wasn't present: The sculptor was away buying marble.

"Never have I seen such cleverness wedded to artistry rendered in edible form," called out Rafaello da Montelupo. "And I was one of the fortunate attendees of the apprentices' fête in Florence!"

Directly before Tommaso, in the center of the banquet table brought up from the dining hall for the occasion, sat the haunted centerpiece. The blood drained from Tommaso's face. For one dizzy instant he thought he too might faint, just as Caterina had.

Even Isabella d'Este was praising it. "Fifteen years ago, on a trip to Naples, that city's queen honored me at a banquet with the presentation of a reproduction of our palace in Mantua constructed entirely of spun sugar. Wonderful as that was, it was not so clever or lovely as this," she said.

Cosimo Ruggiero didn't join in the tribute. He stood bent over the entremet, studying it with an intent frown. Then he glanced up, saw Tommaso, and tried to smile.

Caterina sat in a chair well back from the table, quiet and impassive, holding her cat in her lap. Tommaso knew that from that distance and angle she couldn't see into the mirror.

Beroaldo pushed Tommaso forward to accept the accolades. Coming close enough to begin to make out the reflections in the mirror, Tommaso saw forms move swiftly across the false lake's surface. He flinched.

Cosimo followed Tommaso's gaze. Then Cosimo's eyes widened. He looked up from the centerpiece again, this time at Caterina. Tommaso couldn't fail to notice the bitterness of Caterina's slight smile.

But when Tommaso steeled himself to look at his creation again, he saw reflected in it nothing but a roomful of happy revelers gathered around a charming model, vying with each other to guess all its theological, astrological and literary allusions.

Tommaso made his escape as soon as he could, but not before pulling aside the Salviati servingman. "I thought I told you to cover that accursed thing," he hissed.

The servant shrugged. "I would have, but when I arrived the *Duchessina* had already declared her intention to present it."

The man blinked. "Why do you object so, Signor Arista? You could have hardly have garnered such praise if it had remained hidden away."

15

Tommaso still wanted to bury himself in his cot as soon as the celebration was over—now as much to hide as sleep. But he had a foreboding he might be summoned again that night, so he forced himself to stay awake.

A messenger finally came for him, very late. Not the flamboyant Beroaldo, but Domenico, as if to point up the bleakness of the hour. "Come with me. You're wanted," was all the Tartar said.

Tommaso sighed and followed him. Domenico led him to Ambassador Venier's old suite. Although it wasn't quite ready for Cosimo, it had been decided he must move in right away, in case Caterina needed his medical attentions. Since Cosimo arrived with no entourage, not even a secretary or a single man-at-arms, accommodating him hadn't proved a problem.

Cosimo was writing by the light of an oil lamp when they arrived. "Thank you, good Domenico, for your aid," he said when they entered. "And thank Ippolito for me also," he said by way of dismissing the Tartar. Cosimo set down his pen and came around the corner of the writing desk to clasp Tommaso's hand.

"It's good to see you again, my friend. You're sorely missed in Florence." He gestured Tommaso to a chair. "Sit, please. Forgive this tardy summons, but I know how late kitchen help works, especially after an event like tonight's. I called for you because I have something for you from your family." Cosimo turned around to his desk and picked up a packet of papers, then handed them to Tommaso.

Tommaso took the parcel. It was a slight bundle of letters, like the one Michelangelo had given him at the Salviatis' hunting estate. Tommaso smiled in relief that this was the reason he'd been summoned.

"Thank you, young master," Tommaso said. He stood to go.

Cosimo motioned for him to sit again. The young astrologer's face was grave. "Pray, stay and talk with me a while."

As Tommaso sank down again, so did his heart.

"Your entremet was a thing of beauty and wit, and very remarkable, perhaps more than you know," Cosimo said. "Yet I overheard you telling one of the servants that it was cursed. Why did you say such a thing?"

Tommaso didn't know how to respond. He dropped his head and tried to find an answer in the patterns of the wood grain of the flooring. Surely they contained more meaning than the chaotic visions he'd seen in the mirror-lake, the unnatural power he'd felt from it.

Cosimo coaxed him. "I spoke with the *Duchessina* about her, uh, seizure, after I'd been brought to examine her," he said. "Of course, one of our sex must never be left truly alone with a young woman of her stature, quality and reputation. But we were in her bedroom, *just* the two of us together. The door was left open so her ladies could be sure no impropriety occurred, but they were at some distance and I'm certain couldn't hear our conversation, we spoke so quietly.

"Caterina was completely frank with me, Tommaso. She told me of the images she saw in the mirror, the forces she felt from it."

Tommaso still didn't know what to say, but he looked up at Cosimo.

"Tommaso, did you see anything in the mirror of your centerpiece?"

There it was. How could he deny it when Cosimo asked so directly?

"I know your father doesn't believe in the ephemeral world," Cosimo said gently. "However, I *am* an occultist, Tommaso. I won't laugh or think you mad. You can tell me what you saw."

"I'm not certain I saw anything," Tommaso muttered.

"Then tell me what you think you saw."

Tommaso wanted to swallow, hard, but his throat was too dry. "I saw the moon, and members of my family."

Cosimo leaned forward. "Which members?"

"My mother, and my sisters and brother: Ginevra, Beatrice, Pietro," Tommaso said.

Cosimo leaned back. "Ah, so it was like looking into the past. Like seeing memories in one's mind's eye."

"Just like that," Tommaso agreed gratefully.

"And what about when Caterina called you back to be lauded by the guests? Did you see anything then?"

"At first I thought I did," Tommaso said. "Just dark amorphous shapes moving across the mirror. Then I realized it was the reflections of people's clothing, their sleeves as they reached over the centerpiece to point at this or that detail."

"That's most observant," Cosimo said. "But what you saw before, the first time—it made you afraid, didn't it?"

Tommaso nodded.

Cosimo smiled. "Your beautiful creation wasn't cursed."

Tommaso wasn't reassured by Cosimo's easy words.

Cosimo saw the doubt lingering in Tommaso's face. "Do you believe I'm reasonably accomplished in what I do?"

"Most certainly," Tommaso whispered. He remembered the strange noises, smells and lights that often issued from the study of Cosimo's father Ruggiero the Old, in Florence.

"Try to think of it like this," Cosimo said. "For years, by eating your family's cooking, I've availed myself of your skills. Tonight is when you begin to avail yourself of *my* family's skills."

Once Tommaso took his leave and returned to the kitchen, Cosimo sat down behind the desk and took up his pen again. He'd begun to write a letter to his father, but he'd wanted to interview Tommaso before finishing it.

"Honored sir," he wrote. "You once likened the *Duchessina* de' Medici to a book, with the pages representing her presence in many planes of existence, and the binding symbolizing her origins in *this* plane, from which she participates in all the others. You also wondered to what extent she might come to know of her true nature, if ever.

"I can report to you that she already knows something of that nature, and with the onset of her maturity and her powers she's likely to gain in that knowledge every day, with or without our help. Therefore, I find

it advisable to extend my visit and stay here in Rome with her indefi-
nitely.

"I did not arrive at my conclusions concerning her state through
careful divination of elusive signs, but rather as the result of a confrontation with a manifestation immediately upon my arrival here at the
Salviati mansion, and a frank conversation with an understandably upset
Duchessina.

"It appears that just before a party to be given in my honor, the
Duchessina encountered an accidental speculum; either that, or she projected her latent talents onto an ordinary mirror. With no attempt at
evocation or invocation on her part, she glimpsed a succession of possible
futures—some tragic, some triumphant, some tranquil, and including the
one you foretold at her birth. It was as if she'd pick up the pan-existential
book that is herself and riffled through its pages rapidly. Then some
force from one of those pages, one of those other planes, used the
speculum to try to reach out to her, perhaps to change the course of the
'chapter' it's a part of."

Something slid softly, silently against Cosimo's leg. He jumped in
his seat. A couple of drops of ink splattered his letter. Shivering, he
sprinkled fine sand on them to blot them, glad of the chore, not wanting
to look down and see a nothingness, though he still felt a *somethingness*
there.

The light touch came again, this time followed by a "Prrrowr?"

Cosimo chuckled shakily. He reached down and picked up the *Duchessina*'s cat. The bold creature had the run of the house. How had it
gotten in here? Tommaso must not have closed the door behind him
when he'd left.

The cat settled in his lap and looked up at him with adoring eyes.
Cosimo was utterly charmed. "Since when did any cat adore anyone but
herself?" he murmured as he stroked her jawline and chin. The cat
breathed a sighing purr of pleasure and curled up to sleep. Cosimo found
if he stretched his arms a little he could still reach the desk to write
without disturbing her.

When he'd first seen the cat upstairs in Caterina's suite he'd been
startled. She was the exact replica of the cats that roamed the kitchen
compound of the Ruggiero home in Florence. He couldn't remember a
time when such a cat hadn't prowled somewhere in the background of
his childhood. His father once told him that that had been the case ever

since Gentile Arista had brought his young bride Piera Befanini to come live in the household. She'd brought the first of the cats with her, a dowry for the kitchen.

Cosimo recalled that Piera had made a gift of one of the kittens to the *Duchessina* to brighten the little girl's life when she'd been cloistered against her will in the dreary convent of Santa Lucia.

Piera Befanini. That reminded Cosimo of what he wanted to write next to his father.

"But on further reflection I question whether the matter of the *Duchessina*'s intersection with the speculum was entirely accidental. The mirror was part of a dinner entremet commissioned by Caterina from Tommaso Arista, whom you know well." Cosimo then briefly described the centerpiece. "According to the *Duchessina*, the concept for this creation, and the inclusion of the mirror, originated with Tommaso.

"When I viewed the entremet at the celebration and in the company of the *Duchessina* and her other guests, I perceived a residue of the visions she experienced. She insisted Tommaso be brought to her suite, ostensibly to receive the well-deserved praise of the gathered company, but also to make a point to me.

"With Tommaso's added presence the ghost of the illusion intensified. Besides the three of us, no one else there appeared to see anything. I queried Tommaso this evening, and he admitted noticing something in the mirror. But unlike the *Duchessina*'s plethora of futures, he only glimpsed the past. From this I glean that in some way he acted as an anchor to the *Duchessina*'s forward-looking visions. Because of this I'm now reassessing Tommaso as a previously unconsidered factor.

"When the *Duchessina* came to us before her move to Rome and conveyed her desire to employ Tommaso, we assumed it was because of his obvious loyalty and devotion to her and his equally obvious growing talents, both culinary and artistic. Now I'm beginning to believe there might be more. Tommaso is innocent of the occult. I sense no ability on his part to initiate any sorcery. But just as toads and cats serve as *streghes'* familiars, I think Tommaso may act as a similar tool for the *Duchessina*'s powers.

"Knowing this honest boy all my life, I could not at first imagine from whence he'd gotten such an ability. But then I remembered that his mother's family's name is Befanini. Befanini are small pastries, true, but as you know, also another term for the practitioners of the Old Religion. And the Befaninis have served the *Duchessina's* ancestors for generations."

Cosimo sat bolt upright, recalling something else. His movement disturbed the cat, who grumbled. Caterina as a book: The first night his father explained that analogy to him had been the night Tommaso was waylaid by the Arrabiati. Ruggiero the Old had drawn back the velvet wrapping on the great speculum in the Ruggiero studio to show many wonders to Cosimo, some still unexplained to this day.

To *this* day. But on the morrow ... There was something Cosimo must do, but he wouldn't be able to enter Caterina's apartments until the next morning. Too excited to sleep, Cosimo absently patted the cat in his lap.

Exhausted as he was, Tommaso couldn't sleep either. He sat reading his letters by an oil lamp in the kitchen.

The first was from his father. Most of the letter conveyed news about Piera's cousin Francesca.

Francesca had always claimed that the father of her little boy Paolo was a soldier gone to foreign lands with his brigade. No one gave her story much credence. Everyone expected that at some point she'd claim to hear news of her husband's death in battle, allowing her to shift seamlessly into the state of *viudad fantasma*, the marginal respectability of phantom widowhood.

To the Ruggiero cooking staff's vast surprise, one evening a worn-looking man wearing a tattered uniform arrived at the kitchen's alley entrance, introducing himself as one Marchetto Beccacce. He begged to see Francesca. Gentile wrote, "From the instant I laid eyes on him, I was struck by his resemblance to little Paolo."

A tearful reunion with Francesca followed. Marchetto declared himself sick of war and killing. He wished to find honest work and live in peace with Francesca and his little son, who until then he'd never seen.

"He seems a good, honest man," Gentile wrote. "Now that Florence is recovering from the siege, the Ruggieros are entertaining lavishly again, as they did in the old days. I miss both your own and Ottaviano's skills and will to work. Although Marchetto lacks the skills as yet, his will to work can't be faulted. We're all teaching him as we go along. If he found employment elsewhere he'd take Francesca away, and over the last few years she's become indispensable here."

Piera's letter mentioned that she knew Gentile was writing about Francesca, then she went on to touch on other topics.

She'd visited with Elissa Pecorino recently, so most of her news concerned Tommaso's old friends in the art community.

Vittorio, Il Tribolino's journeyman, had at last been elevated to Master. Tommaso's fellow apprentices Salvatore and Bertino were now journeymen. Pagolo di Arezzo had returned to the Aretine—everyone hoped for only a short while.

After all this, Piera added an item that made Tommaso smile.

"At last one of Gattamelata's daughters—the lame one—has borne a litter. I can't describe to you how enjoyable it is to have kittens underfoot again. Luciana and Paolo are quite in heaven. They spend all their time playing with the catlings and taking care of them, so for a little while, at least, no one need spend time watching *them.*"

Piera's next news, however, pulled the corners of Tommaso's smile down into a frown.

"I have one more thing to tell you. You are the first to hear of it, my son. I haven't even let your father know yet, though within the week I'll draw Gentile aside to inform him. I'm pregnant again. I'm well and strong this time, so pray be happy for me."

Tommaso let the pages of the letter droop in his hand. He wished his mother well, but how could he be happy? He was gone from that life.

His father was replacing him in the kitchen. Amado would take the place he'd always thought of as his. Or perhaps it would be filled by this new fellow, Francesca's husband.

Ginevra, Beatrice and Pietro were irretrievably departed. Apparently all four of them were replaceable, as long as Piera could bear children. It was as if it didn't matter that he and his three lost siblings had ever existed. Luciana was, what, four years old now? Then this new one, then how many more? At least two more, until all the original children had been replaced?

Tommaso squeezed his eyes together, sealing them against the tears he felt forming. He refused to cry. Ginevra, Beatrice, Pietro. Was he the only one left to bear witness to their short lives? Is that why he'd suffered that dreadful vision?

During the interview with Cosimo he realized that Cosimo, for all his arcane skills, was unaware of Tommaso's first vision, before Caterina entered the room to view the centerpiece. And in spite of Cosimo's analysis of Tommaso's later illusion as simply memories, Tommaso knew that was not the case. His mother—looking young and unworn by recent travails—had looked at him directly, had seen him as clearly as he saw her, as if they gazed at each other across the years through an open window.

And then later, in Caterina's presence, the visions he'd suffered of his lost sisters and brother had also not been memories. For he'd been privy to something he had *not* seen in the past, had never wished to see— their agonized deaths of the plague in the dark, empty Ruggiero farmhouse.

16

Cosimo paced his room. He mustn't arrive too early, but if he were late he might find the centerpiece dismantled and evacuated from Caterina's dressing room. When he heard the first quiet sounds of the household maids going about their rounds, he hurried over to Caterina's suite, her cat following at his heels. The two of them then loitered in the corridor. Passing Salviati servants looked at him. But only with mild surprise, since he was one of Caterina's doctors.

He waited until he heard someone stirring inside. He forced himself to linger about fifteen minutes more before knocking. A maid opened the door. She was startled to see him. The cat took advantage of her surprise to glide into the room.

"I've come to examine the state of the *Duchessina*'s health," Cosimo said, putting on his most solicitous physician's manner. "It's best to observe her physiology first thing after she wakens, before the activity of the day causes her choler to rise."

"The *Duchessina* and her ladies are yet asleep," the maid whispered.

"Perhaps I could wait in her reception area?" Cosimo suggested.

The maid still looked doubtful, so he added, "I wish to be sure that there's no repetition of yesterday's unfortunate episode."

The maid nodded and let him in. Cosimo took comfort in the fact that he hadn't really lied. He did eventually want to examine Caterina this morning.

He sat down in a chair close to Caterina's bedroom doors and stared fixedly until the maid became nervous. This was the cue he'd been waiting for.

"I see I'm discomfiting you," he said in his most courteous manner. "You're worried the *Duchessina* or her ladies might enter here in disarray before you can warn them that a man is present."

The maid nodded apprehensively.

Cosimo pretended to search his brain for a solution. "I tell you what," he finally said, "if that unusual centerpiece from last night is still about, I could while away the time by viewing it and enjoying its charm, until the ladies wake."

The maid considered his suggestion. "Well," she said, "it *is* being stored in the wardrobe room, from which the ladies will eventually need their dresses for the day. But I could at least intervene in the reception area and bring their clothing to them, so you wouldn't chance upon them or they upon you until they'd made themselves decent."

That agreed upon, she let him into the dressing room. As soon as she shut the door behind him Cosimo opened the drapes to the room's window. The entremet was balanced on a chest. Cosimo crouched beside it. The women must scent their clothing. He smelled a blend of cinnamon and cloves.

He imagined away the room's accouterments—the chests, the cabinets, the scattered women's apparel—and focused on the scene in miniature before him. Tommaso had done a beautiful job. Scrutinizing the centerpiece in these close quarters, it wasn't hard to believe one stood at the edge of a lovely park, and that one step would take him within its boundaries.

Now that Cosimo understood what he saw, he recognized the scene. It was precisely one of the unexplained visions his father had conjured in the great Ruggiero speculum in Florence four years ago—a still and clear lake, festooned with classical statues, masses of foliage in the distance.

Cosimo shook his head in wonder. He remembered that his foremost thought, that night years ago, was that the lake's surface was so perfect and reflective that it could pass for a mirror.

He was glad he hadn't signed the letter to his father yet. He'd have much more to write to him.

        ✳   ✳   ✳

For the next few days Caterina was weak and unsure of herself. Her ladies tiptoed about and spoke only in soft, soothing voices.

On Wednesday the *Duchessina* received a letter waxed with the papal seal that did more for her health than all of Cosimo's and Dr. Rastelli's ministrations and all of Ippolito's worried care.

Bearing a pot of herbal tea for her nerves, Tommaso accompanied the retinue of servants carrying breakfast up to Caterina's rooms. Instead of the usual sickroom hush, they were greeted while still well down the hall from the *Duchessina*'s suite with the sounds of breaking furniture and angry shouts. The shouts were in one voice only: Caterina's.

The doors to the suite burst open and a lady-in-waiting ran out, holding her hands to her ears. Several chess pieces came flying out after her. Tommaso heard a furious, shrieked, "I will *not* be compelled!"

The breakfast procession slowed to halt, uncertain whether they should proceed. "What on earth is going on?" Tommaso asked the woman as she hurried past them.

"Her Grace wishes me to fetch her uncle and aunt. She just received formal notice from His Holiness the Pontiff that He, the Pope, and the Duke of Albany, have arranged a betrothal between her and the second son of the King of France. The *Duchessina* is most displeased."

Tommaso and the rest of the household staff tiptoed around the palazzo for the next two days, trying not to draw the attention of the irate *Duchessina* or any of the senior Salviatis, who were displeased themselves with their charge's behavior. Even Ippolito's charm failed to soothe. Whenever Caterina saw him she burst into tears. She called Cosimo Ruggiero to her suite three and four times a day. None of the servants could make out their heated, whispered conversations, but Cosimo always left Caterina's rooms scowling, his brow furled.

On the third day Caterina ordered everyone out of her rooms except for her cat, declaring she wished to fast, meditate and pray until the next morning.

Late that evening Tommaso took it upon himself to carry a tray of food up to Cosimo's room.

"Who is it?" Cosimo said loudly when Tommaso knocked on the door.

Tommaso had never heard Cosimo sound so brusque.

Tommaso felt his shoulders hunch up toward his ears. "Tommaso Arista," he replied timidly.

Cosimo opened the door. His face was tired and drawn, but he smiled. "Forgive my rudeness, good friend. Please, come in."

"I noticed you haven't been eating well," Tommaso said. "I presumed to bring you a little something."

Cosimo drew back the linen covering the tray, revealing a plate of pasta covered with *savore sanguino*, a bowl of salt cod and leek soup, and a carafe of red wine. "Hearty Florentine dishes," Cosimo observed. He took the tray from Tommaso and set it on a table by his bed. Then he poured himself a goblet of the wine. He took a small sip. Cosimo's eyebrows raised. He looked at Tommaso. "Could it be?" he asked.

Tommaso nodded. "Yes. *Vermiglio*. From the Medici vineyards and cellars. The Salviatis have several casks."

Cosimo's wan smile warmed. "You must indeed be worried about my health. How could I refuse such concern?" He waved Tommaso to a chair. Then he sat on the edge of the bed and slid the small table carefully around to face him.

When the rich, hot broth, with its chunks of toothsome cod and tender leeks, brought color to Cosimo's face, Tommaso relaxed.

"Are you all right?" he asked.

"The last few days have proved sorely trying for all of us. But I believe my health isn't in jeopardy. Nor will be, after partaking of this nourishing fare," Cosimo said, between blowing and sipping at a spoonful.

"Sorely trying for *all* of us," Tommaso repeated, musing. "So Caterina is also well, not weakened by her distress?" Cosimo was one of the few people in front of whom Tommaso could call Caterina by her given name.

Cosimo chewed on a meaty morsel of cod. "Hardly," he said drily. "Anger affects our young mistress like a tonic. I don't believe I've ever seen her in such ferocious good health."

The first thing next morning, the upstairs staff brought news that the *Duchessina* was awake, dressed, desirous of going riding and in the sweetest mood imaginable.

Throughout the day, reports trickled down to the kitchen that

Caterina had apologized first to her servants and ladies-in-waiting, and then to the Salviatis, Ippolito and Cosimo for her ill humor. She sent for Tommaso in the afternoon.

"Don't look so worried," she told him. "I'm quite myself again. Did you bring your slate with you? Good, we have some planning to do. Let me have that." She reached for the slate and chalk. "I'll explain the occasion, and what I had in mind."

While she wrote, one of her maids hurried off to fetch some moistened cloths for wiping the chalk off.

"There. Tell me what you think." Caterina handed the slate back to Tommaso just as the maid returned.

The slate read:

> *Don't fear for me, my gossip. The French betrothal is just my cousin the Pope's first move in the game. I knew it would come sooner or later. I shouldn't have been so taken aback. Now that I know Clement's strategy I can develop my own. All the information you've gathered, all the alliances I've forged, now come into play. But we need more: more information, more alliances. First I must mend the ill-advised rift I've caused between myself and Uncle Jacopo and Aunt Lucrezia. I've invited them for a small, intimate supper tomorrow in these rooms. In that short amount of time, what magic can you concoct in the kitchen that would help to win me back their hearts? What do you suggest?*

Tommaso took one of the moistened cloths, wiped the slate clean, and without hesitation wrote down a menu. He'd now cooked enough for the Salviatis to know exactly what was called for.

17

June 24, 1531

It had taken Tommaso a while to accustom himself to Cellini's *bottega* after the spaciousness of Michelangelo's. Here were no enormous free-standing blocks of marble, extensive architectural models or large foundry facilities—crowding on a vast scale.

In Cellini's studio, apprentices' workstations squeezed together; some of their surfaces cluttered with polishing tools, others with everything necessary for melting and carving hard wax, still others set up for beating sheets of gold or silver into rounded forms, or inlay work, or winding precious metal wire into tiny, tight, pleasing patterns, or the engraving of gems. There was a foundry—Cellini cast far more pieces than Michelangelo. But instead of one great structure there were several small furnaces designed for the jeweler's dainty craft.

In spite of his initial reluctance, Tommaso found himself enjoying his apprenticeship at Cellini's. For one thing, the goldsmith had at last made long overdue amends to those he'd abandoned in Florence and sent for Paulino and Cencio to join him. With his old friends working along beside him, and Michelangelo and Ascancio dropping by frequently, Tommaso could almost imagine himself back in Florence.

And he was surprised by how much knowledge he gleaned from the goldsmith. Cellini might suffer from an overweening sense of self-importance, but at least his narcissism led to an obsession with perfection in his craft.

Whether the item produced was as important as a reliquary for the

Pope or as insignificant as a hatpin for some young blade, it had to meet Cellini's exacting standards. Therefore, the goldsmith took care in instructing his apprentices in every facet of the trade. Every piece had to bear the mark of the master's own hand. Tommaso grudgingly admired how, when an apprentice finished with a *chiavaquore*, Cellini took the silver bride's girdle and incised into the figures sculpted in half relief that decorated it—there, and there, with a few small precise movements—correcting a few errors in the apprentice's work, imparting a liveliness that had been lacking.

Tommaso found other advantages to Cellini's training. Compared to sculpture, the smaller size of most of Cellini's commissions was more in scale with Tommaso's decorative work in the kitchen.

And his methods more suited to Tommaso's occupation.

Michelangelo had mastered every technique and medium he'd turned his hand to, but he preferred the glyptic arts, where the sculptor subtracts matter away from the original material. Cellini, too, was adept at every phase of *his* art, but his strong suit lay in augmentive techniques. As Tommaso studied the way Cellini built up models in soft wax or clay, he found it perfectly analogous to the forms he created with butter or dough or the molds he'd built for casting jellies.

So his sojourn in Cellini's studio proved far more pleasant than Tommaso had envisioned it would be.

Except for this afternoon, and that was no fault of the goldsmith's. What Florentine exiled from his homeland wouldn't feel melancholy on Saint John's day? The Romans observed the occasion as a feast day, of course, but where was the pageantry, the celebration?

The apprentices attended religious services early in the morning. They'd been granted a half-day holiday, but found themselves back at their workstations at the *bottega* hours before they were due.

Cencio worked on engraving a cardinal's seal with listless fingers. "I miss the water displays beneath the bridge of Santa Trinita'—the delight of it, the miracle of fluid water taking on fantastic shapes, the way the most far-cast droplets reached us where we stood and watched, cooling our brows under the summer sun," he said softly.

"I miss herding my little sisters to view the processions through the Piazza del Duomo"—Paulino sighed—"their eyes big as apples when they caught sight of the angels and saints, the gilded model castles, the giant puppets. This is the first time in four years our Florence will put on a pageant worthy of her former glory, and I shan't be there to escort my darlings. In another year or so they'll be too big to find the wonder in it," he said forlornly.

Tommaso couldn't bear to think of younger sisters. "I love the way the whole city celebrates," he said. "Every shop festooned with gonfalons and streamers, dressed even more gaily than the girls during *Calendimaggio*. Each citizen, whether a performer or not, takes care to brighten their appearance with ribbons, or a cloth scarf of gold stars on a dark blue ground, or a cheerful mask. Each street fills with music and dancing."

"Well, what *I* like and miss about this day," Cellini's voice, a loud sword, cut through the morose atmosphere, "is when the riderless horses are cut loose to run from Porta al Prato clear down through the city to the Porta alla Croce. The spiked iron balls swinging from their sweating, panting sides have been known to knock down any number of dull, gloomy apprentices, the kind who let their dismal sensibilities affect their work adversely.

"My, I wonder when my cheerful Roman assistants are going to return from their half holiday and brighten this *bottega* with their presence?"

The three young expatriates fell silent and tried to immerse themselves in their work. The atmosphere of dejection didn't disperse.

Finally Cellini gave up. "How can one work in such an ambience?" For emphasis he waved about a steel poniard he'd been engraving, then stood up from his workstation and stomped out of the studio, down the long hallway to his living quarters.

Tommaso cringed, then looked at his friends, who shrugged.

"Benevenuto claims Florence as his own, but he always leaves our city easily enough," Cencio muttered.

Then from somewhere, faintly, came the sound of a flute. It was playing a cheerful tune, the kind of melody that makes the heart hum with pleasure. Its bright notes grew louder. In spite of his gloom, Tommaso found himself keeping time with his feet. The music drew closer. Where could it be coming from? Tommaso raised his eyebrows, silently asking the question of Paulino.

Paulino looked as surprised as he, but he knew the source. "It's the master," he said. And a moment later, Benevenuto Cellini waltzed into the room, flute at his lips.

Cencio pushed his chair away from his worktable and began to sing in accompaniment. Master and apprentice were amazingly good together.

"I had no idea that Maestro Cellini played, or so well," Tommaso whispered to Paulino.

"Oh, yes," Paulino started, but was interrupted by the end of the tune.

"If the lot of you aren't going to work in good spirits, then at least try to make merry," Cellini admonished. "Now, *everybody* sing." He launched into another melody, this one an old Tuscan song. The three boys joined in, trying to harmonize. Midway through, more voices joined them. They turned to find Michelangelo and Ascancio standing in the doorway.

"I knew if there were other Florentines to be found we could make a decent day of it for Saint John's sake," Michelangelo said when the last stanza finished. "You play as well as ever, Benevenuto. Your sainted father would be pleased."

"I play *better* than ever," Cellini said. "Although I still mourn my father's passing"—he crossed himself, an awkward gesture while holding a flute—"its one benefit is that without *Pater*'s constant pressure to turn my talents to professional musicianship, I find I enjoy making music again."

"In spite of your talent, this celebration still lacks. These youngsters need to invest more effort into it," Michelangelo said. "Is it possible to put Florentines and music together and not have dancing?"

Cellini's next tune skipped and capered. While Michelangelo and Cencio sang the melody and clapped the beat with their hands, Tommaso, Ascancio and Paulino jumped up and began moving through the steps and figures that were as much as part of their heritage as the Duomo, or the lions in the piazza, or Florence's symbolic lilies, or *cibreo*.

They were still dancing when the studio's Romans arrived for work. Cellini's partner Felice stared in wonder and shook his head. "I always knew you Florentines were mad. Now I have the proof of it. For sweet Jesus' mercy, what *are* you doing?"

"Have you Romans no music in your souls?" Cencio said. "Don't you ever play tunes, sing and dance?"

"Play tunes, yes. Sing, yes. But that leaping and jumping is dancing?" Felice replied.

"You look like a bunch of young goats bouncing around," blurted Filigno, the youngest apprentice.

Cellini laughed so hard at that he had to stop playing.

That night Tommaso wrote a letter to his parents describing how he'd managed to celebrate St. John's day in spite of himself.

At the same time, Cosimo Ruggiero was also writing to his father.

"It's almost midnight of Florence's saint's day and nothing untoward occurred. The *Duchessina* attended services at the Vatican with her relatives the Salviatis. Afterward they took part in quiet festivities held by Fillipo Strozzi and his sons at the Strozzi palace.

"My greatest fears were for two days past, on the summer solstice, but I discerned no sign of our enemies from the other plane. It appears your prediction was correct, that their power has trouble extending this far unaided, and remains centered in Florence.

"Your most dutiful son, Cosimo."

In her bed, Caterina was not yet asleep. Gattamelata curled at the foot of her bed and Ginevra lay warm over her heart. A heart that felt it was breaking.

Two days ago I endured the great day of celebration of life and growth, the marriage of the God and Goddess. It should have been the day Ippolito and I made promises to each other, now that I'm a woman, Caterina mourned. *Yet the workings of Intialo reach as far as France to outflank my maneuvers, betroth me to another beforehand.*

That is a strategy your enemies will come to regret, one way or the other, Ginevra soothed. *They've picked tools they're unfamiliar with.*

While I sharpen ones I know, and find others at every turn, Caterina agreed, the thought comforting her a little. *But to kneel in prayer today before my cousin Clement, He who is the source of all my woes—oh, that I were a man, or as strong and brave as Aunt Clarice! Every second I wished to leap up and tear His throat out, plunge a poniard into His heart. How can I be so weak in this world, when you tell me I'm so strong in others?*

Ginevra's laughter quivered against Caterina's skin. *What a delicious scandal that would have been! The young, small, female cousin of the Pope rends Him asunder before all of Rome! But alas, you know His use to Them is over. He may have been one of the founts of our predicament, but now He's nothing more than an empty husk, no longer even worthy of revenge. Your danger lies elsewhere, in Florence and beyond.*

Beyond to France, Caterina thought.

No, much farther than that. Beyond this world.

Caterina sighed. *I shall never be safe, never be strong.*

Ginevra's assurance came as comforting heat. *How could you not be safe, beloved, with a* Fata *purring at your feet and a* Lasa *lying on your heart?*

18

The grand hall of the Guild of the Pasta Makers of Rome was grand indeed. Minor damage inflicted upon it during the *reiters'* sacking had been used as an excuse for extensive renovations.

A tesserae floor from the imperial age had been moved entire from a recently excavated ancient villa. Its tiny tiles still bright after so many centuries, it was a classic *asaroton*, depicting scattered remnants of a banquet—soft brown-and-ocher crusts of bread, red-purple pomegranate skins, some spilled black olives, turquoise-and-silver fish heads.

Small artillery fire had broken windows and pitted the major columns. The pillars had been repaired and then set with gold-and-azure tile to complement the flooring. The windows were reglazed with accents of red, green and purple leaded glass bordering clear central panes. They cast red, green and purple mottled shadows across the tessaraed floor.

Tommaso felt grateful for the opportunity to visit such a splendid edifice. The annual meeting of all the food guilds was attended by only Rome's culinary masters, their journeymen, and their most senior apprentices. Messers Spada and Ramerino included him as a courtesy. Besides acting as a useful professional opportunity, the occasion served to distract his thoughts from Caterina.

She'd recovered from the debacle of Cosimo Ruggiero's gala and her fit of temper at the news of her betrothal. But she was still pensive and withdrawn on some days. Like this morning. One of Caterina's maids told Tommaso that the *Duchessina* suffered from bad dreams. Her ladies often heard her crying or talking in her sleep. The mornings after those nights were when she suffered these fits of melancholy. Those were the mornings Tommaso worried about her.

He'd had a hard time putting her out of his mind when he, Ramerino, Spada and Averardo left the Ruggiero mansion in the early afternoon. Finally the necessity of paying attention to Messer Spada's monologue forced him to forget her for the moment.

"The honor of hosting this event rotates every year," *Ser* Spada informed him as they walked to the church services held before the guild function. "Last year the Bakers' Guild performed the honors.

"You're fortunate that you're a resident in Rome *this* year instead, Tommaso. The bakers possess a fair but modest guildhall. The pasta makers' hall will put on a far finer affair then the bakers did last year."

Bindo Ramerino, walking beside Averardo and just behind Tommaso and *Ser* Spada, took umbrage. Although he supervised the making of all grain-based foods in the kitchen, including pasta, Bindo's official guild affiliation was with the bakers' hall.

"It's the cooking at these events that counts," he said angrily. "Not the grandiose overexpenditure on the hall. Last year the bakers offered magnificent appetizers as examples of their art—a multitude of delicacies that could be picked up and nibbled with one's fingers. There's only a handful of pasta recipes that can be eaten that way."

"Ah, but if you're going to argue for quality, then it's not the number of offerings that count," Messer Spada countered. "Why the meat-stuffed fried ravioli alone..."

The quarrel lasted until they reached the church of San Lorenzo. Both master cooks managed to hold their tongues during the services honoring Saint Lorenzo, whose feast day it was. But they shot furious looks at each other throughout the liturgy, much to the amusement not only of Tommaso and Averardo, but also the other carvers, cooks, pastry chefs and bakers standing near them in the nave.

As soon as the service concluded and they left the church the argument began anew, with Bindo Ramerino taking a new tack.

"You Romans confound me," he complained. "You claim to be the greatest cooks in the world. While such a notion makes me laugh, I will concede that, taken all together, the combined cooks of all the Italian states comprise the greatest culinary force in the world. So why do you choose a Spaniard as your patron saint?"

"Saint Lorenzo was Spanish?" asked Averardo.

"Yes, and his sole claim to our profession was not as cook but as one *cooked*," Bindo said with satisfaction. "He piqued the Roman emperor of the time, who reciprocated by torturing Lorenzo in various ways, eventually killing him by roasting him on a gridiron. It's said that before he expired Saint Lorenzo said, 'you can turn me over. I'm done on this side.'"

Marcus Gavius Spada made the sign of the cross and rolled his eyes heavenward. "How can you show such disrespect for a saint? Lorenzo may have been born Spanish, but he lived here in Rome, serving as loyal deacon to Pope Sixtus II."

Bindo Ramerino shrugged his shoulders. "So? He still was no chef. Why didn't the guilds here choose someone more appropriate, like Saint Martha? She was not only an excellent cook, but the sister of the Virgin Mary and aunt to our Lord."

"What? You'd have us represented by a woman?" *Ser* Spada was scandalized. "I don't care how sanctified she was..."

And so it went until they, along with all the other culinary professionals who'd attended church services, reached the pasta makers' hall.

Mercifully the adversaries needed to refortify themselves after their efforts. A buffet was already laid out with *primi servizi di credenza*. Apprentices hurried to lade plates for their masters. Bindo Ramerino decided it unpolitic to continue with a discourse that could be construed as insulting to their hosts, especially since in reality he was as much a pasta maker as a baker. He wandered away to strike up a conversation with some *tortellini* makers.

Tommaso at last had time to study and enjoy the great hall. While appetizers were served all the cooks except the guild officers mingled, nibbling on grilled polenta, stuffed gnocci and the fried lasagna Marcus Gavius Spada had mentioned. A troupe of sword dancers capered about as the entertainment.

Meanwhile, the officers of the various guilds met in a separate room, debating issues like the regulation of imported spices, or quotas that had been set on fisheries. Once policies were decided, the masters of all the guilds were called and assembled before the officers to be notified of any changes. That left the apprentices and journeymen to finish the appetizers and help the apprentice pasta makers clear the buffet table and ready it for the next course. After the meeting was over a competition among the journeymen pasta makers would be judged and *la matta cena* served.

Once *Sers* Spada and Ramerino left for the general assemblage of masters, Averardo felt free to speak to Tommaso about the one subject never far from his mind.

"I swear to you, love so distracts and exhausts me that I'll soon die."

In truth, Averardo didn't look healthy. Unable to sleep well, he'd grown pale. He was too thin. His complexion had worsened.

Tommaso sympathized. At the same time, he was grateful he slept in a lonely cot by himself, rather than in the big apprentices' bed. Averardo's sexual longings for Laudomia had grown so severe that the other apprentices' well-being also suffered. Tommaso woke many a night to one or another of the younger boys cursing and shouting, "How can we sleep with you sweating and thrashing about? It's disgusting! Get out of this bed, this room. Go batter your pole in private!"

The next morning invariably found the younger apprentices as drawn-looking as Averardo and surlier than Bindo Ramerino and Marcus Gavius Spada when quarreling.

Averardo's statement that he suffered unrequited love wasn't precisely true. Laudomia pined for him as desperately as he pined for her. Her methods of suffering weren't as rude as Averardo's, but just as irritating, judging from the other young maidservants' petulance. Tommaso heard them complaining on several occasions that they were sick to death of Laudomia's sighing and moping.

It seemed to Tommaso that if something didn't happen to change the situation soon, the Salviati kitchen would explode like a fireworks display.

"Why don't you just go to her family and beg for her hand?" he asked Averardo.

"Laudomia is the only girl in her family. They all dote on her: mother, father and three *large* older brothers. Although they're craftsmen and far from wealthy, they harbor expectations for her. That's why they placed her in service with a family as esteemed as the Salviatis. They hope her surroundings will refine her, compensating for her small dowry. They trust she'll be exposed to a better class of people at the Salviatis'— including potential husbands.

"She told me her family expects her to marry a man no lower in status than journeyman, and preferably a master with a good established position. By the time I've improved my lot it'll be too late. I know for certain that she's caught the eye of more than one of the men-at-arms."

Averardo twisted in anguish. "Tommaso, what shall I do? I have never loved another. I swear there is no other woman in the entire world for me but her."

Although Tommaso thought Averardo overly melodramatic, he had to admit that at this point in his own life he couldn't imagine ever loving anyone but Michelangelo. He did have the perspective, however, of at one time desiring Filomena.

He looked at the thoroughly miserable Averardo. There were ways of manipulating these situations. His own mother had brought about the marriage of two of the Ruggiero servants, Enzio and Massolina, and at the same stroke achieved protection for Filomena.

"If you're willing to stoop to some small deceptions in the service of honor, I have a few ideas I could share with you," Tommaso offered. "But only if my part in it remains anonymous." If he became known as a meddler in the servants' circles he risked losing his efficacy as the silent, neutral, almost invisible observer Caterina needed him to be. That efficacy required he be well liked by those of his own class, but not drawn into their squabbles and dramas—for those too often reflected the squabbles and dramas of their masters.

Averardo instantly agreed to Tommaso's terms.

Tommaso started to explain his plan, but only got midway when the masters' meeting let out. Then, as journeymen set out dishes for the pasta judging, Vieri, one of Bartolommeo Scappi's apprentices, approached them.

"Begging your pardon, *Ser* Arista, but the master asks if you'd join him for a few moments over there." Vieri pointed to where Scappi stood talking to a tall young man.

"Look who Maestro Scappi speaks to!" Averardo struck his forehead with his hand. "Of course we'd expect to see one or more of them here!"

Mystified, Tommaso looked at his friend.

Averardo grasped Tommaso's forearm. "Remember what you asked me, soon after you arrived here? The confusion regarding your name? Well, that's one of them. One of the Roman Aristas."

Tommaso studied the fellow as they crossed the hall to greet Messer Scappi. The man appeared to be in his mid-twenties. He was as tall as Tommaso's father Gentile, but possessed an entirely different build, with narrow sloping shoulders and a waistline that would turn to paunch in his middle years if he wasn't careful of his diet.

Bartolomeo Scappi brightened when he saw Tommaso. "I'm pleased to see you, young friend. I believe we can throw light on the mystery of the multiple Aristas. Allow me to introduce Signor Ardingo Arista."

Tommaso performed a short, polite bow, searching the man's face for any familiar features. Ardingo Arista's eyes turned down at the edges, and his coloring was almost identical to Gentile's, but besides that and his height, Tommaso perceived no similarities.

Until he spoke, that is. "It appears we may be cousins," Ardingo said. "My grandparents moved to Rome from Florence approximately forty years ago." In spite of his Roman accent, the timbre of Ardingo Arista's voice exactly matched Gentile's.

Tommaso's mouth hung open for a moment. He flushed and clapped it shut at Ardingo's amused smile. "Forgive my astonishment," Tommaso said. "But in speech you sound much like my father."

"Then we must indeed assume ourselves related," the other man said. "I wonder how distantly?"

"My father and his family have for a number of generations worked as cooks and carvers for the Ruggieros, physicians and occultists of great repute in Florence," Tommaso offered as a reference.

Ardingo shrugged. The name Ruggiero obviously meant nothing to him. "I was born and raised here in Rome. I know little of Florence's culinary deposition other than that my father's family hails from there. I am the third generation of Aristas, beginning with my grandfather, to enjoy the employ of the Cavalieri family. In fact, when Maestro Scappi here first spoke of a fair youth called Tommaso, I was somewhat confused, as one of the Cavalieri heirs also bears that name."

Tommaso vaguely recollected the name Cavalieri. It belonged to one of Rome's aristocratic families. No wonder Ardingo Arista looked so unimpressed at the mention of service to physicians and mages, no matter how exalted they might be.

"My grandfather is still alive," Ardingo continued. "Although ancient, his mind remains lively. You must come visit us and solve this interesting mystery. Most of the Cavalieris depart for the country for part of August and early September to escape the worst of Rome's heat. Our work slackens at that time. Let me send for you then. Where can you be found? At Maestro Scappi's?" he said with some condescension.

Tommaso's spine straightened. "Thank you for your generous hospitality. I'm sure Maestro Scappi wouldn't object."

Bartolommeo nodded. He appeared quite entertained by the interchange.

"But rather than impeding on any of his precious time, why don't you send word directly to my place of employ, which is also my place of residence while I remain in Rome," Tommaso said smoothly. "That would be the Salviati mansion. And let me beg for your forbearance in advance: I'll need sufficient notice so I can rearrange my schedule with my employer. I work as personal chef to the Pope's cousin, the *Duchessina* Caterina Romola de' Medici."

Catching sight of Bindo Ramerino and Marcus Gavius Spada standing together, not fighting but casting searching glances about, Tommaso bowed again. "Please excuse me and Averardo here. I notice that the Salviatis' senior cooks appear to be looking for us. It would be discourteous not to rejoin them at once. I look forward to receiving word from you, Maestro Arista."

Tommaso marched off with a straight back, but Averardo glanced around. "Now it's the other Signor Arista who's slack-jawed," Averardo said. "Maestro Scappi appears to be barely holding in his mirth. Well done, Tommaso."

A moment later Averardo glanced back again. "The other Arista is walking away, joining some other men who look somewhat like him. He's pointing and nodding in your direction, Tommaso. You made quite an impression."

Tommaso imagined that he had. He was sure he'd hear from his possible cousins in the future.

Tommaso inquired after Caterina's well-being as soon as they returned to the Salviatis'. The *Duchessina* was not only much improved, but she intended to attend a *commedia* the next day with her aunt and uncle. And the day after that she wanted Tommaso to serve a luncheon for herself and a few of her Roman acquaintances.

Madonna Spada handed Tommaso the list of courses Caterina requested. "When I brought her some porridge this afternoon, Her Grace asked if I would give you this. She ate with a better appetite than I expected. I understand she cheered considerably after going through her correspondence earlier in the day. She must have found good news there."

19

The next morning Tommaso shopped early at the market before leaving for Bartolommeo Scappi's. Scappi was still in good spirits from the revelry at the pasta makers' hall. While working on a butter sculpture centerpiece of Romulus and Remus suckling on the she-wolf for a dinner being hosted by Gregorio Magalotti, the governor of Rome, he joked with Tommaso about obscure relatives.

When Tommaso went home he began preparing for Caterina's affair the next day. He set soup stock simmering, shelled a large quantity of fava beans, boiled a potful of pork tongues in wine, and set a cleaned, plucked crane to roast. By the time he finished he was so tired he scarcely remembered sliding into the bedding of his cot.

He woke late the next morning. He'd barely finished bathing and dressing before the Ramerinos arrived for work. Tommaso felt refreshed by the good night's sleep and relaxed about the hours before him. All he had to worry about today was his service to Caterina.

He worked at a steady but unhurried pace. By the appointed hour the dishes Caterina required were ready. She'd chosen them to stimulate Roman rather than Tuscan palates. They included among other things: the pork tongues cooked in wine sliced and served cold, a seafood salad, a truffle salad, roast crane and turnips napped with a *dulceforte* sauce, and fava beans de' Vitellius, the last from a recipe Messer Spada swore came from the ancient gourmet Marcus Gavius Apicius.

Tommaso commandeered two of Spada's oldest sons, who were

about eleven and twelve years old, to help with the service. The number of guests was mercifully small. Caterina had requested specific dishes but provided none of the visitors' names: this was now her code to Tommaso that he either didn't know them or didn't know them well enough to be acquainted with their tastes, or they weren't important enough to favor with individual attention.

Tommaso had come to realize over time that with the kind of politics Caterina was involved in, too much courtesy shown to insignificant people could be as injudicious as too little courtesy shown to those with power and connections.

In Caterina's suite Tommaso and his assistants cleared several small tables, arranged them in a line, threw clean cloths over them and set up the cutlery and dishes for the first course.

Most of the guests were old Roman acquaintances of Caterina's, except for the Gondis, who sat together on a settee, holding hands.

When Tommaso walked past them, Antonio waved him over. "I know you're busy, Tommaso. Let me take but an instant of your valuable time. I wanted to let you know that we'll now be the closest of neighbors. Madonna Lucrezia has invited us to stay as guests, and the *Duchessina* requested my darling"—Antonio glanced adoringly into his wife's sweet, honest face—"as one of her ladies-in-waiting. I must confess myself relieved. My usual bachelor lodgings here in Rome are far too crowded to accommodate a growing family." Antonio's gaze dropped to his wife's belly, rounded with another pregnancy.

The news gladdened Tommaso's heart. He knew what good folk Antonio and his wife were. They were among the few that Caterina completely trusted.

"I rejoice that you're joining the household," Tommaso said sincerely. He called over one of his assistants and ordered him to serve a particularly fine wine to Antonio to celebrate the news. Then he surveyed the rest of the guests.

Ippolito and his entourage weren't present—Ippolito had Cardinal's work to do that day at the Vatican. Only Pier Antonio Pecci remained behind to watch after Caterina, a task Ippolito often assigned him. Pier Antonio stood conversing with one of Caterina's ladies-in-waiting, the pretty Reparata, in a corner. He looked distracted. He kept glancing in Caterina's direction with a worried frown.

Caterina sat in a grand carved chair which, since her royal betrothal, she'd taken to referring sarcastically as "my throne." A man sat before her in a much lower chair, so that if she leaned forward she'd hover over him. She didn't. She lounged well back. It was her visitor who had to bend toward her.

The fellow's back was to Tommaso. He appeared young, and no one Tommaso knew. His clothing was clean, but plain and a little threadbare.

When the tables were ready, Tommaso and the Spada boys brought up the dishes for the first service. Caterina waved to Tommaso to approach her. "Come, Tommaso. There's someone here I want you to meet. Let your assistants finish that task."

Tommaso dutifully walked over to stand before her. The youth she'd been talking to turned, so Tommaso at last saw his face.

"This is my cousin Lorenzaccio de' Medici, also called Lorenzino. He lives here in Rome. We just discovered his presence."

Lorenzaccio bowed his head perfunctorily. He couldn't have been more than a year older than Tommaso, with a thin sallow face and a somewhat dreamy manner. He looked vaguely familiar, but Tommaso couldn't think of where he might have seen him before. The *mercato*, perhaps?

"Lorenzaccio, this is my master-chef-in-training, Tommaso Arista. Tommaso's mother's family have attended the Medici for generations. But of course, you'd have known that if only you'd had the opportunity to be raised at the family palazzo in Florence, as you should have been. What a pity."

Caterina had never referred to Tommaso in such a way before, as if he was almost chattel, merely part of her status. Tommaso couldn't help himself. He flushed with displeasure.

But when Lorenzaccio turned toward him, Tommaso's high color blanched clean away. On the other youth's face was such a look of bilious envy that Tommaso caught his breath. Now he recognized the fellow. This was the young man he'd seen on his very first day here, whom he'd help lock out at the gates.

"Lorenzino, I want you to be acquainted with Tommaso. I mean to find out what pleases you. We'll start with food," Caterina said, all tranquil graciousness. "As a Medici and my cousin, you deserve to be treated with the highest regard."

Caterina's words acted on the youth like one of Cosimo Ruggiero's spells. The look on Lorenzaccio's face melted from rancor to gratitude.

All the way back to the kitchen to fetch the second course, Tommaso shook his head. What was Caterina up to?

20

Third week of August, 1531

Laudomia disliked Tommaso's plan. This didn't surprise him. She disliked it so intensely he was glad he'd made Averardo swear that it was Averardo's idea and no one else's.

The scheme was based on information Tommaso'd learned soon after he joined the kitchen staff: Bindo Ramerino's family's early-morning arrival was a relatively recent habit.

A distant cousin of Laudomia's, Madonna Ramerino was the connection that had secured Laudomia's position in the kitchen. Therefore, she acted as Laudomia's guardian in the household. So when young Alessa informed her that Averardo and Laudomia appeared on the verge of trysting, Madonna Ramerino initiated the preemptive early-morning appearances.

After a year of this, only Madonna Ramerino and Alessa remained keen on keeping the lovers apart by this method. Bindo Ramerino and the rest of his children longed to return to the extra half hour or so of sleep in the morning.

"So give them a reason to sleep in," Tommaso advised Averardo. "Let it appear you've lost your ardor for Laudomia."

"Then when they're lulled, my love and I can meet again at dawn," Averardo said enthusiastically. "That way we'll endure until I qualify for journeyman and can ask for her hand."

"No, no!" Tommaso said, alarmed. "You must *not* meet with

Laudomia in the morning. Madonna Ramerino surely has talebearers in the staff spying on the two of you."

When Averardo told Laudomia the plan, she not only doubted it, but him.

"You think to trick me into conspiring in my own abandonment?" she wailed, pounding her fists on Averardo's chest and pushing him away. She couldn't push him far enough to suit her fury, since he'd chosen to tell her in the privacy of one of the pantries. Averardo fell back, banging his head on several long hanging sausages, then tripping over some sacks of barley piled on the floor. "Ow!" he said loudly as he fell.

Tommaso, standing guard outside, flinched and looked around to be sure no one heard.

"No, I swear, my gentle *paloma*, this is only to allay Madonna Ramerino's suspicions. I pray it won't be for long."

Laudomia stormed out of the pantry. Averardo followed at her heels, whispering pleas of patience.

"And you, what's your part in this?" Laudomia turned on Tommaso. Tommaso backed away, both hands up and shaking his head in denial.

"Tommaso just agreed to stand watch while we spoke. And he'll act as our courier, so we can still send messages back and forth to each other," Averardo said.

Tommaso had agreed to no such thing. But in the face of Laudomia's fury it suddenly seemed like a good addition to the plan. He nodded vigorously.

Acting indifferently toward Laudomia was torture for Averardo. But since he believed in his goal he performed passably well.

Not believing in Averardo, Laudomia's performance was far better. No one in the kitchen could miss her tear-filled, red-rimmed eyes, the furious daggered glances she launched at her former inamorata.

Although Tommaso initially viewed the situation with humor, he felt guilty for the anguish he'd caused her.

"I swear to you Averardo's heart is true," he whispered as she assisted him in pounding some veal for a dish of *biancomangiare*. "Look how well the plan proceeds: It's been less than a fortnight, and already the Ramerinos arrive later in the morning."

Laudomia looked over her shoulder to where Alessa buzzed like a

fly about Averardo at his workstation. "I see how well this plan proceeds," she hissed, thwacking the veal a great blow with the back of a
cleaver. "If Averardo's love for me stands fast, tell him to act soon. To
my eye, it appears as though Alessa Ramerino is striving for her own
betrothal to him. Bear him this message for me: If such is the case I
promise he'll hear of *my* betrothal to someone else before *his* to her.

"I've told my parents I'm ready to think of marriage. They're beginning to cast about for a suitable husband." She wiped her hands on
her apron and glared at Tommaso. "There, I'm done," she said, and
stalked off.

Tommaso stared at the mound of pulverized meat she'd left behind.
I've never seen anyone, not even my father, reduce hard muscle to pulp
in such a short time, he thought, both impressed and appalled. The man
who thinks women are weak is a fool.

Serving Caterina's weekly soirée didn't provide Tommaso much relief
from the kitchen's tension. When he arrived at her suite with his assistants, filled platters and serving bowls, who should number among the
guests, as he did frequently these days, but Lorenzaccio de' Medici.

The fresh linens, plates and cutlery for the place settings were kept
in Caterina's wardrobe room now. Tommaso helped his assistants carry
all the necessities out and set up the *biancomangiare*, black cabbage rolls,
spinach-and-fennel salad, fresh peaches soaked in wine and honey, all the
while keeping an eye on Lorenzaccio.

"I don't understand it," he said to Leone Strozzi, who'd strolled
over to admire the well-laden table. "Why does she keep inviting him?"

Leone shrugged. "He is a cousin, after all, no matter how distant.
The Pierfrancesco branch of the Medici haven't done badly, even if
they're not descended from Cosimo Pater Patriae and Lorenzo il Magnífico. Look at Giovanni del Bande Nere."

"Who gained much credit by joining il Magnífico's line when he
married Maria Salviati," Tommaso pointed out.

"True, but his accomplishments as a great soldier were his own,"
Leone countered. "And even Lorenzino's family, although not wealthy
now, is not unaccomplished. Lorenzino's sisters are lovely. My father is
considering a match between one of them and my brother Piero."

"Really?" said Tommaso, astonished. He looked over to where

Fillipo Strozzi, a bearded, grave-looking man with a broad high forehead and close-cropped curly hair, stood talking to Lorenzaccio. That explained why Signor Strozzi was so attentive to Lorenzaccio, though the younger man was already tipsy.

"Look at him," Tommaso said. "Nothing you've said convinces me he's fit company for the *Duchessina*."

Leone did look, then sighed. "You're right, my friend. I don't know why I try to be kind, except that I endeavor always 'to be cautious and reserved rather than forward, and take care not to get the mistaken notion that I know something I do not know.' I'm not acquainted with this fellow well enough to judge him. 'I will not be careless in speaking words which can offend.' "

"You know your *Courtier* well." Tommaso smiled.

"Doesn't everybody?" asked Leone. "And I do mean everybody." He nodded toward Lorenzaccio, who was waving in their direction. "I believe Lorenzino requires you bring him more wine. Come, do as he bids, then listen."

Tommaso's mouth thinned to a tight line. It was inappropriate to his position at this kind of social event for him to pour wine for anyone but Caterina. Even Lorenzaccio must know that. But Tommaso did as Leone asked and fetched a bottle from the sideboard. Leone walked over to Lorenzaccio with him.

Leone clapped Lorenzaccio on the back as Tommaso filled the glass. "Young Medici, since you're a cousin of sorts, let me warn you—beware of this vintage. It's appetizingly smooth and therefore treacherous, likely to nourish those 'thorns and tares of our appetites which so often overshadow and choke our minds.' "

Lorenzino blinked, taken aback by the warning. Then his lips rounded in a faint cat's smile. And, like a cat, he lapped delicately from the goblet. "Delicious indeed," he pronounced. "A true pleasure. It would make me suffer not to drink it. Remember, fair cousin-of-sorts, 'true pleasure is always good and true suffering always evil.' "

Even sober, avuncular Fillipo Strozzi looked impressed by Lorenzino's ability to duel quotes from Castiglione.

Tommaso was more struck by the youth's ability to hold himself in as tightly as a spring, in spite of the amount of wine he'd drunk.

And though Lorenzino gave the illusion of forthrightness, he revealed none of his true emotions. His eyes might be shining brightly from the combination of too much wine and the pleasure of well-countered repartee. Or they might shine in outright hostility that Leone had tried to tweak him. It was impossible to tell.

Leone bowed low. "Anyone who can quip thus needs not fear an 'overshadowed mind.' Come, chef Arista. Let's see if there are others here who need savor this vintage," he said, propelling Tommaso away from his father and Lorenzaccio.

Safely out of earshot Leone held out his own glass. Tommaso filled it gladly—the act of a friend, not a servant.

"You see what I mean?" said Leone. "Young as he is, Lorenzino possesses a quick mind. He works hard to educate himself for that stratum of society he believes himself entitled. It's too bad he's already incurred the displeasure of Roman authority and of his immediate family.

"I'm as ill at ease as yourself regarding Caterina's desire to patronize him, but I'm not sure yet if I can fault her." He winked over his goblet at Tommaso. "Families—a mystery, are they not?"

Tommaso thought of the invitation he'd received earlier that morning, posted from the house of Cavalieri. Tonight, after this soirée, he'd at last meet and break bread with the Roman Aristas.

"To mysterious families," he agreed with Leone Strozzi, clinking the bottle of wine against Leone's in a toast.

21

The Cavalieri mansion's kitchen differed little from the Salviatis' in its particulars: a great hearth equipped with ironware furnishings for roasting and hooks for hanging cauldrons and smoking sausages; a broad *fornaio* for baking; stone-framed grills; kneading troughs; worktables; shelf upon shelf laden with serving platters, mixing bowls, all sorts of cooking pots and pans, stoneware jars for preserving pickled meats and vegetables; and on the ground under the tables sat baskets and sacks filled with grains, fresh fruit and vegetables.

The dinner for the Cavalieri family and then the other domestics had been served, cleared and cleaned up after. The cooks were just beginning to concoct their own supper from the leftovers. A complex fragrance hung veil-like in the air, hinting at marinated and roasted meats, the clean crispness of greens, unctuous sauces, and the high sweet notes of burgundy-skinned pomegranates, flaxen pears, amber figs, purple plums and cool-scented icy green melons.

Tommaso, with his connoisseur's nose, appreciated the differences between the attar of this kitchen and that of the Salviatis', with its Florentine and Bolognese influences. This was more of a purely Roman kitchen. The savor of pork cooked a dozen different ways and the sharp iodine essence of seafood dominated the aromatic mix.

A Cavalieri gatekeeper had escorted him to the kitchen. Ardingo hurried over to greet Tommaso, then introduced everybody in the crowded, busy room. Tommaso tried to catch the flurry of names: Franceschetto, Diomede, Alamanno, Boccolino, Guglielmo, Grazia and more. Were these all relatives? Some must be scullery boys and maids and apprentices. By their looks, several were obviously Ardingo's brothers or cousins. Were all the women wives, or were some unmarried sisters? Tommaso did grasp that Franceschetto and Diomede were Ardingo's uncles.

"And this," Ardingo said, drawing Tommaso over to one of the long tables where several girls were laying down settings of majolica and cutlery, "is our patriarch, Galleoto Arista. Grandfather, let me introduce our guest and possibly a member of our family—Tommaso Arista of Florence."

The elderly man seated at the head of the table looked at Tommaso during Ardingo's introduction. Tommaso searched those still keen eyes for some similarity to his own Arista grandfather, whom he'd last seen years ago on a visit to the Ruggiero's country property. This man was older and more frail, his hands trembling where they rested on the table, but the set of his jaw and mouth resembled Tommaso's grandfather.

"So you're from Florence, eh?" The words came out clear and very loud, startling Tommaso. He'd expected the mumbling, shaking voice he associated with the very old.

"Y-y-yes," Tommaso stuttered.

"Speak up," Ardingo whispered on his other side. "Grandfather's a little hard of hearing."

"Yes, I'm from Florence. I'm in Rome serving as cook to the *Duchessina* Caterina Romola de' Medici." It was excruciating blaring all this out in front of a crowd of strangers.

"Were you born to the trade or apprenticed in?" Galleoto brayed.

"Born to it. My mother's family have served the Medici for generations. Gentile Arista, my father, works as master carver and cook to the physician Ruggiero the Old."

"Hah! Hah!" Galleoto crowed. "Gentile Arista? That little *furafante*! A master carver now, you say? And the Ruggieros! That pack of nefarious sorcerers!" The old man shook his head in astonished delight. He turned to Ardingo. "Why didn't you tell me of this, of Gentile and the Ruggieros?" he demanded.

"I met Tommaso only briefly at the guild meeting. In truth, he mentioned those names, but I forgot them," Ardingo admitted.

"Sit down," Galleoto urged Tommaso, patting the place setting to his right. He looked up at the gathered family. "What are you doing standing there? After a long day you're not hungry? And even if you're not, what about our cousin-guest here?"

The solid wall of people broke apart. Everyone but Tommaso and Galleoto went back to preparing supper.

Galleoto beamed at Tommaso. "So little Gentile grew up and had a family? What about that rascal Marcantonio? Does he yet live? Or did he die years ago at the hands of some irate husband?"

It took a moment for Tommaso to realize that Galleoto meant Gentile's father, Tommaso's grandfather.

"He still lives," Tommaso said. "Though members of his—our— family were lost to the plague that ravaged Florence and the Tuscan countryside. Grandfather manages the Ruggiero country estate, and alas, the farmlands weren't spared." This was a subject Tommaso couldn't bear to speak of.

Galleoto might be deaf, but he wasn't unobservant. "Sad, sad," he commiserated loudly. "We too have known grief these last few years. My eldest son Ludovico, who was Ardingo's father, died defending the city against the *landsknechte* during the Sack. And my beloved Ilaria, who bravely left Florence with me so long ago, passed away last spring."

Galleoto reached over and patted Tommaso's hand. "The priests tell us we all shall die. And if we've been good march up to and through Heaven's gate. Since all of us here are good cooks—which no matter what our sins, qualifies us for a sort of goodness—we can be certain with glad hearts of our final destination. So while we live let's be merry. Tell me how my native Florence fares. How are the Ruggieros? Did young Ruggiero turn into the great sage his father predicted?"

Considering that Ardingo hadn't recognized the Ruggiero name when Tommaso talked to him at the guildhall, Tommaso was amazed that old, deaf Galleoto had heard of Cosimo's auspicious talents.

"Indeed he has," Tommaso said. "And more than that. He's admired as a gentleman of great tact, courtesy and warmth."

"Truly?" said Galleoto, surprised. "He was such a studious youth— so shy and reticent that many thought him cold."

Tommaso realized with chagrin that the young Ruggiero Galleoto referred to was Ruggiero the Old. "He is still of grave demeanor," Tommaso said, recovering quickly. "But perhaps the lessons life teaches all of us warmed his disposition over the years. He's prosperous in his work. His house thrives."

"Thrives, eh?" Galleoto shook his head. "I'd be working in that house's kitchen yet, if greater opportunity hadn't arisen here."

"I wondered why you left Florence," Tommaso said. He waved his hand to indicate the huge, well-equipped kitchen. "Although this is a far grander situation than the Ruggieros' employ."

"It is," Galleoto said cheerfully. "Much as I've missed Florence, I've been happy here. I reached a position I could never have attained at the Ruggieros', though circumstances shifted back there in ways I couldn't have foreseen." He winked at Tommaso. "We Aristas aren't without our ambitions."

"What do you mean? What circumstances?" Tommaso asked.

"Inheriting the Master Cook's position in the Ruggiero kitchen, of course. Though it was always intended for my oldest brother Ambrogio—and he did attain and hold it—for a while it appeared that I'd succeed him. You still look mystified. Your father never told you of these things?"

Tommaso shook his head.

Galleoto looked thoughtful. "Perhaps Ambrogio never thought to explain it to Gentile. My brother might have forgotten how young Gentile was when he came to us."

Platters of food were set before them on the table. The kitchen staff seated themselves.

"Ah, supper at last," Galleoto said. "What do we have tonight?"

The younger uncle, Diomede, stood and pointed to each dish or bowl in turn. "For the *primi*: seafood and barley soup with striped mullet, gilthead and bream; lettuce *patina* serves as the egg dish; olive paste *crostini*; a salad of seasoned melon."

The food smelled and looked delicious, but Galleoto's story intrigued Tommaso. He wanted to hear the rest of it more than he wanted to eat.

Galleoto noticed the expression on Tommaso's face. "No one should look so letdown with a fine meal before him," the patriarch said in his carrying voice. "I'll continue the tale while we eat. It will be good for these youngsters to hear this story, since it's part of their history too." The desultory wave of his hand included everyone in the room.

"All those who would have remembered any part of it are now gone, one way or the other: my beloved Ilaria; my eldest son Ludovico, who was chief kitchen apprentice at the Ruggieros' when we left Florence; my eldest daughter Bernardina, who is not dead but more or less happily married. You, Franceschetto, were too young to remember. And you, Diomede, weren't born until after we arrived in Rome."

In between spoonfuls of soup, Galleoto began his tale.

"There were three of us Arista brothers, separated by intervening years and intermittent sisters. The oldest by far was Ambrogio. After him came my elder sisters Cornelia and Caia. Then I arrived. I was followed by two more sisters, Boadilla and Fillapella. The last born, much later, was Marcantonio, our guest Tommaso's grandfather. By that time Ambrogio was twenty years old and clearly the heir to the kitchen."

Galleoto scraped up his last spoonful of soup. One of the women, perhaps a daughter-in-law, took away the bowl and filled his plate with small portions from the rest of the *primi* service. Galleoto kept talking.

"We three brothers differed greatly in more ways than just our ages, especially in our temperaments. I believe that came about from our positions within the family. Ambrogio possessed a sober diligent nature, as befits a first son. I did my best to follow his example in all things, not just in cooking. But I felt myself nowhere near his match, as middle children are wont to do. Marcantonio, on the other hand"—Galleoto stopped to roll his eyes—"played out the role of youngest son to perfection. He was our sisters' darling, their poppet. No surprise that as he grew up women followed him the way cats follow catnip.

"But in spite of our differences there were traits we shared. We each showed an aptitude for our trade and an affinity for the fairer sex.

"When he turned twenty-five, the proper time for Florentine gentlemen to begin considering marriage, Ambrogio's ardor was awakened by a lovely maiden from a family esteemed within our trade. Both sets of parents rejoiced at the prospective match.

"Alas, it was not to be. The girl became pregnant out of wedlock. Evidently the child wasn't Ambrogio's, for though he urged haste in posting the banns, in the end she refused him."

Galleoto shook his head. "No one knew why, since that's the time-honored way for a woman to escape such a fix. Her reasons may have been estimable: that she didn't want to cast aspersions on Ambrogio's honor nor place him in the position of caring for a rival's bastard. She seemed fond enough of Ambrogio that these could have been the reasons.

"On the other hand"—Galleoto shrugged—"she may have still been infatuated with her paramour. No one knew for certain his identity, but rumors abounded.

"Whatever the reason, Ambrogio was heartbroken. He withdrew into silent pride and refused to court another. It appeared he'd remain a bachelor his entire life."

The scullions cleared away the empty *primi* platters and set the *secondo servizi* on the table. After everyone filled their plates Galleoto continued.

"Some years passed. Then it was my turn for affairs of the heart. As I said before, throughout my life I imperfectly followed Ambrogio's example. I fell in love as truly as he had, but when I met Ilaria I was only twenty and considered too young to marry. Ilaria was almost eighteen and her parents already casting about for a husband for her. Luckily for me, Ilaria loved me as truly as I loved her.

"We despaired that fate might contrive to keep us separated. In desperation we decided that our choice was between a life apart on earth or a life together in Heaven. To that end, we took to our respective beds in our respective homes and ceased to eat, determined to waste away."

Galleoto chuckled. "This was considerably easier for Ilaria. Her family worked as armorers. But for me—hah! Day and night I lay tortured as the kitchen's sweet bouquet wafted about me, tempting me. My parents, once they knew the source of my 'illness,' took care to prepare my favorite foods. They left meals fit for a duke on the table by my sickbed." Galleoto pounded his chest. "Do you see me? Then you see a good Christian, for I know already the torments Hell promises—how seductively the devil can tempt one. I suffered through such torments then, but I remained constant.

"At last, seeing that Ilaria's and my minds were made up, our parents relented and let us wed. We proved to be the happiest couple in Florence. In time we were blessed with four children: Ludovico first, then you, Franceschetto, and your two sisters. No, no."—Galleoto shook his fork at his youngest son. "I haven't forgotten you, Diomede, but remember that you were born here, practically in this very kitchen.

"Anyway, young Marcantonio grew up in the intervening years. Although gifted in the kitchen he lacked concentration. His restless nature yearned for expression in physical things. He loved *calcio*, swimming, dancing, wrestling and spear casting. Every chance he got to abandon stove and hearth he'd flee outdoors.

"Our father took that aspect of Marcantonio's nature into consideration. At the time the Ruggiero family was in the habit of visiting their country property often. Since there were more than enough of us working in the kitchen in Florence, and since Marcantonio attracted far too much attention from the fairer sex and there was bound to be trouble from that, our father assigned him to accompany the Ruggieros as their cook whenever they traveled to their estate.

"This arrangement made everyone happy, most of all Marcantonio. It allowed him the physical life he loved, offered him more responsibility and challenge in his work, and he could still enjoy all of Florence's pleasures. And yet"—Galleoto shook his head—"in the end he couldn't curb his nature any more than a blade of grass can stand up to the wind.

"There came a day of great tension in the kitchen during one of Marcantonio's interims back in Florence. Heads shook in dismay, rumors abounded. Marcantonio had impregnated some young woman. There was hell to pay. No one knew the identity of the unfortunate girl. When our father hauled Marcantonio into a room in the mansion to discuss the matter away from the kitchen and behind closed doors, Marcantonio shouted loud enough to be heard through the wall at one point by some, uh, passing house servants, 'I don't care what her father desires! I love her! I want to marry her!' Our father's reply couldn't be heard, but evidently he disapproved of the match. The rest of us inferred there must be a disparity of status between Marcantonio and his inamorata, although it just as easily could have been his age—he wasn't even twenty.

"The next morning he was gone, banished to the country. Maestro Ruggiero was kind enough to facilitate the situation by awarding him the position of cook and chief steward there. As luck would have it, fate lent credence to Marcantonio's departure. One of the Ruggiero children came down with an illness and needed a protracted convalescence in the clean country air. Madonna Ruggiero and one of the elder Ruggiero daughters left for the country with all the little Ruggieros and stayed there almost a year, so Marcantonio had the excuse of necessary employment."

Galleoto helped himself to a second helping of salted pork tongue napped with a date sauce. "About half a year later we learned the truth of the matter. We received a formal but cordial letter from Marcantonio announcing he'd married a country maid and that they were the proud parents of a beautiful, healthy newborn son, your father Gentile," Galleoto nodded at Tommaso.

Tommaso flushed at the clear implication: His father had narrowly missed coming into the world as a bastard. And his grandmother, obviously seduced on one of Marcantonio's forays into the country, had been considered too lowly of birth to be worthy of marrying an Arista.

Although Ardingo smirked a little, Galleoto evidently hadn't intended to humiliate Tommaso. He loudly sailed on with his narrative, the story of Tommaso's lineage a necessary aside in his tale.

"All of our futures now appeared assured. Three of our sisters had been married off long before. The youngest, Fillapella, begged to join a convent and take her vows. Ambrogio assumed more and more responsibilities from Father. Although Ambrogio was destined for the position of chief carver and cook in the house, I felt content. Since Ambrogio had no heirs, all future employ would fall to my children. The Ruggiero household was socially connected and large enough to accommodate two cooks who were guild-designated masters. Especially two cooks who worked as well together as Ambrogio and I.

"Then the stars shifted in the heavens." Galleoto rolled his eyes upward for emphasis. "Our fates shifted with them. The first change was that Ambrogio, upon turning forty, decided to wed after all. This time the woman wasn't young or flighty. In fact, she owned her own business. She ran one of those shops on the Ponte Vecchio that procure wild game for the city. Although she was too independent for my taste, she was otherwise a good, sober woman. As content as I was in my own marriage, I couldn't resent Ambrogio's chance to experience similar joy."

Galleoto stopped to drum his fingers on the table. Several different emotions played across his face. Clearly he was unsure how to continue.

"Well," he said at last. "I *was* happy for my brother. But this wife, Constanza Sedani, although not young, was not too old to bear children. A year and a half after they wed she produced a fine baby girl, who they named Leonora. Constanza decided that if this girl showed any aptitude, she'd follow Constanza into the game-shop business.

"This did little to assuage my fears. Where there was one baby, more would follow. I saw the legacy of employment for my own children slipping away and myself relegated to a minor position in the kitchen even before I reached old age.

"Meanwhile, Marcantonio's country wife died from some illness. Marcantonio mourned for a barely decent amount of time before marrying again. Perhaps he'd come to resent his first wife for his lost opportunities. Or maybe he succumbed to his youthful nature again. He was barely in his mid-twenties." Galleoto looked thoughtful. "It must have been the latter; his second bride was also a country wife, and their baby, a daughter, *also* entered this world less than nine months after the marriage."

Galleoto waved his hand, indicating his empty plate. Everyone else, listening to him, had finished long ago. Several of the women cleared the table and set bowls of a single *dolci* out: leftover fruit sliced thinly, napped with sweet wine and sprinkled with macaroon crumbs. Galleoto took a bite, smacked his lips, and pronounced the dessert satisfactory.

Everyone helped themselves to some of the fruit while Galleoto continued the story.

"There are advantages to having a premonitive employer. Maestro Ruggiero rarely bothered with our affairs out in the kitchen. But perhaps he had a vision of paying exorbitant wages to too many cooks, for he asked me to meet him in his study one day. There he reminded me that among the last group of visitors he'd hosted was a highborn Roman couple. They'd loved the food during their sojourn at his palazzo. They now sought a cooking staff for a new mansion they were building in Rome. They wrote him entreating that he recommend some Tuscan cooks equal in skill to his own."

Tommaso stifled a smile. The supper he'd just eaten had been excellent, but there was little of Tuscany left in it.

"Maestro Ruggiero said at first he'd been at a loss how to reply," Galleoto was saying. "What did he know of cooking and cooks? But then he considered his own kitchen and how crowded it was becoming. 'What about you, Galleoto? Would you be interested? This job would be quite a challenge. These people are aristocrats, far wealthier than we Ruggieros. They entertain frequently and lavishly, but you are easily the equal of your father and brother in culinary matters. Of course, every Florentine hates to leave Florence, so I understand if you don't wish me to recommend you.' With these and many other fair words he made me see the attractiveness of this opening.

"Still, I hesitated. I felt an obligation to my parents and Ambrogio. If I left, I'd be taking not only my talents, but also those of Ilaria, who since our marriage had worked alongside me and become very skilled, and Ludovico, who was now first among our kitchen's apprentices. I feared I'd leave the Ruggiero kitchen in opposite distress—understaffed.

"I expressed my trepidations to Maestro Ruggiero."

"'If those are your only doubts, calm yourself,' he said. 'They are easily solved. Your father may be slowing down, but he is still capable at his work. It appears Ambrogio and his wife may yet produce more children to raise in the trade. In the meantime, we already employ several scullery maids. The guild can be contracted and a journeyman hired. As for an apprentice to replace Ludovico, I know of just the boy.'

"'On my last trip to the country I observed tension between your brother Marcantonio's wife and Gentile, his son by his first marriage. It's evident she feels the child reminds Marcantonio of his first love overly much, for Gentile *is* the apple of Marcantonio's eye.'

"Then surely he won't relinquish the boy. And how old is Gentile now?" I asked. "Five? That's too young to begin an apprenticeship."

"'He's six, a strapping boy from all that fresh air, healthy outdoor exercise, and hearty food. He could easily pass as eight,' Ruggiero replied. "'You're right, of course, in that Marcantonio is reluctant to lose him so young. At the same time, your brother confided in me that he wants the child to have the kind of decent public education that a life in Florence provides, and better chances to learn the culinary trade.'

"'As you know, in the last few years my children are mostly grown. We rarely visit the estate as a family anymore. So occasions for refined cooking out there are infrequent. Besides,' my employer added, 'though he wouldn't admit it, I believe Marcantonio wishes for peace with his new wife.'

"So we agreed upon a solution," Galleoto said. "A journeyman was hired, the Romans notified of my interest once their home was completed, and Gentile sent for from the country, the idea being to see if the situation was amenable to everyone before taking final action."

Galleoto shrugged. "Within six months I had cause to be grateful for Maestro Ruggiero's suggestions. Constanza became pregnant again. I knew if I wished ever to have a kitchen to master that we needed to leave." He pushed back his chair from the table. "So I did. And here we are."

"But my father, rather than one of Ambrogio's children, now runs the Ruggiero kitchen," Tommaso said.

Galleoto shrugged again. "Sometimes fate plays little tricks on us. Ambrogio and Constanza's second child was also a girl, who I later heard eventually married someone outside our art. All of Constanza's children after that were stillborn, but Ilaria and I were well settled here in Rome by then. Gentile grew up to fill the role of son for Ambrogio.

"When our parents died Ambrogio and I wrote less and less to each other. After he, too, died, I lost all contact with what was left of the family in Florence. Your father probably barely remembers us."

"So if you'd stayed you *would* have finally become the head cook and carver there," Ardingo said.

Galleoto smiled at his grandson. "Yes, but though even now I miss my beloved Florence, I don't resent the fate the stars chose for me and for you children." He swung his arm, his gesture encompassing their surroundings. "We serve a grander house and work in a grander kitchen than that of the Ruggieros'." He looked at Tommaso. "Am I right?"

"Yes," Tommaso admitted.

Galleoto winked at him. "And we make grander wages. I told you we Aristas are ambitious." He reached over and patted Tommaso on the shoulder. "Ardingo says that in that particular you've proved yourself a member of the family. Tell us what it's like to work for the Pope's little cousin. The *Duchessina* must keep you busy in her service."

"At first that was true," Tommaso said. "But since her betrothal she's much in demand socially by those eager to cultivate a connection with the French court." He knew it was more the Arista ambition Galleoto referred to that had led these cousins to invite him here than a desire to renew family ties.

"Most evenings she accompanies her aunt and uncle to a banquet, or pageant, or theater party, or a fête in her honor. Therefore, except for special commissions on her behalf, the bulk of my labors consists of assisting the Salviati master chefs and learning the art of exceptional culinary presentation from Bartolommeo Scappi."

Tommaso talked a little more about what it was like working at the Salviatis'. His cousins wanted to know of his plans for France. What sort of entertaining would be expected of the *Duchessina*? Did Tommaso expect that he'd like living in France? What sort of position would he occupy within the hierarchy of the royal kitchens?

Tommaso deflected their questions with a pose of modesty. As a mere servant, he couldn't say what his *Duchessina* intended, or what would be expected of her. And what did he know of France, other than what he'd read and heard, which wasn't much.

He couldn't tell them the truth—that he didn't expect to move to France, for he didn't expect, in the end, that Caterina would marry Henri, Duke of Orleans.

In the first place, Pope Clement was playing too dangerous a game. Emperor Carlos V would never tolerate such a potentially powerful match to the son of his premier enemy, François, King of France. The Pope's action was intended more as a gesture to win François good faith. The proof of the marriage's unlikelihood was that Emperor Charles didn't exact any revenge on Clement when he heard of the betrothal. The Emperor took the arrangement no more seriously than Tommaso did.

Secondly, standing in for Caterina's deceased parents, the Pope offered far too modest a dowry for a king of François's stature to accept. Rumor at the Salviati household had it there was a secret addendum to the marriage contract for an "invisible" dowry: the promise of several Italian cities and territories which Clement had no power to deliver.

The whole arrangement was so insecure that there'd already been a postponement of at least eighteen months and the actual date for the nuptials hadn't been set.

All of this without even taking Caterina herself into consideration. She was determined to have a say in her own future. Tommaso was one of the very few who knew of her and Ippolito's plans for a life together.

So Tommaso hedged with his relatives as best he could. He was grateful when several lovely, merry children—he guessed Cavalieris from the satin and embroidered linen they wore—descended on the kitchen. In spite of the housemaid trailing behind them who scolded that they should be going to bed, the youngsters pleaded for late-night treats, distracting Tommaso's audience's attention away from him.

Tommaso smiled. The scene reminded him of the countless times the Ruggiero children had come wheedling for sweets at the kitchen back home in Florence.

The Cavalieri youngsters were led by their oldest member, a boy of about twelve or thirteen. Tommaso'd never seen such a beautiful youth in his life. The boy's perfect, silky skin glowed. His hair was a glossy russet brown. His features were even and classic, pleasantly animated; his eyes were a bright light blue rimmed with black; his physique was slender yet already well muscled.

As Franceschetto, Diomede and some of the women good-naturedly threw together some morsels for the youngsters, Tommaso drew Ardingo aside.

"Is that Tommaso Cavalieri?" Tommaso asked, pointing as surreptitiously as he could manage. "The one whose name caused confusion when we met?"

Ardingo looked, then laughed. "No, that's Tommaso's younger cousin. Tommaso Cavalieri is probably a year or two older than you, and so handsome he makes that child look ugly."

Tommaso stared at Ardingo and then back at the lovely boy. He was so beautiful that even Michelangelo would yearn to sketch him. Then Tommaso dropped his head, embarrassed at the thought.

After bidding farewell to his cousins, Tommaso followed the night watch most of the way back to the Salviati mansion. He no longer felt nervous about walking Rome's streets, but the hour was late and he didn't like taking chances. At the top of the road that led to the Salviatis', the watch turned in the opposite direction, waving to Tommaso as they left him. It was still a long stroll home, but here and there oil lamps lit the avenue. Halfway down, the street opened up onto a small piazza containing a pleasant little fountain, a marble bench for any passersby who felt weary, and a few modest statues of alabaster *putti* coyly posing on bases formed from satyrs' heads carved from porphyry. The satyrs' heads themselves decorated the tops of short supporting pillars.

As he approached the small square Tommaso saw someone enter it from the opposite side, coming from the direction of the Salviati mansion. The fellow was almost enshrouded in his hat and long cloak. He walked with a peculiar stiff gait, so controlled that he made headway very slowly. Yet in spite of his efforts to govern his body, every few steps he lost his balance and tripped.

As the man came fully into the light of the piazza's single oil lamp Tommaso recognized him. It was Lorenzaccio, only now finally leaving the Salviatis. By the looks of him, he'd kept drinking after Tommaso had served him that afternoon. His eyes, though open, were blind and unfocused. As Tommaso watched, Lorenzaccio tripped again, barely catching himself before he crashed to the pavement.

Tommaso saw no way of getting past the inebriated youth without risking a confrontation. He slipped into the shadow of a deeply recessed doorway, trusting that Lorenzaccio's wine-soaked eyes wouldn't detect him there.

The near fall jarred Lorenzaccio out of his stupor. He spun about, glaring so hostilely around the empty piazza that Tommaso was glad he'd hidden. Then Lorenzaccio reeled about the square, squinting and examining the bench, the fountain, and the sculptures in such a manner that Tommaso could only guess he was pretending, with drunken logic, that he'd planned all along to be scrutinizing the piazza in such a state at such an hour.

He was also delivering some sort of soliloquy, though Tommaso couldn't hear the garbled words. Evidently Lorenzaccio's discourse dealt with a martial theme—every now and then he punctuated it by drawing out his sword and waving it about. Then he'd sheathe it back in its scabbard shakily. Tommaso cringed, waiting for him to plant it in his thigh instead.

At last, after pulling forth the weapon and brandishing it about yet again, Lorenzaccio became distracted by one of the statues. He lurched up to it, holding the sword so slackly that its tip dragged, bouncing and ricketing, along the paving stones behind him. Tommaso winced. A cook would never treat his carving tools with so little consciousness and so much disrespect.

Lorenzaccio circled the sculpture, staring up at the little *putti* on top. He muttered at it at first, then his speech cleared.

"Little feathered fat thing sent down from Heaven—grinning at me, are you? Since when has Heaven ever smiled on me to my advantage?" Lorenzaccio launched up on his tiptoes to examine the cherub closely.

"This time the joke's on you, *putti*. You never should have descended here to mock me. Say farewell to Heaven—I'm about to send you on your way to Hell." Lorenzaccio lowered his heels, stood for a moment with his face gone slack. He turned and started to walk slowly away. Tommaso concluded he was in such a stupor that he couldn't remember himself from one moment to the next.

Tommaso was wrong. Lorenzaccio walked a distance of twenty paces, then spun around. He brought his sword up and narrowed his eyes, looking back at the *putti* with hatred. To Tommaso's horror, he saw that Lorenzaccio meant to attack the sculpture.

Tommaso tried frantically to think of what he should do. Most likely Lorenzaccio's sword would bounce off the statue, perhaps chipping it and surely damaging the sword. What if it bounced back onto Lorenzaccio? If the fool injured himself Tommaso would have to come to his aid and get help. And then Tommaso would be hard-pressed to explain why he'd done nothing to prevent Lorenzaccio's actions. But if he interrupted him, the chances were good that Lorenzaccio would take after him instead.

Before Tommaso could come to a decision, Lorenzaccio began loping toward the cherub. With a movement astonishingly graceful and controlled, he swung the sword in a perfect horizontal arc. A loud *clang!* rang out. Tommaso saw the sword embed itself momentarily at the joint between alabaster and porphyry. The cherub tilted up and away, falling, crashing to the ground and shattering into several large fragments.

Lorenzaccio stared, then began laughing, his face a perfect match to the foolish mirth on the denuded satyr's head. Lorenzaccio waggled his finger at the satyr. "I could push you over too, you know. But I see by the look on your face that you're a man after my own heart, and grateful to boot for the burden I've released you from."

Lights lit at several of the windows facing in toward the piazza. Lorenzaccio looked up and saw them. He came to his senses. He pulled his hat low and took to his heels without taking the time to sheathe his sword, passing Tommaso's hiding place at a run.

Tommaso waited until several householders arrived in the square to see what the commotion was about before he left the doorway to join them, as if he'd just chanced to stroll by. One man sent his servant for the night watch. When questioned, Tommaso said he'd been walking down the street when he heard a loud crash, then a man holding a sword ran past him, but that he was unrecognizable, concealed by his cape and hat. Tommaso was glad he'd walked most of the way with this same night watch: He fell under no suspicion himself.

As the commander of the watch questioned the neighbors Tommaso looked at the vandalized sculpture. Lorenzaccio had cut precisely between the cherub and satyr with enough force to snap the joint between the two and tip the cherub over. Tommaso shivered. It seemed an impossible feat for the slender drunken youth, and as neatly executed as a skilled butcher jointing a carcass. Lorenzaccio was even more dangerous than Tommaso had realized. The first thing I do tomorrow, Tommaso thought, is tell Caterina, warn her.

22

Caterina turned a deaf ear to his warnings.

"By all that's holy," he cursed in a seething whisper. "I should have turned him in to the guards and saved you from misguided compassion."

Tommaso never spoke to her that way. Anger sparked in Caterina's eyes, but the hand she laid on his arm was gentle.

"No, you did the right thing in sparing him, my friend. Don't mistake my sentiments toward Lorenzino for compassion. I know full well what he is, far better than you do."

Tommaso blinked at the iron in her voice.

Caterina sighed. She withdrew her hand. Her face softened. "Tommaso, your carving knives—they're sharp, are they not?"

Tommaso blinked again. "Of course. How else could I do my work?"

"Precisely," Caterina said. "Could one say your carving knives are sharp to the point of being dangerous?"

"Yes," Tommaso agreed. "But over the course of years, over the course of my whole life, I've trained in their usage, that I might someday achieve a certain mastery."

"I assume part of that mastery is learning never to turn the blade on yourself?" Caterina asked.

"Of course."

Caterina leaned forward, bracing her forearms on her small desk.

"We're not so different. I, too, have trained my whole life for a certain mastery. People are the materials, the tools I've been provided with. Some act as spoons for stirring things up. Others serve as platters, bringing me information. A few are no more than pretty garnishes.

"Lorenzino is a carving knife. The keener I hone him, the better. Yes, he's dangerous, and will become more so. But just like you, Tommaso, I would never turn a sharp blade against myself."

23

Tommaso's new relatives invited him over again a week later, while their employers still lingered in the country. This time Galleotto didn't entertain with reminiscences. The conversation centered on Tommaso's prospects in France: The cousins had thought up new questions. Ardingo, in particular, seemed fascinated by employment in a king's household.

Tommaso returned to the Salviati mansion late enough that he had to ring for the gatekeeper to let him in. When he walked through the herb garden to the back entrance to the kitchen he found a small, dark form sitting in front of the door.

Tommaso grinned at the rather cross-looking cat.

"Did Reparata tire of waiting for you to come in from your evening prowl?" he asked her.

The cat ignored him. She slipped into the kitchen as soon as he opened the door.

Tommaso thought for a moment. The maids would have locked up Caterina's suite from the inside hours before.

He didn't want to leave the cat here, either. Three other cats already claimed the Salviati kitchen as their territory. Though they gave the *Duchessina*'s cat a wide berth when she visited their garden and tolerated her daytime foraging, they might take umbrage if she invaded the close quarters of the kitchen at night, when the kitchen was theirs alone. Even now one of them—a big, long-haired orange female who'd been sleeping on a bench near the fireplace—raised her head to fix the *Duchessina*'s cat with a cold stare.

"Perhaps you'd better spend the night with me," Tommaso whispered. He thought he might have to pick her up, but perhaps she, too, felt it wiser not to invade the other cats' territory. She followed him willingly into the apprentice's room. She leapt up to curl herself on his stomach when he settled himself into his cot.

The night was chilly. Tommaso welcomed the extra warmth she provided. He stroked her a few times, then laughed silently as the vibration of her purr resonated against his belly. The reverberation followed his fading thoughts down into sleep.

These rugs are so fine that my feet don't feel the ground. I could be floating, Tommaso thought. He peered downward. The floor of the Salviati hallway stretched out far below him. I *am* floating. No, he moved too swiftly to be floating. I'm flying.

He heard a whistling close by. Very close by. He turned to look, the motion making him tumble. The sound changed into a tousling, riffling noise as he rolled, weightless, through the air. Tommaso laughed at the sheer pleasure of the sensation. The whistling returned, and Tommaso realized it came from himself. It was his own laughter.

I'm a wind, a breeze. I'm dreaming. If I'm dreaming, I can do anything. He looked down toward his feet again. He couldn't see them. Of course. Who can see the wind's feet?

He stretched, feeling himself flatten and become as thin as spilled wine, as flexible as a whip. He sped on, an undulating carpet of air. He wrapped himself around corners, skimmed against ornate wooden ceilings. Their deeply carved marquetry riffled his aeolian form into bumptious waves.

He explored every room as he glided through the palazzo, marveling at the way he could surround himself around vases, chairs, statuary. Locked doors posed no barriers. Tommaso poured through keyholes, slid under doorsills. Whisking over sleeping servants, he made them shiver and pull their covers up to their chins. The few sounds he heard matched his own soughing exhalations: Jacopo Salviati's lusty snore; an old housemaid's wheezing sighs; the in and out of each small, personal tide of breath.

Faint articulations broke the natural susurrance. Curious, Tommaso followed the distracting mutter to its source—a spill of yellow light oozing out from under a bedroom doorway. He squeezed himself in through the crack, against the outpouring light.

Inside the room, one of the Salviati's visiting Greek scholars sat on the edge of a bed, speaking to a late-night guest. It was the scholar's strongly accented voice Tommaso had heard.

"I do not understand," the Greek said. "Why not simply let the Pope sell her off? Surely the prestige cannot hurt the family?"

"If His Holiness lived forever, or even for years hence, that might be true." The Greek's visitor was a Roman in his mid-twenties. His dark, nondescript clothing gave away nothing about his rank or occupation.

"You've seen the Pontiff," the Roman continued. "He grows weaker and weaker, yet fails to face his own mortality. The Duke knows once Clement dies, the French will use the *Duchessina* against Florence. As the one Medici's legitimate heir, the French will use her as their excuse to overrun Florence and supplant His Excellency. So she'll always be a threat."

"But an assassination? Of one so young?" the Greek protested. "Surely there's another way."

The Roman shook his head. "Other means have been tried. They failed. Do you not want the commission? You have no desire to follow in Argyropoulos's and Chalcondylas's esteemed footsteps and enjoy, with the Duke's support, a position at the Florentine Academy? Since that day when the Turks swarmed over the walls of Constantinople, has the employment of Greek scholars been so assured that you'd refuse?

"No, it's just that..." The Greek scholar shivered. "Do you feel that sudden draft? Surely it's an omen." He stood, walked over to the door and pushed against it, trying to seal it more tightly. This didn't stop Tommaso's agitated movement.

The Roman rolled his eyes and made a face, clearly wishing to be spared professorial scruples. "This *shall* happen, whether you help us or not," he drove his point home. "You must decide now whether you want to reap the benefits, or continue to exist on the scraps of rich men's patronage."

The scholar finally nodded his assent.

The Roman held out a small pouch to the scholar. "You tutor her this week, yes? Does she not always offer you refreshment? Find a means to slip some of this into her drink, or even better, her soup, if any is served."

The scholar's reaching hand recoiled away from the bag. "You mean for me to poison her?"

"Not exactly, though the effect will be the same," the Roman said. "The pouch contains diamond dust. Once in her system, it will attach there, killing her slowly, undetectably. She'll seem to suffer from a digestive ailment. If any blame falls at all, it will fall on the cooks, not you."

Tommaso woke up sweating. He felt too hot. A weight lay heavy over his heart, compressing it. He cranked his chin downward. The cat lay curled on his chest. Tommaso sighed. No wonder he'd suffered such a terrible nightmare. He gently picked the cat up and placed her at his feet instead.

24

Several days later Tommaso had the opportunity to consider the strange manner in which dreams linger at the edge of one's consciousness. He'd forgotten his nightmare, but now, while he arranged a light repast in Caterina's suite, it all came back.

A Greek scholar, resplendent in exotic robes and long, flowing beard, sat reviewing Socratic discourse with Caterina. The man was the scholar from Tommaso's dream.

Tommaso looked down at the food he'd brought. He experienced a strange mixture of befuddlement and vertigo: He hadn't made any soup. He always cooked soup as one of the courses for the intermission in Caterina's lessons. Had the dream reached out from insensateness to shift his working actions?

The scholar got up and strolled along the sideboard, inspecting the dishes.

That's nothing to be alarmed at, Tommaso chided himself as a frisson shivered up his spine. He always does that.

The Greek turned to Tommaso. The man seemed a little pale. "Where is the soup?" he asked. "Aren't we having soup?"

"An excellent shipment of rice arrived at the market this week," Tommaso said. "So today, for the *primi* course, I decided to cook a lovely risotto with fresh greens and seafood." Tommaso pointed to the dish.

Was it his imagination, or did the scholar appear flustered?

What if I make a game of this, and pretend to myself that my dream was in some way prophetic?, Tommaso thought. As long as I tell no one, who can it hurt?

The risotto made a poor vehicle for diamond-dust poisoning. It was a bright, cloudless day. Sunshine poured through the windows. Even well mixed into the rice, diamond dust would surely glint in that strong light.

What else had the Roman assassin suggested in his dream? That the poison dust could be slipped into Caterina's beverage.

Today Tommaso had brought up three decanters with the meal: one of white wine, one of cinnamon water, one of almond milk. Caterina never drank wine so early in the day, especially during her lessons. The flavored water was distilled with cinnamon oil, so it was as clear as the wine. The almond milk, on the other hand, was opaque to the eye and somewhat granular on the tongue: the perfect agent for disguising not only diamond dust's sparkle, but also its texture.

Tommaso felt better, and foolish for his suspicions. Caterina always drank cinnamon water. She complained that almond milk left a coating in her mouth; an unpleasant sensation when she had to recite for her tutors. It was her ladies-in-waiting who always requested the beverage.

The very moment this occurred to Tommaso, the Greek scholar reached to pour himself a goblet of wine. His long, wide sleeve caught the edge of the decanter of distilled cinnamon water.

Tommaso leapt forward as it tipped. It seemed to fall more slowly than snow melts, but he was even slower. It hit the sideboard, flipped over, smashed to the floor. The cinnamon water, splashing everywhere, filled the air with its aromatic fragrance. Tommaso stared at the slivers of glass, so like diamonds, glinting up at him from the soaked carpeting, and had the terrible intuition that his dream was coming true.

Caterina and her ladies leapt to their feet at the sound of the crash.

"My apologies, Your Grace." The Greek scholar was flushed. "I thought I'd pour myself some wine, and these clumsy sleeves..." He waved them helplessly.

Tommaso was down on all fours, picking at the glass, blotting up the cinnamon water.

"Maestro Chrystosophos, there's no need to serve yourself," Caterina said. "The servants are happy for the labor." She waved away his further apologies. "It's just a water decanter, and of no matter. Compose yourself. Sit. Food will relieve your nervous humors."

She looked at the remaining decanters and sighed. "No wine for me, or I'll be the one tipping things over. Pour me some almond milk, Tommaso."

Tommaso froze where he knelt, then scrambled to his feet. "I'll send to the kitchen for more cinnamon water, Your Grace."

Caterina shook her head. "Don't trouble yourself. I can make do for today."

Tommaso started to sweat. He watched the Greek scholar with a hawk's eyes while he served the meal.

The mid-lesson luncheons were informal. Texts continued to be discussed, diagrams and atlases examined. As Caterina, the scholar and a few of the ladies passed papers about the table, Tommaso grew increasingly nervous. He poured an extra goblet of almond milk and set it on the sideboard, his hands shaking.

"Look at this, Your Grace. It illustrates my point about the brilliance of the ancients, especially when one considers how limited was their knowledge of the magnitude of the world around them."

The Greek scholar thrust a book under Caterina's nose. It was opened to a copy of an old map. The scholar's hands were hidden as they supported the broad volume. Tommaso stared. Could the scholar be palming something into Caterina's goblet as he hovered?

Caterina nodded at the point her tutor made. "Yes, I agree, though I didn't argue the point with you before."

The scholar withdrew the book. He set it down, then wiped his hands along the side of his robe.

Tommaso rushed forward, his own hands full carrying a wide platter covered with sculpted morsels of different kinds of melon. "Your Grace, please try some of these. They'll refresh your palate after the risotto."

Caterina looked surprised at Tommaso's vehemence, but picked out several bitefuls. Tommaso carried the platter the rest of the way around the table, offering some to each of the ladies-in-waiting, and even the Greek scholar. Then he bore the platter back to the sideboard. His wrist ached from balancing the dish. His hand was cramped from the clawlike position it had maintained since switching Caterina's goblets and carrying the first goblet, hidden under the platter, away from the table. He covered the goblet with a napkin and set it where it wouldn't be noticed, behind two piles of dirty dishes.

Nothing more of a suspicious nature occurred during the rest of the meal. When Tommaso returned to the kitchen, he decanted the goblets' contents into a ceramic jar with a tight cork stopper. He took the goblet outside to wash it. Was that a slightly gritty texture against his fingers? He held the half-washed goblet up to the light. Was the glinting he saw there from the crystal itself, or something else? He couldn't tell.

25

The Salviatis had assigned a man-at-arms to Cosimo Ruggiero to look after his needs for the duration of his stay with them. It was this fellow, a big, sturdy Bolognese, who answered the knock at the door.

Cosimo looked up from the charts spread out before him and his guest, sitting across the table from him. "Who is it, Fazio?"

Fazio was speaking to someone out in the hallway, out of Cosimo's line of sight.

"One of the cooks, Signor. I told him you were busy with a client."

"We're almost done here. Ask if he can wait."

Cosimo turned back to the man before him, one of the Salviatis' other guests. "That's as much of your horoscope as I can tell you now. I clearly see disaster narrowly averted. As far as your question regarding success in the near future, that's unclear. You may achieve the status you seek, or you may simply come to appreciate the life you lead now."

The client looked bemused. Then he nodded and rose. "Let's consult again soon, as we planned," the man said. "We'll see how the planets then turn."

Cosimo walked his client to the door. Fazio opened it to usher the fellow out. Tommaso Arista stood waiting out in the hallway.

"Tommaso! Come in. It's good to see you." For Cosimo, encountering Tommaso not only engendered the pleasure of seeing a familiar Florentine face, but always brought back memories of home and hearth.

Tommaso stuttered a distracted greeting in return. He was staring at the broad back of Cosimo's client retreating down the hallway.

"Tommaso?" Cosimo tried the retrieve the youth's attention. "Did the *Duchessina* send you about some menu matter?"

Tommaso turned back to him. His face had paled. "No. I come to you regarding a personal matter. I need your expertise. Your skills. If I may?"

Cosimo waved him in, concerned. "By all means." He looked at the pouch dangling from a cord wrapped around Tommaso wrist. He looked at it pointedly. "I wouldn't charge you, Tommaso. And even if I did, you wouldn't need that large a purse for the few *soldi* I'd ask for."

Tommaso slung the bag behind him, looking uneasy. "It doesn't contain money," he said.

Cosimo raised an eyebrow at him, questioning. Tommaso just stood there like a wooden statue. He said nothing further. Cosimo sighed. He didn't know if he should be irked or amused. Whatever bothered Tommaso, it would have to be drawn out. He gestured to the chair vacated by the client. "Come. Sit. Do you need your horoscope cast? Or are you in need of physicking services?"

Tommaso squirmed in the chair. He looked over his shoulder.

At last Cosimo understood. "Fazio, I don't need you for the moment. Have you supped since breakfast? No? Why don't you get something to eat while I talk with my old friend here."

Tommaso looked at Cosimo with grateful eyes as the man-at-arms left the room.

"It's my dreams," Tommaso said, as soon as Fazio closed the door. "Of late I've suffered such strange ones. I worry I might be going mad."

Cosimo suppressed a smile. "I doubt that. What sort of dreams?"

Tommaso thought for a moment. "They start wonderfully, then end with terrible protents."

"Do you dream about places?" Cosimo was intrigued. What sort of dreams would a cook have who could instinctively construct a powerful speculum? "People?"

Tommaso nodded vigorously to the last.

"Who?"

Tommaso looked over his shoulder again. "That man. The one who was just here," he whispered.

"Fazio?"

"No. The other one. Your guest." A thin sheen of sweat filmed Tommaso's forehead.

"Maestro Chrystosophos?" Cosimo laughed at the idea that the stodgy scholar could enter anyone's dreams and cause such terror.

Tommaso looked piqued that Cosimo would find mirth in his misery.

"I'm sorry," Cosimo said contritely. "When did these dreams start? And why are they so frightening?"

"They started a little over a week ago," Tommaso said. He described his transformation into a breeze.

"That's common," said Cosimo. "Many dream of flying."

"That was the splendid part. It's what followed that troubles me." Tommaso repeated the discussion he'd dreamt between Chrystosophos and the stranger.

Cosimo frowned. A troubling nightmare, indeed. "Sometimes we hear things in passing without even knowing we've heard them. Later our dreaming minds knit them together in eerie ways. We *all* worry about Caterina's future. I'm sure we all project our fears for her onto the smallest incidents."

"That's what I, too, thought," Tommaso agreed. "But mere days later reality seemed to mimic my nocturnal vision." Tommaso described the luncheon in Caterina's suite.

"I feared I might be mad, so I saved this." Tommaso drew a stoppered glass jar out of the pouch. Its liquid contents were an opaque white-beige. A thin line of pale green mold had formed at the top.

"I hid this in my clothes chest," Tommaso said. "When nothing happened after the luncheon, I felt like a fool. But after last night..." Tommaso looked up at Cosimo. His eyes were haunted. "Maybe it's good that I saved it, after all. With your science you can prove my fears right or wrong."

"What happened last night?" Cosimo asked as he took the jar from Tommaso and held it up to examine it against the light shining through his window.

"I dreamt again. It started exactly the same way: flying; hearing the Greek talking to someone—the same man; floating into the Greek's room. I thought the dream would proceed as it had before. But this time the conversation was different. It had ... progressed.

"The Roman said there was no downturn in Caterina's health. The scholar protested that he *had* slipped her the poison, even stirred the drink with his finger to be sure.

"The Roman then said more active plans had been laid. They bore greater risk, but would guarantee success.

"The Greek became agitated at that, but the Roman reassured him. He said, 'It's not as if you'll have to do the deed this time. I just need someone inside this house who can apprise us of her comings and goings, her whens and whereabouts. Do you have the means to accomplish that for us?'

"'Not so much the means as the proper acquaintanceships,' the scholar replied."

Tommaso looked at Cosimo. "You can understand why I was shaken to see him at *your* door."

Tommaso's unspoken question stretched taut and quivering in the air between them, like unstruck lightning at the height of a storm.

"You were wise to let me know," Cosimo finally said. He put the jar of almond milk on his desk. "I'll run some experiments on this. The truth of your dreams can easily be proved true or false."

Although dismissed, Tommaso lingered at the door. "You'll let me know? For my peace of mind?"

Cosimo nodded. "Yes, surely. If Fazio is still in the kitchen, ask him to return to me."

Once Tommaso left, Cosimo unstoppered the jar. With a pen knife he snagged and drew forth the film of mold at the top. A bowl of used blotting sand sat nearby. Cosimo flipped the mold onto the inky sand. He replaced the stopper onto the jar.

"With all your science can prove..." Tommaso had said. Cosimo shook his head and smiled. This is why science and religion enjoy such great respect: Because Man has elevated common sense to the level of arcane art.

The Salviatis were among the few wealthy enough to afford to install the indoor pipe systems introduced by Leonardo da Vinci. Cosimo's room enjoyed such a contraption, which was especially useful for his work.

He placed a plain, white ceramic tray beneath the pipe. He turned a spigot. Water, pulled down by gravity from a cistern on the top floor, flowed through the pipe. Every day servants refilled the cistern by drawing up buckets of water on pulleys from the mansion's internal well.

Cosimo let just a little water puddle onto the tray, then turned the spigot's handle closed. He shook Tommaso's jar thoroughly. He unstoppered it once more and poured a small amount of the almond milk onto the tray. He picked up the tray and swirled it, mixing the water and almond milk together, until it made a thin, dilute mix that filmed across the surface of the tray.

Cosimo carried the tray over to the window. He held it up level with his eyes, angling it so sunshine reflected across its surface. Crystalline pinpoints of light sparkled back at him. Cosimo set the plate down and thought.

During Chrystosophos's consultation, the scholar had requested future appointments. He'd been polite, even solicitous. Knowing Cosimo's primary patron to be the *Duchessina*, he inquired after her schedule, not wanting his conferences with Cosimo to conflict with hers in any way.

Cosimo was carefully rinsing the plate out into the waste sump below the water pipe when Fazio returned.

"I was told you need me?" Fazio said.

"Yes. Please go to Cardinal Ippolito de' Medici's suite. If he's not there, leave a message. Tell him I must see him immediately."

Three nights hence, Caterina traveled through Rome, crossing one of Rome's internal bridges over the Tiber as part of her route. She'd been invited to a women-only gala meant to relieve the lying-in of a wealthy young matron.

Ladies enjoyed their own masquerades and salons, where they indulged in feminine versions of coarse language, theatrics, music, and jests, without men's stern disapproval. The party was an informal affair, so Caterina traveled in a plain, light, covered coach, accompanied by only one lady-in-waiting, a man-at-arms and the coach's driver.

The festivities lasted well into the evening, until the young woman who was both hostess and guest of honor declared the merriment so successful that she might commence to go into labor at any moment.

Both quiet and a light fog from the river lay over Rome's dark streets like a muffling blanket as they returned. Quiet, too, was the *Duchessina*'s coach. Perhaps she'd fallen asleep. Perhaps she sat awake and pensive, reflecting that the fate of the pregnant girl she'd visited might soon be her own.

The coach reached the bridge. Light from torches at either end pierced the fog enough to cast the carriage's shadow against the bridge's low balustrade.

When the coach had traveled about a third of the bridge's length, three dark, silhouetted forms ran up behind it out of the fog. They blended for a moment with the coach's shadow, then launched upward to the driver's seat. They struck blows to the heads of the driver and the man-at-arms sitting beside him. Both of Caterina's menservants fell away to lie on the ground motionless beside the coach. One of the assailants leapt forward to catch the two horses' tack, stopping them. A lilting voice from within the coach called out, asking what had rocked the coach, why they'd stopped.

"Remember, no knives," one of the conspirators—a young Roman Tommaso would have recognized—said in a low voice. "It must look like an accident. The horses startled at something, panicked out of control, ran off the bridge. All injuries must reflect that trauma. So just open the door quickly, crush the women's skulls, and we can tip the coach over. That will drag the horses in after it."

"What about these?" One of the other two assassins pointed at the two still men at their feet. "I don't think they're dead yet."

"No, but they're unconscious," the first man said. "As soon as the coach sinks, we'll toss them in the river too. They should drown nicely. Now go."

One of the men yanked open the coach door. Immediately shrill cries issued from within. The second man lunged forward with a cudgel. The cudgel struck something, then was pulled farther into the coach, the surprised assassin yanked in after.

"By St. Agnes's hymen, what the . . . ?" the coach-door holder swore. The rule about no knives not withstanding, he drew his dirk and clambered in after his companion. The coach swayed briefly.

The young Roman, still holding the horses, stared after his disappeared comrades. Something pricked the back of his neck. He turned. A sword tip nicked the skin of his Adam's apple. The hooded man holding the sword was dressed in clothes as dark as his own.

"Ah, a pleasant night for murdering virgins?" the swordsman inquired politely. The hood fell back away from his face, revealing handsome features, black hair and beard. "Domenico, are you all right?" the swordsman called out softly.

The felled man-at-arms rolled over. He got to his feet, rubbing the back of his head. "Yes, but I fear I'll bear this lump for days. I wish I'd known they intended to eschew knives. I could have spared myself at least *this* discomfort." The Tartar unlaced and wrestled a thick leather collar from his neck. "The driver is still unconscious, but I think he'll be all right. You Italians—your skulls are unfavorably thin."

"You can come out now," Ippolito addressed the coach.

The carriage doors opened. First a body rolled out to thump on the ground. Pier Antonio Pecci climbed out after it. Last to emerge was a white, tooth-filled grin, seemingly attached, not to a face, but to a clumsy, distorted double-body. It was Beroaldo, his cloak half-wrapped around one of the assassins.

"I hope the *Duchessina* will forgive me any blood spilled in her coach. I had to stick this one with his own dirk, but I think my cloak stanched most of the blood." The dagger was embedded in the attacker's neck. He wasn't quite dead yet.

"Are both of you uninjured?" Ippolito asked.

"Yes, though my voice feels stripped from those girlish shrieks," Pier Antonio said. He dragged the first body over to the bridge, hauled the top half of it up till it tipped over the balustrade. One good heave on the feet and the fellow fell over the edge. An instant later they heard a splash echo from below.

The clang of horseshoes rang on the bridge. The assassin with Ippolito's sword at his throat tried to turn to look. Ippolito's gaze, however, didn't waver.

"My source was correct, then." Cosimo Ruggiero sat astride one of four approaching horses. Two of the others were also mounted, and he led the fourth by its reins.

"Thankfully so," Ippolito agreed.

Caterina and Reparata rode the other two horses.

"My lady, mercy, please," the assassin at swordpoint begged. "I possess valuable information. I can tell you who wants you dead, and why."

"Your currency is worthless. I know who. I know why," Caterina dismissed him. "Pier Antonio, would you and Beroaldo be so kind as to lay the coachman gently in the carriage and then finish the journey by driving it home? It's such a lovely, misty night that Reparata and I prefer to ride."

Pier Antonio bowed his assent.

"We'll wait for you at the other end of the bridge," Caterina said. She and Reparata rode on.

Beroaldo maneuvered the half-dead man he held up to the bridge. He faced the man outward, toward the water. When he pulled the knife from the man's throat, blood fountained down into the river. The man burbled, struggled weakly. Beroaldo pushed him over.

Ippolito reached forward to the man he held at bay. With one motion he spun his captive around, slit his throat, and shoved him over the balustrade to join the other two assassins.

Cosimo handed Ippolito the reins to the fourth horse. Ippolito mounted.

"Did you recognize him?" Cosimo asked as they rode to join Caterina and Reparata at the far side of the bridge.

"Yes," Ippolito replied. "One Assatore. A friend of Alessandro's, who grew up with him in Cardinal Giulio's court. And, like Alessandro, a cleric's bastard. But not as highly born. I think his father was an abbot."

"How much hue and cry will his disappearance raise?" Cosimo asked.

Ippolito shrugged. "Not much. His father died some years back. He himself enjoyed almost as bad a reputation as Alessandro's. Even if his body floats up, no suspicion will attach to us. He'll have met the end everyone expected." Ippolito looked at Cosimo. "How many more attacks do you think we can expect on Caterina's life?"

"Since she's come to Rome, Alessandro has tried to neutralize her by poison, by arcane means, and now by force. Each time he's failed. We should be on guard, but I doubt he'll try again as long as she's so far out of reach."

26

Mid-October, 1531

Wherever Tommaso looked, wherever he worked, he found himself annoyed, distracted or distressed by love gone awry, love held in abeyance, love tossed and turned by chaos.

In his usual excessive way, Cellini had conceived a grand passion for a Sicilian courtesan. This girl, Angelica, was so young that her mother, a woman named Beatrice, still worked as a highly sought-after member of the same profession. Beatrice added to her own income by acting as her daughter's procurer. Knowing a hooked fish when she saw one, Beatrice milked Cellini for more *soldi* than any girl's standard fee. At the same time she limited his access to his new love.

"What can you possibly be thinking?" Cellini's partner Felice said early one evening. "You're already in trouble with the Pope over that damnable chalice He commissioned from you. If you slip away to Florence it'll appear that you're defying Him and fleeing His ire. Shouldn't you save that alternative for the day when you *will* need to escape His wrath?"

Cellini waved a nonchalant hand. "I'll write to His Holiness and make it clear my departure won't slow down the work on His chalice. I'll take it with me. In fact, away from Rome I'm more likely to complete it, since I'll be free from the meddling of His jeweler, that imbecile Pompeo. You know that's what holds me back on finishing His commission. That and the fact His Holiness won't furnish the gold I need to cast the piece."

Felice didn't give up so easily. "What about that position you begged Him for? You were only appointed to it this last April. After all the fuss you made, you'd leave, turning your back on it?"

Cellini sniffed with disdain. "I didn't beg for the post I received. Clement wouldn't give me the one I wanted—the vacancy in the Piombo—a position worth more than eight hundred crowns a year. Instead He commanded I make do with a mace-bearer's office, forcing me to march before Him like one of the beadles, for less than two hundred crowns a year."

"You're usually exempted from actual service, and two hundred crowns is two hundred crowns," Felice pointed out.

Cellini drew himself up. "A year cloistered in Florence with the exquisite Angelica is worth far more than that," he said.

"But a Pope's wrath is worth . . ." Felice started to protest.

"I'm off to spend the night with my beloved," Cellini interrupted, throwing on his cloak. "Instead of arguing with me, Felice, you'd profit more if you spent your time planning on how work in this shop will proceed during my year's absence. My plan for spiriting Angelica away is almost set." He flourished his cloak and left.

Felice sat down heavily at a workbench and put his head in his hands.

Tommaso, Cencio, Paulino and the other apprentices looked at each other. Felice had reason to worry. He was an honest man with a good head for business and decent enough skills in the craft, but he utterly lacked Cellini's artistry and talent. The shop would suffer if Cellini abdicated for a year.

The youngest shop lad, Guarnieri, tried to comfort Felice. "You know how changeable Master Benevenuto is. By tomorrow he might detest the wench."

Cencio looked doubtful. "I've never seen Cellini this smitten before," he muttered. "You'd think him beglamored."

Paulino shrugged. "His infatuation could lead to an end of our exile. If Cellini's scheme for abducting the girl works, we'll return to Florence with him. You heard him—he intends to keep working even while in amorous exile. I, for one, look forward to his reappearance tomorrow morning exhausted, enervated and brimming with plans for departure."

Paulino was mistaken. Cellini returned within the hour, a shaken man.

"Felice, Cencio, all of you—throw on your cloaks and come with me," he croaked. "I've need of your aid."

"But the work . . ." Felice pointed to a crucible of silver heating in the foundry, waiting to be poured into medallion molds. Guarnieri had set out the steel dies for stamping them on a bench nearby.

"Leave the work," Cellini said violently. "What do I care about fripperies for petty cardinals?"

"You worked hard to gain those commissions," said Felice, astonished. "Why do you say such a thing? What's happened?"

"My angel, my Angelica, she's gone!" Cellini wailed. "One of her wretched brothers overheard us plotting. He informed their mother and she fled, taking my darling with her. Waste no more time. Get your capes. I need your help intercepting them."

"Where? How?" asked Felice.

"They're departing Rome by way of Cività Vecchia. I beat it out of that knavish brother. Two other brothers travel with them as their escort. You must aid me in extricating my angel from their grasp."

Felice looked at the red-hot foundry. "I pity your suffering and I'd help you if I could," he said. "But one of us has to keep his wits. We can't rush off and leave a burning foundry."

"I can't go with you," Tommaso said. "Since I serve the *Duchessina* in the morning, I have to return home at a reasonable hour. Guarnieri shouldn't go either. He's too young to be involved in this sort of a fracas. Between the two of us we can pour the medallions and put the foundry to bed. After I leave he can lock up the shop and await your return."

"Thank you, Tommaso," Felice said, relieved at the solution. He and the other apprentices made ready to go.

Tommaso helped Cencio into his cloak. "I don't return here until next week," Tommaso whispered to his friend. "Find a way to let me know of the outcome of this misadventure before then."

Cencio grinned and winked his compliance.

There was no relief from love deferred in the Salviati kitchen. Laudomia had grown so quiet and subdued that Averardo feared she'd given up hope. He worried she wouldn't resist any betrothal her parents might arrange, or might succumb to the attentions of interested menservants in the Salviati household. He begged Tommaso to dance attendance on her, reassuring her of Averardo's love and keeping potential suitors or seducers at bay.

Tommaso obliged Averardo as much as he could, but though he often had the excuse of needing extra help with his kitchen duties, he found Laudomia's constant presence tiresome. Tommaso did all he could to cheer her up, not so much as a favor to Averardo, but to make his own day bearable.

In the meantime, Alessa continued plaguing Averardo.

At first Tommaso thought Averardo should take advantage of the situation to ingratiate himself with the young girl.

"If your attraction to Laudomia made Madonna Ramerino nervous, think how concerned she'll become at any interest shown in her own daughter," he told Averardo.

Averardo frowned. "It's true the Ramerinos consider me lowly born."

Averardo came from a family of tanners. Like Laudomia, he'd been apprenticed socially upward.

"But in the first place"—he held up his index finger—"I detest that little minx so greatly that any cordiality I could force myself to show her would be so strained and false that no one would believe it, except possibly herself and Laudomia.

"Secondly"—he held up his middle finger—"if Laudomia *did* in any small way believe in my attentions to Alessa I'd lose all hope of holding her heart.

"Thirdly"—Averardo added his ring finger—"Alessa has proved most persuasive with her parents, especially her mother. There's enough of a difference in our ages that in the several years, as she reaches marriageable age, she might wear down her parents and convince them I'd make a suitable husband.

"The only way I could guarantee *that* not happen would be to perform poorly in my apprenticeship which, firstly"—he held up his other hand and began counting off on *its* fingers—"goes against my nature, and secondly"—yet another finger up—"would probably lead to me being dismissed here and sent back to the tannery. That would mean, thirdly"—the other ring finger joined the crowd—"that I'd no longer see Laudomia. That, fourthly"—at last a little finger—"would be just as well, since I'd no longer be employed in the kind of labor that would convince her parents to let us wed."

Tommaso looked at all those outstretched fingers and sighed. "You're right. I didn't think it through. It's a shame, though. I hoped that some attention paid to Alessa might make the Ramerinos nervous enough that a marriage between you and Laudomia would appear a good solution to the problem."

Tommaso considered the circumstances that had brought about Enzio and Massolina's wedding back in Florence. Now that the Ramerinos arrived less early in the morning, it would be easy to arrange an "accidental" discovery of Averardo and Laudomia in a compromising situation. That would force an immediate engagement. All that was necessary was for Alessa to overhear the lovers arranging a predawn rendezvous.

Tommaso, however, was uncomfortable with cold-bloodedly casting aspersions on Laudomia's virtue in that fashion. And Averardo loved Laudomia truly enough that Tommaso believed his friend would be unable to perform the necessary humiliation in public. Therefore, they'd been thrown back on a waiting game, lulling Madonna Ramerino's fears and Alessa's suspicions.

Whenever Tommaso went for lessons at Bartolommeo Scappi's, he mentioned Averardo at every opportunity, praising his hard work and skill, hinting that the master who ended up with him as a journeyman would be fortunate indeed.

If Scappi employed Averardo, Averardo would become a spousal catch Laudomia's parents and even Madonna Ramerino would approve of. Even if Scappi merely expressed interest in Averardo at the guild, it might propel Averardo to journeyman status quickly and cause Marcus Gavius Spada and Bindo Ramerino to consider him with greater favor.

So here we all sit, suffering, Tommaso thought as he worked in the kitchen the morning after the debacle at Cellini's. Laudomia in her misery. Himself having to endure her misery. Averardo sullenly enduring Alessa. Only Alessa was happy, reveling in Averardo's captive company. Averardo looked as though he wanted to murder Alessa.

Laudomia was watching Averardo and Alessa too. She dropped her head. Her shoulders shook.

"Laudomia?" Tommaso said.

She looked up at his, her eyes filled with tears, her cheeks wet.

Tommaso wiped his hands. He reached over to pat her awkwardly. To his horror, she gave a small sob and buried her head against his chest. Her forehead thumped hard as a rock against his collarbone. Face burning with embarrassment, Tommaso glanced around. One of the other scullery maids was staring at him with frank astonishment.

What do I do now? Tommaso thought, frozen. What would the Courtier do? He racked his brain, but he couldn't remember anything in the book corresponding to this situation. The best he came up with was the general admonition that a good Courtier shows women the greatest reverence. Tommaso was fairly certain that Baldessare Castiglione never intended a gentleman to end up in this predicament.

Fate stepped in to rescue him in the guise of Paulino and Cencio, escorted into the kitchen by the gatekeeper's son.

"Messer Arista, we pray you, offer us refuge," Paulino said. Although he was laughing, both he and Cencio looked exhausted.

To Tommaso's relief, at his friends' entrance Laudomia melted away from him as swiftly as snow from the sun.

"Why aren't you working at the *bottega* this morning? Or if Maestro Cellini kept you up all night on his behalf, why aren't you sleeping?" he asked his friends.

"He *did* keep us up all night. To his credit, he granted us the day off to rest. But since he himself does little but wail and lament, there's no rest to be found at the studio."

"He didn't find the girl?" Tommaso asked.

Cencio rolled his eyes. "Didn't find her, and worse than that."

Tommaso noticed that the kitchen's noise level had dropped to an unnaturally low level, work slowed, and the kitchen staff's ears practically stretched away from their heads, so hard were they trying to hear.

"Messers Ramerino and Spada govern this kitchen. It's not in my power to grant you sanctuary," he said. "But if you sit at your ease and tell an entertaining tale of last night's adventures in loud and clear enough voices so all can listen and still labor, perhaps my masters will repay you with a bed to sleep in and some refreshments."

For once the two head cooks agreed on something: They gave their enthusiastic consent. There were few rogues more gossiped about in Rome than Benevenuto Cellini. How delicious to be among the first to hear of his latest escapade—and from the lips of his own apprentices!

Marcus Gavius Spada seated Cencio and Paulino at the largest work-table so the kitchen crew could gather round them. While the two young artists ate the quick repast Bindo Ramerino threw together for them,

Tommaso recounted the beginning of the story up until Cellini's departure with his search party the night before.

Then, since Cencio was still eating, Paulino continued the tale. "We went to the Civitá Vecchia. There the gatekeepers told us that no one resembling Beatrice and Angelica had passed that way. We lay in wait for several hours. Our master carried on like a madman the whole time, swearing he'd beat Beatrice and her sons within an inch of their lives.

"After a long while he became suspicious. He left Felice and three of the other apprentices to watch there and took Cencio and myself back to the inn that served as Beatrice's bawd house.

"Cellini began cursing again when the innkeeper told him that the whoreson he'd beaten earlier had fled. Another courtesan at the inn took pity on our master. She told him she'd heard Beatrice tell her son that after he diverted Cellini he was to meet her, Angelica, and the other sons at the Ostia gate.

"We ran all the way there. The Ostia gatekeepers confirmed our master's fears. Beatrice and her family departed from there hours before. Since night had fallen when they passed, the gatekeepers couldn't say in which direction they'd turned.

"Cellini decided on returning to the inn to see if he could obtain any knowledge of Beatrice's destination from the helpful courtesan. He sent me and Cencio to fetch Felice and the others still waiting at the Civitá Vecchia, with instructions to meet him back at the inn.

"Halfway to the Civitá Vecchia, Cencio was chilled by a dire premonition. At his insistence we raced all the way, gathered the others and ran to the inn."

Cencio had finished his breakfast. He motioned that he wanted to continue the narrative. "I had no idea what my intuition meant," he said, "other than that it boded ill. We arrived at the inn almost too late.

"Upon his return to the inn, our master was informed that the doxy who'd informed to him was busy entertaining a customer. The innkeeper wouldn't tell Master the doxy's whereabouts, so Master went from room to room searching for her. When he finally found her, her customer took umbrage at the interruption of his pleasure, picked up Master and threw him from the room.

"We arrived at the inn just as Master drew his sword on a not only unarmed but naked man. Meanwhile the doxy was screaming that she knew nothing of Beatrice's destination and that she entirely regretted aiding our master in any way. The whole inn was in an uproar.

"The innkeeper sent for the night watch. We convinced Master to leave before they arrived, since nothing could be gained and much lost by staying.

"Next he led us to the nearest church. There he amused several priests by falling on his face before the altar. He made the most outrageous lying promises to God if only his Angelica was restored to him. Finally, a priest told him that God couldn't help but hear him, and that he should return home and wait for God to work His wonders."

"What kind of promises?" Marcus Gavius Spada asked.

Paulino and Cencio looked at each other. Cencio compressed his lips and shook his head.

"*I* don't mind telling." Paulino laughed "The only reputation Cellini possesses honestly is that of a skilled artist and goldsmith. This tale won't tarnish *that*.

"Among the things he swore, so numerous I can't remember them all: That he'd never brawl again, whore again, get drunk again, be late on a commission again, boast again, lie again, nor speak disrespectfully to or of any cardinal or the Pope again."

The whole kitchen burst into uncontrollable laughter.

"So after burdening the priests he finally went home?" Madonna Spada asked, wiping moisture from the corners of her eyes with her sleeve.

"No," Paulino said. "After the church he insisted on stopping at a tavern. There he at once broke one of his vows and drank so much he fell into a stupor and slept. We stayed awake to guard him—he was too heavy and we were too tired to carry him home. By the time he revived enough to be half-carried it was dawn.

"When we returned to the *bottega* he—having had at least some sleep—commenced again in bewailing his tragic romantic fate. At that point Cencio and I remembered that good Tommaso here had requested to be apprised of the outcome of the situation. To that end, and in hope of finding a more restful place, we fled hence."

"You've earned your reward," *Ser* Spada said. "Our apprentices' bed lies empty. If you don't think kitchen noise will keep you awake, sleep there as long as you like."

His friends taken care of, Tommaso returned to work. There he faced the third case of love under duress—that shared by Caterina and Ippolito.

I should feel more sympathy for Cellini, he thought as he finished preparing the midday meal. Since he now suffers the same kind of heart's absence Caterina endures.

If Clement had assumed that Caterina's betrothal to Henri of France would cool Caterina's and Ippolito's ardor, his strategy failed. They acted with discretion in public, but Clement had his sources. He heard how they drew ever closer together.

Tommaso had to admit that the Pope's solution was intelligent and to the point. Clement designated Ippolito to the position of papal legate and promptly sent him off on one mission after the other. These were assignments Ippolito couldn't quarrel with publicly.

Although he hadn't wished for a cardinal's hat, Ippolito's nature was to do any task well. As a result, he was a popular cleric with the other Cardinals—far more popular than Clement was as Pope. So there was logic in the Pontiff appointing Ippolito to act as the Vatican's representative in matters of diplomacy. In fact, it was such an astute move that Clement's reputation rose again briefly with the college of cardinals.

At present Ippolito was gone from Rome on one of many trips.

Caterina wouldn't mind his absence today. She was acting as official hostess at a supper for ten in the banquet hall honoring a visiting relative, Cardinal Salviati, the cleric to whom the textile merchant Vitelli reported. Cardinal Salviati was himself a papal legate, to Parma. He was also one of the Pope's creatures.

Today Tommaso, as Caterina's chef, would perform as master carver and receive public acknowledgement as part of Caterina's entourage. But he was pleased with the assignment for other reasons.

Besides acting as one of Clement's informants, Cardinal Salviati was also one of Benevenuto Cellini's enemies in the papal retinue. In the past he'd meddled with and blocked papal commissions to the goldsmith. Tommaso wanted to see with his own eyes the Cardinal who'd obstructed the irascible Cellini. Cellini always referred to Cardinal Salviati as "that beast of a Cardinal, who resembles a donkey more than a man."

When Tommaso arrived at the banquet hall to supervise the service of dishes from the sideboard, he saw that for once Cellini hadn't exaggerated. Cardinal Salviati was a homely, long-faced individual. From his manner of speaking it was obvious he was the Pope's spy. And in that obviousness, he made for a very poor spy.

"You must all miss the charming Cardinal de' Medici," he said in an attempt at suavity. His remark included everyone at the table but his gaze strayed to Caterina.

In spite of Caterina's status as hostess of the event, Lucrezia Salviati answered. "Who wouldn't feel the lack of such a gallant young man? But as his relatives, we applaud the opportunities our cousin the Pope bestows on Ippolito in the form of these papal missions," she said firmly.

"Do you hear from him much? How he fares?" asked Cardinal Salviati bluntly.

"Too little," Caterina blurted, her voice tremulous. "We hoped you might have word of him for us."

Lucrezia Salviati frowned at Caterina's outburst, then recovered with an irritated smile.

"Forgive the *Duchessina,*" she said. "Ippolito is as a brother to her. A young lady of sensitive nature, she worries about his welfare and yearns for tales of his triumphs."

Cardinal Salviati looked at Caterina doubtfully.

So did Tommaso. Caterina hardly appeared sisterly in her sentiments. Her huge dark eyes beseeched the Cardinal, her cheeks pinked. She could have posed as the model of girlish infatuation.

What game is she playing? Tommaso wondered. Caterina missed Ippolito, and Clement placing more obstacles between them infuriated her. She didn't childishly mope, though. Her response had been to throw herself more diligently into her studies and to develop an impressive correspondence with almost every visitor to Rome she was introduced to. And, with a very few, like Tommaso and Cosimo Ruggiero, she shared her plans.

So why play the role of smitten maiden? Tommaso looked at Cosimo Ruggiero, seated across the table not far down from Caterina. What did Cosimo make of all this? The young astrologer didn't meet Tommaso's eye. In acting as though Caterina's behavior wasn't exceptional, Cosimo was also performing a role.

Caterina appeared contrite at her great-aunt's chastising words. "Forgive me, Your Excellency," she addressed Cardinal Salviati meekly. She resumed the role of hostess. "Would you like some more wine? How do you find your soup? I'd value your opinion of Tommaso's *cipollata*."

At this Lucrezia Salviati stared at Caterina, then rolled her eyes. Jacopo Salviati tried to smother a laugh and ended up gagging on a mouthful of the dish under discussion. Even Cosimo indulged himself with a small, private smile.

Only Cardinal Salviati remained blissfully unaware of being tweaked. He smacked his lips around a mouthful thoughtfully.

"Excellent," he declared. He leaned forward to confide in Caterina. "And I am one to know, for this is one of my favorite dishes."

After the repast Caterina granted Tommaso the rest of the day off. Early that evening he attended an artists' gala. There Tommaso drew Michelangelo aside. He described Caterina's behavior and asked the sculptor what he made of it.

Michelangelo considered Tommaso's story for several minutes. "Why do the *Duchessina*'s actions distress you?" he finally asked. "She's lived a perilous life. Do you feel she shouldn't dissemble when she needs to?"

Tommaso shook his head. "Of course not. But why in this manner? Since Cardinal Salviati is the Pope's creature, shouldn't she use him to lull the Pope? To convince Clement that His plan worked and her love wanes in Ippolito's absence?"

Michelangelo laughed and clapped Tommaso on the shoulder. "You're a bright youth, Tommaso, but your mistress is both bright *and* wily. She knows the Pope is aware that she and Ippolito have been together before, parted, and come together again—Rome, then Florence, now Rome again—and that they grow closer with each separation and reunion. He'd never believe indifference on her part.

"If He Himself observed her acting in the fashion you describe, He'd see through her performance. Clement's weakness is that He surrounds himself with donkeys like the Cardinals Passerini and Salviati. Cardinal Salviati will report what he *thinks* he observed: an impressionable, emotional, immature and easily controlled young girl.

"Thus through her performance the *Duchessina* convinces the Pope, secondhand, of what He *wants* to believe of her. That is how He lets his guard down."

"But how can she be certain of Cardinal Salviati's doltishness? How can she know that will be the Cardinal's report to the Pope?" Tommaso asked.

"I'm sure her jest at his expense reassured her." Michelangelo jerked his chin toward a corner where Cellini bemoaned the loss of Angelica to a group of sympathetic admirers.

"That notorious incident when Cardinal Salviati insulted Benevenuto by comparing Benevenuto's jewelry to the mishmash of *cipollata*, onion stew, is famous, thanks to Benevenuto repeating the story to half of Rome. It also landed Cardinal Salviati in a hot stewful of trouble, once Clement learned how the Cardinal had insulted Cellini: That's a privilege reserved for Clement alone. Yet Cardinal Salviati is so dull that he failed to notice how Caterina made him the butt of her joke by serving him the very *cipollata* he'd insulted Cellini with."

Michelangelo left the party shortly after their conversation. Tommaso waited an hour before making his own departure. He walked over to the sculptor's studio and slipped through the alleyway entrance to Michelangelo's personal quarters.

Michelangelo's cot was too small for two to linger in for long, but Tommaso stayed a while, entertaining Michelangelo with the various tales of thwarted love he'd borne witness to.

"I hope the best for all of them," he said.

"Even Benevenuto?" Michelangelo smiled and raised his eyebrows. "You hope he finds his courtesan?"

"Even Messer Cellini," Tommaso said. "For two reasons: First, he'll be impossible to work around as long as he's beglamored of his courtesan. Second, once he finds her, it's likely that she and her mother will exact some retribution or another from him, avenging all the women he's made miserable during his life. It'll be pleasing to see God's justice done."

Michelangelo threw back his head and roared with laughter.

Tommaso watched him and thought with gratitude that at least what he and Michelangelo shared was simple and true. Love hadn't darkened *his* life with complications.

27

Tommaso returned to the Salviati mansion late that night. He approached the kitchen door quietly. He didn't want to make so much noise in the dark that he woke the other apprentices.

To his amazement, the thick door opened onto a kitchen well lit with oil lamps and still occupied.

Madonna Spada and all the Ramerino and Spada children were gone. Gone, too were the apprentices and younger scullery maids. But Marcus Gavius Spada, Bindo and Madonna Ramerino sat behind the largest worktable, their faces grave. Across from them, their backs to Tommaso, sat another man and woman. These two turned to look up when Tommaso entered. He didn't recognize them. Several of the older scullery maids perched on stools before the dying hearth of the great fireplace. Three strongly built young men lounged against a wall. Laudomia sat at the end of the great table, her eyes downcast.

A peculiar, strained atmosphere overwhelmed the lingering fragrances of a day's worth of cooking. Tommaso couldn't tell if the tension was grim, expectant or both.

"Forgive me for interrupting your council," he said. "I'll retire quickly and silently."

"Hold there, Tommaso," said Marcus Gavius Spada. "It's you we've been waiting for.

Tommaso felt suddenly uneasy.

"Please, sit." *Ser* Spada gestured to a stool not far from Laudomia.

Tommaso saw Madonna Ramerino nudge her husband. Bindo Ramerino coughed. "Yes, of course. The amenities. Tommaso Arista, let me introduce these good, honest people I'm sure you've been anxious to meet: Laudomia's parents, *Ser* and Madonna Gorini. Over there are her three brothers."

Why would I be anxious to meet Laudomia's family? Tommaso wondered.

Bindo Ramerino coughed again and looked with pleading eyes at Marcus Gavius Spada. Spada nodded and settled himself. "Perhaps it's best that I broach the matter, since I'm the least involved and therefore the most judicial," Spada said.

Bindo Ramerino looked relieved and grateful.

The hairs rose on Tommaso's arms. Since when had Marcus Gavius Spada and Bindo Ramerino ceased battling and become each other's advocate?

Ser Spada continued. "I'm sure the delicate subject I raise is one that—due to your youth, and justly so—you deemed unnecessary to broach and pursue until you reached greater maturity and some accomplishment in your career."

By St. John's beard, what is he babbling about?

"But unbeknownst to you and your suit, matters initiated outside your sphere necessitate action and commitment at perhaps an inconveniently early date."

My suit? What suit?

Ser Spada leaned back in his chair and favored Tommaso with a smile as tight as it was broad. "Inconvenient, but maybe not unfortunate. Contrary to popular wisdom, I've observed that marriage at a young age settles a youth, ripens him into manhood and good citizenry. I believe, Tommaso, this will be your happy fate."

Tommaso's uneasiness rose in his gorge, swelling to full-blown panic. "Marriage?" he gagged.

Madonnas Ramerino's and Gorini's eyes narrowed to slits, like those of angry serpents. Marcus Gavius Spada pretended not to hear Tommaso's outburst and sailed on.

"Madonna Ramerino and the Gorinis have been seeking an advantageous betrothal for Laudomia." *Ser* Spada nodded at the girl. "They believe they found an excellent candidate and apprised her of this this very evening when she finished work.

"Imagine their surprise when she informed them she already favored another fellow. Her words, close to exact, were: 'He's fair of face, his prospects excellent. Gentle and kind, he attends my every word, is sensible to my feelings. By every action he shows his fondness for me. No one works harder than he in this kitchen. I've labored long learning this craft, so I prefer a husband whose working days I can share. His only fault, I fear, is that you'll consider him too young to wed.'" Spada turned again to Laudomia. "Is that close to what you said?"

Laudomia nodded.

Tommaso stared at Laudomia. His mouth hung open. That entire description applied to Averardo, not him. Why didn't Laudomia set them right?

"When we asked her who this paragon was, Laudomia said surely we must know, must have noticed—that the other maids could tell us who tendered her affection that, while courtly, bordered on indiscretion. So we asked them." *Ser* Spada pointed to where the other young women sat by the fire.

The eldest stood up. "I'm astonished at your surprise, Maestro Tommaso," she said. "We've all seen how you dote on Laudomia. Her slightest melancholy draws you hurrying to her side—if you're not already there. You spend most of your day with her. Why, this very morning, did I not see you embrace her while she wept? We"—she indicated the other scullery maids—"have noticed the love growing between you. Laudomia didn't deny it when we queried her."

Tommaso whirled to stare at Laudomia. Even with her face still downcast he saw the small smile on her lips. What could she hope to accomplish by dissembling in this fashion?

Madonna Ramerino spoke up. "We pointed out to her that the conditions of your employment will take you not only away from Rome, but out of Italy altogether, away from her home and family. In reply she said her husband will be home and family to her. She prefers a comely man with fine prospects whom she knows to one she doesn't know.

"In short, she spoke with such good common sense, unusual in one of her years, that she dissuaded us out of our objections. All that remained was to confront you with our approval of this match, freeing you to declare your love for her."

Laudomia means to go through with this, Tommaso realized. If she can't have Averardo she means to have me. In this fashion will she avenge herself on both of us?

He stood up, turning to face Madonna Ramerino. "But that's impossible. I don't love her," he blurted.

Laudomia's brothers pushed away from the wall they leaned against.

"No matter what her virtues"—Tommaso put up a hand, backing away as they rounded the table—"how could I when I know she loves another?"

The brothers hesitated.

"Ask her!" Tommaso demanded.

Laudomia only dropped her face lower. Tommaso could no longer see what expression it bore.

"She loves my friend Averardo Fancelli." In desperation Tommaso spoke for her. "If I danced attendance on this young woman it was only as his second, bearing his messages to her, reassuring her of his constancy."

"Is this true?" Laudomia's father asked her. "Why are we just learning of this now? Why the duplicity?"

Laudomia raised her head, her expression meek. "Madonna Ramerino knew Averardo and I yearned for each other, but felt a match between us unpropitious, for altogether sensible reasons. I would never go against either your or the Ramerinos' wishes.

"But I desire to have some say in my fate and not marry a stranger. Tommaso shows me such courtesy that I know I could happily endure being wed to him. I also knew that all here would approve of him. He was my second choice."

Laudomia's explanation made too much sense even to Tommaso's shocked ears. "All the virtues you ascribe to me apply equally to Averardo," he protested. "Averardo is gentle, kind, fair to look at, hardworking, and he adores Laudomia, which I do not. Although he may not become a cook in the kitchens of the king of France, his prospects are bright. Maestros Spada and Ramerino rely on him as on no other."

Tommaso took a deep breath and risked everything. "Even Bartolommeo Scappi takes notice of him and asks me frequently of Averardo's progress."

Tommaso looked at Laudomia. She'd dropped her head and wore her secret smile again. Anger ignited in Tommaso at the way she'd repaid his kindness with jeopardy. He drew himself to stand as tall as he could.

"And when I *do* choose to marry, I'll not be some maiden's second choice; nor will I offer a marriage she'd have to *endure*," he said, his voice acid.

The smile left Laudomia's face.

Laudomia's father looked from her to Tommaso. He waved his sons, who'd been standing at ready, back against the wall. "*Ser* Arista will not have my daughter," he said. "My daughter protests the man we've found for her. Why not bring this Averardo forth? Let's see what he has to say on the matter."

"I'll fetch him, for I think you no longer need me," Tommaso said. He dashed down the short hallway to the apprentice's room. He burst through the door, almost crashing into Averardo. A single oil lamp burned on a chest. By its light Tommaso saw that the other apprentices were awake as well, sitting up together in the big apprentices' bed.

Averardo was beside himself with anxiety. "Tommaso, what's happening out there? Laudomia's family arrived tonight and *Ser* Ramerino ordered us to retire early. Did they discover our plan?"

"No, they came to betroth her to another. She had designs other than ours." Tommaso briefly explained the scene in the kitchen.

"You? She chose you?" Averardo grabbed Tommaso's sleeve with one hand, fisted the other. "Have you ill treated my trust, used it to steal away my darling's heart?"

Tommaso struck away Averardo's threatening hand. "I've never desired Laudomia," he snapped. "Nor given her reason to misinterpret my courtesy. Don't make me regret my recommendations of you to her parents. Dress yourself quickly. They're waiting for you to account for yourself and press your suit for the lady."

Tommaso was tempted to add that Averardo might reconsider pledging his troth to such a fickle, self-serving maid. But for his own sake, Tommaso held his tongue. The last thing he needed was for Averardo to fail in his goal.

Averardo pulled on his clothes and left. Tommaso undressed, extinguished the oil lamp and climbed into his cot.

"This evening's entertainment was worth the loss of sleep." Vittoriano's voice came out of the darkness. "With the final act of the *commedia* drawn to a close at last we'll enjoy some peace in here." The other apprentices sniggered.

"Until, of course, that time when you find yourself suffering from the same besotted affliction," Tommaso said sourly. "Then the laughter will be bought at *your* expense."

That silenced the other boys. Tommaso remembered how a short time ago he'd lain in Michelangelo's arms, congratulating himself on the smooth course of his life and love. He shook his head at his naïveté, turned on his side and slept.

The next morning Laudomia and Averardo glowed with happiness as they accepted the congratulations of the other apprentices and scullery maids, Madonna Spada, and any other servant who happened by the kitchen. Madonna Ramerino wore the satisfied look of a matchmaker triumphant. Messers Spada and Ramerino even clapped each other on the back at the success of what they saw as a collaboration.

Tommaso noticed with a somewhat mean satisfaction that the only person not effusive with joy besides himself was Alessa Ramerino. She sat, a drooped-over shadow, in one corner of the room, dicing aubergines into small cubes. Tommaso didn't doubt that tears streamed down her face as copiously as Laudomia's had the morning before.

He was unmoved. If she hadn't meddled, Averardo and Laudomia probably would have been caught in a compromising position and betrothed to each other before he'd even arrived from Florence.

Tommaso laid a year's worth of misery at Alessa's door. He finished preparations on two trays of breakfast. Caterina had sent word at daybreak that she and Madonna Gondi would sup together in her suite while the rest of her entourage broke their fast in the banquet room.

He was balancing the two trays, getting ready to leave, when Madonna Spada noticed him struggling.

"Tommaso, you can't bear both of those yourself." She glanced around the room. "Laudomia, you help him. Let others in the house have the opportunity to wish you well on your betrothal."

Tommaso gritted his teeth. The last person he wanted to accompany him was Laudomia. He knew why Madonna Spada assigned her to him—she wanted the girl out of the kitchen. With all the romantic commotion going on, work had slowed to a breakfast-imperiling pace.

He and Laudomia carried the trays up to Caterina's suite. A thick stone wall of silence lay between them.

Madonna Gondi opened the door for them. Caterina looked up

from her small desk, piled high with correspondence. When she saw who accompanied Tommaso, her welcome smile broadened to a mischievous grin. Tommaso's heart sank.

"Tommaso, thank you. You arrive exactly the moment I begin to feel pangs of hunger. And who escorts you? The newly betrothed? Laudomia, congratulations on your upcoming nuptials. I wish you every conceivable happiness."

Laudomia brightened that a person as esteemed as the *Duchessina* should acknowledge her engagement.

"You needn't wait while Tommaso serves us, Laudomia," Caterina said. "I have matters to discuss with him and I'm sure they need your skills back in the kitchen. Why don't you return to help with the trays in, say, an hour?"

Laudomia curtsied deeply and left.

Caterina stood up from behind her desk and stretched while Tommaso arranged breakfast.

"So, that's the lovely maid that almost married you instead. You're indeed precocious, my gossip."

Tommaso felt his face heat and flare like a fireworks display. "You heard that part of the farce?" He groaned. "When?"

"Last night, long after dinner. Messers Spada and Ramerino begged for an audience with me. They said they'd just found out that you might have compromised a young woman. That she and her family waited in the kitchen that very moment for a resolution. They said you'd gone to an artists' party for the evening and they didn't know what to do. Since we're so far from Florence and your family, I act not only as your employer but also your guardian. They had no choice but to come to me."

Tommaso was horrified. He dropped to his knees before her. "I had no idea, my lady. They told me nothing of this."

Caterina motioned for him to stand. "Compose yourself, Tommaso. I told them I know you to be a young man possessed of the highest integrity, faithful to a fault—that they should await your return and query you gently. I also told them that should they remain unsatisfied with your comportment in this matter, they could return to address me on the morrow.

"When I woke this morning, the first news to greet my ears, curiously enough, was of Laudomia's engagement to another young cook. It sounds as if she possesses a fickle heart." She smiled. "Should I be offering you condolences?"

"Not at all." Tommaso grimaced.

While Caterina and Madonna Gondi sat down to eat, Tommaso told them the whole story.

"I see," Caterina said when he finished. She was struggling not to laugh. "I thought it might be something of the sort."

She rinsed her hands in her finger bowl, then wiped them dry on her third napkin, the one always kept clean at the side until the end of the meal. Her face grew thoughtful, then grave.

"I wish you to have a good life, Tommaso, with friends and interests and lovers. You're young, like me, so I know your blood runs hot. I wouldn't deny you love's pleasures, and in that matter I believe I can trust your already amply proven discretion."

Tommaso wouldn't have thought he could blush any more fiercely than he had at the beginning of the conversation. He was wrong. He knew Caterina referred to his liaison with Michelangelo.

"It's your friendships and your good heart that concern me," Caterina continued. "You know that until Ippolito and I are ascendant and together in Florence that we all play a dangerous game. To that end, yes, you should ingratiate yourself and gain the confidence of everyone you meet.

"But by the same token, beware of others attempting to gain *your* confidence, attempting to ingratiate themselves with you. Don't let yourself be drawn into the plots and travails of others. In less time than it takes to draw a breath, such circumstances can be turned against you. And then, in turn, perhaps against me.

"What if Laudomia had insisted on wedding you, and we found out later that she was one of Clement's spies? After all, she comes from outside this household. For your safety and mine I'd have been forced to dismiss you."

Tommaso dropped to his knees again. "*Duchessina*, I'm unworthy of your patronage," he said miserably.

"Tommaso, *please* stopping falling down on all fours," Caterina said. She held out a hand to help him up.

He looked up at her smiling face.

"Consider it this way," she said. "Your unhappy adventure was a

lesson provided by those who watch over us from above. Now we all—
not just you—know to be more careful. Yes?"

Tommaso nodded gratefully.

Catherine's smile turned sly. "If you still feel in debt for the dis-
turbance I suffered last night on your behalf, I have a way for you to
make amends. I have an assignment for you. Discharge it well, and I'll
forgive you your little contretemps and more."

Tommaso groaned. This meant it would be an assignment he was
sure to dislike. "I'm braced for your request, Your Grace."

"I need someone to observe the Pope for me."

Tommaso was surprised. "But Ippolito sees the Pontiff all the time."

Caterina shook her head. "Ippolito quarrels constantly with Clement
when they're together. I need someone with a cooler eye to tell me how
my Holy cousin fares."

"But I have no recourse for visiting the Vatican."

"You could," Caterina said. "Clement requires that Benevenuto Cellini attend to him regularly. It might take you a while, but watch for an
opportunity to accompany Cellini.

"Now be so good as to clear the dishes away." Caterina ignored the
face Tommaso made at the thought of more time spent with Cellini.
"My ladies will return soon. And *your* lady-that-almost-was will be back
to help you."

Indeed, no sooner had Tommaso organized the empty dishes in the
tray than Laudomia arrived at the door.

Caterina gave Laudomia a small silver brooch to congratulate her on
her betrothal. Laudomia glowed with pleasure. She immediately pinned
it to the breast of her *gamurra*.

Watching Laudomia's satisfaction, Tommaso could hardly contain
his anger. On the walk back to the kitchen he couldn't bear it any longer.
When they reached an empty hallway, he stepped in front of Laudomia
and barred her way.

"I acted as your friend and advocate, with nothing but your and
Averardo's good in my heart. And how did you repay me, you venomous
wench? By manipulating my life and risking my future!

Laudomia regarded Tommaso calmly and with no more emotion
than a fish she'd just filleted. She shrugged, and said, "So? Now you
know what every woman suffers."

✻   ✻   ✻

Caterina looked at the closed door after Tommaso and Laudomia left. "This *has* been a lesson, in more ways than one," she told Madonna Gondi. "I've known for a while that I must learn to go on the offensive more. All those pitfalls I just warned Tommaso against—being drawn into the plots and travails of others; I can certainly learn to work those pitfalls to *my* advantage, if I'm the one conducting the drawing in."

28

The night of October 31, 1531

The two small, round tables in Caterina's bedroom weighed little. She maneuvered them with ease, but not without making some noise as she lifted them and set them in place before the western-facing window. With each thump or scrape of table legs against the floor she stopped, listening to see if anyone had noticed the sounds.

Madonna Gondi had consented to stay late this evening before returning to the suite she, Antonio and their two small children had moved into. She sat outside in the reception room, playing a game of cards with Reparata, resting her hands now and again on her growing belly— Cosimo Ruggiero had predicted a Christmas baby for her. Madonna Gondi and Reparata were ready to intercept any of the other ladies-in-waiting who might become curious at the sounds of activity coming from the bedroom Caterina had retired to so early.

Caterina heard no footsteps approach, no one ask meddlesome questions. She continued with her preparations.

In the middle of the table closest to the window she placed a bowl and poured seawater into it from a pitcher on her washstand. Tommaso had obtained the brine at her request: He'd decanted it from a tank containing live oysters at the fish market. He also brought another one of her requirements—a pouch of rough sea salt. Caterina poured half the contents of the pouch into the center of the bowl until it peaked above the salt water, forming a small salt island.

From a drawer in the other table she retrieved a carved rock crystal *cassone.* It contained gems she'd bought on the pretext of someday commissioning some jewelry.

She selected a perfectly round moonstone and balanced it on top of the salt island.

"Come witness me here, Holy Mother," she whispered to the moon's full aspect. "I beseech you—lend your bright strong power to this enterprise."

Next she selected nine pearls from the rock-crystal box. One by one, she arranged the pearls from right to left around the bowl in a half circle. The half circle's open side faced the window. Each time she set one of the pearls in place she murmured, "From right to left, Lady Jana; for gaining, not losing."

Then she positioned a white candle to the right of the bowl, at the beginning of the line of pearls, and a black candle to the left, at the end of the line.

To complete the first altar she placed three small censers so they formed an equilateral triangle around the bowl and pearls. Two of the censers paralleled the window frame. The third pointed at the second, still-empty table. "This is for the manifestation of my desire in this world," Caterina prayed.

She arranged the second table in exactly the same manner, using the rest of the sea salt and seawater, adding nine more pearls and another moonstone. But this time she invoked the moon's waxing phase, the phase of beginnings.

"Lady Diana, set me well on my journey. Please bless this enterprise."

The tip of the triangle formed by the censers on this table pointed up toward the tip of the downward-facing triangle on the other table.

"This is for the manifestation of my desire in the realm of the spirits," Caterina murmured.

The altars ready, Caterina picked up an unprotesting Gattamelata and set her outside the base of the first altar's triangle, facing inward. The cat's back faced the window and the rising moon. Gattamelata adjusted herself till she sat comfortably, gazing into the bowl before her.

"I beseech you for your aid, Little Kitchen Goddess," Caterina prayed. "You who've chosen to come from the spirits' dwelling to our world."

Caterina's next action was the hardest. She could hardly bear parting from Ginevra.

You must do this. Ginevra's words echoed in her head. *We both have work to do here. Our separation will only last a little while.*

With reluctant hands, Caterina drew the necklace over her head and placed it so its pendant lay just outside the base of the second altar's triangle.

"I beseech you for your aid, my dearest friend," she whispered. "You for whom it was chosen to transform from our world to the spirits' dwelling."

The Caterina sorted through five small silk pouches, each containing a different herb. Tommaso had also supplied her with these. She sprinkled a little from each bag into the two bowls.

"Rue for our protection. Fennel as our weapon. Coriander for our love. Solomon's seal as our power. Jasmine for our Mother Moon's blessing."

The moon rose high enough to clear Gattamelata's back. It shone down between the portals formed by the points of the cat's ears onto the bowls.

Visions formed in the rings of water circling the salt islands. In the first bowl the images spun lazily counterclockwise, then faded, only to reappear in the second bowl. There they spun clockwise.

Caterina smiled at the first vision. It was one she'd seen before, and a good omen. Madonna Gondi's image floated in the mercurial medium. She held an infant in her gentle arms, caring for it tenderly. Although Caterina saw no accompanying signs or symbols, Ginevra had already told her that the baby was hers, Caterina's.

I will know love. I will bear beautiful children, Caterina thought. With new resolve she continued the ritual, drawing down more images into the bowls from the moon: visages of those she corresponded with, to bind them more closely to her. Their faces shrank and sharpened to bright points, like the stars in the night sky under which she and Ippolito would travel when they made their way together away from here. "Come celebrate *La Festa dell Ombra*, my friends," she murmured. "Tonight we rejoice in the union of the God and Goddess."

In his studio in Florence, Ruggiero the Old sat down to compose a letter to his son in Rome. He held his pen in hand, hesitating before writing. He wondered what Caterina was doing at that moment.

He wasn't sure how specific her knowledge of the occult and her own powers had grown. From what Cosimo wrote to him, Ruggiero the Old knew she'd become sufficiently self-aware to act on her own behalf. She couldn't help but feel the power of this night. This night the Old Religion called shadow fest.

Ruggiero the Old sighed. He knew the inclination of Caterina's heart. He wished she could attain what she desired.

Sadly, all of his studies, all of his clandestine spying on the other realms of existence, every horoscope he cast, pointed to another future altogether, or disaster might befall them all.

But if he moved directly against Caterina, she'd never trust his or Cosimo's guidance and all would be lost anyway. She was so potentially powerful that even he couldn't act against the grain of her nature.

He put pen to paper. "You must teach her and observe her, my son," he wrote. "Do not hinder her. Neither, though it might rend your heart to stand back, may you help her."

Gattamelata curled up at the foot of Caterina's bed. Though the rites had lasted a long time, tiring her old feline body, at her core she felt stronger, her ancient powers replenished. All that night she slept well, dreamt well.

Hundreds upon hundreds of years ago she'd chosen this form, in part because of its ability to dream. Before the Etruscans settled in her land, the small wild cats of the Tuscan hills prowled realms other than their own in their sleep, kept reality knit together with their dreaming. They heard her when she spoke to them in voices of wind and stream. They heard her sisters, too.

Their bright curiosity, so similar to her own, attracted her. She chose to become one of them, knowing that every time she slept she'd return to the life she'd led since the beginning of the world—swimming in the winds, singing in the waters.

Caterina also slept. Unlike Gattamelata, she enjoyed little rest. She flew to other places, became other beings with labors of their own to accomplish.

She woke as a warrior beast in the midst of battle on a strange diffuse world of fog. As she fought, she and other creatures like herself floated more than ran through thick air almost indistinguishable from the smokelike ground.

In another land she was a great mage, with powers and knowledge far greater than that of the Ruggieros, and in possession of a waking knowledge of all her other simultaneous existences. In this life she knew that this was the self that had arranged for her birth as the linchpin entity Caterina de' Medici of Florence. Like the spider it resembled, this sorcerer self continually repaired the interconnecting web lines to her many lives, trying to keep a universe of worlds balanced and whole.

She awoke again as the vast sea of a watery world, floating darkly in an unlit portion of the heavens. Her fluid depths wrapped around a warm core of stone. Within her swam countless tiny flecks of life, flashing motes of phosphorescence. And larger forms floated there— milky-eyed, as vast and languid as giant dreaming women. Everything rested in and upon her waters.

Life after life followed. Finally, she lay in the form of a plain, drab rock on a featureless plain under a violet-colored sky. Three moons coursed across heavens lit not by a sun, but by the bright, glowing shape of a bull with the face of a man.

At last, I am only a stone, she thought. Now I can rest. And she did.

29

Late November, 1931

Cellini glared at the model of the chalice before him. "If the Pope wished me to finish this, he should leave me in peace and not insist that I act as mace-bearer in his processions. I'm supposed to be exempted from that duty."

"Usually you are exempted. He only insists you participate when you avoid him overlong," Cellini's partner Felice pointed out. "You force him to call you into service because it's the only time he can query you on your commissions for him."

"He doesn't query—he interrogates me," Cellini grumbled. "That's why I avoid him in the first place."

Cellini looked around the *bottega* impatiently. "Well, *someone* has to go with me to the Vatican." Cellini could go alone, but he felt his presence lacked importance without a minimal retinue.

Felice usually acquiesced when Cellini took one or more of the shop lads with him on these outings. It was almost impossible for Cellini to walk down the street without getting into a quarrel with somebody. Accompanied by one or more sturdy youths, arguments were less likely to escalate to blows or drawn knives. On those occasions when violence did occur, having an entourage meant there'd be someone handy to run for help, a doctor, or bring word to Felice that once again his contentious partner needed to be released from the city guards.

But today the *bottega* was rushing to finish an order: several sets of ornate silver basins and matching jugs, and ten finger rings of refined steel engraved with gold and set with small shell cameos.

"It's only morning, and already you'd take a pair of good hands, besides the loss of your own, with you," Felice complained.

"If you like, I could go," Tommaso offered. "I'm the most expendable." Here, at last, was the perfect chance to discharge Caterina's assignment to spy on the Pope.

Felice looked relieved. "There, Benevenuto. The perfect solution."

Cellini still appeared disgruntled. "You know I prefer more than one attendant." Then he looked at Tommaso and grinned. "But with that bright red hair, you *will* draw attention to my colors. Get yourself cleaned up, *Ser* Arista, and put this on." He tossed Tommaso a livery decked with Cellini's heraldic device: a lion rampant on an azure field, holding a red lily in its right paw.

Tommaso pulled off his work smock and washed quickly.

It had rained the night before, but today the weather was clear, the sky a strong cobalt blue. The sturdy smell of washed dust and cobblestones filled the air. Bright light from the morning sun glowed off puddles in the street as intensely as fire in the heart of a foundry. Tommaso kept having to put up a hand to shade his eyes.

Cellini talked incessantly all the way to the Vatican. "Have you seen this?" he asked, pulling a letter from his surcoat. "My darling Angelica arranged to have it smuggled out of Sicily."

Tommaso nodded politely. All morning Cellini had been slipping the billet out, regaling each of the apprentices with it in turn. He hadn't gotten around to Tommaso until now, but Tommaso already knew of its contents from Cencio and Paulino.

"She loves me. She misses me." Cellini beamed. He held it up to read it verbatim. "She says she's 'extremely unhappy.' She pines for me, as I do for her."

Knowing it wasn't tactful, Tommaso still couldn't resist tweaking the goldsmith. "Indeed?" he said. "I thought you'd found comfort in the arms of one of Signora Antea's courtesans."

Cellini dismissed the accusation with a shrug. "An unimportant liaison. It serves only to dull the edge of pain of my real passion. Without such slight solace, I couldn't continue to function as an artist and a businessman. The arrangement with Antea's girl will only continue until I contrive a way to be with Angelica again, whenever that may be."

He glanced at Tommaso. "If you put your mind to it, perhaps you could tell me when that would be. Your family possesses the power to divinate, does it not?"

"You're confusing the Aristas with our employers, the Ruggieros," Tommaso said stiffly. It was unsafe even to jest about sorcerous matters on Rome's streets. Who knew who might be listening, waiting to report to the Inquisition?

"Not the Aristas," Cellini said. "Your mother's family. All Florence purports that they're a pack of witches." He threw a comradely arm across Tommaso's shoulders. "Surely at your mother's knee you learned of some little concoction that would allow me a glimpse into the future. Don't be shy—tell me. You know, from my earliest days I've had the most intense desire to learn something of the arcane arts."

Tommaso began sweating. Would Cellini never shut up?

"I believe myself as destined for such knowledge as I am for fame as an artist," the goldsmith prattled on. "Did you ever hear of my encounter with a great scorpion when I was but three? Or of the discovery of a salamander sporting in the burning coals of my family's fireplace when I was five?"

"No," said Tommaso desperately, though he had. "Pray tell me of these wondrous occurrences."

Telling anecdotes distracted Cellini until they reached St. Peter's. There, the ongoing construction on the great basilica distracted him into changing the subject again.

"A noble design of Bramante's, and certainly grandiose enough to satisfy even Pope Julius's ambitions," he said. "But Bramante lacked the technical expertise for his plan to ever come to fruition." Cellini sniffed. "See how there, and there"—he pointed—"Bramante's architect successors and Julius's papal successors have changed the original design." Cellini shook his head. "What's needed is a genius with a singular vision to save it."

"Yourself, perhaps?" Tommaso inquired slyly as they rounded the construction and approached the Vatican.

Cellini snorted. "An educated man should understand and be able to discuss architecture intelligently. But mastering a discipline that, in the end, is endlessly revised by committees holds no interest for me. What glory and artistry is there in that?"

✻   ✻   ✻

In spite of his protestations back at the studio, once Cellini was dressed, bedecked with the insignia of his office, and marching in procession, he fell into the role of mace-bearer with relish. He imbued each slow, measured step with solemn grace. Head held erect, his eyes gazed calmly toward a joyous eternity. His handsome features were set in an expression of tranquil piety. Among the dozens of papal office-bearers, none drew the eye the way he did.

No one performs better, Tommaso thought with reluctant admiration. He guessed that to achieve such an accomplished effect, the goldsmith had convinced himself of the emotions he so ably projected.

I suppose an actor whose own acting tricks him into thinking he *is* the part he plays could be considered in one of two ways, Tommaso reflected. Either that he's a fool, deficient in wit, or that he's one of the greatest actors alive.

The procession paraded down the nave and past the distant, tiny figure of the Pope, who was engulfed in huge, ornate robes. Tommaso stood with his head bowed in a side gallery, along with the rest of the office-bearers' retainers. Religious services followed the procession. The blessing of visiting foreign dignitaries came next, then the granting of dispensations. During the latter, the audience was free to move about and talk quietly among themselves.

"I haven't seen you here before," one young man said to Tommaso. "But I perceive by the device you wear that you serve the notorious goldsmith. How do you find service with him?"

"Never dull." Tommaso smiled, not correcting the youth on the real nature of his arrangement with Cellini. Other retainers were more likely to gossip with him if they thought he was Cellini's man. They'd probably say nothing if they knew he worked for the Pope's little cousin.

The other fellow grinned. "Ah, so the rumors are true?"

"I can't say for certain without knowing which rumors. But yes, most likely," Tommaso answered.

"I always wondered. Cellini acts the sainted lamb on the rare occasion when he participates in the ceremonies here."

"Then a sojourn in God's house benefits his behavior, and, with luck, his soul," Tommaso said. "Have you noticed that effect on any others here?"

"On some, yes. On others, no."

As a naturally curious newcomer, it was easy for Tommaso to ask questions without rousing suspicion. His new acquaintance, who introduced himself as Gaio, gossiped away about all sorts of papal court matters.

"What about all the foreigners I see? Do they attend for political or spiritual advantage?" Tommaso asked.

Gaio nodded over his shoulder to where a group of severe-looking men wearing plain black surcoats stood. "The Spanish there proclaim their devotion. Yet they marched under their emperor and king's banner to sack this sacred city. Even worse, they employed the godless Swiss and Germans to desecrate the churches and clergy. They'd have murdered the Pope Himself if they'd laid their hands on Him. Common knowledge has it that they attend religious services for their emperor. They're here to monitor Clement's actions, not to exercise their faith."

Then Gaio nodded toward a soldier leaning against a nearby pillar. "There, on the other hand, is a visitor whom I believe to be a truly religious fellow."

The man wore a military uniform and insignia Tommaso didn't recognize. He appeared to be in his early twenties, and was both short and homely. Still, he had an alert air about him, and a good carriage.

"Who is this paragon of virtue, and how do you know of him?" Tommaso asked.

"He's a French soldier. One Gasparo . . . no, pardon me, *Gaspard* de Saulx. His companions call him Tavannes. I made his acquaintance at a roadhouse outside the city gates, where I was dining and drinking the other night. He expressed deep regret at France's inability to come to Rome's aid during the Sack. He said one of the greatest regrets in his life was not to have had the opportunity to defend the church.

"Later, when he took leave to answer nature's call, his friends who were with him, from his regiment, spoke highly of him. They said that although he shares the traits of wit and cynicism with all other Frenchmen, he was the most devout and brave young man they'd ever known."

"Who are these other Frenchmen who vouch for *Ser* de Saulx? Can you point them out to me?" Tommaso asked.

Gaio craned his head about, looking. "A Gilles Gerard, Etienne Romard, and Louis something-or-other. I don't see them anywhere here."

He nudged Tommaso and laughed. "Which only goes to prove their contention that Gaspard is the most devout among them."

Tommaso's responding chuckle was genuine. He couldn't have chanced on a better-informed or more voluble tale-bearer than Gaio. "How did you make their acquaintance?"

"They needed my help. Can you imagine it? They didn't know how to use their forks! Everyone else at the establishment was making gibes at their expense, so I offered to instruct them." Gaio nudged Tommaso again. "It only proves that virtue and valor are no substitute for manners and good breeding."

After the ceremonies, Cellini hastened to doff his ceremonial robes and slip away. To no avail: Two of the Pope's chamberlains were waiting for him.

"His Holiness requires an audience with you, Benevenuto. He wishes to discuss some matters regarding the commissions He placed with you," one of them said.

"Signor Pier Giovanni, today I spent time discharging my mace-bearer's duty that could have been put to better use working on the Pontiff's chalice. Surely His Holiness can see that requiring my attendance will only put the possession of that which He desires further into the future."

Signor Pier Giovanni looked amused. "Nonetheless," he said firmly, sweeping his arm to indicate the way.

Cellini sighed. Flanked by the two chamberlains, he marched to the Pope's apartments. Tommaso trailed behind.

Tommaso knew that Jacopo Salviati often visited and stood in the role of advisor to Clement. Let him not be here today, Tommaso thought nervously. Jacopo knew him well enough to recognize him, but since he was only a servant, Tommaso doubted that Jacopo knew of his apprenticeship with Cellini. If Jacopo saw him, Tommaso was sure he'd be surprised and likely ask Tommaso what he was doing there, wearing Cellini's livery.

They at last finished climbing what seemed like an interminable series of stairways and reached the papal suite. Tommaso was relieved that Jacopo Salviati was nowhere to be seen.

Like Caterina, Clement held his private audiences in his sitting room. Of course, Clement's was far larger. Tapestries alternated with gilt-framed paintings. Tommaso recognized pieces by Raphael, Mantegna and Titian. Servants stood at ease back by the walls, but not so close as to touch the paintings and tapestries. Damask-covered chairs and settees were scattered about, but except for a few very elderly gentlemen who sat in the far, shadowed corners of the room, everyone else but the Pope was standing. Tommaso guessed them to be grateful for the thick, padded rugs covering the floor. Rome might have lost much during the Sack, but the Pope had recovered well.

Clement sat in a thronelike chair, talking with the Spanish contingent Gaio had pointed out to Tommaso earlier.

Cellini brightened. "Ah, see—His Holiness entertains important visitors. Surely He wouldn't wish my presence as an interruption," he said to Pier Giovanni.

"My dearest Benevenuto—last year, when you were so ill and said you suffered most grievously in your eyesight—I see now the truth of your claims. Evidently you fail to see that those the Pontiff speaks to are the Emperor's men. Rumor has it His Holiness has not felt any fondness for the Spanish since the Sack of Rome," Pier Giovanni said dryly.

"What would you like to wager that part of your purpose here today is precisely to serve as an interruption? And a long-winded, boring interruption at that." Pier Giovanni motioned Tommaso to go stand with the other attendants against the wall.

The two chamberlains and Cellini approached the thronelike chair. The Pope looked up, saw Cellini, and fixed the goldsmith with a vulpine grin. "Ah, gentlemen. Here is the master artisan I was boasting of to you."

Cellini flinched at being labeled a mere artisan. Tommaso knew he must be glowering inside, but the goldsmith let no trace of annoyance show on his face.

"Have you brought with you the model of the chalice? Or, even better, the partial or finished piece?" the Pope asked.

Cellini didn't rise to the bait. Instead, he countered.

"How could I? Since it was necessary to discharge my duty as mace-bearer, there was nowhere on my person to carry it."

The Pope's gaze veered toward Tommaso, so resplendent in Cellini's livery.

Cellini added smoothly, "And of course I would never entrust such a valuable piece, executed to your specific commission, to even my most trusted apprentice. I have come prepared, however. I brought a copy of the plans with me so we could discuss my progress on the project."

Cellini took a roll of parchment from inside his surcoat. He untied the ribbon binding it, then spread it out on a small table that Pier Giovanni and the other chamberlain hastened to set before the Pope.

Tommaso had to admire Cellini's comportment. Though the goldsmith had hoped to avoid the Pope, he'd come prepared for an encounter. The Pope must know from Cellini's answer that the chalice wasn't finished. If it were, Cellini wouldn't have been able to bear not to flaunt it. But Cellini had easily avoided telling the Pope where work actually stood on the chalice. If Clement wanted to know, he'd have to ask Cellini directly, and risk looking petty and foolish in front of the Spaniards.

The Spanish gentlemen gathered around the table while Cellini explained the chalice's designs.

"You can see here, good Signore, how instead of the usual plain top chased with designs, I'm fashioning three figures sculpted in the round, representing Faith, Hope and Charity. Corresponding to these, complementing them, the base will exhibit three circular histories in bas-relief. The first is the Nativity of Christ, the second the Resurrection, the third is Saint Peter crucified head downward."

With all eyes on Cellini, Tommaso could at last study the Pope. He'd never seen him in the flesh before today, but there were several paintings of him as a youth in the Medici mansion back in Florence. The Salviatis owned a decent copy of Raphael's portrait of Pope Leo X with Clement, who was only Cardinal Giulio then, standing in the background with another cardinal. Black-haired and clean-shaven in that painting, Tommaso had been uneasily struck by the then-young cardinal's resemblance to Grandfather Befanini. Giulio could have passed as Tommaso's grandfather's callow, more slender brother.

Tommaso had seen a more recent portrait, by Bronzino, so he knew not to expect the still-promising young cleric from Raphael's picture. After Clement escaped from the Castel Sant' Angel wearing servant's clothing and ragged, long, false beard, Clement had grown his own beard out just as long and scraggly. What shocked Tommaso was that it was almost white. The man himself looked frail, his foxlike features gaunt, though Tommaso knew he was only fifty-two or fifty-three years old.

Illness wasn't uncommon in the Medici family. Lorenzo il Magnífico had died of gout at the age of forty-three. But Tommaso had never heard of any member of the family aging in this manner. Tommaso's grandfather, at most a year or two older than Clement, looked twenty years younger.

Cellini was now describing the model for the chalice that he'd constructed out of wood and wax. The Pope asked knowledgeable, technical questions as to how Cellini intended to translate the design into precious metals.

Cellini appeared to have forgotten that he'd resisted this trip to the Vatican. He was thoroughly enjoying expounding on the complexities of his profession. The Spanish gentlemen, who appeared genuinely impressed when first shown the design for the chalice, now looked bored.

Near to Tommaso stood a couple of the Spaniard's servants. They, too, looked austere and wore all black. They were whispering in Spanish to each other. Tommaso could barely make out their words, make sense of what they were saying. He was grateful they weren't speaking in French or German, which he wouldn't have had a prayer of understanding.

"May I have a word with you, young sir?"

Tommaso looked up, startled. He'd been listening so closely to the Spaniards that he hadn't noticed Pier Giovanni approach him.

"Certainly," Tommaso said, recovering.

Pier Giovanni drew him aside. "I respect your master and love his work well. Convey this warning to him for me: Tell him it's in his best interests not to tarry over the chalice's completion.

"Clement is making plans already to meet with the Emperor in Bologna. When He does, He'll recall Cardinal Salviati from Parma to serve as the legate in Rome during His absence. Salviati's duties may include overseeing the Pontiff's personal business. If that happens, your master will have a hard time of it. Salviati bears Benevenuto such ill will that he's sure to turn over any unfinished commissions to his own favorites, and cause as much strife between Benevenuto and His Holiness as he can."

Tommaso promised to pass along the warning.

The Spanish diplomats interrupted Cellini's endless discourse as politely as they could by bowing low. "We always enjoy an education in the finer things in life when we visit You, Your Holiness," the senior member said. "Unfortunately, we have other appointments this afternoon. We'd be guilty of extreme discourtesy if we were tardy. Please forgive us."

Clement gestured a dismissal, then turned back to Cellini. The goldsmith launched once again into his complicated explanation.

As soon as the Spaniards and their servants left, Clement waved His hand again, this time to stop Cellini.

"Enough, friend Benevenuto. Once again, you've served me well." The Pope smiled.

Cellini bowed. "My pleasure, Your Holiness."

Clement grinned.

Tommaso shivered. There was more malevolence than mirth in that grimace.

"The rest of Italy sings Baldessare Castiglione's praises, but if he weren't dead already I'd be tempted to excommunicate him," Clement said. "He extolled the Spanish as the masters of courtiership in his book, even praised them for their 'calm gravity.'

"Pah!" Clement spat. "They're no more than lowly informers and curs. They lack the basic intelligence necessary to follow a prolonged discourse on the arts ... Thank Heavens!" The Pope beamed at Cellini. "I can always count on you."

The rest of His court laughed. Tommaso, however, thought the Spaniards remarkably patient and restrained.

"Let me further prove your confidence in me," Cellini said. "I understand another post in the Piombo is vacant. Allow me to resign my mace-bearer's commission and take that up instead."

Clement tried to humor Cellini. "That Piombo post is worth more than eight hundred crowns a year. If I gave it to you, you'd spend your time scratching your paunch. Thus your magnificent handiwork would be lost and I would bear the blame."

Cellini didn't give up that easily. He responded at once. "Cats of a good breed mouse better when they are fat than starving. Likewise, honest men who possess some talent exercise it to far nobler purport when they have the wherewithal to live abundantly. Princes who provide such folk with competences, let Your Holiness take note, are watering the roots of genius—for genius and talent, at their birth, come into this world lean and scabby."

The Pope's only reply was a stony gaze.

Cellini shrugged. "Very well. Your Holiness should also know I asked for the Piombo position with no hope of getting it. Only *too* happy am I to have that miserable mace-bearer post." Cellini's words were sarcastic, their tone spiteful.

Tommaso saw Pier Giovanni put one hand over his eyes and shake his head.

"Since you don't care to give it to me, bestow it on some other man of talent who deserves it, and not on some fat ignoramus who *will* spend his time scratching his paunch, if I may quote Your Holiness's own words." Cellini paused to glare about the chamber at individuals who Tommaso assumed fit the description—in Cellini's mind, at least.

"Follow the example of Pope Julius, of illustrious memory," Cellini chided Clement, "who conferred an office of the same kind upon Bramante, that most admirable architect." Cellini then bowed low, turned on his heel, and marched out of the room, his face scarlet with fury.

Tommaso stood stunned for a moment. Then, heart in throat, he raced after the goldsmith.

Cellini had managed to turn the Pontiff's agreeable, flattering words into ill, had presumed to lecture Him, and compared Him unfavorably to Julius, the great warrior pope and patron of the arts. Tommaso expected the papal guard to come running up from behind at any moment to arrest them. He knew if that happened, Cellini was in such a rage that he'd draw his sword.

Nothing happened. They clattered undetained down the great stairway. Courtiers and clerics ascending the stairs made way when they saw Cellini's stormy countenance. Tommaso also saw small smiles of amusement. Evidently Cellini's tantrums were as common in the Vatican as they were in the *bottega*. The goldsmith's pace slowed by the time they reached the base of the stairway, and he looked more vexed than angry.

Jacopo Salviati and a friend were just approaching the steps. "Ah, Benevenuto. Another dispute with Clement?"

"Indeed," Cellini glowered. He launched into an account of the incident.

"I'm sorry I missed it. My wife's grandniece, the *Duchessina*, detained me with some questions pertaining to the proper etiquette for some visitors she's expecting. If I'd been here, perhaps I could have intervened in some small way," Jacopo said pleasantly.

His gaze fell on Tommaso. He looked puzzled. "I know you," he said. "But from where?"

Tommaso flushed. "From your own household, Signor, where I customarily wear your livery, rather than Signor Cellini's here. I work for the same aforementioned *Duchessina*. I came with her from Florence as her chef-in-training. My name is Tommaso Arista."

Jacopo struck his head with his hand. "Of course!" he said. "But what on earth are you doing here with this notorious rascal? Is he instructing you in the fine art of seducing wenches, or merely demonstrating how best to drive Popes mad?" He poked Cellini with one finger. Both Cellini and Jacopo's friend laughed.

"Well, an education of a sort," Tommaso said. "My mistress, the *Duchessina*, will eventually depart for France. There, the people, though vivacious, think 'that letters are detrimental to the profession of arms,' and in general esteem education but little, if we are to believe Signor Castiglione. Therefore, before she leaves, she wishes even her least servant to be availed of some tutelage.

"In my profession as chef I must know not only what is pleasing to the palate but also what is pleasing to the eye. Therefore, she'd deemed it advisable to place me under the tutelage of the inestimable Signor Cellini here, for one day each week."

Jacopo clapped his hands in delight. "A chef who can quote *The Courtier* at will and who studies with master artists. Caterina is growing into as wily a Medici as any born. I predict she'll take the French court by storm." At that, he and his friend took their leave.

Cellini's ill temper was alleviated by the encounter with Jacopo Salviati. In particular he liked being referred to as a "master artist" by that powerful and respected man. The goldsmith referred to this compliment several times on the walk back to the *bottega*, and gave Tommaso permission to go home early.

Tommaso accepted the offer gratefully.

30

The first person to greet Tommaso back in the Salviati kitchen was young Alessa.

"It's lucky you're back earlier than expected, Tommaso. The *Duchessina* sent word she'd like to speak to you."

"Thank you," Tommaso said. "I need to wash up and change into a fresh shirt. Then I'll report to her."

Alessa put a hand on his sleeve to stop him. "The *Duchessina* has visitors this afternoon. She's holding audience with them in the garden. One of her maids said Her Grace wanted to take advantage of the fine weather to take in some fresh air. You'll need your jacket."

"Thank you again," Tommaso said, looking down at Alessa. In the last week or so she seemed to have recovered from her infatuation with Averardo and her dejection at his engagement to Laudomia. She'd returned to her natural state: that of a happy, vivacious young girl. Now that their all lives were back to normal, Tommaso forgave her. Her actions had almost precipitated disaster, but she was young and didn't know any better.

"If the *Duchessina* suggests refreshments to her visitors after her walk, I can help you serve them," Alessa said, smiling prettily.

Charmed, Tommaso was about to accept her offer when he caught sight of Averardo smirking at him from across the kitchen.

Tommaso's eyes widened. Averardo nodded in response.

"A thousand thanks. I'll let you know," Tommaso told Alessa hastily. As he headed toward the apprentices' room he gestured for Averardo to meet him.

Tommaso was scrubbing his forearms and face in the washbasin when Averardo joined him. With water dripping in chill rivulets down his arm, Tommaso turned to glare at his friend. "Tell me I mistook your look," he said.

Averardo grinned, leaned against the wall and folded his arms. "I doubt that you did," he replied. "It's clear Alessa has transferred her affections from me to you."

"No, it's nothing like that," Tommaso protested. "She's recovered from her disappointment and reverted to her usual high spirits."

Averardo shook his head. "You're wrong," he said. "You forget you arrived here to a well-developed scenario. Alessa is behaving *exactly* as she did when she first became infatuated with me. In some ways it will be worse for you. I was already smitten with love for Laudomia. In your case, you appear to have no inamorata, unless you frequent some doxy when you stay out for your artists' soirées. With no evident obstacles, Alessa will head in as straight for the kill as a falcon."

Tommaso groaned and put his head in his hands. "I suppose I should thank your for your warning...and I do. But try not to enjoy so much humor at my expense."

Averardo just laughed.

The late-afternoon sun still shone unseasonably bright in the garden, but with an illusory warmth. Tommaso, walking along the pathway skirting the garden wall, felt the true nature of the day in the winter chill cast by the high wall's shadow.

Though the Salviati garden wasn't large, it made artful use of its space with a maze of pungent-smelling juniper hedges that opened up here and there onto small alcoves suitable for trysting. The murmur of voices, both men's and women's, let Tommaso know where he'd likely find Caterina. By standing on his tiptoes and hopping a bit, he could see the tops of several gentlemen's heads near the center of the garden.

Tommaso reached the end of the pathway where it opened up. He hesitated. This was the section of the garden with the largest open space. Small, well-pruned fruit trees with a few bright leaves left on their limbs partially shaded a number of benches circling the space. A lovers' knot bed of herbs graced the very middle.

Caterina strolled close by. One of her hands rested lightly on the arm of her escort, Cosimo Ruggiero. She wore an ensemble Tommaso hadn't seen before: a high-collared silk dress with a doe gray bodice. Its collar and sleeves were cut from midnight blue velvet. The ensemble looked fashionable, but of a style far more conservative and mature than the clothing Caterina usually wore. She faced away from Tommaso at a slight angle. With her features half-turned she appeared taller, thinner, older.

The visitors she and Cosimo were conversing with were the Spanish contingent from the Vatican. Farther around the circle of benches three of Caterina's ladies-in-waiting sat playing lute, viola and flute for the Spaniard's retainers.

Tommaso drew back against the hedge. If the diplomats saw him, there was a chance they might remember him from the Vatican.

Caterina saw his movement out of the corner of her eye. She turned, smiled and gestured for him to approach. In that instant she became again the charming girl who commanded his devotion.

Tommaso tried to signal her to stop. Too late. The Spanish gentlemen saw her motion. Curious, they too turned. By the expressions on their faces, Tommaso knew they recognized him.

"Forgive the interruption, Signores," Caterina said. "This is my chef, Tommaso Arista. I asked that he be sent to me. I thought your appetites might be stimulated by this fresh air and require some refreshment. You can tell Tommaso your preferences."

The senior diplomat's eyes narrowed as he continued to gaze at Tommaso. "This is most unusual, Your Grace. I'd swear by my sword that we saw this youth's twin in the Pope's chambers this very day," he said.

"No twin at all," said Caterina, smiling graciously. "You saw Tommaso himself." She explained the circumstances of Tommaso's tutelage with Cellini.

Then she added, "Messer Cellini is one of my cousin the Pope's favorite but most difficult artisans. Therefore, it's necessary for the Pope to confer with him frequently, keeping the goad to the horse, so as to speak. And Messer Cellini, like any gentleman, requires an attendant on such occasions. Cellini chooses his from among his students."

"An interesting addendum to their education," the Spaniard said thoughtfully. "Who knows what they might hear in such august company?"

"Who knows, indeed?" Caterina agreed.

The Spaniard bowed deeply. "To my regret, Your Grace, we're unable to tarry for refreshments. We must leave forthwith. We're being fêted this night by the Procurator-Fiscal, Signor Benedetto Valenti. The Pope's associates take their hosting seriously. They appear determined to entertain us so constantly we scarcely have time to think. But I'm grateful for this time to confer with you. You've told us much of interest. May we call on you again?"

"Of course," Caterina said gravely. She extended her hand to him. He bent to kiss it.

Caterina waved for her ladies to escort the Spaniards out. Once they left, she plopped down on the bench in a most unladylike fashion and grinned up at Cosimo. "That went well, don't you think?"

"Better than anyone could have expected," Cosimo replied with grudging admiration. "Did you know Tommaso had penetrated the Vatican this day and would return here in time to make an appearance?"

Tommaso had the uneasy feeling Cosimo might not be referring to Caterina's acquiring that knowledge through the usual avenues of information, such as other spies or messengers.

"No, I just hoped," Caterina said. "His arrival validated my contentions. I believe we sowed the necessary seeds of concern in the Emperor's men." She turned to Tommaso. "Tell us everything about the Vatican."

Tommaso reported on what he'd seen and heard. "I was in a position to eavesdrop on the Spaniard's servants too," he said. "If I understood them correctly, the Spanish know Clement betrothed you to the royal house of France. They apparently broached the matter to Clement before Cellini and I arrived. Clement made light of it, claimed there were many suitors petitioning for your hand, including the Emperor's choice, the Duke of Milan." He coughed. "They said something about an analogy the Pope made—about bees' attraction to a flower—the more bees, the more honey."

Caterina appeared thoughtful rather than insulted. "That's something the Spanish could well believe about Clement—his greed; his desire to gain as much as he can from as many as he can. Such homilies on Clement's part would go a long way toward convincing them not to take the rumors of my betrothal seriously."

She looked at Cosimo. "We were correct to put them back on their guard."

Cosimo nodded.

"Tommaso, you did well in your discourse with my Uncle Jacopo," Caterina said. "At every like opportunity, don't hesitate to express and convey the impression that I've acquiesced to the French betrothal, that I'm committed to it."

Tommaso bowed briefly. "*Duchessina*, what Cosimo asked you ... *did* you by some means ascertain that I accompanied Cellini to see the Pope? By other informants, or ... ?"

Caterina looked nonplussed.

"You see," Tommaso said hastily, "each moment I feared your uncle might arrive in the papal quarters. If Signor Salviati had recognized me before those gathered there, the Pope would have instantly known me to be your agent."

"Oh, *that*." Caterina laughed. "I have no cadre of agents to rely on, Tommaso. Only my own wits. If whenever my Uncle Jacopo announces he means to call on Clement happens to fall on one of your days with Cellini, then I contrive some matter of etiquette or diplomacy on which I *must* seek his advice. How unfortunate that it invariably delays him. Of course, I ask his advice on other days and at other times as well. It wouldn't do for Uncle Jacopo to decipher that I detain him only on certain specific occasions."

Cosimo folded his arms and frowned. "A clever ruse, but what would you have done if Signor Salviati had left to attend the earlier religious observances? He wouldn't have failed to see Tommaso then."

Caterina laughed again. "My most excellent Cosimo, what good is all your learning if you lack perceptiveness? Surely you've noticed by now that Uncle Jacopo detests religious ceremony. He believes it a waste of time better spent on more useful pursuits, such as making money, practicing diplomacy or attending a good *commedia*. He *always* waits until later in the day to attend the Pope, when the courtiers gather and the intrigue thickens."

Cosimo shrugged. "If Signor Salviati wants for intrigue, he should have stayed here and watched you manipulate the Spaniards."

Caterina folded her hands demurely in her lap. "Intrigue indeed, Cosimo. You wound me. I only wished to persuade them of the truth."

"What truth?" Tommaso could no longer stand being ignorant of Caterina's and Cosimo's game.

"The truth all Rome knows. The truth the Spanish had heard of and were beginning to entertain suspicions about: that my cousin Pope Clement means to gain great advantage by marrying me off to France, specifically against the interests of Emperor Carlos. Of course, in private, Clement assures Carlos's Spanish diplomats that the marriage will never occur.

"I've been doing my best to convince the Spaniards of Clement's inconstancy. But since I'm a young, somewhat cloistered woman, they gave insufficient credence to my words.

"But now, thanks to you, Tommaso, they see I have my own agents in place in the very heart of the papal court. Before my very eyes I saw the seeds of belief planted in their hearts."

"You wish to bring the Emperor's wrath down on Rome again?" Tommaso was aghast.

Caterina's face stiffened. "Clement brought about the sack of this city four years ago for reasons that had nothing to do with me. He continues to be intemperate in his politics. That's not my fault."

Caterina's expression softened as she looked at Tommaso's stricken face. "I also truly believe, my gossip, that if this marital plot is exposed *before* it's implemented, the Emperor will be inclined toward leniency. He'll take out his wrath on Clement alone."

"Are you sure of your success here today?" Tommaso asked. "I was your only agent at the papal court, and it was only my first time."

Caterina grinned. "The Spaniards don't know that. The one brief glimpse of you today provides me with a hundred shadow informers in their minds."

Tommaso didn't know what to say. He noticed that Cosimo looked impressed.

"Ah, I see my ladies returning to escort me to supper." Caterina rose from the bench. "If you gentlemen will excuse me?"

Tommaso remembered there was something he still had to tell Caterina. "If it please Your Grace, there's one thing more I need to speak with you about," he said.

Caterina looked at him. "Yes?"

Tommaso glanced at Cosimo and flushed. "It doesn't relate to this afternoon at the Vatican. It's a private matter."

Cosimo raised a quizzical eyebrow. Caterina looked intrigued. "Then by all means. Cosimo, please tell my ladies I need to confer with my chef a few more minutes. Could you amuse them with some legerde-main?"

"Perhaps," Cosimo said. "But I'll need some accouterments. Tommaso, do you have some *soldi* on you I could borrow for the occasion?"

Tommaso fumbled at the pouch hanging from his belt. "I'm not sure. I don't usually carry money. Rome is full of cutpurses."

"So is that why you hide your money in such unusual places, that thieves would never think of?" Cosimo reached up behind Tommaso's ear and pulled forth a coin.

Caterina rolled her eyes. "I trust you know better parlor tricks than that. My ladies are not so unsophisticated."

Cosimo laughed and bowed. "I'll do my best, Your Grace." He strolled over to Caterina's ladies-in-waiting.

Caterina sat back down on the bench. "What is this about, Tommaso?"

"After that unfortunate farce concerning Averardo and Laudomia, you warned me about unconsidered involvements in my personal life. I'm doing my best, but a situation has arisen that I have little control over," Tommaso said. He told Caterina about Alessa's attraction to him.

"You say this infatuation is just beginning?" Caterina asked when he'd finished.

Tommaso nodded.

"You've done well to come to me. I have no influence over another's heart, but as your employer I can make certain you're not trapped in a compromising position again. Leave it to me. In a few days all will be resolved."

She glanced around. Cosimo must have come up with better tricks. The women clustered around him.

"Meanwhile, since Cosimo has my ladies so entranced, I *would* like to speak with you about culinary matters. Ippolito returns home in three days. And of course I wish to hold a fête to welcome him and his entourage home."

31

Early December, 1531

The Salviati mansion bustled. Servants opened and aired rooms closed off for the last few months. Bindo Ramerino ordered extra food supplies from the market. Older servants who'd remarked on the blessed peacefulness of the house when Ippolito and his companions left now welcomed the return of their cheerful high spirits.

Tommaso remarked on this to Madonna Spada.

"Of course." That good woman smiled. "Don't think such retainers inconstant, Tommaso. For those of us who've worked long years for the Salviatis, the coming and going of guests is like the coming and going of the seasons. In the countryside autumn is welcome after the heat of summer, but with the labors of the harvest it eventually becomes tiresome. Winter offers rest at last and an end to autumn's employment. Months later, one wearies of the cold and yearns for spring's rescue. And so on, through the year.

"Here in the city, the ebb and flow of visitors defines our toil's tenure. Now that we've had some respite from Cardinal Ippolito's retinue, we can rejoice in their return."

In spite of the whirlwind of festivities welcoming Ippolito, Caterina didn't forget her promise to Tommaso. Two evenings after Ippolito's return, Tommaso met Caterina in her drawing room after dinner. As always, she sat on a long-legged chair behind her desk, writing letters. She didn't stop as she greeted him.

"Your timing is excellent, Tommaso. Please draw up a seat." She stopped to glance around, then pointed. "Take *that* chair, and sit at my right hand. Wait, though." She gestured again. "First place those two other chairs directly across, facing us."

As Tommaso carried out her instructions, Caterina called over one of her ladies-in-waiting, a pretty young Florentine. "Reparata, pour Messer Arista a glass of wine. Then go to the kitchen, please. Inform *Ser* and Madonna Ramerino that I'd like to see them. I understand they return to their own home at night, so tell them I only need to speak with them briefly."

"Tommaso, when they arrive, it's only necessary for you to bear witness to what I have to say to the Ramerinos," Caterina said, then picked up her pen and resumed her correspondence.

Tommaso sipped at his glass of wine and tried not to fidget. He wasn't used to being idle at the this time of night. Back in the kitchen the apprentices still cleaned up after dinner, and preparations for the next day's breakfast were under way.

He looked around the drawing room. Most of the ladies-in-waiting weren't there. Caterina excused them to pursue more pleasant occupations when she was involved with her correspondence. Nannina sat reading on a settee, where an oil lamp on an end table shed the most light. Three other women clustered around another table, engrossed in a card game. Madonna Gondi wasn't present. She was close to full term now. Cosimo Ruggiero had prescribed as much bed rest as possible.

Tommaso glanced at Caterina. *Up* at Caterina. Her chair stood higher than his. She wore a burgundy taffeta gown with black sleeves embroidered with gold-and-saffron threads. She looked mature and capable, yet not severe.

Tommaso took another sip of wine and looked at the empty chairs facing him. They were shorter than Caterina's. And if he wasn't mistaken, shorter than his own.

"How go the preparations for the celebration? Did you find sources for everything I requested?" Caterina asked, still deep in her paperwork.

"The eel and cabbage for the pies are easy to procure at this time of year. The young squab you desire present some difficulty. Even the best breeders can't make their pigeons mate when the days grow colder and shorter," Tommaso told her.

"Then we'll alter our plans," she said. "Settle for somewhat older birds—the nestlings from the end of summer. Instead of grilling them

whole, poach and then grind them into a forcemeat, with whatever sea-
sonings you think best. Serve them in nests of steamed..."

"Spinach," Tommaso interjected, half-teasing. Caterina loved spinach.

"Of course," she said. During this entire exchange she hadn't looked
up even once from her writing. Tommaso was always amazed at the way
Caterina could perform several tasks at once. This skill resembled Cosimo Ruggiero's magic.

Reparata returned, the Ramerinos trailing behind her.

"Madonna and Maestro Ramerino, please, take a seat." Caterina
tipped one hand toward the empty chairs. With the other she gestured
to her ladies to retire. One of the doors out of the parlor led to their
own reception and common room. As Caterina straightened her letters
and put them away, her ladies retreated there but left the door open.
They were out of earshot but not out of eyesight.

Bindo Ramerino perched on the edge of his chair. He smiled at
Tommaso nervously. Madonna Ramerino was inscrutable. Tommaso had
guessed correctly about the height of the chairs. He and Caterina looked
down on the Ramerinos.

Caterina folded her hands together on the desk. "A matter has been
brought to my attention concerning which, as a responsible employer,
I'm forced to intervene, though I'm reluctant to do so.

"Messer Arista"—she nodded toward Tommaso—"is being
groomed for the position of my head chef. To that end, he has not only
spent his entire life attaining culinary skills, but has acquired more than
the mere rudiments of a classical education and has apprenticed in the
arts under some of the finest sculptors and craftsmen of our time—all
at my expense and encouragement.

"In addition, anyone who is not blind can see he is well favored in
form and face.

"But his qualities I value most, even beyond his considerable talent
in the kitchen, are his loyalty and integrity."

Tommaso thought he'd melt away into a cringing puddle of embarrassment under the weight of so many compliments.

"Such a man will someday make an exemplary husband for some
young woman."

Tommaso watched Madonna Ramerino's eyes take on a calculating
gleam.

Caterina must have seen the same thing. "I said *someday*." Her voice sharpened. "Tommaso is still too young to negotiate a marriage without his parents' consent, even if he were so inclined. Which he's informed me he's not."

Madonna Ramerino's gaze dropped.

"As his employer, I act as his guardian in the absence of his parents, to whom I must answer," Caterina said. "He's already been drawn unwittingly into one compromising situation in this house. I speak of his near entrapment as a substitute spouse in the matter of the betrothal of the servants Averardo and Laudomia.

"Recently I've been apprised that your eldest daughter Alessa has contrived an infatuation for Messer Arista."

Bindo Ramerino appeared surprised by the allegation. He turned a questioning look at his wife. His eyes widened when she refused to meet his gaze.

Caterina continued. "This in spite of the fact that he assures me he harbors nothing more than a brotherly affection for her. Have either of you marked anything in his comportment that would lead you to believe otherwise?"

"Of course not, Your Grace!" Bindo Ramerino said. Madonna Ramerino only muttered, "No."

Caterina drummed her fingers on her desk. "I cannot allow the integrity of a valued servant to be questioned a second time. If needs be, I'll bring up the matter with my Great-aunt Lucrezia."

Bindo Ramerino shook his head vigorously.

"Then I trust the two of you will make sure Tommaso's position isn't jeopardized?" Caterina's expression was stern.

"Of course not! I mean, of course!" Bindo Ramerino said again.

Tommaso sat up straight and still, but inside he shrank. Bindo sounded both terrified and furious.

Caterina's voice and mien softened. "Be firm but not harsh with your daughter, Messer Ramerino. A young girl's heart can be as fragile and precious as a fine Venetian goblet. In this case, no harm's been done. Don't make her suffer unnecessarily."

Tommaso blinked. He'd come to pity Alessa after Averardo's betrothal to Laudomia. But considering how quickly she'd recovered and made him the object of her affections instead, he wagered that her heart, far from being fragile as glass, more likely resembled the toughness of leather.

"Rest assured, Your Grace. I'll make certain my daughter brings no dishonor to Tommaso, our family, or herself," Bindo said.

"In that case, the matter is settled," Caterina replied. "You may retire with my heartfelt thanks."

Seeing the Ramerinos rise from the chairs, Caterina's ladies drifted back into the room.

Tommaso glanced at Caterina beseechingly. He didn't want to walk back to the kitchen with Alessa's parents. But Caterina had pulled out her paperwork and wasn't looking at him. He got to his feet to follow the Ramerinos.

"Where are you going, Messer Arista?" Caterina said. "We haven't finished discussing the menu for my gala."

Tommaso sat down again quickly. He began to suggest substitute dishes for some of Caterina's choices as he watched the Ramerinos leave.

Caterina shook her head when he finally finished. "I've done my part, Tommaso. You work with those people. You're going to have to speak with them eventually."

Tommaso sighed. "I know. I just wanted to wait a little while to give them a chance to sort it out. Perhaps by tomorrow morning it won't seem so embarrassing."

"Possibly. Or possibly not," said Caterina.

Reparata saw Tommaso out. "It was wise of you and Her Grace to deal with the matter so promptly," she told him. "If you could have seen the look of maternal avarice on Madonna Ramerino's face when I fetched her and her husband here! I'm certain she was conspiring with her daughter toward your entrapment." Reparata smiled. "You're far too comely a youth to be lost to marriage so soon."

Tommaso blushed. He could see why all the men-at-arms and most of Ippolito's entourage were enamored of this pretty young woman. He stammered his thanks for her compliment. This was the first time he'd ever actually spoken to her. He decided to take his courage in hand.

"May I ask you something?"

"Of course," she said.

"I know I'd never met you before you joined the *Duchessina*'s entourage, yet you look very familiar. How can that be? Do you have any idea?"

Reparata looked surprised. Then she laughed. "That's none of the questions I thought you might ask, but yes, I can answer you. You've met my younger sister, who I've been told resembles me closely. You wouldn't have known us to be related, however. Though we're devoted to each other, we're as different as night and day. She's a novice at the Murate; Sister Anna Maria. She told me about meeting you, and about your part in keeping the *Duchessina* from harm when the *Signoria* came for her."

Tommaso stared. Now that he knew, the likeness was striking. Where Sister Anna Maria's loveliness transposed itself into an ethereal serenity, Reparata's beauty, in contrast, was as sensuous and delectable as a perfectly prepared and waiting banquet.

He blushed again as he realized that Reparata was the first woman he'd been attracted to since the slave girl Filomena. Then he thought of Michelangelo and felt shame. Michelangelo had warned him that eventually he'd be drawn to women again. Guilt wrapped Tommaso's heart as hotly as if he'd betrayed his lover in deed, instead of so briefly in thought.

32

The next few days proved awkward. Tommaso and Bindo Ramerino avoided each other—neither could meet the other's eye in the kitchen. Tommaso hated the discomfort between them; Bindo was a good, honest man.

Rumors circulated throughout the household. Caterina's ladies might not have been able to hear Caterina speak to the Ramerinos, but they were good at guessing. When they talked with the maids who roomed with the scullery girls and heard of Alessa's newest infatuation, they drew their own conclusions. Wherever Tommaso happened to go in the palazzo, other servants teased him about his fatal charm.

It could have been worse. Madonna Ramerino and Alessa didn't return to the Salviati kitchen for a week. Tommaso hoped Madonna Ramerino kept the girl home to instruct her in more appropriate behavior.

The Salviati kitchen was too busy for awkward sentiments to last long. With the holiday season commencing, the Salviatis hosted extra festivities and guests. Tommaso and Bindo were working side by side again by the time Madonna Ramerino brought a chastened Alessa back to the palazzo. Alessa also wouldn't look Tommaso in the eye. She made a point of working at opposite ends of the kitchen from him.

Tommaso was relieved at first. But on those occasions when he was out in the house, away from the kitchen, delivering or picking up trays of food, he frequently crossed paths with Alessa, busy on the same sort of chore. She always acted circumspectly, so he couldn't complain. But he stayed on his guard.

Madonna Gondi gave birth to a healthy boy two weeks earlier than Cosimo's prediction. Caterina took a great interest in the infant, and spent considerable time in the Gondis' suite.

This pleased the younger of her ladies-in-waiting. It freed them for more time to play as the holiday festival season began. Tommaso knew from listening to housemaids' gossip that most of Caterina's ladies liked their *Duchessina*, but thought her entirely too studious and serious for a girl her age. It was clear they'd expected a more, rather than less, active social life when they agreed to become her attendants. So when Caterina tarried in the Gondis' suite, it freed them to abandon her for their own pursuits. Nowadays Caterina was often accompanied only by Reparata and one or two of her older ladies-in-waiting.

Lucrezia and Jacopo Salviati were also pleased by this new, domestic aspect of Caterina's. Tommaso was circling the banquet-hall table one evening, serving slices of venison, when he overheard Lucrezia saying in a soft aside to her husband, "See? We know she'll make her mark as a great court lady, but look at her. Someday she'll be a lovely mother as well."

Tommaso glanced over at Caterina. She'd insisted on holding Madonna Gondi's baby a while so its mother could eat in peace. Caterina's head bent, a curtain of gilt-colored hair veiling the baby, who lay asleep in her arms. Tommaso couldn't imagine a prettier sight.

As he finished serving the venison, he noticed that Ippolito also watched Caterina and the baby. The look on Ippolito's face wasn't that of a disinterested cousin or celibate cleric. It was the look of a man who yearned for the day when the child Caterina held in her arms was his own.

Three days before Christmas Tommaso struggled up to the Gondis' suite balancing three stacked trays. He had no hands to knock with, so he thumped his head on the door to announce his arrival. Madonna Gondi opened the door immediately.

Once inside, a slim, blond youth relieved Tommaso of part of his burden and gave the top two trays to Reparata, who put them on a nearby chest. Tommaso set the third tray on a waiting table. It was laden with a light late repast for Caterina and Madonna Gondi: warm almond milk, fried cream wheat cakes with honey, poached partridge and a dried fruit compote. Gattamelata, sitting on a cushion on a chest, jumped down and circled the table, sniffing at the aroma wafting from the tray.

"What do you think?" the blond youth asked, turning slowly around with arms outstretched. Tommaso took in the Salviati livery worn over a blousy beige shirt and surcoat, short violet breeches, jaunty floppy amethyst-colored cap, but could hardly make himself look at the somewhat baggy tan stockings.

"Will I pass undetected in the hallway? Do I make for a good servant boy?" the youth asked in Caterina's voice.

"Unnervingly so," Tommaso said. The leggings belonged to him. He'd smuggled in an extra kitchen livery the day before. Reparata had furnished the rest of the costume, probably in bits and pieces from her numerous suitors. The gathered clothing was slightly oversize, hiding Caterina's blossoming figure. The cap hid her pinned-up hair. Tommaso assumed from the shape of her chest that she'd wrapped her breasts flat.

For over a week Caterina had studied the stride and movements of various men in the house. At night, after she retired to the privacy of her bedroom, she practiced mimicking their walk.

All these elements failed to explain the manner in which Caterina had disappeared and this youth stood in her place. She looked taller, her facial features longer and utterly lacking in the little-girl plumpness and delicacy she hadn't yet grown out of.

Ever since they'd come to Rome, Tommaso knew that others saw Caterina differently than he did, not merely in terms of personality and temperament, but in her actual physical characteristics. He explained away the phenomenon by thinking to himself, The Venetian ambassador is tall and stout, so of course he perceives Caterina as short and thin. Or, The Milanese ambassador is small and thin, so naturally he thinks Caterina large. Anything to quell his uneasy suspicions that when she chose to Caterina could shift her shape.

At times he, too, glimpsed some aspect of her changing nature. But before this he'd always found a means to explain it away. A change of hairstyle, the cosmetics she'd begun to wear, new styles of clothing: Any of these factors could make a woman seem like a different person.

But now before him stood a boy. To all appearances a real boy, not Caterina.

Caterina pulled up on the leggings. "I fancy these. If I could but wear these out riding, I'd hunt all day. Do you think these too loose, Tommaso? Will they draw attention?"

Tommaso clapped a hand over his eyes. The last thing he wanted to do was ogle his *Duchessina*'s legs.

Madonna Gondi and Reparata giggled at him.

"I cannot do this," he said.

Caterina pulled his hands away from his face. "You must. With all the holiday festivities and all the extra guests in the house now, Ippolito and I have had no opportunity to speak in private since his return, and time grows short. Come, Tommaso. You've done braver things than this. And you'll do braver things in the future. All you have to do is walk down a few hallways with me. If my appearance disturbs you, fear not. I'll walk the whole way behind you."

Tommaso appealed to Madonna Gondi, who was usually so calm and correct. "Can't you dissuade her from this action?"

When Madonna Gondi laughed, Tommaso remembered that she was still a very young woman too. "This is only a small adventure, *Ser* Arista. If you're apprehended, it will be considered one of Her Grace's small pranks. No onus will be laid on you, me or Reparata, since we must acquiesce to the *Duchessina*'s wishes."

"See?" beamed Caterina. "It's all been thought out."

"What if someone comes looking for you?" Tommaso said.

"My Salviati relatives are out attending a gala hosted by the Cavalieris," Caterina said. "I intended to go but"—she coughed—"my delicate constitution suffers from this season's damp, chill vapors.

"And if someone should call for me"—she shrugged—"I'll have drowsed off watching the baby. Though both baby and I will be asleep, Madonna Gondi might allow those who seek me, if they're *very* quiet, to peek into the bedroom."

"How is that possible?" Tommaso asked. "Have you conjured up a double?"

"Yes. Of a kind." Caterina took Reparata by the hand and drew her forward. "Notice that Reparata wears a dress similar in style and color to the one I wore at supper. In the dark, draped with the new red cape

Aunt Lucrezia gave me for the holidays, and facing away from the door, no one will be able to tell us apart. And if someone should ask for Reparata, La Gondi will invent errands that I've sent her about the house on."

"Her hair is amber, not golden," Tommaso pointed out. "If any light at all shines into the bedroom, even just enough for a peek, the difference will be obvious."

"Not with these." Caterina reached into a brocade purse. She pulled out a number of slender blond braids and gave them to Tommaso. The color matched her hair exactly. "A few of these pinned to the back of Reparata's long locks will do the trick nicely."

Tommaso was begrudgingly impressed. "Ah, the false tresses some ladies use to make their hair look fuller or to add to an elaborate coiffure. Where did you find such a perfect match?"

"So you think these false tresses?" Caterina smiled. "Don't you recognize them? Did you think, though I cut my hair, that I'd part with it so easily?"

The braids felt like heavy satin in Tommaso's hand. His breath caught in his throat. "From that night in the Murate?"

Caterina nodded. "I knew I'd have use of them someday." For an instant she looked like herself again.

Tommaso gave the braids back to her and picked up one of the two remaining trays. Caterina had totally disarmed him by invoking the memory of the night Florence's *Signoria* came to kill her.

"Then let us go," he said. "The sooner we embark on this enterprise the sooner we'll return from it."

He thought of one other thing. "Madonna Gondi, what of your husband and your other children?"

"Antonio knows of the *Duchessina's* plans tonight," La Gondi said as she handed Caterina the other tray. "Another banker, Réne Birago, hired a puppet show for his own children and their friends, to be followed by a Christmas party. My children were invited and their father escorts them. They'll sleep over there."

Before Reparata could close the door, Gattamelata slipped out after Tommaso and Caterina.

Tommaso swung around to knock for Madonna Gondi to retrieve the cat.

"Let it be," Caterina said. "There's no harm if she accompanies us."

"Except that everyone knows she's your cat. She's a clue to your identity."

"Not at all. She often stalks the house at this time of the evening, knowing that scraps of food are more likely to come her way at the end of the day. She'll make our little deception all the more convincing."

"*Your* deception," Tommaso corrected her.

Tommaso felt foolish by the time they reached Cosimo's room. Earlier, he could have sworn that Alessa was trailing him to Caterina's room. But they'd hardly come upon anyone in the hallways, other than a few servants, who passed them without a second glance.

As he reached up to knock on Cosimo's door, Caterina whispered in his ear, "Say nothing to Ippolito. He doesn't know about my subterfuge this night. Cosimo told him you're stopping by with refreshments. He expects me to arrive later with La Gondi, the baby and Reparata, under the pretext of consulting with Cosimo about casting our horoscopes for the coming year."

Cosimo opened the door and bade them enter. He didn't even blink as Caterina marched past him. He waited for Gattamelata to glide in last. "I've cleaned a space on my desk for the food," he told Tommaso.

Ippolito sat in an armchair, leaning over a map on a small table before him. An oil lamp on the table reflected a warm rosy hue up onto his lean features from the scarlet Cardinal's robes he wore. He looked up, nodded at Tommaso, smiled at Gattamelata and acknowledged Caterina not at all. He returned to studying the map. Tommaso looked around the room. He saw none of Ippolito's usual companions.

Cosimo walked over to stand next to Ippolito's chair. "What was it you were saying about the northern road?" he asked Ippolito.

Ippolito half glanced over his shoulder to where Tommaso and Caterina laid out the food. "Let's wait to continue our discussion after we eat and after your other visitors arrive."

Ippolito knows me well. He's reticent in the presence of another servant who's a stranger, Tommaso realized.

"Then in the meantime, let's sup," Cosimo said. "With the Salviatis rushing off to their gala, I didn't have the appetite to dine at so early a dinner." He leaned over and rolled up the maps, then waved for Tommaso to serve them.

With the various stops he knew he'd have to make along the way, Tommaso hadn't attempted to bring any warm food. The repast consisted of cold dishes made from dinner's leftovers: stuffed eggs, fish rissoles, grilled cardoons, and cold sliced duck with boiled turnips. For after dinner and to soothe the night's chill, he brought chestnuts Cosimo could roast in the small bedroom fireplace.

As Tommaso placed the dishes before Ippolito and Cosimo, Caterina poured their goblets full from the bottle of good Tuscan wine Cosimo always kept on his desk. Then she stood behind and to one side of Ippolito's chair, ready to decant more when they emptied their goblets.

She waited until Ippolito had finished several of the stuffed eggs and a fish rissole. When he paused to wipe his hands and beard, she bent to place the bottle of wine on the floor behind her. Then she bent over and wrapped both her arms around Ippolito's neck. Her velvet cap rested against his cheek.

Ippolito's eyes flew open. He stood bolt upright, shedding Caterina. Cosimo, who'd been watching, grabbed Ippolito's plate as it started to flip over.

"What in the name of...?" Ippolito exclaimed. His face flamed as bright as his robes.

"Alas, Signor, I fear I've offended you," Caterina said. She bowed low, sweeping off the cap, which pulled out several of the pins holding up her hair. Half of it tumbled along one side of her face. She looked like Caterina again, charmingly tricked out in boy's clothing.

Like a chameleon, Ippolito's face went from scarlet to ivory to scarlet again. His mouth opened, closed, opened. Nothing came out. Finally, he whirled on Cosimo. "You knew of this?"

Cosimo put Ippolito's plate back down on the table. "She insisted. Her plan differs from yours somewhat. Among other particulars, it requires her to pose as a young male servant. It sounded like madness to me, but she's just proved me wrong. If she can fool you, Ippolito, she can fool anyone."

Ippolito looked back at Caterina, and finally smiled a small, crooked smile. "You make for a very brash, bold, fetching young man, my darling cousin. What are these plans of yours?"

"I've been hard at work in your absence," Caterina said, grinning. "I'll show you on your map." She reached to push Ippolito's plate out of the way.

Cosimo coughed and made a twirling gesture to one side of his head.

Caterina put her hand up to her own head. "Of course. How could I forget? Tommaso, I need your aid in putting my hair back up. If anyone happens by, I'm still just the assisting servant boy."

While Tommaso helped Caterina repin and stuff her hair under her cap, Ippolito cleared the table and rolled the maps out. Cosimo stood out of the way, nibbling at his plate of food.

"First, let's reprise your scheme, Ippolito. Then I'll show you how mine builds on that," Caterina said. She held down one of the map's curling edges. Ippolito placed one of Cosimo's volumes on the occult on the opposite edge, anchoring it.

Caterina pointed north and east of Italy. "In the last year you've mostly been stationed in Venice on your tours. Now Clement has announced he's sending you to the Kingdom of Hungary immediately after the new year."

Ippolito nodded. "I can make strong enough alliances in Hungary to assure our safety from Clement, once I wrest you from his control."

He tapped his finger on the Republic of Venice. "I've cultivated useful friendships in Venice. Michelangelo Buonarotti put in a good word for me with the satirist Aretino and their mutual friend Titian. The *Unico* Aretino hates Clement for trying to sheathe his swordlike pen and for banishing him. He'll do anything he can to pique Clement. He and Titian can arrange safe passage for us from the Republic to Hungary."

"When *do* you plan to claim me?" Caterina asked.

"Clement says he wants you returned to Florence prior to the wedding in France. That works to our advantage. I have more friends and far greater power in Florence than here."

"But Alessandro and his allies also reside in Florence," Caterina said softly. "They'll expect just such an attempt."

"I know," Ippolito responded. "That's always been the greatest point of contention between you and me. So I've come up with an alternate plan. We won't wait for you to be installed back in Florence."

Caterina clapped her hands. "Yes, Ippolito! That's what I've been saying all along."

"Instead I'll intercept you on the trip back to Florence," Ippolito said.

Caterina's hands stopped in mid-clap.

Ippolito was too involved in explaining the rest of his plan to notice. "The best place to ambush Clement's men is near Arezzo. Then we'll start to head due north. This is what Clement will expect, so we'll separate into two groups.

"Antonio Pecci will lead most of my men toward the city of Venice, escorting a curtained coach, which Clement's forces will assume carry the two of us. In the meantime, you and I will race on horseback with just Domenico and one or two others this way,"—his finger cut abruptly east on the map—"past Urbino, to here." His finger stopped at the coast on the town of Rimini.

"From there we'll sail for Istria." His finger swam across the Adriatic Sea to the peninsula that, though part of the Republic of Venice, was separated from the rest of Italy by the band of land that provided the Kingdom of Hungary with access to the sea.

"Before Clement can detect our whereabouts, we'll cross over the Venetian border to Hungary and the city of Trieste." Ippolito leaned back and flung out his arms. "Then I shed these cursed vestments and wed you in French Henri's stead. That should spoil all of Clement's plans for you.

"We'll rest, regroup and bask in love a while in Hungary. The people of Florence chafe under Alessandro's rule. The people of Rome detest Clement—they'll not soon forget the Sack. When the time is right we'll regain Florence together."

Caterina smiled lovingly at Ippolito's bravado, but her smile was strained. "What you propose sounds bold, but comes too late. The time for us to move is now, as you go to fulfill your commission to Hungary."

"I know almost no one of consequence in Hungary at this juncture. I can't assure our safety there yet," Ippolito protested.

"Which is why we'll catch Clement unprepared. He'd never believe us ready to act." Caterina leaned forward to place her palm over the Kingdom of Hungary, blotting it out. "You don't need to assure our safety in Hungary because we're not going there.

"Most of your men will still ride up toward the city of Venice, as if conducting you to your post in Hungary. They'll escort a carriage part of the way. The carriage will turn toward Urbino and Rimini." Her fingers traced the route to the east.

"Ippolito's cadre has the excuse of accompanying him north, to give to the watchmen at Rome's gates as they leave," Cosimo interjected.

Caterina nodded. "You, Ippolito, will of course openly depart with them," she said. "Then you and a select few will split away from the coach under the cover of darkness and circumnavigate around the outside of Rome."

"But on what pretext does the coach leave?" Cosimo persisted.

Caterina looked up at Tommaso. "With the holidays at last over, the *Duchessina* Caterina Romola de' Medici sends her trusted chef on a trip to the coast to purchase depleted culinary supplies. After my disappearance is discovered, it will be remembered that there were sufficient empty sacks and baskets in the coach under which to hide a young woman."

Ippolito waved his hands in frustration and confusion. "But if all my planning for Hungary serves as nothing more than a decoy, where *are* we going?"

Caterina's hands slid across the map in the opposite direction, to the west. "To here."

Cosimo, Ippolito and Tommaso stared at the map.

"To *Spain?*" Tommaso finally said, in a faint voice.

Caterina nodded again. "Another element Clement would never expect."

"But how?" asked Ippolito.

"The Spanish delegation leaves for home soon. With some persuasion on my part, they've decided to host a great masque on the evening before they depart—the night of the Epiphany.

"I and some members of my entourage will infiltrate their palazzo during the course of the festivities, hide amongst them, and decamp with them for Spain in the morning. They didn't wish for information on any of the particulars—it's safer for them that way. But I know they believe I'll arrive as a guest—incognito and separately from the Salviatis—then change costumes and camouflage myself as one of their maids."

"But you're not going to do that," Cosimo guessed.

"No. Both for their protection and my own I want a disguise that allows me flexibility of movement should our plans go awry. At the same time, should anyone stumble onto our escape attempt, the Spaniards would suffer if I were detected as an attendant to one of their ladies. Every lady knows those who serve her: It would prove the Spaniards' collusion in our scheme."

"Which explains the rehearsal of your disguise tonight." Ippolito leaned forward on the edge of his chair, intrigued.

Caterina nodded. "Since the Spaniards are leaving the next morning, their own cooks have too much to do in the way of packing to provide adequate refreshments for such a grand masque. Among many other suggestions for their gala, I told them of a most excellent caterer here in Rome, who attends to the wants of only the finest clientele—one Bartolommeo Scappi. I even sent a note to Scappi just yesterday. I informed him that, knowing how overstretched his resources would be for such an occasion, I'd lend him the services of my own good chef, who, coincidentally, has been studying with him."

"I thought I'm supposed to be on a coach headed for Rimini," Tommaso interrupted.

"I'd never send you away from my service, Tommaso," Caterina said. "You won't depart on that coach. We just need word spread that you *will* be on the coach, as soon as you've finished with your duties that night. At the last minute I'll instead send Reparata with a note to the coachman and an order for him to deliver to the agent in Rimini, with the excuse that your duties at the Spanish masque would delay you too long, so the coachman will have to depart without you."

"But what about *you*?" Ippolito asked her impatiently.

"A new Salviati kitchen apprentice will accompany Tommaso to the masque, loaned to Maestro Scappi courtesy of the Salviatis and the kind *Duchessina*." She jumped up and bowed. "At your service, Signore."

"This seems too risky," Cosimo mused. "The Salviatis are invited to that masque, as are you. What excuse can you make for not attending? Another case of the sniffles and coughs? And what if they see you there? Ippolito may not have recognized you immediately here in my dim room, but I wouldn't wager on Lucrezia Salviati's eyesight in a brightly lit ballroom."

"I wouldn't either," Caterina agreed. "But since I'll be attending as a new apprentice under Tommaso's guidance, he can keep me busy back in the kitchen doing menial work. I won't be considered presentable enough to go out and serve guests.

"And I can pose as a servant boy safely that night because the *Duchessina* will retire early, immediately after the Epiphany service in the family chapel. She'll wish to devote herself to private prayers for the souls of her dead parents. Everyone will of course understand that she's really melancholy because of the absence of her dear cousin Ippolito.

All mirth left her eyes. "Ippolito, it's imperative that you meet us and the Spanish delegation at the end of the day after Epiphany in Ostia. That's where I'll reveal myself to the Spaniards. Without you by my side, in their eyes I'm only a headstrong, foolish girl. *With* you as my advocate I become a *Duchessina* guarded by her Cardinal cousin, trying to spare Rome from yet more disaster at Clement's hands.

"I have copies of the betrothal and dowry documents as proof that Clement means to betray Emperor Carlos by marrying me to the royal house of France. Besides promising my own lily white hand in marriage— which might not concern Carlos that greatly—Clement vows to deliver Parma, Pisa, Livorno, Reggio and Modena up to King François."

Even Cosimo looked startled. "Clement lacks the authority to surrender those cities," he said.

Caterina nodded. "Of course. But at France's insistence, He may try. The documents are proof of His treachery to both the Italian states and Emperor Carlos. Once I deliver them to the Spanish royal court, no contracts that Clement negotiated anywhere will be honored. Not my betrothal to France"—she looked at Ippolito—"nor Alessandro as Duke of Florence."

Cosimo raised his eyebrows and ran his hands from his forehead back through his hair. "A brilliant plan, Caterina. So brilliant it may actually work."

Ippolito still looked concerned. "Brilliant, yes. But there's too much time when you'll be unprotected. Don't forget what the Spaniards are capable of. They held France's king and then his two sons hostage.

"And though Rome's populace hates Clement there are plenty of men willing to spy for Him and do His bidding. I don't know if it's wise to snatch you from the heart of His power."

Caterina drew in the sharp breath Tommaso recognized as her way of biting back an impatient retort. "Ippolito, my love, you lived only a short time with your father, gentle Giuliano, before he died. Since then our family's popes have controlled your destiny. You've been close to Clement for too long. I don't believe you possess the eyes to see Him truly anymore."

She turned toward Tommaso. "While you were away, Tommaso attended the papal court several times as Benevenuto Cellini's page. Tommaso, how does the Pope strike you?"

Tommaso thought the world of Ippolito. It pained him to see Ippolito stung by Caterina's words. But there was truth in what she said.

Tommaso cleared his throat. "His Holiness appears shrunken. Like a sad, hollow puppet. Cellini throws temper tantrums, storms off, and Clement does nothing. He has no power over even a puffed-up jeweler."

Ippolito still shook his head. "If only there were more time. Epiphany is less than two weeks away. There's still much to arrange before then."

Caterina knelt before him and took both his hands in hers. "Now is the time, my love. We may not have another chance."

33

The evening of the Epiphany, January, 1532

Caterina lit three candles in her bedroom window. Her excuse that she wished to retire to her chambers early to pray hadn't been completely spurious.

"Tonight, Wise Three, special guardians of my house, look down upon my efforts. I beseech you to guide them and reward them.

"Tonight is the night each year when you especially bless my lineage.

"Tonight, oh Little Kitchen Goddess . . ."

Gattamelata wound herself, purring, around Caterina's ankles.

"Tonight, oh Mother Aradia . . ." Caterina lifted her eyes to the rising moon.

"Tonight, oh Sacred Maiden . . ." Caterina's hands sought the red stone at her breast. It warmed at her touch.

"Tonight all the stars align to bless my destiny. Tonight the dark forces aligned against me will taste the beginning of defeat."

Caterina shut her eyes tight. She knew that at that moment, in Florence, Piera Arista wandered throughout the Ruggiero household, hiding colored pebbles here and there. She knew that in the de Medici palace kitchen a gray-haired crone sprinkled herbs over a boiling cauldron, whose steam sent a fresh, cleansing scent throughout the palazzo. In the hills above Florence a circle of women and girls chanted below the moon. Here in Rome, Pope Clement, officiating at ceremonies for the Epiphany at the Vatican, dwindled thinner and thinner, a paper-skinned shadow.

Caterina counted her allies, blessing them all: her sisters in faith in Florence; her friends among the nuns of the Murate; Isabella d'Este, who'd helped facilitate the counterfeit plans for fleeing northward; Michelangelo, Titian, the *Unico* Aretino; Reparata and a few other of her ladies-in-waiting; her Strozzi cousins; Ippolito's merry band; Tommaso; Lorenzino de' Medici; Maria Salviati and her son Cosimo; the Gondis, who, with Cosimo Ruggiero, she'd sent on holiday to Sardinia after Christmas for their safety; and secret friends both here in Rome and abroad.

She asked for blessings especially for Ippolito.

She knew full well why Clement had sent Ippolito off to Hungary before the Epiphany. On this night of the entire year, when the Wise Three's powers were at her disposal, He couldn't risk her and Ippolito pooling their resources. Even now, Ippolito was doubling back to meet her in Ostia on the morrow.

Caterina said her last prayer and blew out the candles.

A soft knock came at the door.

"Mistress?" Reparata's voice came from the other side. "Lorenzaccio de' Medici is here to see you."

"Just one moment," Caterina replied. She lifted the top of a waiting basket. Several flat cushions softened its wickered flooring. Gattamelata jumped in. Caterina fastened the latch on top. Carrying it by its straps, she went into the sitting room to greet Lorenzino.

The sallow young man bowed low. "Allow me to pay my respects on this night, so sacred to our family," he said formally.

Caterina nodded solemnly. "May there be nothing but good omens this evening, to ensure success for all our endeavors." She passed him the basket. "You know what to do with this."

He bowed and took it from her carefully.

After he left Reparata helped her change into her costume for the ball.

34

Highborn guests could be seen wearing dazzling, jeweled costumes of silk, satin and velvet through a wide set of doors that led from the kitchen to the rest of the Spaniards' rented mansion. They danced, laughed, ate and guessed at each other's identities.

Meanwhile, the kitchen resembled one of the crowded, busy lower circles of Hell. The Spanish cooks were constantly underfoot as they pushed crates of their packed supplies out back to be loaded onto wagons in the yard. Scullery maids, on their hands and knees mopping up spilled liquids and grease, yelled as chefs tripped over them. Pans clanged and banged, music only to a demon's ears. Two apprentices bumped elbows, spilling cinnamon, flour and nutmeg. A Spanish steward, hurrying by, erupted into aromatic sneezing. There were altogether too many Spanish stewards, poking their long, sharp noses into each cook's business. Tommaso shook his head—couldn't they see they were defeating their own purpose and slowing the work down?

Cooks, apprentices and scullery maids, wearing any one of at least five different heraldic devices on their liveries, quarreled over precious working space. This masque was so grand that the Spaniards had hired three separate services to cater it: Bartolommeo Scappi for the elaborate presentation pieces and two others for the rest of the fare. All of them had borrowed extra help to fill out their work forces.

Luckily Scappi, by necessity, constructed most of his presentation pieces at his own facility. He only needed to assemble them, perhaps do a little last-minute baking. The other caterers had been ensconced in the Spanish kitchen since morning. They complained when Scappi's journeymen, carrying in a massive butter sculpture of the Three Wise Men bowing in homage, tried to commandeer sufficient space to set it down. It took the intervention of the Spanish stewards and some men-at-arms to make them give way.

Tommaso found a place for Caterina in a corner. He set her to work cutting food feathers from fronds of silverbeet for an angel's wings. Reparata washed, cleaned and beat sauces to a froth with a strong arm, as if she'd worked as a scullery maid her entire life. She only surprised Tommaso when she suddenly leapt up and smashed at some grain sacks with a pot she was washing.

"What ails you?" a passing Spanish steward asked. "Are you possessed by spirits, to thrash around like that?"

" 'Twas a rat, sir," Reparata replied. "It's not right, sir, to let them chew on food meant for the guests."

Caterina tugged at Tommaso's sleeve. "Go out to where the coaches are being loaded near the stables. Someone will give you something there. Bring it back and tell the steward it's a loan from the stables for his vermin problem."

The yard beyond the kitchen's back door was as chaotic as the kitchen. Tommaso ducked around draft horses, oxen and mules being backed into wagon traces. He dodged a cask that tipped over and rolled across the cobblestones, then wended his way around crates piled so high he couldn't see in which direction the stables lay. He found it by letting the pungent odor of manure lead his nose.

Wagons and coaches were taking on freight here, too. Tommaso peered in along the line of stalls for a stableboy to question. One of the dusty, scruffy men hoisting loads onto the carts separated himself from his crew. "Cook Arista? I have what you've been sent to fetch."

Tommaso whirled around at the voice and peered into its owner's grimy face. Lorenzaccio de' Medici reached into an empty stall and pulled out a strapped basket.

"Let me guess," Lorenzaccio said with his familiar sly smile. "The kitchen suffers from rodents and the barn can provide the solution." He handed Tommaso the basket.

Which shifted in Tommaso's hands. He was momentarily startled at the familiar sensation. He knew immediately what the basket contained.

He grimaced a smile back at Lorenzaccio and trudged back past all the drayage to the kitchen. "I should have known she'd never leave without you," he spoke down to the basket. He made a face at Caterina when he handed it over to her. She grinned and let Gattamelata out.

"Aren't you worried she'll stray, or get lost, or get injured in this tumult?" Tommaso asked as he watched the cat disappear among some crates of vegetables.

"She won't stray far or long," Caterina said. "The masque will last for hours more. After that she'll suffer a long, confined journey. Let her stretch, relieve herself and hunt up something to eat in the meantime."

"She was handed to me by Lorenzaccio," Tommaso whispered in Caterina's ear.

"Yes. It would have been too conspicuous for me to bring her. This way she arrives from the Spaniards' own stables."

"But *Lorenzaccio*," Tommaso hissed.

Caterina leaned away to look at him. "I know you dislike Lorenzino, but for now, at least, he rallies to our cause. As Ippolito pointed out, at the moment I'm vulnerable. I can use men about me who are good with a sword."

Tommaso ground his teeth. He picked up a slicing blade and whetted it. He'd trust himself to protect her before he let Lorenzaccio near her.

Behind the scenes, the banquet and masque passed like every banquet Tommaso had ever labored over. He was aware of every slice of meat he cut, as if it were the perfectly placed stroke of a paintbrush; every daub of butter he molded as though he were caressing a sculpture into existence.

But another kind of consciousness eclipsed these movements. His skin listened for any sign of Clement's agents. His eyes tasted for flavors of shadowy men who might be in Clement's employ. Tommaso thought of how he'd probably never again see Bindo Ramerino, Marcus Gavius Spada or any other of the kind folk in the Salviati kitchen. When he'd left they all bid him farewell for just a few days, wished him Godspeed for his supposed trip in the coach to Rimini.

The night crawled by in an agony of slowness.

Tommaso was shocked when the last platters of *dolci* and fruit left the kitchen. The worktables lay empty of platters filled with lovely food and started to pile up with dirty dishes instead. Gattamelata walked past with a mouse hanging by its tail from her mouth. She ate it and jumped into her basket. Reparata passed Tommaso carrying a tray laden with empty bowls. She smiled at him. He tried to pretend his heart didn't melt a little at the attention she gave him.

"Only the dancing and more pageantry remains," she murmured.

Tommaso's heart began to beat with anticipation more than fear. It was going to happen. In a few hours they'd take off their liveries and mingle among the Spanish servants, climb onto the departing coaches, and be gone.

He was still afraid. He'd had mere days to accept the idea he'd soon live in a foreign country, leaving behind Michelangelo and any chance of seeing his family for years. He wondered if the Spaniards were all like the austere delegates he'd seen at the Vatican and in the Salviati gardens, or like the plethora of somber stewards with their searching keen eyes that kept ducking in and out of the kitchen.

Their searching eyes. Tommaso stopped scraping food from the platter he held. His heart clanged louder than the clamoring of the pots and pans. A flush of embarrassment flared across his cheeks. He was an idiot. How could he have not seen it? So intent had he been on detecting Clement's agents that he'd failed to notice the real purpose of these far-too-many stewards.

They were trying to ascertain who were Caterina's infiltrating retainers among this evening's influx of Italian guests, servants and cooks. And who and where Caterina might be.

That was why, at this very moment, one of the Spanish gentlemen stood in the wide doorway that led to the banquet hall and stared at Reparata. The furrow rifting between his eyebrows resembled that of a gazing hound sighting for prey. Could that maid, with her honey-colored hair, be the *Duchessina*? Was she young enough, her hair golden enough? It hadn't occurred to Tommaso that they might need to be wary of Spaniards as well as of Clement's agents.

Out of the corner of his eye Tommaso watched the Spaniard move away from the kitchen entrance and back toward the banquet hall and ballroom, to continue the search for Caterina there.

A masked guest almost bumped into the steward, then ricocheted into the kitchen. Tommaso had to smile as the lost drunken reveler flirted with and bowed to each scullery maid he crashed into. The poor sot must have had no luck with the ladies at the ball. He enjoyed no better luck here. The scullery maids rolled their eyes and shrugged him off.

Tommaso glanced at Caterina to see if she was similarly amused by the buffoon. She wasn't. She stared at the man, her whole body rigid. She started to move around the table toward Tommaso.

Tommaso looked back at the fellow. What alarmed her so?

The drunkard tripped and sprawled, caught himself by flinging his arms around Reparata. Reparata grimaced in distaste and put her own arms up to push him away. The man dropped his face to her neck and mumbled something. Reparata's head snapped upright. She turned toward Caterina, panic in her eyes.

Caterina grabbed Tommaso's sleeve. "It's Antonio Pecci. Something's wrong. Get to him before anyone else does."

Reparata was gesturing to Tommaso urgently.

"Allow me to help you, Madonna," Tommaso said as he flung down his dishrag and dodged around a page carrying in a tray stacked with dirty dishes. "Surely this fine gentleman means no offense. A breath of fresh air might bring him to his senses." Tommaso gestured imperiously to Caterina. "You, boy. You don't have much work left. Come help me escort this man outside."

Caterina scurried over. Between the three of them they managed to haul a loose-limbed Antonio Pecci out the kitchen's back door. They walked him away from the kitchen and propped him up against the wall outside. Tommaso shivered. The night was cold.

"What are you doing here?" Caterina said fiercely. Her breath came out in foggy puffs. "You're supposed to be leading most of Ippolito's cadre toward Hungary."

Antonio Pecci pushed the mask up from his face. He still lolled drunkenly, but his eyes and voice were clear.

"Ippolito sent me back to warn you, to stop you from your plan. Your Grace, forgive me—he's not coming."

Caterina's face turned more pale than ice. Her knees started to buckle. Antonio Pecci and Tommaso both reached out to catch her.

"This is not possible," she whispered. "What happened? Has Clement discovered us?"

Antonio shook his head. "No. Not to my knowledge. We headed

northward as planned. We stopped to rest when we reached the juncture where we'd part company—Ippolito heading south to meet you, myself heading north with the others as the decoy. Ippolito paced back and forth for hours, then decided.

"He fears if he follows your plan, that even if it succeeds, the two of you will become hostages in Spain. The Spanish could force you into a marriage to their benefit, to one of their own. And with their arm of the Inquisition so much stronger than Rome's, Ippolito might face life as a cardinal to the end of his days. He wants you to wait until he establishes autonomy for the two of you in Hungary.

"He sent me back to stop you from beginning this venture, but it took me too long to lie my way through the watch at Rome's gate. When I reached the Salviatis' I couldn't ask for an audience to see you: If you were already gone that would have exposed you. Thankfully, I remembered that Tommaso here was to act as your escort on this adventure. When I found him gone from the kitchen I knew I was too late. Then I had to search for a costume so I could infiltrate the gala."

They stood together in a shocked, silent tableau for a moment.

"Your Grace, we can still do this," Reparata urged. "If you flee to Spain, Ippolito will have little choice but to follow."

"Let me think," Caterina said in a daze. "I..."

"Is everything all right there?" came a loud voice behind them. A Spanish steward stood silhouetted in the well of light pouring from the kitchen doorway.

"Yes, it's fine," Tommaso called out. "This gentleman drank a little too much. He stumbled into the kitchen. We feared he might vomit so we helped him out here."

The idea of vomit gave the steward pause; then he started walking over to them.

"I can't stay here and force Ippolito's hand. Without him, my plan *is* too dangerous. The Spanish will hold me as they did King François and his sons," Caterina murmured. "Antonio, you must tell the Spaniards what happened, but draw it out in the telling. I have retainers scattered throughout this palazzo who must be warned."

Antonio Pecci pushed Caterina, Reparata and Tommaso away from him. "My pardon, Signor." He stepped forward to meet the Spaniard. "I was trying to explain to these servants that I'm not, in fact, drunk.

That was a ruse to gain access to the house. I'm Antonio Pecci. I bring urgent news to your Viceroy from the Cardinal Ippolito de' Medici and Her Grace, the *Duchessina* Caterina Romola de' Medici."

The steward tensed. He bowed curtly. "Then by all means, let me introduce you to the Viceroy forthwith." He took Antonio by the arm in a gesture only marginally courteous and walked him swiftly to and through the kitchen.

Caterina pushed Reparata and Tommaso back into the kitchen. "For a few more minutes we have to look like servants returning to our chores. I'll retrieve the basket and then we'll slip away."

But at the entrance to the banquet hall, the steward turned and looked back at them. He snapped his fingers. Two more Spaniards appeared. The steward pointed a finger to where Caterina, Tommaso and Reparata stood.

Caterina muttered an oath. "I wish the Spanish were stupid! They're coming after us."

To Tommaso's amazement, Reparata broke away. She started dodging the Spaniards around tables, sacks and cooks.

"Rep...!" Before Tommaso could finish calling out to the maid not to panic, Caterina grabbed his sleeve again, this time pinching the flesh on his arm. He gasped.

"She's drawing them away from us," Caterina muttered. "Look as amazed as everyone else is at the chase. Go back to your station, pick up the basket and return to me."

"They're distracted *now*, so it's *now* we must leave," Tommaso whispered back. "I know you love that cat but..."

Caterina pinched him harder. Tommaso bit his tongue to keep from yelping. Sharp pain and the taste of warm iron flooded his mouth.

"The proof—the copies of the dowry and the marriage contract—they're sewn into the bottom cushion of that basket," Caterina hissed.

Shaking, Tommaso went back. He retrieved the basket. His butcher knife lay on the table before him. With one hand he wrapped it in a dish towel and tucked it into his livery. He reached Caterina again just as the stewards finally trapped Reparata, who'd crawled under a table to escape them. As they dragged the maid out the front door of the kitchen, Tommaso, the basket, and Caterina slid out the back door.

In the cobbled yard behind the kitchen, the last of the loaded oxcarts lined up to begin their journey to the seaport at Ostia. It was easier for the huge, slow carts to negotiate Rome's streets at night.

The rest of the Spanish contingent would catch up with them by the end of the next day. The other mostly loaded coaches lined the edges of the compound so the muleteers and drivers could reharness their animals into the traces easily in the morning.

"Walk slowly," Caterina said under her breath. "Talk to me gaily. We're merely two apprentices going home." She raised her voice. "So, do you think Master will make good his promise of a bonus after all the extra work tonight?" she asked as they passed a muleteer taking off his animals' gear.

Tommaso couldn't think of anything to say other than a mumbled, "Yes, surely." He slung the basket over his shoulders and left it to Caterina to maintain a stream of patter until they reached the stables.

Caterina peered through the crowd of muleteers and horse drivers cleaning and hanging up their tack until she spotted Lorenzaccio. "Ho, stableboy." She pointed at him. "A word with you a moment about our lady's steed."

Lorenzaccio sauntered over. He had to know something was amiss, but he kept his insolent and lazy look. Tommaso felt a stab of envy for Lorenzaccio's composure.

"The air outside is cold. Let me fetch my cloak," he said, grabbing a bundle behind a bale of hay.

Caterina explained what had happened as they crossed back across the yard to where the oxcarts were passing through the gate.

Lorenzaccio rubbed his forehead. "What about the others who were going to leave Rome with you? What of them?"

"Most were attending as invited guests at the ball or disguised as hired help. They'll see Antonio Pecci being escorted for questioning and realize the plan has gone awry. The Spaniards won't know whom to retain. I worry only for Reparata."

They fell silent as they scuttled around the side of one of the last oxcarts, out of sight of the gatekeeper on the other side. They walked alongside the cart until it turned, then they dashed across the street to hug the shadows of the buildings there. They scuttled down the street till they came to a recessed doorway.

"I thought you were cold," Tommaso said to Lorenzaccio.

"I am. But I couldn't risk dropping this to put my cloak on," Lorenzaccio peeled back a fold of cloak to reveal a sword scabbard. He strapped the sword on and slung his cloak around his shoulders. "I trust your basket keeps you as warm, Chef Arista." He smirked.

Caterina peeked out of the doorway. "It should be safe. Only a little farther to the corner. We must stop skulking—it'll draw suspicion. Remember, if we come upon the watch, we're just tired servants kept working too late."

Lorenzaccio frowned. "Pray that the watch *doesn't* come upon us. Too many of them know and dislike me."

With plodding feet they walked down the road. They were almost at the corner when shouts rang out behind them.

"Keep walking," Caterina said through gritted teeth as Lorenzaccio glanced behind.

"It's the Spanish stewards," Lorenzaccio said. "They're waving for us to stop. There are six . . . no, seven of them."

"Wave back at them," Caterina said. "The stewards saw us wearing the Salviati livery and deduced we might be connected to the *Duchessina*."

They reached the corner. The Spaniards kept shouting. Lorenzaccio glanced back one more time. "They're starting to trot after us."

They rounded the corner. "Now run!" Caterina cried. "Our lives depend on it." They put considerable distance between themselves and the Spaniards before the stewards turned the corner behind them.

"Follow me," said Lorenzaccio. "I know these streets better than you two." At a dead run he turned sharply at the next corner, leading them away from the broad straight avenues and onto narrow, winding streets intersected by numerous alleys.

"I hope we *do* run into the watch," Tommaso panted. "We could complain we're being pursued by a pack of murderous Spaniards. That excuse would suffice to set the guard on them for revenge for the Sack." He'd gone from cold to swelter. Now as the sweat dripping down his ribs cooled he began to feel chilled again.

"Stop for a moment and listen," Caterina commanded. They heard yelling, clanging swords, pounding feet on cobblestones, from both the street to their right and to their left. "They're going to wake the whole city at that rate," she muttered.

"They've split up their group," Lorenzaccio said. "This alley doubles back up ahead and converges with the street to the left. We could run right into them."

Caterina thought for a moment, breathing hard. She held one hand to her side. "Then we'll turn back here, retrace our steps, and flee by a different side street," she decided.

No more sounds of running feet or shouts reached them. "They're listening too," Lorenzaccio guessed. "Or hiding to watch for us."

They crept down the street the way they'd come. Lorenzaccio peered around the corner. "There's no one ahead of us." They moved out, dashing from shadow to shadow.

Now Tommaso heard something else: a soft, familiar thrumming he could feel through his back. Ahead of him, Lorenzaccio came to a dead halt. "What's that?" he said, turning and staring at Tommaso. "Is that the cat? Purring?"

Tommaso nodded.

Lorenzaccio barked a short, muted laugh. "Well, I don't suppose that will give us away."

A large, round fountain graced the end of the next street they turned onto.

"Just a few droplets to sprinkle on my face," Caterina said as they neared it.

Suddenly the cat's purring stopped.

Caterina halted in mid-stride. "Back up slowly," she whispered. "Don't make a sound."

They'd retreated halfway back to the corner when four dark silhouettes loomed up from behind the fountain.

"Ambush!" Caterina shouted. "Run!"

As they crossed the bottom of the first street, the three other Spaniards turned in at its other end and pelted down to join their comrades.

"We're younger than any of them. We might be able to outrun them, but we won't get out of their sight again," Lorenzaccio gasped. "There's a church ahead. If it's open we can beg for sanctuary. Surely priests would be happy to grant it against the Emperor's men."

The Spaniards might be older, but they were fit. They gained on the three fugitives. For all her hunting and dancing, Caterina was unused to sustained running. She started to lag. Tommaso grabbed her hand and pulled her along.

They reached the base of the steep church steps. The way to God had never stretched so far away before. Lorenzaccio unsheathed his sword as he ran. "Get her to the door. I'll hold them off." His eyes shone. He looked as deranged as the night he'd attacked the statuary.

Tommaso pulled Caterina the rest of the way up, then jumped back down a step. He swung the basket off his shoulders and into her arms with one motion. "Pray that the door opens," he said as he yanked the butcher knife from his livery and free of the towel.

Caterina didn't have time to either pray or open the door before it pushed outward on its own.

A short, homely man stepped out. "By all the blessed saints, what passes here?" he said in an atrocious accent. He wore a uniform and a sword.

Tommaso's mouth dropped open. He knew the man. It was the devout little Frenchman from the Vatican.

"As you love God, please help us, Signor," Tommaso blurted. What in the devil was the fellow's name? "These Spaniards attack us. We fear for our lives. We're young, and there are only three of us against seven of them. This youth"—he pointed to Caterina—"is a cousin of His Holy Excellency, the Pope." Then Tommaso remembered that Lorenzaccio was a de' Medici too. "As is that one." He pointed to where the Spaniards were closing on Lorenzaccio. "Save us from these same men who sacked this Holy City."

The Frenchman grinned like a devil at the prospect of battling the plunderers of Rome. Short as he was, he leapt down the steps three at a time. Tommaso ran down after him as Caterina wrestled the heavy church door farther open and slid herself and the basket through it.

Lorenzaccio was staving off the Spaniard's attack by swinging his sword wildly and unpredictably. The Frenchman leapt out of the way to avoid a backward cut, then slipped forward to stand next to Lorenzaccio. "Shoulder to shoulder, in a half circle," he commanded Lorenzaccio and Tommaso. "That gives them no opening."

Sword, sword and butcher blade turned outward, they shuffled up the steps together toward the church door. A Spaniard tried to slide behind them, but the Frenchman lunged out and drove him back. The Spaniard yelped, dropped his blade and clutched at his arm. Lorenzaccio parried another attacker's thrust. Their swords tangled. The Spaniard threw his weight forward. Tommaso saw a drawn dirk in the man's other hand. Tommaso's butcher blade came down like a stone toward the man's hand. The Spaniard saw the broad blade descending and dropped the dirk just before the butcher blade embedded itself in his hand. He lost his balance and tumbled down the steps.

Caterina opened the door behind them and they plunged backward into the church one at a time; first Tommaso, then Lorenzaccio, the Frenchman last.

"We claim sanctuary," Lorenzaccio shouted as the door thudded shut and Caterina dropped the bar across the door. Lorenzaccio's cry echoed through an empty church.

Tommaso leaned over, hands on his knees, trying to catch his breath. "Where are the priests?" he panted, looking down the vacant nave.

The Frenchman shrugged. "All gone to bed. They tire, waiting for me to finish my prayers. This way."—He led them toward the altar, then diverted off to the side. "I think you'll not want to wait until morning on those fellows out there. Let them stand outside till the priests wake, if they like. I know all these churches: I know the back ways out."

He escorted them home to the Salviatis. They lingered for a while to be sure no Spaniards lay in wait there. Before taking his leave, the Frenchman bowed low. "If ever the family of the Holy Father needs aid, seek out again Tavannes." He swirled his cloak with a flourish and swaggered up the street.

Tommaso looked around, but Lorenzaccio had already slipped away into the darkness.

Caterina ducked her head as the gatekeeper let them in. They returned as chef and new apprentice.

"How was the masque?" the gatekeeper asked.

Tommaso smiled wanly. "Tiring."

"It must be a most excellent event. Only Signor Jacopo and Madonna Lucrezia have so far returned. They say they expect the dancing to continue till dawn. Who'd have expected those dull Spaniards could provide such excitement?"

Tommaso drew in a deep, shaky breath. "Who indeed?"

He escorted Caterina to her suite. With the terror of the chase worn off she looked exhausted and numb. Tommaso's heart broke for her. Then it flared with anger at Ippolito. If Ippolito could have seen what she'd just endured . . .

"You'll be safe in your rooms until your ladies return from the masque?" he asked her.

She nodded and set her key in the latch—the key she thought she'd never use again. She leaned her head against the door.

"Tommaso, before you go, there's something I must tell you. I never intended that we return here, so there was no point in divulging this: After you piled the empty sacks and baskets in the coach for Rimini, I sent Reparata back out with the note for the coachman and a few other things. While Reparata spoke with the man and gave him the note, she saw someone slip into the coach."

Tommaso waved his hand wearily. What did this matter to him?

Caterina turned toward him and bit her lip. "It was Alessa Ramerino."

Tommaso stood stock still. His tired mind turned like a slow wheel. "What were those other things you sent Reparata out to the coach with?"

Caterina's head hung so low he could see the back of her neck. "A jug of water. Some biscuits. And a new red cape very like the one Aunt Lucrezia gave me, for keeping warm."

"And for letting anyone who might glimpse into the coach while it was on its way think that they saw a young, golden-haired—or red-gold-haired—maiden, wearing a distinctive red cape," Tommaso finished for her.

Caterina looked up at him. "I didn't cause or encourage Alessa's obsession with you. I just took advantage of it. No one told her to hide in that coach to entrap you, but I guessed that she might.

"Do you think she ever cared or considered whether you might love someone else? Did she care about Laudomia, or even Averardo, whom she professed to love? Alessa will come to no harm. Other than that, she'll do no more than reap what she's sowed."

35

The worst repercussions to the misadventures of the night of the masque fell on Alessa. Her frantic parents spent two days searching for her. Tommaso was in agony for them, but could say nothing about her whereabouts.

A terrified, tearful Alessa wasn't discovered until the coachman stopped at the agent's in Rimini. When the coachman returned both her and the fish he'd picked up to Rome, Bindo Ramerino packed her off to a convent.

Caterina had been correct in her assessment, but Tommaso was nevertheless racked with guilt.

"Surely *Ser* Ramerino doesn't expect a girl like Alessa to accept a nun's life?" a horrified Tommaso asked Madonna Spada.

"No, I don't think so," that good woman replied. "But perhaps a few years of seclusion, without men, will temper her spirit. Or at least her judgment." Madonna Spada patted Tommaso's shoulder. "You're too kindhearted, Tommaso. Don't forget that she meant to compromise you. Don't plague yourself with guilt."

Reparata returned to the mansion near dawn after the night of the masque, as gay as ever. Antonio Pecci had rescued her.

"Of course I told the Spanish everything," she told Tommaso and Caterina with relish, winking. "I couldn't deny I was one of your retinue, Your Grace. And since we all knew the same thing—the Spaniards, *Ser* Pecci and I—that you meant to escape, taking many of us with you . . .

well, I explained to them that I simply panicked when Antonio told us that the *Duchessina* and Ippolito had abandoned the scheme.

"Much later, a pack of the Viceroy's men returned from chasing three youths they'd wanted to detain for questioning. I said that yes, the three of you were servants of the *Duchessina*. You'd undoubtedly fled in fear when you saw them chase and ill use me so. Antonio vouched for me and declared I was an innocent. He refused to leave the premises without me."

"What *about* Signor Pecci?" Tommaso asked. "Everyone at the masque saw him. Yet it was widely known he was meant to accompany Cardinal de' Medici to Hungary. Didn't he risk rousing Clement's suspicions?"

"The Spaniards were concerned about that too," admitted Reparata. "After our long session with them, Signor Pecci went out among the other guests to make merry. He answered all inquiries gaily, saying that since Cardinal Ippolito had left so early for Hungary, he'd asked for and received permission to return to Rome to finish out the social season. Then he spent several hours dancing before smuggling me back here just before the younger Salviatis returned." Reparata giggled. "Now the gate-keeper believes we're lovers. He entirely approves."

From the way Reparata spoke of Antonio, Tommaso believed that was a state of affairs of which she, too, would approve.

Glad as Caterina was that Reparata had returned safely, it did little to assuage her feelings of abandonment. Few people in the household knew she'd left the palazzo that night. Almost everyone believed she'd retired early and melancholy the night of the masque, wakened sad the next day and even sadder each subsequent morning.

Antonio Pecci called on her several times. In private he pleaded Ippolito's love and devotion. His visits failed to cheer Caterina. Whenever he left she retired to her bedroom and sobbed for hours.

She ceased to come down to the banquet hall. Tommaso excused himself from his lessons with Cellini and Maestro Scappi to tend to her. He devoted his days to concocting dishes that would have tempted a dead man's appetite: *cibreo, arrosto morto*, pheasant terrine, delicate ices flavored with hazelnut syrup and honey. He delivered the food to her room himself and stayed until she ate.

A letter arrived from Ippolito. Caterina refused it. She handed it to Antonio Pecci unopened when Antonio next visited her. Antonio might have been unflappable before the Spaniards, but this alarmed him. He must have written immediately to Ippolito. Letters began arriving daily from Hungary. Caterina handed over each one to Antonio, its seal unbroken.

So the situation remained until Cosimo Ruggiero and the Gondis returned from vacation. Caterina cloistered herself with Madonna Gondi for the better part of a day. Much weeping was heard from behind closed doors. Caterina emerged looking pale but determined. She demanded a consultation with Cosimo Ruggiero. Afterward she didn't appear as disconsolate.

"In fact," Antonio Pecci told Tommaso one afternoon as they took a brisk walk together in the now winter-barren gardens, "she at last looks angry. I never thought I'd find pleasure in facing a furious young woman . . ." He shrugged. "At least that fury is directed at Ippolito, not me."

"Antonio, tell me truly. Do you think Ippolito was correct in deciding not to flee to Spain?" Tommaso asked.

Antonio Pecci knitted his brows. "When it comes to his other pursuits, Ippolito often acts recklessly. Too recklessly for my taste. When it comes to the *Duchessina*, I believes he errs to the other extreme. He knows Caterina is as courageous as he. But instead of joining forces, adding his courage to hers, he tries to maintain a balance with too much caution."

"Look at their lives," Tommaso said sadly. "They'll never be together if no risk is taken."

Antonio Pecci nodded soberly. Then he grinned. "Perhaps Caterina will goad him to that risk. When I left her today, she was preparing to write him at last, detailing all her grievances with him. I leave soon to join him. I expect, when I arrive, to find him nursing blistered eyes from the reading of it."

Whatever Caterina wrote, and whatever contrite reply she received from Ippolito, it seemed to make amends between them. She resumed her lessons and social responsibilities, much to Lucrezia and Jacopo Salviati's relief. They were so pleased they even consented to let her take instruction in perfumery, something she'd desired to do since arriving in Rome. This lifted her spirits but displeased Tommaso. He hated serving food in her suite when the strong attar of alcohol, roses and musk inundated the subtle aromas of his cooking.

But though Caterina seemed to rally, Tommaso noticed she wrote fewer letters to her many correspondents, sent him out on culinary reconnaissance less. He relied on his one great secret sin to tell him the lay of her heart: For as long as she'd sent him to spy on others, he'd also spied on her. She trusted his presence, leaving letters out when he was about, instead of locking them away as she usually did. In those glimpses of correspondence he learned of concerns she didn't think to share with him.

From Isabella d'Este, who'd once written long, cheerful missives devoted to the circumstances a wellborn lady must deal with in traveling, now came pensive advice on marriage and motherhood. Isabella wrote:

> "You ask about the affection one tenders one's children. I regret not a whit the love I've squandered on my sons, especially my splendid Federico. But I'm sorry I didn't care for my daughters more."

On the subject of marriage:

> "Almost every man with time and wealth enough takes on a mistress. In spite of this occurring more commonly than the sun shines in summer, I know of not a single wife who loves her husband who lives content with this circumstance."

Tommaso's heart sank. Ippolito, wed to Caterina, would have been one of those few men not in need of a mistress. Isabella was trying to prepare Caterina for marriage to another.

In February Tommaso received a letter from his father. Piera had given birth to a new son. "I'm naming him Ambrogio," Gentile wrote, "after my uncle who raised me like a son."

Tommaso knew all about this from old Galleoto Arista's family history. It reminded him of Gentile's base birth and only served to depress him more.

The place in the Ruggiero household that would have been mine will be inherited by this child, he thought. I've been as displaced of home and homeland as Caterina.

Tommaso found solace only in his return to Michelangelo's arms, and in the fact that Caterina sent Lorenzaccio de' Medici away from Rome, to Florence.

*   *   *

Flanked by Reparata and Madonna Gondi, Caterina faced Cosimo Ruggiero. A speculum covered most of the table between them.

"Is the only future left to me that of a pawn?" she asked stiffly.

Cosimo shook his head. "The queen has the greatest potential for movement of any piece on the board. But she must move like a queen. She can't move like a knight, for example.

"You know many of your opponent's pieces. Your weakness is that you don't know where they are or how they intend to move."

"Then how can I know what strategy to play?" she asked.

Faint lines began to cohere into a grid on the speculum's surface.

"By observing how your opponent tries to capture or maneuver other pieces on the board." Cosimo tapped a shape emerging in the speculum. "We know Benevenuto Cellini was born to play a pawn who acts as mimic to a far greater piece, the rook that is Michelangelo Buonarotti." Cosimo next patted a horse-headed figure. "We know Tommaso Arista is a knight." As the chess set materialized in the speculum, Cosimo gave each piece a name and attribute.

"Watch over all of these for any indication that your opponent is manipulating them or attempting to take them out of play."

Caterina looked at Cosimo. "You still insist you cannot help me in this endeavor."

"Not entirely, no." Cosimo spread his hands, indicating the board. "I'm forbidden to offer advice. However, as I am doing now, I can inform you. Above all, that's how your fate and mine are inextricably entwined."

"But if I yield to your father's prophecy for me . . ." Caterina let the bitter words hang in the air between them.

Cosimo drew back at the acid in her voice. "You almost succeeded in your attempt to change that prophecy," he said softly. "No would have been happier than I if you'd been successful. It failed not because the stars aligned against you or because of your opponent's efforts."

Cosimo hated the way his words brought tears to Caterina's eyes. Her plan had failed for only one reason: Ippolito's misguided caution.

"I can't predict that you won't succeed in the future. Once you pass that particular juncture, I'll be free to help you, and perceive the rest of your future clearly."

36

March, 1532

One day, while Tommaso worked in Cellini's shop, a priest came to visit. Tommaso had never seen the man before, but Cellini appeared well acquainted with him. The goldsmith hurried over to greet him, according the cleric great respect, almost fawning over him. Cellini's partner Felice, however, turned pale and excused himself from the shop to go run an errand.

"Who is he?" Tommaso asked Paulino.

Paulino glanced over his shoulder at the cleric and grimaced. "Some priest. Supposedly quite versed in Greek and Latin letters. Master Cellini thinks him a genius."

Tommaso raised his eyebrows. It was rare that Cellini thought of anyone besides himself as genius. "You don't seem as impressed," he said to Paulino.

Paulino glanced again to where Cellini was showing the priest a number of the *bottega's* current projects.

"His reputation isn't based on his talents as a cleric so much as his talents as a necromancer. Felice is out of his mind with worry that Master Cellini would associate with such a man." Paulino shrugged. "But we all know how the master is convinced that he possesses untapped mystical powers. It's not surprising he's drawn to this priest."

Tommaso nodded. He remembered too well Cellini talking loudly about witchcraft on the day he'd first accompanied the goldsmith to the Vatican.

Even now, Cellini was leading the conversation with the cleric around to supernatural matters.

"There's a lady I love to distraction who's been spirited away from me. Would you possess the arcane means to divinate when next our stars will cross again?" Cellini asked the mage.

The priest appeared nervous. He looked about furtively, to see if the apprentices were listening. "I can't speak of such matters casually," he said. "My arts are complicated, and with good reason veiled in mystery."

"But throughout my whole life I've had the most intense desire to see or learn something of your craft," Cellini protested.

The priest-necromancer frowned. "A stout soul and steadfast must the man have who sets himself to such an enterprise."

Cellini drew himself up. "Of strength and steadfastness of soul I have enough and more to spare, if I could only find the opportunity to make use of it."

The priest looked solemn. "Then if you have the heart to dare it, I'll amply satisfy your curiosity," he said. "But let us not discuss such matters in a public place."

Cellini appeared amused that the man was suspicious of his apprentices, but he acquiesced. They retired to Cellini's private quarters.

After the priest left, Cellini boasted to the entire *bottega* that they'd agreed on a time and place to meet to conjure up spirits for Cellini to question. "Who among you is brave enough to accompany me?" he challenged the apprentices.

No one came forward

Cellini shook his head. "You are all young. Your blood should crave adventure and danger. What about you, *Ser* Arista?" he asked Tommaso. "Aren't you in the least curious to dabble in your ancestral legacy? Surely you don't fear such things?"

Tommaso shook his head. "I'm not afraid of any demon romantic or indulgent enough to guide you to your Angelica. I fear more powers on *this* side of reality's vale: I fear investigation, torture and imprisonment by the Inquisition."

"But if we're discovered, the Church will grant an exemption," Cellini argued. "Our guide and mentor is a priest."

With a laugh, Tommaso still declined. "I've learned my lesson about meddling in the love affairs of others. As for the rest, I'm not curious."

Later, though, he asked Paulino if he thought the priest-necromancer could actually help Cellini in his quest.

"Of course," Paulino said, surprising Tommaso. "In fact, I'll wager you ten *soldi* that the sorcerer succeeds. But not because of any occult powers. Those he may or may not possess."

"Then why?" Tommaso asked.

"Because Angelica and her mother Beatrice are Sicilians. They fled from here to Sicily. Our fine priest who just left is also Sicilian, and just returned from that island. He met Master Cellini through an astounding series of coincidences—*too* astounding to be believed. What I'd guess is that he saw Angelica and her family in Sicily and knows full well the whens and wheres of their future plans. He'll put on a spectacular show of thaumaturgical marvels, and in the end 'miraculously' elicit the information our master seeks from some foul-countenanced demon."

A week later Cellini regaled the *bottega* with an account of his adventure with the necromancer. Despite Paulino's prediction, Cellini was no wiser as to the whereabouts of his inamorata.

The goldsmith had persuaded a friend of his, Vicenzio Romoli, to accompany him to a site chosen by the priest. The priest, in his turn, brought with him another practitioner of the black arts. The priest required Cellini to bring certain materials for the ceremony: semiprecious stones, costly perfumes, fetid-smelling drugs and herbs and some means for making a fire.

After he had recited many incantations for over an hour, hordes of devils at last appeared. The necromancer instructed Cellini to ask them whatever he wished, but the devils declined to reply.

He might not have gained what he wished, but the experience was convincing enough that Cellini wished to attempt it again.

Tommaso knew the tale would amuse Cosimo Ruggiero. Upon returning from the *bottega*, he visited the young astrologer in his room. To his surprise, Cosimo received the news gravely.

"Cellini means to conjure with that man again?" Cosimo asked, fiddling aimlessly with one of his obscure, enigmatic tools—a device made of four flat sticks of wood fastened together with screws to form the flexible outline of a square.

"Yes. This priest-necromancer says he must ascertain what the first ceremony lacked, the reason why the demons wouldn't speak. While he undertakes some scholarship in the matter, Cellini assembles more expensive perfumes, more gems, more drugs and herbs."

"And you say he asked you to join him on this expedition?"

"Yes. Of course I refused."

Cosimo flicked a fingernail against the framework device. He stared past Tommaso as if at horizonless vistas.

"When it appears Benevenuto means to conjure again, find a way to attend with him," Cosimo said at last in a reflective voice.

Tommaso was aghast. That was the last thing he wanted to do. He straightened his spine. "Maestro Ruggiero, all my life I served in your family's house. You were both my master and friend during that time. But now I serve Caterina. I do only her bidding." The words felt like chips of ice tumbling over his tongue.

Cosimo woke from his reverie with a start. He finally really looked at Tommaso. "Of course," he smiled. "You're right. Your duty lies with Caterina. Forgive me, Tommaso, what was I thinking?"

Tommaso left Cosimo's room relieved

His relief didn't last long. The next day, as he served light refreshments to Caterina's ladies after a perfumery lesson, she called him to her side. On a small table by the settee was a small, carved rock crystal *cassone*. She opened it and took something out of it.

"Tommaso, I understand that Benevenuto Cellini has embarked on a new project that requires some trifling gems. Please give him this small token from me to aid him in his enterprise." She opened her hand. In it lay a moonstone. Its milky glow shadowed pearled light against her palm.

She fished around in the *cassone* and drew out a little leather pouch. She slipped the gem into the pouch. "Tell Cellini it's a *Duchessina*'s whim to aid the course of true love." She looked Tommaso directly in the eye and held his gaze. "Tell him also that I'll aid him in any way I can: that my resources, including the help of those who serve me, are at his disposal."

Tommaso started to give voice to an inarticulate sound of protest.

Caterina cut him off. "All those who serve me, except, of course, those who will be away from Rome accompanying me on the hunting trip I'll soon be taking with my uncle."

Tommaso closed his mouth abruptly. Since she'd almost been gored by the boar while he stood by helplessly, nothing could induce him to attend another hunt. Not even the alternative of accompanying Cellini on one of the goldsmith's rash adventures. Tommaso sighed.

"Good. Besides the gem, I'll write Cellini a few lines specifying my support. If he should ask for aid at night, whoever helps him will be excused from duties the next day. This whole household knows, thanks to the tale borne by your apprentice friends, of the labor he exacts from those who assist him in love's quest." Caterina finished the note with a flourish. "I know this doesn't please you, Tommaso. But you did well to speak to Cosimo about Cellini's difficulties."

Cellini received the moonstone and read the note with delight. Tommaso knew the goldsmith assumed that Tommaso regretted not joining in the first expedition and had articulated this to Caterina.

"According to Her Grace, I can make a claim on your time, *Ser* Arista. In three nights hence, meet me here after your dinner duties."

Tommaso tried not to look glum. Caterina was due to leave for the country on the morning of Cellini's adventure: March 21. He knew he wouldn't be able to talk her out of her determination to send him along with the goldsmith by then.

Cellini misread his expression. "Fear not, you won't lack for company on this endeavor. Vicenzio Romoli agreed to participate again. My friend Agnolino Gaddi and young Guarnieri here"—Cellini clapped the youngest apprentice on his shoulder—"will also join us."

Guarnieri smiled uneasily.

Tommaso walked up to Cellini. He thrust his face within inches of the goldsmith's. "Attend my words well," he said. "Because my mistress bids me to, I'll go with you. But if you or any of your comrades ever mention my participation, you'll live to regret it. You declare you believe my mother's family to be witches. Would you risk running afoul of them? And you enjoy friends in high places who'd turn their backs on you if you foul my reputation."

Even Cellini had to realize he'd misread Tommaso's sentiments. He held up his hands in protest. "A reasonable request. One I can honor."

Tommaso knew it wasn't the warning about his family's occult powers that won the goldsmith's acquiescence, but instead the veiled threat that Michelangelo could be convinced to forsake Cellini.

Later he drew Paulino and Cencio aside.

"Why does Cellini want to take Guarnieri?" he asked them. "He's just a child. Surely one of the other apprentices would be more appropriate. Didn't anyone step forward to spare the boy?"

Paulino shuffled his feet and looked embarrassed. Cencio, however, was forthright. "No one wanted to go the first time, and no one changed their minds for this second excursion. But it wouldn't have made a difference. All of us have endeavored to eavesdrop as much as we can on what passes between Master and the priest-magician. We heard the magician tell Master that what they lacked the first time was a young, *virginal* assistant. Guarnieri is only twelve and looks even younger. I'm sure he's the only one of us that Master is certain meets all the qualifications."

Three nights later, Tommaso returned to Cellini's *bottega*. While they waited the arrival of Vicenzio Romoli and Agnolino Gaddi, Cellini loaded two satchels with the supplies the necromancer had requested.

They heard a tentative knock on the door. Cellini peered out. Romoli and Gaddi stood outside, shrouded in dark cloaks and large, flopping caps that hid half their faces, even from the light of the lanterns they carried. Cellini handed a satchel apiece to Tommaso and Guarnieri. Then they made their silent way through Rome's streets.

There was no moon. It had set early. Tommaso'd seen its slender sliver ghosting through the sky at noon. The air they breathed seemed thin, as if it, too, had retired early. Leaving the Bianchi, where Cellini had his studio, they passed through built-up sections of the city. Then the buildings grew less crowded, interspersed with the ruins of older structures. Finally they clambered over rubble and around forlorn, roofless columns, half-buried in brambles. Tommaso saw an occasional glint of campfires in the wasteland. He wondered who huddled around them. Homeless beggars? Drunken revelers? Thieves and murderers? He shivered.

At last they reached a huge, long, curving structure. Although it was disintegrating along with everything else in the vicinity, enough of it stood intact that, giant high, it towered over them.

"Our destination," Cellini whispered. "We conjure fate within the Coliseum itself. Where gladiators once fought for their lives, I will fight for my beloved Angelica."

*   *   *

At almost the same moment, Caterina crept away from the hunting lodge. After the long, exhausting journey, she found it easy talking her two ladies-in-waiting into retiring early. A pleasant, spicy infusion slipped into their after-dinner libation assured them of agreeable dreams and deep sleep. She slid past them and out the door to her suite. Like Tommaso, she carried a satchel. Hers was small and light. The two instruments she needed most posed no burden. One rested in a silver medallion on her breast. The other stalked beside her.

With no moon abroad, she walked under the guidance of Tana, the spirit of the stars.

Cosimo Ruggiero might have doubts about Cellini's necromancer. She did not. True, he was almost certainly a swindler of some sort. But that he'd chosen to stage the second act of his confidence game on the night of *Equinozio della Primavera*—the ascent of the Goddess—a fact unnecessary for the mere deception of Cellini—told her that he possessed more talent than Cosimo, or Tommaso's friend Paulino, gave him credit for.

Mountebank or true sorcerer, she'd soon know the truth of it. Ginevra and Gattamelata were prepared to fly this night to Rome.

Cellini led his little band to an arched opening in the Coliseum. Tommaso couldn't tell if it was a door or, with the foundation half-buried in silt, a window in one of the lower floors. They wound around catacombed corridors until they reached another arched opening. They stepped through, and stood in the bottom of a great bowl, its sides stubbled with row upon row of staggered worn stone seating.

The priest-necromancer was arranging piles of wood. He'd already set one fire out in the middle, where in ancient days lions dined on Christians.

"Where's your associate?" Cellini asked, looking around as they drew near the magician.

"We don't need him," the necromancer said. "When I meditated on the limited success of our last venture, I determined that one of the problems was that *you*, Benevenuto, should have performed the tasks I set for my colleague, since the questions whose answers we seek are yours."

"How can I discharge those tasks?" Cellini asked. "I possess many skills: as an artist, a marksman, a swordsman, even as a musician. But I know nothing of your craft. That is what I hoped to learn from you."

"Tonight is the beginning of that process," the magician reassured him. "As you yourself pointed out to me, you were born with a latent affinity for the occult. On our last adventure, I had ample opportunity to observe your emanations, the way the apparitions I invoked were drawn to you. Our quest will enjoy greater success with your raw aptitude than with all my colleague's hard-won learning."

Even under the flickering light of the oil lamps Agnolino Gaddi and Vicenzio Romoli held, Cellini's pleasure at the sorcerer's words were evident.

If this errant priest can charm spirits but a tenth as well as he charms Cellini, then he isn't the sham Paulino thinks him to be, Tommaso thought. I wonder what's the real reason his fellow necromancer chose not to join us tonight?

The priest donned robes of scarlet, azure and violet, festooned with cabalistic symbols embroidered in gold thread. He gave Cellini's two friends several censers and instructed them as to which herbs he wished to have burning in each. To Cellini he handed a pentacle.

"You saw what I bid my assistant sorcerer do with this the last time. Tonight will not be the same. Await my instructions."

He directed Tommaso to the piles of wood and set him to laying five small fires around what would be the perimeter of the ceremony. He also ordered him to keep the large fire in the middle alive.

The necromancer settled himself to begin the ceremony.

"What about me?" Guarnieri asked. "What shall I do?"

The necromancer patted him on the head. "Fear not. You have a most important part to play, in a little while."

Guarnieri, already uneasy, looked more nervous at these words. When the magician drew forth a long, curved ceremonial knife, the boy's eyes flooded with fear.

The priest started chanting and singing. He drew mystical symbols in the air with the knife. Tommaso recognized fragments of Greek and Latin, and another language he assumed was Hebrew. Holding the dagger before him, the priest shuffled forward, scuffing circles in the dust as he dragged his feet. Now and then he stooped to place one of the gems just outside the outline of the five circles he was forming around the smaller fires. Agnolino and Vicenzio followed exactly behind him, swinging their censers.

Then the necromancer ascribed a larger central circle around the biggest, central fire. He bid everyone gather their supplies. Then he led each by the hand, one at a time, within the circle.

"No matter what comes to pass, do not leave this circle," he warned them. "It is our fortress. It protects us. If any of you depart before the bells for matins sound, your lives are forfeit to whatever demons come this night."

He set out packages of the herbs and perfumes. Then he commenced, with many complicated and theatrical gestures, his invocations. Occasionally he sprinkled herbs on the flames. They smoldered and billowed in oily, rancid-smelling clouds of smoke.

Tommaso's eyelids felt rimmed with scalded grit. He could scarcely breathe. Nearby he heard Vicenzio Romoli cough and Guarnieri whimper, but he could scarcely see them through the smudgy air and his watering eyes.

Tommaso recognized some of the scents, though he'd never smelled them in a burning state before: wormwood, mugwort, vervain, mandragora, aconite, cinquefoil. His mother kept these on a high shelf in the Ruggiero kitchen, away from children's hands and not to be mixed with the cooking herbs and spices. He'd only seen her bring them down to treat illnesses. A few of the smells—the worst ones—he'd smelled in faint whiffs when he sometimes passed Ruggiero the Old's *studiolo.* But nothing had smelled so ghastly as the sulphurous stench he now endured.

When he thought he could bear it no longer, a sudden flash of light and a new scent—too strong and too sweet—burned away the rime of smoke from inside his nostrils. The necromancer had thrown perfume onto the fire.

So it went for more than an hour. The necromancer threw herbs on the flames, then followed that with precious perfumes. Occasionally he ordered Tommaso to add more wood to the central fire.

Tommaso tried peering out into the darkness. The five smaller fires, without his attendance, burned down to glowing beds of coals. Only a few flames licked upward now and then, like thin, flickering, orange tongues. They barely lit the sable shadows beyond. Tommaso looked upward at the Coliseum's row upon row of seats. They seemed farther away than at the beginning of the ceremony.

One of the peripheral fires threw up a spray of sparks, illuminating the upper reaches of the stadium. Tommaso blinked. The tiered seats suddenly rushed downward, threatening to topple in on him. He threw up a futile arm to protect himself.

A dense cloud of fumigating herbs drifted past, blinding him. When it cleared, the seats were rushing away again. Tommaso felt dizzy. He sat down on the ground with a thump.

"Now, Benevenuto. Have the virgin child stand before you," the necromancer commanded. Cellini drew an unsteady Guarnieri in front of him.

"Hold the pentacle directly over his head." The necromancer instructed Cellini to turn the point of the pentacle in five different directions, toward the outlying fires, keeping Guarnieri beneath the star the entire time.

"Join us, join us, oh Belphegor, Belial and Balaan," the necromancer droned. "Join us, Focolor, Forneus and Fistolo. Join us, Razanil, Rintrah and Ronove. I call you by name, all you demon captains of Hell's legions. I summon you by the virtue and potency of the Lord, the Uncreated, the Living, the Eternal!"

Shadows bulged outward from recesses in the Coliseum's windows and doors, from between the seats. Some separated and oozed toward the fire. Amorphous globs took shape. Tommaso saw here a horned head, there a goatlike form. Sweat stung on his forehead and into his already irritated eyes, trickled under his arms. The shapes drew closer. They stayed as flat and black as ink spots. An ethereal glow lit them from behind.

"They come, they come," the necromancer whispered his chant.

Suddenly the five small dying fires erupted, throwing up shards of color and stuttering light: flashing solferino, madder, amber, emerald, jade, magenta, peacock blue.

"Just as before," Cellini breathed.

Small explosions went off outside the perimeters of the circles, like slowly igniting strings of firecrackers.

"*Not* like before," Cellini said. "What does it mean?"

"That we shall be successful this night," the necromancer said. "The effluvium from the astral plane consumes the gems we laid down as it forges a connection between the demons' realm and our own. Tonight we shall hear them speak.

"Heap more wood on the fire," he told Tommaso. "And you two, pour more perfume on the flames when I tell you to," he said to Vicenzio Romoli and Agnolino Gaddi. Then he instructed Cellini to turn the pentacle again over Guarnieri's head while he sprinkled herbs over the fire.

Incomprehensible sounds growled out of the darkness.

"Ask your questions, Benevenuto!" the necromancer cried.

The goldsmith took a deep breath. "I demand to be reunited with my beloved Angelica!" he shouted. "Tell me when I shall see her again!"

The garbled snarling grew louder as the demons drew closer. Glints of firelight played over their bodies, revealing burnished, deep red skin. Now Tommaso could make out their features.

What a wonder, he marveled. They look just like the demons portrayed at masques and festivals, except that these are real. He would never doubt again the priests of the Holy Mother Church. Truly they must be able to see both Heaven and the Nether World, to describe the legions of Hell to us so accurately.

He glanced at his companions. Were they as dumbfounded as he?

They weren't looking at the devils. All of them, even the necromancer, were staring with open mouths at the pentacle Cellini held, and beneath it, young Guarnieri. Light poured in a star-shaped column from the pentacle down onto the boy's head. Guarnieri clenched his mouth, eyes, and hands tightly.

"What do you see, boy? Speak to us," the necromancer's voice shook.

Guarnieri's mouth opened first. Light, as well as words, poured out of it. "I'm afraid," he said. Each syllable glowed.

His eyelids rose. From his eyes, too, light streamed forth.

"This is most unusual," the necromancer said weakly. "Can you see?" he asked Guarnieri.

"They approach. They are watching. We're in danger," Guarnieri sobbed.

Tommaso whirled around. More dark shapes oozed from the far reaches of the Coliseum, flowing like water. When they reached the edges of the light they broke apart into droplets and pattered upward; black rain falling upside down. The wet flecks melded, rounding into objects, as though clear glass pitchers had been standing there waiting to be filled with ink. The "pitchers" stretched, contorted, became creatures Tommaso recognized.

The raven-headed men formed first—perching, birdlike, wherever a good view could be had.

Other shapes bulged and twisted, grotesquely clownish, settling at last as the beasts Tommaso had once thought resembled *buffoni*.

More forms stretched upward, became angular. Some of their sharp surfaces silvered and turned pale: black, white, black, white, up their laddered skeletons, till their skull-knobbed heads popped out like ivory finials. The *arlecchini*.

Tommaso breathed in and held the air tight within his lungs. There was yet one creature missing. He peered out into the growing throng. He didn't find the one he sought. His breath, when he at last released it, trembled.

The first red demons had vanished beneath the growing dark battalions. Tommaso looked at his compatriots, huddled together in the fragile protection of the dirt-scuffed circle. Did they see the same specters he did?

Vicenzio Romoli and Agnolino Gaddi couldn't. They crouched close to the fire, their arms and hands over their faces. Cellini and the necromancer surely saw something. They stared, straining, back toward the farthest reaches of the stadium, where the darkest shadows were lumpy with emerging revenants.

"There must be a hundredfold more than the first time," Cellini whispered.

"Heard you what they replied to your question?" The sorcerer tried to sound assured, but his voice was feeble with fear. "They said that in the space of another month you shall be where your love is. Now that they've answered your request, it behooves us to be civil and dismiss them gently, for we've conjured the most dangerous of all the denizens of Hell. Signore Romoli and Gaddi, raise yourselves and pour more perfume on the fire."

The necromancer started chanting and pleading with the demons to depart.

Would the necromancer's ceremony persuade the spirits? Tommaso looked back out at the hordes. Something *was* happening. Before, the creatures stood still where they'd coalesced. Now they swayed rhythmically, marching in place, though no sound accompanied their movements. Tommaso felt nauseous. Their silence was horrible. In one area they began to shift from their positions, moving closer together, gathering.

Something emerged from the middle of that throng: a six-legged creature with four legs below and two appendages above. It resembled a man riding a steed. It rocked forward with a graceful, sober gait. Its upper limbs pounded in cadence against its flat, round sides. Still no sound came forth. This was what Tommaso had sought before: the *Obby Oss*.

The hordes of other creatures fell in line behind it. In a great, slow wave, they swelled toward the circled fire.

Guarnieri screamed. He reached out his arms blindly in front of him. "I see them. A million and more come this way."

The necromancer's chant quickened, grew more desperate, more pleading. Vicenzio and Agnolino splashed more perfume on the fire. It flared, threatening to scorch them, but they wouldn't turn around and risk seeing the wraiths threatening. Tommaso was amazed at the steadfastness of Cellini's hands as they held the pentacle over Guarnieri's head.

"What is this?" Guarnieri shrieked. "Now more join them—Titans. We're doomed."

As the boy spoke, Tommaso saw four giant figures coalescing above the Coliseum like thunderheads. They settled on the top of the bleachers, one from each direction. From the south, a figure fashioned from flame. In the west, an enormous waterspout. In the east, a colossus made of wood, draped with vines and leaves. To the north, the largest of all, but so amorphous Tommaso could hardly make it out—a silhouette composed of blowing sleet and snow.

"Have pity," Guarnieri sobbed. "Spare us."

The giants moved down through the Coliseum. They passed through the dark legions as if the demons were less substantial than thought.

The wraiths are etheric, Tommaso realized. We can see them and they can see us, but they aren't actually here. They look at us as if through clear glass, or are spying on us from afar.

The giants reached the floor of the Coliseum and strode up to the fire's circle. From this perspective, they lost all semblance of form. To look up at them was to look up the vast lengths of nebulous columns of water, fire, plant and wind.

They're protecting us, Tommaso thought. The *Obby Oss* and its hordes halted.

Guarnieri sank to the ground. He stuck his head between his knees. "This is how I will meet death, for we are certainly dead men." As he spoke, his glowing words shone out in faint sheets of light from the cave he'd made of his body.

Tommaso knelt and tugged at the boy. "Raise your eyes. What you see is only smoke and shadow." He tried to comfort him.

When Guarnieri peeked upward, his eyes fell on the fiery column. "The whole Coliseum is in flames. It advances upon us. I can endure the sight no longer." He covered his face with his hands again.

Cellini, however, took heart from Tommaso's words. "If these creatures are only smoke and shadow, then they're inferior to us," he said.

The necromancer muttered something to the goldsmith. Cellini turned to Agnolino Gaddi, who'd at last turned to see what threatened and now stood paralyzed with horror. "Agnolo, put your eyeballs back in their sockets. We mustn't yield to fright. Look through the herbs until you find the asafetida. Fling a handful upon the fire."

Though Agnolino shook like an aspen leaf, he did as Cellini bid him. Just as he bent over and flung the noxious herb on the coals, a horrendous noise and stench burst forth. It took a moment for Tommaso to realize that the sound and smell erupted from Agnolino's pants, not from the asafetida exploding on the coals.

Cellini shouted with laughter, his hands finally dropping the pentacle away from over Guarnieri's head. Agnolino looked even more mortified than he had been afraid.

"See, my gossip," Cellini said, gingerly clapping his friend's back from as far away as he could and still reach him. "Even a crap in the pants is more fearful than these fiends. Whew! What a stink! It's worse than the asafetida. I knew you'd be useful on this adventure. If that doesn't drive the fiends away, nothing will."

Guarnieri raised his head—perhaps because of Cellini's laughter, perhaps because of the unbearable fetor. "They're leaving. They're flying away from us," he said. The light was fading from his eyes. Only the barest glow issued forth from his mouth.

The black shapes were dimming, melting into the shadows. The *Obby Oss* stopped its slow capering forward. Just as slowly it started floating backward.

The necromancer kept up his mumbling. The rest of the little troupe huddled together, except for poor Agnolino Gaddi, ostracized to the outer edge of the circle. They stayed that way until they heard matins bells in the distance.

"What do you see now?" The necromancer asked Guarnieri.

"Just a few are left. They seem a great distance away," Guarnieri replied.

The necromancer looked relieved. He concluded his ceremonies and took off his robes. Then he gave his permission to leave the circle. All six of them scuttled across its borders and over the floor of the Coliseum, huddling together. Guarnieri was in the middle, clutching the necromancer's gown on one side and Cellini's cloak on the other. Agnolino Gaddi clung to Cellini. Tommaso, on the other outer edge, hung on to Vicenzio Romoli. As they passed between two of the five smaller circles, he noticed small scorch marks on the earth. All the gems were gone.

They made their lopsided way back to the Bianchi. Early-morning peddlers stopped and stared at them.

"As often as I have entered magic circles, I've never met with such a serious affair as this," the necromancer babbled. "Truly, Benevenuto, I've never met one who could naturally draw the ethereal powers the way you do, with a soul so firm."

The magician's eyes narrowed. "You know, love affairs such as yours are nothing but vanities and follies without consequence. Collaborate with me again, my friend, on matters of greater importance. These fiends know where all the hidden treasures on earth lie. With both our occult talents combined, I know we could compel them to reveal untold wealth."

At the mention of fiends Guarnieri's eyes bulged. "I still see two of them," he whispered. "There they are." He pointed upward. "Skipping along the rooflines." He pulled back and gasped. "They just leapt down and gambol now before us." He wept. "Can't you see them?"

Agnolino Gaddi was too distracted by his laden pants to bother with more devils. Vicenzio Romoli was too afraid to look. Cellini and the necromancer looked at each other and shrugged.

"Without the pentacle in place, we're denied the gift of sight," the necromancer said.

Tommaso saw, though he said nothing. One of the spirits accompanying them flitted like autumn leaves in a breeze, pounced as playfully as a cat. Though it was gaily particolored in amber, ivory, gold, russet and black, it was clearly not one of the *arlecchini*. The other spirit was a single color of red. Unlike the first red demons of the invocation, it was featureless, though possessed of a woman's form. And unlike the devils' flat, madder hue, this spirit glowed with a deep, true, translucent garnet light.

I know her. Somehow I know her. The thought ached in Tommaso's heart.

37

By the time he returned to the Salviati mansion, Tommaso felt ill. His eyes were swollen and sore. So was his throat. His chest felt hollow. Every breath he drew ached. He stumbled often; his feet, though not numb, possessed no connection to the ground. He wanted to crumble like stale old bread into his cot in the apprentices' quarters.

Instead he reported to Cosimo Ruggiero.

Cosimo opened his door as soon as Tommaso knocked. "I've been waiting for you..." he started. From the look of Cosimo's haggard face, Tommaso guessed he'd been waiting all night.

Cosimo's eyes widened. "By all the saints in Heaven! My friend, what have we done to you?" He reached out to support Tommaso as Tommaso tripped into the room.

"Nothing. It was all done by Signor Cellini and his sorcerer friend," Tommaso said, as Cosimo eased him into a chair.

Cosimo walked over to his washbasin, dampened a towel, brought it back and bathed Tommaso's face with it. To Tommaso's embarrassment, the towel came away streaked with soot and dust. He took the towel away from Cosimo and wiped his hands and forearms with it as well.

Cosimo wanted to examine him, but Tommaso waved him away. "I'm weary to the bone. Let me relate the night's adventures while I still have the strength for it."

Cosimo nodded. "You're right. But first sip some of this to ease your throat." He poured Tommaso some wine from a carafe on his desk. "You're croaking like a frog."

Tommaso told Cosimo everything. He hesitated when he reached the point of the tale when the demons appeared. Perhaps it hadn't happened. Perhaps he'd only suffered visions. But in that case, so had all the others in that foolhardy little band. He told Cosimo. The only detail he left out was that he'd seen the latter hordes of dark spirits before, in Florence.

He finished. At first Cosimo said nothing. Instead, the young mage pulled jars of herbs from drawers and began measuring them out and weighing them in small amounts.

"What do you think?" Tommaso asked anxiously. "To see such things . . . were we all mad?"

"No. Not mad. Drugged," Cosimo replied. "The herbs the priest threw on the fire alter the mind and eye. Inhaling them by way of fumigation is an effective, though unhealthy, way of administering them." He poured the herbs into a mortar and ground them with a pestle.

"But that means that when he drugged us, he was drugging himself as well," Tommaso protested.

Cosimo nodded. "He undoubtedly imbibes those drugs frequently and is familiar with their effects, so therefore can discount them. He also knew what would happen, having arranged for it beforehand."

"So there were no demons?" Tommaso was incredulous.

Cosimo looked grave. He took Tommaso's goblet, decanted the herbs into it, added more wine and stirred it well. "Yes and no. Drink this. It will counteract the effects of the opiates you inhaled."

Tommaso forced himself to sip at the bitter mixture.

"Those first scarlet devils you saw . . ." Cosimo explained. "You had good reason to wonder at their resemblance to the demon masks we see at festivals. The second necromancer whose absence Benevenuto remarked on was indubitably skulking nearby, orchestrating the tableau. It's easy enough to hire a band of rascals for a few *scudi di moneta* and dress them up as devils, with a dim lamp attached to their costumes behind to provide eerie illumination. Then one instructs them how to slink, creep and crawl at a bunch of drug-dazed adventurers. Performed at night in a huge, shadow-riven site like the Coliseum, with flickering firelight and other effects, and the collusion of the victim's own vision-driven minds..." He shrugged. "You enjoyed a production far more convincing than any held at a mere *teatro*."

"But to what end?" Tommaso asked

"The usual. Wealth. Greed. You say darkness had fallen before you even left for Cellini's. When you arrived at the Coliseum the necromancer had already begun his preparations. I'd wager the circles he tramped into the ground had been lightly scribed in much earlier, and outside their edges small piles trailed of a mixture of gunpowder and those elements fireworks manufacturers use to color their dazzling displays. Later, with you and your fellows distracted by the scarlet devils, it would be easy for a second sorcerer, dressed all in black and moving under the cover of darkness, to scoop up the gems and light the gunpowder. Thereby effecting the supposedly miraculous fiery consumption of the jewels as a means to forge a connection to the nether realms."

"So I was just a dupe and a fool, as were the others," Tommaso said miserably. He drank the last, most bitter dregs at the bottom of his goblet. "That priest-necromancer *should* take to the stage. I've never seen a better actor. I could have sworn, with that second greater wave of wraiths, that he was as terrified as the rest of us."

"I believe he was terrified," Cosimo said quietly. "Remember, to your query of the presence of demons, I said both 'no' *and* 'yes.'

"So no, your growling scarlet devils were certainly not the denizens of Hell they pretended to be. And I cannot say for certain that the dark legions that followed them were either. But I do believe the dark legions weren't men. I believe they hail from realms far from our own."

Tommaso couldn't stop the shiver that started at the base of his spine and sped straight up to his scalp.

"Not expecting them, of course," Cosimo continued, "your priest-necromancer was terrified. Later, when he'd had time to recover from his fright and reconsider events, he became anxious to repeat the experiment with Benevenuto.

"He and his cohorts conspired to acquire treasure through elaborate deceit. But if the stories about conjured demons helping to find lost booty are true, in Benevenuto he may have found the means to acquire real wealth."

"*You're* a mage," Tommaso said. "*Is* that true? About using devils to find lost treasure?"

Cosimo smiled. "I'm a humble astrologer, not a necromancer."

When Tommaso cocked an eyebrow at him, Cosimo laughed lightly and shrugged. "All right. Yes, my studies encompass a few more arcane arts than just those of the stars. But I've never come across demons, spirits or revenants so generous or knowledgeable that they'd point me to secret riches."

He gently tugged upward on one of Tommaso's drooping eyelids. "Are you getting sleepy yet? Good. You'll sleep here today and sleep well. When you wake you'll suffer no ill effects. Which is more than I can say for your fellow adventurers."

He pulled off Tommaso's shoes and eased the young cook between the covers.

Tommaso sighed. Cosimo's bed was so much softer than his little cot. The sheets smelled of lavender and aniseed.

Cosimo pulled up a chair next to the bed. "Before you fall asleep, we must speak of one more thing. This is important, Tommaso. You said the counterfeit fiends growled and made noise. This allowed the necromancer to claim he'd extracted knowledge of Cellini's inamorata from them. But that second group that filled the Coliseum—did you ever hear any kind of sounds at all from them?"

"No, though I strained to hear," Tommaso said. "The last figure before the Titans arrived, the one resembling an *Obby Oss*—the way it drummed its sides—I kept expecting, kept fearing, to hear its pounding."

Cosimo got up and wrung the towel out in the washbasin. He looked pensive. "That's good. You were very lucky. You surmised correctly. It meant that, close as they seemed, they actually remained a good distance hence, perhaps gazing in at all of you from their own realm. And those four giants *were* protecting you."

"So, in a way, the second vision was an illusion too," Tommaso said. His eyes grew heavy, blurring Cosimo's room into a dream.

"Yes," Cosimo said. "But barely. If you'd heard those creatures marching, heard the *Obby Oss* thrumming, they'd have been close upon you and no one could have saved you."

"What about the two sprites afterward?" Tommaso heard his own voice come from somewhere far away. "The ones only Guarnieri and I could see?"

Cosimo's grim look lessened. "Did you fear them, like you did the others?"

"No, not at all," Tommaso said wistfully.

Cosimo leaned forward and ruffled his hair. "Trust your instincts, Tommaso. They're good."

But as Tommaso felt himself melt at last into sleep, a sudden uneasy thought almost drew him back up from the lovely, warm, heavy depths. His fine intuition that Cosimo said he should trust told him that those faraway realms from which the dark wraiths came were not too much farther away than Florence.

38

Tommaso had to return to Cellini's for his usual session of instruction only four days later. To his surprise, Guarnieri exhibited great good spirits. The boy laughed and joked with the other apprentices as if the horrible events at the Coliseum had been no more than an idyll in the country.

"I confess myself amazed," Tommaso told Cencio. "Did Guarnieri or Cellini tell you anything of our adventures the other night? I doubted Guarnieri would ever recover from them, let alone make merry so soon."

Cencio drew Tommaso around the side of one of the foundries and out of earshot of the others. "We shared your sentiments. When Guarnieri first returned here that dreadful morning after Master's venture into the occult, he was incoherent with fear. His condition lasted for two days, not helped by the fact that cursed necromancer returns here every afternoon, trying to persuade Master Cellini to repeat the experiment.

"Poor Guarnieri couldn't eat or sleep, so in terror was he that he'd be forced to act as their tool again. So the rest of us apprentices put our heads together and came up with a solution." Cencio leaned out from the foundry and nodded toward a cheerful Guarnieri. "There you see the result."

Tommaso was astounded. "You are better magicians than the necromancer! What on earth did you do?"

"Pooled together enough *soldi* to send him to one of the best whorehouses in Rome. He'll never be put to supernatural use again. He's no longer a virgin."

Tommaso laughed. He reached into his purse. "What good, clever friends. Of course I wish to contribute to such a fine cause, even if a few days late."

Cencio reached over and stopped Tommaso. He shook his head. "We'll accept no money from you, Tommaso. You were the only one who protested that Guarnieri was too young and should be spared that dreadful night. You were the only one of us brave enough to join Master's expedition."

Tommaso blushed. Guarnieri or no, he wouldn't have gone either if Caterina hadn't made him. But he couldn't declaim Cencio's admiration without betraying Caterina's interest in the matter.

"Besides, for what money we gathered, Guarnieri enjoyed a bargain," Cencio said ruefully. "At the whorehouse, when we explained the ill use made of him and why it was imperative they initiate him immediately into manhood, all the whores were touched by his travails.

"The youngest and prettiest doxies insisted on making him their pet for the entire night. To save a young boy's soul from demons—rarely can such virtue be ascribed to the plying of their trade. Guarnieri enjoyed such a glorious deflowering that we *all* wish, virgins or not, that we'd gone in his stead with Master."

"What about the Master? Don't you fear his wrath when he finds out Guarnieri's lost his purity?" Tommaso asked.

Cencio shook his head. "We did, but as it happens, there's no reason to fear. Master Cellini steadfastly refuses the necromancer, no matter how much the man pleads, no matter what he promises. Master claims that now that he's assured he'll rejoin his Angelica, he has no other desires, no need to dabble further in mystic matters."

Tommaso looked down and scuffed his foot on the dusty stone floor. "I've never cared for Cellini, so know that I say this grudgingly: That night I could tell by the look in his eyes that he was as frightened as the rest of us, which means he's not completely the conceited, impenetrable fool I've always believed him to be. Yet he never gave way to his fear, and did what he could to rally the rest of us."

"Still—with danger threatening all of you, he never attempted to call the endeavor off?" Cencio observed.

"That's true—he didn't. But I only said he's not *completely* a fool. Not that he's not a partial ass," Tommaso replied.

Caterina returned a week later. While her ladies unpacked her things, she requested an immediate consultation with Cosimo Ruggiero. Madonna Gondi and Reparata accompanied her to the astrologer's room. While Madonna Gondi and Reparata played with the Gondi baby, Cosimo quietly told Caterina of Tommaso's adventures in the Coliseum.

Caterina received the news with no evidence of surprise. She shook her head sadly. "I never should have put Tommaso to such risk. And for nothing, too. I received a letter from Ippolito while I was at the hunting lodge. He'll return to Rome in early May."

"Surely that's good news," Cosimo said.

Caterina looked at him steadily. "I have other sources in this house than just you and Tommaso. I know that while I was gone a letter arrived here from Clement. Uncle Jacopo may be breaking its seal this very moment. He will read that I'm to be returned to Florence immediately, to prepare for my marriage to France. I'll miss Ippolito, and any chance he had to rescue me, by scant days."

"I, too, received a letter while you were gone—from Antonio Pecci," Cosimo said. "He tells me Ippolito still prepares to spirit you away once you've returned to Florence. Your being returned there is the first step in his plan."

"Why do you speak to me so disingenuously?" Caterina's voice was cold. "Do you think I don't know the true meaning of Cellini's misadventure? Settrano, Meana, Alpeno and great Tago reach out to protect us even here. As long as I remain in Rome I can contrive to escape Clement's power. The forces that strive to keep Ippolito and myself apart are still confined to Tuscany.

"Ippolito lacks my particular powers of perception. That's why he's allowed himself to be trapped in this folly. But you, Cosimo, share my talents. You know that once I return to Florence my choice of fate likely narrows to only one. Write and tell your father that it's *his* prophecy that will triumph," she said bitterly.

Cosimo hung his head, closed his eyes. "I don't know that for a certainty. Neither do you. Yes, the possibilities diminish, but do not yet vanish. Yes, my father forbids me to either help or hinder. But remember this—no matter what may come, my fate is tied to yours. So do you really believe I wouldn't want the best, happiest future possible for you?"

"You did try to help, a little," Caterina admitted grudgingly.

Cosimo sighed. "Once back in Florence I can't aid you even that much. I'll be restrained until your life takes its final course, one way or the other. Till then, Caterina, I beg you, don't abandon all hope."

That evening Caterina summoned Tommaso to her rooms. For once he found her not at her desk, writing endless letters. Her papers were put away. The desktop lay empty. Caterina sat in an armchair in front of the fireplace, absently petting her cat curled up on her lap. Her ladies-in-waiting were all silently embroidering. It worried Tommaso to see Caterina so quiet, so empty.

"My gossip, our lives are changing again," she said, motioning him to sit on a footstool by the fire to warm himself. "Uncle Jacopo summoned me this afternoon to read me a letter from the Pope. By His orders we return to Florence by the end of the month."

Caterina looked at Tommaso with red-rimmed eyes. They made her look as brittle and fragile as dry, scorched paper.

"I've drafted letters to Maestros Cellini and Scappi, terminating your instruction with them. You return to Florence as a full-fledged chef. There's only one new set of lessons I require of you: You must learn how to speak French."

II

Florence

39

Last week of April, 1532

Caterina returned to the Murate rather than to her family's ancestral palazzo. On the journey back to Florence she told Tommaso, "Now that I'm grown, Clement dare not put Alessandro and myself under the same roof. It would be too dangerous."

The nuns hurried out of the convent when Caterina's carriage arrived, greeting her with mutedly joyous quail-like cries. Caterina could no longer live in a simple novitiate's cell. She was a *Duchessina* awaiting her wedding day. The Abbess arranged for a comfortable suite in the convent's guest quarters for Caterina and two of her attendants.

Besides the nuns, Maria Salviati and her son Cosimo de' Medici also waited to greet her. "We're staying at Il Trebbio," Maria told Caterina, kissing her on both cheeks. "We wanted you to join us there, but Clement refuses to hear of it. We'll come into Florence to visit you often."

Of course Clement doesn't want Caterina ensconced in Il Trebbio, Tommaso thought. It would be too easy for Ippolito to rescue her from there.

Cosimo welcomed Caterina solemnly. He'd grown even taller since Tommaso had last seen him in Rome. He now looked much older than Caterina. Neither of the two cousins appeared only thirteen.

Tommaso lingered, greeting some of his friends among the nuns. Sister Teresa Lucrezia stood back to look at Tommaso. "How tall you've grown, Messer Arista! Who'd have thought that vaporous Roman air could put such length in a young man's bones. You only need good Florentine cooking to put some flesh on them."

"That's just what I've lacked, especially the Murate's plumpening pastries," Tommaso jested in return.

Sister Anna Maria no longer wore a novitiate's attire, but rather the robes of a fully fledged nun. Her lovely young face shone with radiant tranquillity. Tommaso was tempted to joke how marriage seemed to agree with her, now that she was a bride of Christ, but her serenity was too lovely for jest. He could barely stammer out his regards to her.

Reparata swept past him, pushing him out of the way. She threw her arms around Anna Maria, who hugged her back. Tommaso couldn't tear his eyes from the sight of the two embracing sisters, one so saintly and eternal in her beauty, the other so sensual and temporal in hers.

Once Caterina, Reparata, and one other lady-in-waiting settled into the Murate, the rest of the entourage disbanded. Most returned to their family homes, the Salviati drovers dropping them and their goods off on the way to the stables at the Salviati palazzo. Tommaso, Caterina's falconer, her perfumery tutor, her groomsmen, and a number of others were lodging in the de' Medici mansion. For the duration, Tommaso thought grimly. He joined the others trudging alongside the last horse-drawn wagon.

The streets of Florence seemed narrower than when he was a boy, the buildings not so tall. Edifices that once awed and overwhelmed Tommaso struck him now as perfectly proportioned and genteelly welcoming.

The upper floors of the Palazzo della Signoria, cantilevering outward, appeared to nod down on him in approval, while its tower, the tallest in the city, yearned upward to God and the heavens. The Baptistry, Florence's octagonal heart, with its facing of green-and-white marble, stood as steadfast and stalwart as Saint John the Baptist, the saint it was dedicated to. What a pleasure to cross the civilized spaciousness of the great, paved piazzas: the Piazza Santa Croce, the Piazza della Signoria, the Piazza Pitti.

And the smells! Odors of food and cooking poured from the buildings they passed. Faint, when drifting down from the upper-story galleys of older homes. Stronger from the lower kitchens in more modern buildings, wafting straight into Tommaso's nostrils.

Near the leather-working shops he breathed in as deeply as he could the humble heartening aroma of *scottiglia* melding with the rich scent of the hides its meat had been scraped from. A whiff of the off-season scent of chestnuts meant that in some upper kitchen a mother cooked *necci* with the last of the past winter's supply of chestnut flour. Tommaso wondered if the unseen matron served the ember-baked cakes spread with ricotta, as his mother Piera did. The smoky perfume of steak grilling over smoldering grape vines drifted toward him from the entrance to an alley.

Over every other odor, like a complex garnish, mild breezes swept the scents of spring: the licorice smell of cut fennel fronds; the deep green smell of steamed young spinach; the aromatic medley of the season's first zucchini blossoms stuffed with fresh sheep's cheese and fried in strong, absinthe-colored olive oil. The very air itself was just as it should be—cool, tempered with an underlying blush of warmth.

And yet, something was wrong. At this youthful time of year Florence's ambient light should shine as fresh, sweet and clear as the flesh of a ripe melon. It should glisten off the Baptistry's bronze doors, mellow the Palazzo della Signoria's stern granite colors.

Instead it barely glimmered as a translucent dull ocher, intensifying toward opacity the closer they drew to the de' Medici palazzo.

How can a building so hemmed in by other buildings look so set apart? Tommaso thought when he saw the mansion. The church of San Giovanni degli Scolopi next door appeared to draw in on itself, away from its neighbor, like a young nun gathering her skirts about her in unsavory quarters.

Tommaso and the others trudged to the back entrance of the palazzo. There they unloaded their boxes from the wagon and parted company. Arnolfo, the falconer, headed for the mews. The groomsmen sought the stable. The rest entered the back door to the household servants' quarters. Tommaso stood alone by his piled *cassones*.

The palazzo's aura of sadness and fear made the short walk through the kitchen garden ponderous. Each step up the steep kitchen stairs felt as though it lasted an hour. Just before Tommaso reached the top, the back kitchen door opened. A thin young man stepped out. He slung a bucket of waste water over the side of the stairs, then looked at Tommaso and smiled.

"It's good to see you. We've been expecting you," he said.

The voice was familiar. The face and form were not.

"Cousin Umberto?" Tommaso asked incredulously.

The young man smiled more broadly and slapped his flat belly. "It must be in the Befanini nature to grow tall and thin quickly, whether we start out stout or slender as children. Like you, I've spent the last few years sprouting like a sapling.

"Come in, come in. Once we learned of your impending arrival, we've talked of little else," Umberto said, ushering Tommaso into the kitchen.

As soon as they saw him, Grandmother and Grandfather Befanini, the aunts and their husbands, and the cousins rushed to welcome Tommaso.

"You've had a long journey," Grandfather Befanini said when they at last stopped embracing and kissing Tommaso and slapping him on the back. "I'll wager it's been a while since you've eaten."

"Not since daybreak, when we departed from our last encampment on the journey, in Sienna," Tommaso admitted. "But before I break my fast, I have some chests to bring up."

Umberto helped Tommaso haul his belongings up to and through the kitchen and down a hallway. Tommaso noticed Umberto shiver when they left the confines of the kitchen.

The journeyman's room was large. It contained a single broad bed. Tommaso thumped down on it appreciatively. "At the Salviatis' I slept on a thin cot," he said. "This feels soft and solid."

"You'll have plenty of room to yourself," Umberto said, leaning back on the other side of the bed. "By adding you, there will still only be four sleeping here. No cook of journeyman status outside the family wants to work here anymore.

"Surely you noticed the absence of Aunts Vanozza and Chiara and their husbands and children? They left soon after Duke Alessandro occupied the house. With the plague and the siege, Florence suffers a shortage of capable cooks—they had the good excuse of opportunity for leaving."

"So life under Alessandro is as bad as I've heard?" Tommaso said.

Umberto shrugged his shoulders. "Less so in our kitchen than in the rest of Florence. I shouldn't complain. We work in his employ and he relies on us, so he can't act as high-handed as he does with every other soul in Tuscany. Is that worth having to suffer his presence every day? I'm not sure.

"We cook as before. Alessandro is determined to play out his role as duke, so he holds banquets as splendid as any in the old days, though he himself eats little."

"Truly?" Tommaso said. "I don't recall him suffering a poor appetite when he lived here under Cardinal Passerini's guardianship. We used to make fun of his gluttony and slovenly table manners."

Umberto smiled ruefully. "Evidently he fears us. One of his gossips—a sly, slinky fellow—acts as his food tester. You'd think Alessandro would dismiss our family, but he fears more the public's opinion. He's trying to appear the brave, bold, blue blood and knows he'd look the fool if he admitted his terror of a covey of cooks."

By the time they returned to the kitchen, a plate overflowing with *pan lavato* salad, wedges of deep-fried spelt polenta, and a bowl of *garmugia*, a hearty soup from Lucca, awaited Tommaso. He sat down and drew the food toward him with gratitude. Until that moment he hadn't realized how hungry he was.

"Tell us of your adventures in Rome," Grandfather Befanini urged him.

His mouth full, Tommaso waved his fork helplessly. He swallowed the bite of polenta, and said, "I'll be underfoot here night and day for months. There's plenty of time to recount all my Roman escapades. Instead, while I eat, tell me of Aunts Vanozza's and Chiara's husbands' new employ."

Tommaso had ample time to look about as they did so.

The kitchen was quieter, less exuberant than he remembered. But though his Befanini relatives spoke more quietly, it was with no less warmth than before. The room possessed the feeling of a country cottage sealed up tight against winter's weather; its inhabitants content to endure together until spring.

Tommaso realized he'd failed to notice his missing aunts, their husbands and children because the kitchen was more crowded than ever. But not with cooks. Longtime de' Medici retainers that he remembered well—maids, men-at-arms, a few groomsmen—sat on stools as much out of the way as they could, or helped with easy tasks like stirring. They'd taken refuge in the protection the kitchen offered against the gray and chill atmosphere that had startled him when he'd stepped beyond the kitchen's door into the mansion itself.

Something brushed against Tommaso's leg, making him jump. He looked down. Caterina's cat gazed up at him. Tommaso blinked at the impossibility. Caterina's cat was with Caterina at the Murate. He felt something tap his elbow on the other side. He turned to find a second identical cat standing up on its two back feet, balancing against his chair and reaching out toward his plate with an outstretched paw. Tommaso smiled with relief, remembering at last that two of Gattamelata's kittens had been left behind as a gift to the kitchen.

"Favor shown by the Daughters presages well for any cook. Look how they beg you to start working, that they might taste your wares." A tiny old woman, snowy hair bound back in a tight coil, stood just behind Tommaso. Though her cheeks were as fissured with wrinkles as sun-dried peaches, her eyes sparkled.

Tommaso glanced at her, wondering who she was.

Grandfather Befanini came up and put his huge hands gently on her bird-boned shoulders. "Tommaso just arrived after a long journey. He needs to rest. The *Duchessina* Caterina gave him leave to spend several days with his family before he starts his work with us," Grandfather Befanini said.

"But we *are* his family," the old woman objected.

"You know what I mean, Mother: his parents, his brother and sister."

Mother? Tommaso stared as Grandfather Befanini shepherded the old woman away. This was Angelina Befanini? Tommaso knew from his father's letters that the old woman had staged a remarkable comeback from old age's worst ravages. Seeing her, though, it seemed more as if some impish *Foletti* had stolen his great-grandmother away, substituting another crone in her place.

The Angelina Befanini he remembered sat immobile on her kitchen stool, her face's flesh hanging slackly from the bones, her eyes as dull as dead oysters. The muscles of *this* woman's face were firm with expression and intelligence. She might move with the careful steps of the aged, but move she did. Gone were the last vestiges of gray and dulled red in her hair. Although now pure white, it shone with vitality.

Tommaso struggled to come to terms with these disparities while his cousins told him of Florence's recent adventures and misadventures. When his cousin Maddalena took his empty plate away, the kitchen's ambience intensified as the Befaninis began final preparations for dinner. Tommaso realized he should take his leave soon if he intended to enjoy some respite with his family at the Ruggieros.

"Walk swiftly to your destination," Grandfather Befanini said as he left. "Darkness comes unseasonably early to Florence these days."

Grandfather Befanini spoke no less than the truth. The sun might not actually set before its ordained time, but gloom erupted from the stony pores of every building. It pooled as an ashen miasma that saddened day into night. At this hour the aromas of cooking dinners and the sounds of cheerful, hungry anticipation should fill the air. Instead, all odors were muted, all noises muffled.

Then a melody thrilled up Tommaso's spine. He felt rather than heard a lilting echo of happy voices. It could only come from some bright, sunlit place. Tommaso shivered. The nonsound seemed to originate from somewhere nearby, yet impossibly far away.

The alleyway door to the back of the Ruggieros' was barred from the inside. Tommaso stared at the door handle. In the past it had almost never been locked during the day, except during the height of the siege, when anyone's meager food storage might be plundered by the starving. Tommaso pounded on the door without much hope of anybody hearing him. He'd have to trudge around to the front and gain admission there.

Then someone called out, "Wait a moment. I'm coming," from the other side of the door. The bar was lifted. The door opened. A good-looking man in his late twenties, clean-shaven, with dark brown hair and sienna-colored eyes looked out and smiled. "Welcome, Tommaso. Everyone awaits you."

Tommaso stared at the fellow. He'd never seen him before in his life. Amado hurried up behind the fellow. Amado might have grown from boyhood to youth in Tommaso's absence, but at least Tommaso recognized him.

"Why are you just standing there?" Amado scolded the stranger. "Let him in. He's late."

The stranger stepped aside and smiled sheepishly at Tommaso by way of apology. "I'm Marchetto Beccacce," he introduced himself. "Your cousin Francesca's husband. I've heard so much about you that to find you standing there is to see legend come to life."

Tommaso was nonplussed. He was even more amazed when he walked into the kitchen. Gonfalons painted with lions hung from the ceiling. Several strings of fresh spring flowers crisscrossed over the doorway, brushing the top of Tommaso's head as he passed under them. People crowded everywhere: his family, the scullery maids, Massolina and Enzio, cousin Leonora and her dark-eyed, dark-haired daughters. Three cats circled about the floor, identical to the ones he'd just left at the Medici palazzo, except that one of them limped.

Tommaso was about to ask what the occasion was that he was late for when everyone bore down on him in a mob, shouting and laughing. Piera, her eyes shining with happy tears, hugged him, then pulled away, then hugged him again.

"Gone less than two years, but it feels like ten. How you tower over me! You're as tall as your father now!"

Tommaso looked over to where Gentile hovered tentatively on the outskirts of the crowd. Piera was right. Their eyes met at exactly the same level. Surely he couldn't have aged so much in only a year and a half, Tommaso thought. It's just my absence that gives me the eyes to see.

The others stepped back so father and son could greet one another. In Gentile's eyes Tommaso saw the humble, downcast gaze of one who no longer even tried to ask for forgiveness. It wasn't wrong of me to judge him, Tommaso thought. But what he did he'll never do again. It isn't my right to forgive or not forgive him. That right belongs only to my mother and Filomena.

Tommaso'd seen much in the last few years. He'd seen how men come to fail those they love: Tribolino's betrayal of Florence and Michelangelo, Bindo Ramerino's near-disastrous lack of attention to his daughter, and worst of all, Ippolito's abandonment of Caterina on the eve of their escape together. We men are frail creatures. Who knows what sins I'll need to beg forgiveness for someday? And will I have to pay for them as dearly as my father has for his?

Tommaso's heart finally went out to Gentile in compassion. He reached for him and embraced him fully, and felt his father begin to sob.

Someone laid a hand on Tommaso's shoulder, gently separating them. "Gentile, we'll have him all to ourselves for several days. Right now we must share him with others who've arrived to welcome him home," Piera said in a soft voice.

Tommaso turned around to find Bertino, Salvatore and Gherardo crowding in the doorway like a troupe of grinning monkeys. Vittorio stood behind them like their keeper.

Piera pushed him toward them. "Go, tell them tales of your adventures and listen to tales of theirs. Get out of our way while we finish fixing supper."

"But I can be of use," Tommaso protested.

"This is your holiday. If you want to be of use, stand out of the way and help yourself and your friends to some wine."

Tommaso handed Vittorio the first glass. "I understand you were elevated to Master. Belated congratulations are in order," he said. "Do you own your own studio now?"

"No, but soon," Vittorio said, accepting the wine. "I still labor for Il Tribolino. With the extra commissions farmed out by Michelangelo, I've almost saved enough to equip my own *bottega*." Vittorio slapped Salvatore's back, almost causing that young man to spill the wine Tommaso had just poured him. "I won't have to waste time searching for help once my studio is ready. Salvatore here begged to come work for me as my chief assistant."

Salvatore spun his glass, catching the wine. "I recall that it was you who begged me," he said to Vittorio.

"What about you, Bertino? I heard you made journeyman too. Will you leave for a new studio?"

Bertino laughed. "There's no need to anymore. With those two *furafantes* departing, I'm slated to replace Vittorio as Il Tribolino's chief assistant. Gherardo here only finally passed his journeyman's test. He'll be under *my* heel for quite a while."

Gherardo calmly shrugged off Bertino's gibe. "And the new apprentices will be under mine."

"Is Pagolo di Arezzo returned? Elissa Pecorino told my mother that he went home to the Aretine," Tommaso said.

"That's our only sad news," Bertino answered him. "Pagolo's family suffered financial reverses from the plague and the siege. They need him working at home until they recover. He writes us now and then from his exile. He misses being in the thick of things."

Vittorio scowled into his glass. "Sometimes there's benefit to not being in the thick of things. There are many these days that wish they could flee Florence for Arezzo."

"Hush," said Salvatore. "Speak not of such things. Today we're here to celebrate Tommaso's homecoming, not dwell on politics we have no say in.

"Tommaso, I've never been in a kitchen with a whole household's worth of cooks before. How do any of you accomplish anything in such anarchy?" Salvatore changed the subject as he looked out over the tumult before them.

"It only looks like chaos from here," Tommaso assured him. "In the eye of that storm exists efficient calmness. It only tends to buffet out here where we've been expelled, at its edges."

Tommaso and his friends weren't the only ones banished to the outskirts of the kitchen. The children too young to help, or who were visiting, scurried about or huddled around the art apprentices' feet. The eldest, one of Leonora's daughters, was minding a baby that the other children were trying to distract with songs or funny faces. It was hard to compete with their noise and the kitchen's general cacophony. Tommaso finally gave up with a laugh. He waved his friends to refill their own goblets. "Go see what it feels like to leap into the tempest."

He turned to the girl holding the baby. "You're one of Cousin Leonora's girls, aren't you?" he asked.

She nodded. She looked about eight or nine. Her hair was glossy and nearly black, her eyes a warm dark umber. There was something about her grave serenity that reminded Tommaso of Ginevra. His heart clenched as he realized that this young girl was nearly the same age as Ginevra had been when she died.

"What's your name?" he asked to divert his sorrow.

"Teodora," she said.

"And what about your baby there? May I hold her?" The infant looked unlike any of Leonora's other daughters. It had fair skin, blue eyes and bright, chestnut-hued hair.

Teodora handed Tommaso the baby. "It's not my baby, and it's a boy. His name is Ambrogio."

Tommaso crossed his eyes, enjoying the way it made the baby laugh. The meaning of Teodora's words sank in just as Luciana, who'd been standing nearby watching, spoke up and said, "He's not Teodora's baby. He's mine. He's my brother."

Tommaso looked at the happy baby in his arms. It squeezed its eyes almost shut, chortled, and reached out a tiny, perfect hand toward his face. Tommaso felt ashamed of the jealousy he'd felt for this infant, of his fears that it had been conceived merely as his replacement in the family.

"He's my brother too," he murmured to Luciana.

"Come, dinner is ready," Gentile called.

Tommaso looked at the large central worktable. Platters waiting to be carried over to the main house should cover it. Tommaso knew that today the Ruggieros would be celebrating Cosimo's return from Rome too.

Instead the table was graced with place settings. Chairs, stools, even crates, had been pushed up to it to provide seating for everyone. Gentile waved Tommaso to a chair at the head of the table.

"But the Ruggieros . . . what about their supper?" Tommaso asked as he sat down.

"They welcomed the young master home with a midday feast. The Soderinis invited the entire family over for dinner tonight," Piera said. She and Francesca began serving up soup and passing it around.

"It's my belief that for months we'll be feeding young Cosimo little other than breakfast," Gentile said as he accepted a bowl from his wife. "He'll be in great demand. He returned from Rome with a growing reputation."

Tommaso leaned over his own bowl, breathing in the soup's complex steam of clove, cinnamon, red wine and rich meat stock. It was *brodo al Chianti*, his favorite.

"A reputation Cosimo worked hard for," Tommaso said. "Besides his official position as the *Duchessina's* personal tutor, physician and occultist, with her permission he availed himself of as many requests for his services as he could manage.

"I believe most approached him in the interest of forming a connection with someone who seems destined to hold a firm place in the French royal court, but I knew of none who came away unimpressed with his skills."

Gentile nodded. "And those are the same reasons he'll be courted by every major merchant family here in Florence. They might mock the French, but not a single one would mind acquiring a favored trading status with the royal court."

Finished with his soup, Gentile pushed his stool away from the table. He returned carrying a platter laden with a large venison roast.

"On this day our employer, Ruggiero the Old, rejoiced in the return of his eldest son, Cosimo, who acquitted himself in Rome with distinction," Gentile addressed the crowded table. "In the same manner my own eldest son, Tommaso, is restored to us. We are just as deserving of the right to celebrate. Tommaso, would you honor us by carving the roast?"

All these people had gathered together because they loved him. I thought I was unnecessary, forgotten, Tommaso thought. His face burned with shame.

Next to the platter Gentile placed a hoisting fork, whetstone, two sharp carving knives, a small dish of salt, several damp cloths and a rectangular majolica serving plate. Tommaso stood. "The honor is mine," he said.

He rinsed his hands in his finger bowl and dried them on one of his napkins. Then he sharpened the knives on the whetstone, wiping them carefully with a damp cloth.

The roast had rested while they'd dined on the soup. It was ready for carving. Tommaso cleared his mind. He settled his stance. With a clean flourish he impaled the roast with the hoisting fork and raised it. He picked up a carving knife. As he rotated the boulderlike form of the meat, the knife slid in.

Thin even slices fell along the outer borders of the serving plate in a fish scale pattern. Tommaso laid down four overlapping rows of this framing device.

He picked up the second knife. It melted in to join the first. He wound around the platter. The collops of meat, shedding in tandem, formed an intricate knot. The last pieces fell into place just as he finished the pattern.

Only a small stub of irregular flesh remained on the hoisting fork. Tommaso extricated it back onto the original platter with one of the knives. He cut it into three portions and threw one to each of the cats, who'd waited devoutly at his feet, more rapt an audience than even his spellbound family and friends.

Then with a graceful motion he swirled the pooled juices from the first platter onto his creation. With an identical movement he did the same with the salt. He wiped his hands on a clean damp towel and bowed.

The roomful of people, respectfully silent during his performance, erupted into applause.

Tommaso remembered back to another, less successful carving attempt. While he'd struggled with hoisting fork and carving knife, his father and Cosimo Ruggiero had contrasted the ephemerality of the occult world with the concreteness of the physical world. Looking at the glowing faces before him, Tommaso wished he'd known then what he knew now.

The connection that exists between these people and myself—I cannot taste it, smell it, feel it on my skin, or even truly hear or see it, for words are inadequate and sight can't reveal the specificities of a man's heart or mind. Yet that connection, that love I somehow perceive, is the most real thing in this room.

All the visitors left late. The Aristas and the rest of the kitchen crew put away the last dishes and utensils. Piera glanced over at Tommaso. As the honored guest of the evening, he hadn't been allowed to participate in the cleaning. He sat asleep on a bench, leaning back against the wall. He'd tried to entertain them during the cleanup chores with stories of the people he'd come to know in Rome, but the long day of traveling and return finally took its toll on him. His words softened, blurred, with longer and longer pauses between them, until at last they faded away. Marchetto and Francesca nudged each other and smiled at the sight.

All three cats gathered about Tommaso. The lame one curled up in his lap. The other two settled themselves on either side of him. Piera nodded to herself at this sign of acknowledgment by the Little Kitchen Goddess's daughters. She expected no less. Hadn't Tommaso, uneducated though he was in the Old Way, instinctively honored Her and Hers by offering them the first morsels of the hunt?

40

Like Tommaso, Cosimo Ruggiero was overwhelmed by friends and family. It wasn't until two evenings after his return to Florence that he and his father were able to meet together in Ruggiero the Old's studio.

Cosimo blinked at the dazzle that greeted him. Oil lamps hung everywhere, each one's glow overlapping the next. No shadows interrupted the brightness. The flat, depthless glare laminating all the room's surfaces disoriented him. As did the sense of walking into a room filled with sky.

Instead of tapestries, Ruggiero the Old had always preferred to surround himself with paneling in his workrooms. The studio boasted the rarest woods, carved or inlaid by Tasso and Florence's other fine woodworkers into portraits of ancient philosophers, mathematicians and doctors: Socrates, Plato, Euclid, Diogenes, Zeno, Democritus, Anaxagoras, Archimedes, Aristotle and more.

The magnificent woodwork had vanished, covered over by brocaded cloth of a deep, bright blue. Only the dark purple velvet that still shielded the great speculum relieved the eye.

Cosimo went up to one of the hangings. Its pattern consisted of interlocked, repetitive symbols he knew well. He looked down at his feet. An azure rug covered the floor. It was so large that it ran, like a high tide, several inches up the sides of all the room's walls, except for the wall the door was set in. There it met the edge of the room precisely, with no gaps.

Cosimo's skin prickled. He looked up. To his relief, he saw that at least the ceiling was as it always had been—a gridwork of carved, gilded, down-hanging finials. He pointed to it and smiled at his father. "For a moment I thought I had cause to fear."

His father didn't smile back. "*Do* fear. The floor above is covered by an identical rug to this one, thereby sealing off this room.

"I couldn't find such carpets and tapestries here in Florence. An agent in Venice purchased them for me from Muslim lands. They originate from a far older religion than either Mohammed's or Christ's. The Muslims repudiate their old gods in the same way we no longer believe in the gods of the Greeks or Romans. So when these rugs are sometimes discovered, they're sent off to the Western world for a handsome profit."

Cosimo thought about the old oriental sages who'd devised the protective symbols woven into the carpet: Such men as the three magi who'd searched for the infant Christ, and whom the Medici family claimed as personal protectors. Cosimo fancied he could feel the rug's power sealing off the soles of his feet from any evil influences wafting up from the rooms below them.

"Tell me what you've perceived since your return," his father said.

"The shades that emerged as soon as Alessandro took power have changed," Cosimo said. He noticed himself frowning, as if that would help him think any more concisely. He made a conscious effort to smooth his brow.

When he'd left for Rome, Florence had been populated with two towns' worth of citizens. Raven-visaged observers perched on every cornice. Shadows with no forms to cast them crawled everywhere. Knobheaded creatures crowded among everyday Florentines, till it seemed impossible that the *popoli* not feel their jostling presence. A low, not always unpleasant thrumming rose from deep beneath the Tuscan soil, vibrating up through one's heels, up through the body, until it shimmered in one's ears.

Now, after his return, he saw few of the otherworldly creatures, other than an occasional raven-headed man peeking down from a rooftop. Florence seemed worse for their absence, not better, however. The shadows of buildings, fountains, men and women as they walked across the piazza—all appeared unnaturally dense, possessing a greater dimensionality than the objects casting them. The thrumming sound had grown stronger, clearer. It had lost its slight seductive resonance and taken on a pounding cadence that echoed in Cosimo's skull and made his teeth ache. He described these differences to his father.

Ruggiero the Old nodded. "The beings who crowded into Florence when Alessandro took control constituted his invading army. Now that we've been conquered, there's been no need till now for them to patrol our streets or maintain an armed presence.

"They absorbed into the bricks that make up the substructure of our buildings, the cobblestones lining our streets. Florence is a thoroughly occupied country, but for small oases like this," Ruggiero the Old said, nodding around at the blue-draped room. "But today things changed yet again."

"I returned," Cosimo said.

His father favored him with a sarcastic glance.

Cosimo felt himself blushing as hotly as poor Tommaso Arista. "Caterina de' Medici returned."

His father smiled his distinctive dry smile. "I don't mean to disparage your importance, my son, or my own, or the power manifested by our talents working together. But you must always keep in mind that Caterina is the hinge about which the door of our reality swings."

Ruggiero the Old threw back the purple velvet covering the great speculum. The reflection of all the room's reflected blue nearly blinded Cosimo. He flinched back. His attempted grin felt thin and watery. "It's like standing naked under God's own sky," he said.

His father scowled at him. "Naked, yes. But we'll stand under a sky unrecognized by any god we might call our own. Prepare yourself to foray into other worlds. The enemies' weaknesses are that they've invested everything in one linchpin—Alessandro—and that they think *we've* invested all in Caterina and Ippolito. It's time to strengthen the other, invisible players on our side of the chessboard."

41

Tommaso enjoyed three days at the Ruggiero household before returning to the de' Medici mansion. When he approached it he experienced the same sense of compressed gloom he'd felt on his first day back in Florence. Tommaso guessed it would always be thus as long as Alessandro de' Medici held sway. Only the Befanini-run kitchen retained its peculiar status as a light-filled refuge within a shadowed territory.

He arrived early enough to help with the last of that day's breakfast preparations.

Unlike the Ruggieros, the Medici family had always been wealthy enough to maintain a serving staff separate from the kitchen help. Some kitchen senior member, however—Grandfather Befanini or Great-uncle Giacomo—always accompanied the procession of food to the dining hall to be sure everything was presented properly.

No one accompanied breakfast as it left the kitchen.

"Is this a new custom?" Tommaso asked Umberto while they prepared the secondary breakfast for the servants.

Umberto nodded. "We help clear away a meal when all the diners depart, but almost never enter the hall when Duke Alessandro is present. When he hosts a large banquet he might trot out Uncle Giacomo for a display of carving skills, but other than that he forbids us to enter his presence. His personal steward negotiates all the weekly menus."

"If Duke Alessandro feels such anathema for the Befaninis, why hasn't he dismissed the family and hired other cooks?" Tommaso asked.

Umberto's smile was bitter. "I'm certain he'd like to. I told you before that he fears looking the coward—a Duke frightened by some cooks! And, I expect, because he knows he'd have trouble hiring anyone else." Umberto shrugged. "Even if he could, they'd be as likely to poison him as we would."

"Has anyone here been tempted?" Tommaso whispered.

"All of us," Umberto replied. "Fortunately or unfortunately, Great-grandmother Angelina's powers of reasoning revived sufficiently for her to point out that, with Clement in power in Rome as Pope, and Gucciardini still in power here in Florence as Clement's emissary and Alessandro's advisor, whosoever nobly murders Alessandro will surely die soon afterward themselves. And likely their entire family as well. She also persuaded us that Florence needs the Befanini alive more than Alessandro dead."

Umberto shook his head. "Some of us aren't convinced such is the case, but abide by the family's decision. For now." Then Umberto grinned. "Of course, Duke Alessandro knows nothing of our discussion or resolution. To be on the safe side he dines out as much as possible."

The other Medici servants usually ate in their own dining commons. A sideboard was kept supplied with food so they could help themselves as their work schedules allowed. Tommaso assisted Umberto in delivering bread, covered bowls containing pulses, cured meats and fruit to this room. Then he followed Umberto to clear away the breakfast dishes in the banquet hall.

As they loaded their trays, a group of men passed by in the hallway beyond the open banquet hall doors. From their attire Tommaso could tell they were departing for a day of riding, perhaps some hunting in the nearby hills. In the midst of them strode Alessandro de' Medici.

In the years since Tommaso had last seen him, Alessandro'd grown only a little taller, but he had filled out. His lips, always full, now looked blubbery. Perhaps to draw attention away from them, he'd cultivated a thin, scraggly beard. His unruly hair was frizzy.

Seeing him thus, Tommaso understood the rumors regarding Alessandro's parentage: that in the field, during the Roman *Campagna*, Clement—then still Cardinal Giulio—had begotten his loathsome progeny on some unwilling Nubian or Blackamoor slave. Tommaso thought the allegations insulting. The Nubians and Blackamoors in Ippolito's entourage were of an unusual but beautiful appearance. Their lips were also full, true, but finely etched over taut, firm skin. Their hair was a lustrous black, with an appealing crinkled texture. In no way did they resemble the repulsive Alessandro.

Tommaso had only an instant to think all this as Alessandro passed by. A young man on Alessandro's other side, his arm slung across the Duke's shoulders, glanced around and into the banquet hall. He saw Tommaso, smiled and winked at him.

Tommaso dropped the silver platter he'd picked up. It clattered and bounced, its metallic clamor echoing throughout the banquet hall. The few *bomboloni* left on it flew briefly. Then like fat, wing-clipped pigeons they tumbled to the ground.

The man so companionable with Duke Alessandro was Lorenzaccio de' Medici.

The terms of Tommaso's employment required that he meet with Caterina each week, bringing her some small treat. The Murate possessed several secular salons where noncleric guests could receive visitors. Tommaso expected to find her in one of these. When he arrived, however, Caterina had left word that he should join her in the garden.

"The *Duchessina* says it would be a sin not to enjoy this lovely spring day Our Lord has granted us," Sister Teresa Lucrezia told Tommaso.

Tommaso found Caterina, Reparata and a middle-aged nun who was one of Caterina's tutors sitting on some blankets in the lower part of the Murate's garden, down near the river. All three wore broad-brimmed straw hats to protect their fair skin from the sun.

"What have you brought us, Tommaso?" Caterina looked so tranquil that Tommaso momentarily forgot how piqued he was with her.

Tommaso's arms were full. Reparata took the large basket he carried in one hand so he could set down the serving dish he carried in the other. He lifted away the dish's cover. "*Pasticcio di riso e mele.*"

Caterina clapped her hands at the sight of the firm-baked rice pudding, its amber crust covered with wafer-thin apple slices. "Where did you get apples at this time of the year?" she exclaimed.

"My mother sliced and dried these last fall. I reconstituted them by first soaking and then poaching them in *Vin Santo*," Tommaso said. From the big basket he unpacked the plates, napkins and cutlery Sister Teresa Lucrezia had assembled for him.

Caterina wrinkled her nose at the decanter of almond milk Tommaso set before them. "That's all very well and good," she said. "But surely we should then also have some *Vin Santo* to drink with the *pasticcio*. Sister Helena, would be you be so kind as to beg us a small flask from Sister Teresa Lucrezia?"

To Tommaso's surprise, the dignified nun graciously accepted the rather subservient chore that should have been assigned to him or Reparata.

"Sister Helena is a Ridolfi," Caterina said by way of explanation, when she saw Tommaso's puzzled expression.

This baffled Tommaso even more. The Ridolfi were among the most esteemed families in Florence. They possessed a far more ancient lineage than the Medici.

"Sister Helena begged her family to allow her to join the convent. She's a formidable scholar and wished to be spared the burden of married life and childbearing. Still, she misses the free access to some of the niceties she enjoyed freely in her secular youth, such as fine dessert wines." Caterina winked at Tommaso. "She knows full well that as both a paying guest and a *Duchessina* I can afford her good access to those small temptations.

"While she's gone, tell me how things fare at my ancestral home."

Tommaso remembered the indignation he'd nursed for several days.

"Your cousin Lorenzaccio now resides there as Alessandro's closest gossip."

Caterina didn't look surprised. "Indeed."

"Couldn't you have warned me?" Tommaso couldn't keep the irritation from his voice.

"If I'd known for a certainty I would have." Caterina didn't react to his angry tone. "I received several letters from Lorenzino soon after he departed from Rome. Then nothing. I hoped he would gain Alessandro's confidence. Because of his silence I guessed that to be the case: Lorenzino wouldn't be able to write to me safely once he succeeded in taking up residence at the Medici palazzo."

"You *want* him to curry Alessandro's favor?" Tommaso was incredulous. "Lorenzaccio is a dangerous individual, no more trustworthy than a jackal. He's attained a position of power with Alessandro. I'm told

Alessandro calls him 'the philosopher' and 'my philosopher.' Do you truly believe Lorenzaccio will continue in his loyalty to you when his own ambitions are better served by allying himself with Alessandro?"

"I don't rely on Lorenzino's loyalty," Caterina replied calmly. "I rely precisely on his vaunting ambitions. It was those, in Rome, I as carefully nurture in him as you nurture me with your divine cooking. Lorenzino grows close to Alessandro not to aid him, but in hopes of supplanting him. As long as Lorenzino believes I abet his cause, I have nothing to fear from him." She nodded to Reparata, who started slicing the *pasticcio*.

"But now that *you* are in the palazzo," she continued, "I want you to meet with Lorenzino, convey messages between him and myself." Caterina raised her eyebrows at Tommaso. "I don't ask you to seek him out. He'll find the means to contact you. On to other matters. Tell me what you hear in Florence of Alessandro."

Tommaso opened his mouth. He wanted to protest, but the subject of Lorenzaccio had been closed.

"Most of what I learned was during my holiday with my family at the Ruggieros. That was the only time I've had to be out and about in the streets," he said. "Since the melting down of the *Vacca*, Francesco Gucciardini has held Alessandro more or less in check, requiring him to consult with the various city councils. This leads some citizens to hope that Alessandro might yet grow from arrogant youthfulness into an at least passable ruler. When Clement eventually dies, they pray Alessandro will be intelligent enough to realize he's lost the Vatican's power and become a more humble and rational man."

Caterina rolled her eyes. "Citizens with such hopes and prayers are fools. Alessandro will indeed eventually lose the resources of the Throne of Saint Peter. They forget, however, that if Alessandro finally weds Emperor Carlos's bastard daughter he'll enjoy a far more effective, more dangerous protector than Clement." She popped a piece of the *pasticcio* into her mouth.

Tommaso nodded in agreement. "Then there are those on the other side. They fear Clement's death will free Alessandro from all constraints. They believe Florence will suffer even more than when it bore Passerini's yoke. They rumor that Alessandro intends to build himself a fortress within the city walls. But surely that's untrue."

"Why do you say that?" Caterina asked.

"For several reasons. First, such a thing is unheard of in a free Italian city, whether ruled by republic or aristocracy. Second, these rumormongers claim to have discovered the plans for this fortress. These plans prove the impossibility of it, since the supposedly intended site is already occupied by the convent of Saint John the Baptist."

"But if there *are* plans . . ." Caterina said.

Tommaso shook his head. "I believe Alessandro had them drawn up and then arranged for their discovery as a thrifty way of instilling fear and compliance.

"One thing all agree on: Alessandro's intolerable personal behavior. Outside of the kitchen help, there's not a woman of comely age in the entire Medici palazzo that's gone unmolested by him or his companions. This is an accomplishment of sorts, since Alessandro spends little time at home. He prefers to gallop recklessly through the streets with his unsavory friends. They've trampled any number of helpless beggars.

"He passes his nights drinking and whoring. Decent men keep their wives and daughters hidden from view, afraid to let them even attend Mass. Alessandro publicly insults everyone he can, crafting the dubious art of rudeness to new heights. He's found ways to rifle the funds of some of the minor guilds, and 'borrows' from the old banking families with no intention of repayment. He'd have been assassinated long ago if the siege weren't so fresh in everybody's hearts."

Sister Helena appeared at the top of the garden, carrying a flask. She started to walk down toward them.

Caterina leaned forward. "Tommaso, I'm sorry I must assign you distasteful tasks involving distasteful people. It's for the final outcome that we *all* must suffer through these times. Remember, no matter what my eventual destiny, you'll be by my side.

"To that end," she raised her voice as Sister Helena came within earshot, "you need to start searching for suitable staff. You can't do all my cooking by yourself when we leave here, and relying on recruiting foreign chefs could be disastrous.

"Ask for the advice of those in your profession who you respect. Seek out invitations to guild functions and attend as many of these as you can. Sample the wares. Assess the wares-makers. Look for skilled Florentine cooks, but they must possess another quality as well: a willingness to work under you. This is important, for you'll be an unusually young head chef."

Sister Helena reached them. She handed the flask to Tommaso, who poured the *Vin Santo* for the three women. He nodded and listened as Caterina continued.

"Seek in prospective helpers also a willingness—nay, even a desire—to travel and live in strange, foreign countries. Seek flexibility in their craft: I fear we may journey to lands that don't enjoy our Tuscan bounty, so my chefs will have to cook all the more brilliantly to make do.

"And above all, Tommaso, choose to please yourself. These are the people you may be working alongside for the rest of your life. Be sure you pick companions you love well."

42

As much as he could, Tommaso stayed within the haven of the de' Medici kitchen. There he enjoyed a respite from both the sadness permeating Florence and the menace lurking only a stone wall's width away.

In his youth he'd spent only brief months at the end of Passerini's rule working with his Befanini relatives. Now, with his own skills matured, he better appreciated the depth of their shared knowledge.

Great-uncle Giacomo still functioned as master carver, though he was called in to perform his art in the dining hall rarely these days—only on those occasions when Duke Alessandro felt compelled to put on a grand banquet. Giacomo kept his skills honed by carving roasts for his family's and the other servant's entertainment before the finished platters were sent on to Alessandro and his cronies to sup on.

If Tommaso hadn't so despised anyone who chose to associate with Alessandro as a compatriot, he would have pitied them. To see and eat the finished masterpiece of intertwined rose and mauve roast petals was the smallest part of the pleasure they afforded. It was the watching of old Giacomo's thaumaturgical prowess as a huge haunch melted magically away in gold-leaf-thin sheets, wafting down through the air, that made the eating of each tender morsel of meat so delicious. One could close one's eyes and imagine Giacomo's sorcerous skill dissolving into one's soul as the petals of meat dissolved on the tongue.

Giacomo handled roasts as large as any Tommaso'd seen his father

Gentile carve. Tommaso paid close attention to his great-uncle. Giacomo knew tricks of moving efficiently that Tommaso had never seen Gentile use.

"You possess a sharp eye," Giacomo said, when Tommaso queried him. "Your father doesn't move like me because he doesn't have to yet. He's a big man, and in his prime. I move with the knowledge that comes with age *because* of age. If I hoisted roasts the way I did in my youth, I'd be a crumbled pile of bones by now."

Giacomo knew other tricks of the carver's trade. He taught Tommaso his secrets for aging and curing meats. Giacomo packed the meat of different kinds of animals, different portions of the carcasses, with various combinations of herbs and spices, honey or sugar. "And of course the age of the game makes a difference—whether it's a young lamb or full-grown mutton." he told Tommaso.

Tommaso thought he knew the uses of spices well, but the diversity of Giacomo's curing recipes overwhelmed him.

"Did you learn all this over the years too?" he asked

Giacomo shook his head. "I've added knowledge as I've gone along, but I'd been taught the foundation by the time I was your age."

"By your father," Tommaso stated rather than guessed.

Giacomo laid a forefinger callused from decades of wielding butcher's knives along his long, bumpy nose. He bent toward Tommaso as if Tommaso were a small child, though in fact Tommaso bent over him, like a tall young tree over an ancient, scraggly shrub.

"My father was a fine carver, but a merely adequate preparer of meat," Giacomo said. "He felt quite satisfied with himself because he carved for the great Cosimo Pater Patriae, and for Cosimo's sons, and finally for Cosimo's grandson, Lorenzo il Magnífico. You couldn't tell my father anything.

"My knowledge of the proper marriage of meat and herb comes from one person." The finger left its resting place against the nose and pointed across the room. "From my older sister Angelina."

Tommaso looked over to where his great-grandmother sat peeling garlic at the main table.

"But how would *she* learn such things, if not from your father?" Tommaso asked.

Giacomo kneaded more spices into the prosciutto he was preparing to hang.

"Angelina and I were the youngest children. As I'm sure you've noticed, the Befaninis run strongly to girl children. My father was the only son in *his* generation. For us, we had many older sisters, only one older brother. Our mother, between all the work, and our father's high-handed ways, and so many children, had little energy to spare for shepherding us.

"As the baby of the family and the only other son, I garnered a good deal of attention. Angelina, though, often ran wild in the streets. If the Befanini name wasn't so well respected we would have been censured for letting a daughter behave so.

"No one feared for her safety. I was told that when she was still very little she possessed such a ferocious temper—which, in addition to her red hair, made her appear at times a small demon—that no one in all Florence dared touch her."

Tommaso thought how much that sounded like his younger sister Luciana in her infancy.

"By the time I grew old enough to know her," Giacomo continued, "she'd become the toughest, most pragmatic female I'll *ever* know.

"Angelina spent a good deal of time with the women who ran the wild-game shops on the Ponte Vecchio. Our mother even permitted her to travel with them to the country on their buying and supplier-acquiring trips. Angelina learned the secrets of curing meat from the game-shop women. Luckily for me, she taught me those secrets too.

"Besides her other virtues, Angelina is unfailingly generous, a trait that caused even our self-absorbed father alarm when she reached the age of nubility." Giacomo winked at Tommaso.

The mating habit of his elders was a subject Tommaso didn't want to learn more of. "And now you're willing to instruct me," he diverted his great-uncle.

Giacomo tapped his finger against his nose again. "Of course I am, but why not learn from the master herself? You're favored with an opportunity that just a few years ago seemed lost. Angelina was slowly leaving us. Now she's back, as sharp as ever."

Giacomo grinned at Tommaso's hesitation. "I saw how she frightened you when you were a child. You had nothing to fear then from that sad old empty shell. True, there's far more to be afraid of now that she's returned to the woman she was. But not for you, Tommaso. Not for any Befanini. Do what you wish, Tommaso, but it would be a pity to pass up such a chance to learn."

Tommaso knew his great-uncle meant well, but Giacomo's words didn't engender any desire in him to seek out Angelina. Besides, there were so many others in the kitchen to learn from.

His grandfather's wife, Grandmother Befanini, came from a long line of pastry cooks who originally hailed from Sienna, the only city-state in Tuscany with a strong tradition in desserts and sweet baked goods. She tutored Tommaso in making fried custard, *pan con santi*, and cookies like crisp, snowy *ricciarelli* and spicy *cavallucci*, which was also her own family's surname.

Tommaso felt comfortable with his grandmother. From family lore he knew she'd been much courted by journeymen cooks in her youth, for both her beauty and her skills in the kitchen. Years of work and childbearing had changed but not diminished her loveliness. All his life, Tommaso had known her as a plump, serene woman whose sweet disposition and fine, porcelain skin reminded him of the meringued *ricciarelli* she was so fond of baking.

But even in his grandmother's presence Tommaso couldn't escape Angelina Befanini.

"I began baking as a toddler," his grandmother said. "My family is esteemed as pastry-makers—more skilled in that art than even the Befaninis. When I came here as a young bride, though, I worked little with my new family, especially my mother-in-law.

"You see, my parents were of two minds about my marrying your grandfather. No culinary family was more admired than our rivals, the Befaninis. The exception to that high esteem, however, was my sweetheart's mother Angelina. It was bad enough she'd borne her son out of wedlock, but such things weren't unheard of, even in good families. However, on top of that she'd been so brazen as to refuse the hand of a good, honest man. Well!" Grandmother Befanini sniffed.

"Though my parents liked your grandfather, they preferred I marry some other suitor. Only my stubbornness and love for him won the day. After we wed, I arrived in this house simmering with resentment for the discord Angelina had caused within my family.

"My new husband made sure word of my pastry talents reached the highest levels of the household. Soon even Lorenzo il Magnífico, who was in his last, pain-racked years, sent down personal requests for my *fritelle di crema* and my *panforte*. I gloried in my triumphs, which I took care to be sure were mine alone! I was certain I'd humbled the Befaninis with my prowess, particularly my mother-in-law."

Grandmother Befanini smiled ruefully. "Then the novelty of my wares wore off. Soon the Medici family again asked for sorbet, cheese and fruit at the end of their meals: strawberries in wine, poached figs, well-ripened pears and unsweetened cakes like *castagnaccio*. I sat alone with my pride in the small corner of the kitchen I'd marked off as my own. I brooded, unworking, for weeks, growing sadder and sadder in my lonely arrogance. Your grandfather was at his wits end as to what to do with me.

"It was Angelina, my despised mother-in-law, who reached out to me. She approached me one day and said she'd been eating poorly for weeks—which was probably the truth, for all the suffering I'd caused her. She said she'd heard *fritelle di crema* was easy to digest and would put the flesh back on her bones. Humbly she asked if I'd teach her my recipe.

"Poisoned by my angry bile I, too, had been unable to eat. I showed her how I prepared my fried custards. Meanwhile she worked alongside me at the stove poaching fresh peaches and apricots in *Vin Santo* and spices, as only she knows how to do. We sat down together to eat. We said not a word. No one else spoke to us. It was as though we dined in silence at a table set at the bottom of a well." Grandmother Befanini paused. Her eyes looked far, far away and long, long ago.

"Never had I tasted such a sweet medley of flavors. The soft creaminess of the custard melded with the perfumed savor of fruit, wine and spices on my tongue and lingered there. I knew instantly it was because my mother-in-law possessed special wisdom. I saw how my pride had kept me from accepting my new family and my true place in this kitchen. If I'd continued as I was, I'd have rotted and soured like unused fruit. I would have deprived myself of so much and would have never attained happiness here."

Grandmother Befanini's dreaminess evaporated like fog in the sun. She looked at Tommaso squarely. "I hope you never cheat yourself in like fashion."

Tommaso ducked his head away from her gaze. Her meaning was clear, but he still didn't want to seek out his great-grandmother.

"Why do I hear nothing but 'Angelina Befanini this,' and 'Angelina

Befanini that,' and 'Angelina Befanini possesses the wisdom of the ages'?"
Tommaso complained to Umberto one morning while they picked salad
greens and young herbs in the garden. "Why do they pressure me to
seek her out?"

"Because she knows so much." Umberto shrugged at the sight of
Tommaso's sour face. "If you didn't want to know, why ask me? Since
Great-grandmother's 'return' to the land of cognition we've all spent time
at her side, absorbing whatever she felt like sharing."

Umberto picked a tender leaf of *dragoncello* and worried it between
his teeth. "Why do you fear her? If anyone should be terrified of the
woman . . ." He tapped his chest to indicate himself. "She came back to
us in front of me alone. I was in the kitchen late one night snacking on
quince pastries when the room filled with a storm of laughter. *Her* laughter." Umberto shivered.

"Now I can't face a quince pastry, let alone eat one," he said sadly.
He looked at Tommaso, his face moody. "I overcame my fright. Are
your delicate sensibilities so much more refined, so less callused than the
rest of ours that you can't master your qualms? The old woman is a
treasure house of lore, and a pleasant enough teacher." Umberto
shrugged again. "Cheat yourself of her wisdom to your own professional
peril."

Tommaso blushed. "You're right, of course," he mumbled. Although
his friends and family expressed joy at his return, in the last few weeks
he'd felt another sentiment rising: resentment that he'd escaped to a
carefree life of work, play and achievement in Rome while his family
and compatriots remained behind in Florence to be ground under Alessandro's heel. The fact that he'd survived the plague and siege counted
for little in the light of the current state of affairs.

Tommaso knew too that Umberto would think him petty if he tried
to explain why he dreaded Angelina Befanini: All his life people had told
Tommaso how much he resembled her in her youth. She'd been tall and
willowy, and shared his striking coloring. He'd always secretly feared
that, as if in a cracked, twisted mirror, her shrunken, decrepit visage
afforded him a glimpse of his own eventual future.

Angelina wasn't the only person in the Medici palazzo Tommaso wished
he could avoid. One day soon after his conversation with Umberto,

Alessandro's wardrobe master stopped by the kitchen with some alterations to the week's menu. And, oh yes, a request from "the Philosopher."

"Signor Lorenzaccio de' Medici understands a cook from Rome
recently joined the staff. Since Signor Lorenzaccio resided in that city
for so long, he misses its cuisine. He wants to order some specific dishes
from your new man. This afternoon would not be too soon to meet
with him." The wardrobe master nodded at Tommaso.

Tommaso suppressed a grimace and executed a curt bow of compliance.

Lorenzaccio's room proved to be sparsely furnished, but Tommaso took
note of the big bed, an ornate desk, a fair number of chests for clothing.
Lorenzaccio certainly dressed better in Florence than he had in Rome.
He wore a knee-length brocaded amber surcoat, its chest cut low to
show off the high-collared white lace shirt beneath it. His leggings were
madder-colored silk and his belt tooled Spanish leather. Evidently the
position of chief gossip and poison-taster to Alessandro de' Medici paid
well.

Lorenzaccio stood talking to a guest, who sat with his back to
Tommaso and the door.

A man-at-arms—one of the old de' Medici retainers—waited on
Lorenzaccio: yet another indication of the callow youth's rise in the
world.

When Tommaso entered, Lorenzaccio looked up from a portfolio
he was paging through.

"Ah, our visiting cook has arrived." Lorenzaccio snapped the portfolio shut. "We'll return to this later," he told his seated guest. "I promised the Duke an evening of dining on traditional Roman fare soon. He
says he misses the hearty food he enjoyed as a child in Cardinal Giulio's
court."

The guest reached out to pick up the portfolio. He stood, bowed,
turned to go. He almost walked right into Tommaso.

Tommaso blanched. The portfolio-bearer was Giorgio Vasari.

Giorgio had the grace to drop his head and look shamed.

Michelangelo had told Tommaso months ago that Giorgio had become one of Alessandro's creatures. Knowing that hadn't prepared Tommaso for the changes in his old friend.

Like Lorenzaccio, Giorgio's lot in life also seemed improved. He wore a linen shirt dyed an expensive dark lapis-blue. His surcoat alternated between stripes of the same blue and deep maroon. His breeches were also maroon, his leggings black silk. The ensemble proclaimed its wearer's prosperity. At the same time, the cut of its cloth and darkness of its colors fell within the parameters of sober Florentine good taste. As did the black woolen *lucco* Vasari gathered up from a chair.

The colors of Giorgio's garb might reflect a refined nature, but they were an unfortunate choice for him. His complexion had always been dry, easily irritated by exposure to the chemicals and other materials present in artists' studios. Since Tommaso had last seen him, Giorgio's skin had worsened. The backs of his hands were red and lined with welting scratches. Flakes of dried skin dappled the sleeves of his dark shirt. Dandruff lay like a dusting of coarse flour on the shoulders of his jacket.

"I see you know each other," Lorenzaccio said.

"I used to cook at the *bottega* of the artist Il Tribolino," Tommaso said stiffly. "I met many of the city's artists during my tenure there, including *Ser* Vasari, who was at that time apprenticed to Andrea del Sarto."

Lorenzaccio clapped Giorgio around his shoulders. "Vasari has come a long ways since those days. He now enjoys honor as Duke Alessandro's favorite young artist." Lorenzaccio tapped Vasari's portfolio with his free hand. "The Duke has entrusted me to work in concert with Vasari to design a series of medals glorifying our Medici family ancestors."

Giorgio still didn't raise his eyes to meet Tommaso's. He patted his portfolio instead. "I'll proceed on these sketches according to those changes we agreed on, Signor Lorenzaccio. I know other concerns press upon you." He bowed, his eyes cast low, and left.

Lorenzaccio shook his head and poured himself a goblet of wine from the decanter on the desk. "There's a sad excuse for a man," he said. "I was told he practically came begging at the door within weeks of Alessandro's arrival in Florence."

Tommaso held himself in tightly. "The Duke is fortunate to have Giorgio Vasari in his service. I knew no other apprentice who worked harder at learning his craft, or who struggled so to overcome the obstacles of poverty, death in his family, and the ill luck of bad timing," he defended his former friend.

Lorenzaccio laughed. "Well, for once his timing proved superb. When Cousin Alessandro decided to take up the Medici mantle of art patronage, he found to his dismay that Florence's sculptors and painters were all busy with reconstructing the damage from the siege. Or with commissions from de' Medici supporters returned from exile. Or with all that work Michelangelo Buonarotti farmed out. Strange that in all the history of Florence, this is the era that finds *all* its good artists fully employed. Alessandro was finally forced to hire Vasari." Lorenzaccio took a sip of his wine and winked at Tommaso. "Not that Alessandro now regrets it. One couldn't find a more satisfyingly boot-licking cur than young Giorgio."

Tommaso remembered all that Caterina had said about Lorenzaccio. He bit down the words he wanted so desperately to blurt out: that it took one toady to recognize another. This man is a tool, not a man, Tommaso reminded himself of Caterina's words.

The "tool" surprised him by seemingly reading his mind.

"How fares our *Duchessina*?" Lorenzaccio asked. "Surely by now you've visited her in her cloisters." Lorenzaccio pulled up a chair. He swung his leg across the front of it so that he sat in it backward, his arms folded on the top of its back, the hand holding the goblet crooked outward.

Tommaso chose what he said next with care. Caterina might trust this man. He did not. "The *Duchessina* is deprived of the social life she knew in Rome, but stays busy continuing her education. She finds living at the Murate tolerable, even pleasant."

"Pleasant enough, I'm sure, but yes, more constrained," Lorenzaccio said, stirring his wine with one finger. "No more romantic interludes with handsome Cardinal Ippolito. No more exciting escapades posing as a boy. Our *Duchessina* made quite the fetching youth, don't you think?" Lorenzaccio drew his finger from the wine and sucked on it suggestively.

Tommaso felt himself grow pale with rage.

Lorenzaccio didn't notice. His musings took a different turn.

"With her lineage, intellect and education, think what Cousin Caterina might have accomplished if she *had* been born male. There'd have been no doubt about her future. How Clement must have breathed a sigh of relief when he learned the news that Madeleine de la Tour's and his cousin Lorenzo's only progeny had been born female!

"Perhaps that's when it first occurred to His Holiness there might be a way to maneuver His own bastard into this mansion." Lornezaccio sloshed the wine in a circular motion within the goblet and frowned.

Tommaso tried to keep up with Lorenzaccio's abrupt mood swings.

"You have no idea, *Ser* Arista, how truly depraved Alessandro is," Lorenzaccio said. "I may drink too much and suffer overboisterous impulses at times, but I'm a lamb in the fold compared to our duke. The man who someday lifts Alessandro's foot from our necks, who liberates Florence, will go down in history as a savior."

Lorenzaccio emptied his goblet in one draught. He peered into its empty depths, then held it out for Tommaso to refill.

Tommaso complied. The more Lorenzaccio drank, the more freely he'd speak.

"Maybe it's just as well Caterina wasn't born a boy," Lorenzaccio said as Tommaso poured. "Did you know it was Clement who Pope Leo sent here to fetch her to Rome after her parents died?"

Lorenzaccio waved his hand. "How easy it would have been for a baby to die of the croup or some other infant malady on the way. You must have noticed how Clement's enemies tend to die conveniently, their constitutions unusually frail and prone to mortal illness." Lorenzaccio laughed into his glass. "Except, of course, the unfortunately robust Emperor Carlos. No, I'm certain only her extreme youth and gender saved Cousin Caterina.

"On the other hand"—he sighed—"women possess powers we can't fathom, or so Duke Alessandro insists. For all that he compulsively beds them, they terrify him. He's sure each and every one is a *strega*."

Lorenzaccio's eyes focused for a brief moment. "Maybe *that's* why he's such a whoremonger. In possessing women he hopes to possess their abilities What a fool!" Lorenzaccio looked up at Tommaso. "Alessandro is quite mad. He'd be frightening and appalling in any walk of life, but as Florence's ruler..." He took another sip of wine and shuddered.

To Tommaso, the conversation itself had become frightening and appalling. He wished it would end. "You summoned me to discuss a meal with Roman dishes," he said. "Let's settle that before I leave here."

"Yes. It's important that I stay in Alessandro's graces." Lorenzaccio held out his glass for yet another refill. "The Roman supper... I wish to start with oysters in a cumin sauce. Then pork stew with citron. Are you familiar with the dish?"

Tommaso nodded. "Very familiar. It's attributed to the great Roman chef of ancient times, Marcus Gavius Apicius."

Lorenzaccio looked impressed.

Tommaso knew the dish because of Marcus Gavius Spada's insistence on teaching him every extant recipe of Spada's namesake's repertoire.

They finished discussing the menu. Tommaso hesitated to take his leave. Caterina expected a report from him on this encounter. As yet he had little to report that she didn't already know. He took a deep breath.

"I visit the *Duchessina* the day after tomorrow. Do you have any words of greeting for her?" he asked Lorenzaccio.

Lorenzaccio's eyes hazed over. He appeared to be searching through his memory.

Tommaso sighed inwardly and wondered at the wisdom of cultivating a drunkard informant.

Lorenzaccio's face lit into a smile. He'd remembered something. "Yes, tell her I send her salutations, and there's something she should know. That's really why I sent for you. Alessandro intends to impose another tax on the city, for thirty-five thousand *scudi*. Officially its purpose is to improve Florence's fortifications. But once collected he'll spend it on preparations for the *Duchessina's* wedding."

Tommaso absorbed the implications of this news. He turned to go. Lorenzaccio clutched at his arm. "Tell my little cousin this, too. I'll never forget her kindness and encouragement in Rome." Lorenzaccio's eyes shone with wine-soaked sentiment. "Tell her no matter how far away fortune takes her, she can rest assured that someday soon a *deserving* Medici prince will rule Florence."

That night Tommaso sat at one of the smaller worktables near the roasting pit and wrote a letter to his art apprentice friends in Rome. He addressed it to Ascancio at Michelangelo's *bottega* rather than to Cencio and Paulino. He didn't want it lying about where Cellini might find it, especially because he wrote about Giorgio Vasari's change of fortune, for both better and worse.

Tommaso paused for a moment to mourn his once friend. Couldn't Giorgio see his error? His disintegrating skin alone lay like the mark of the devil upon him.

But far worse were the dark shadows that lay behind Giorgio's eyes, which he'd tried to hide from Tommaso with his downcast gaze. Whatever the pestilence was that gripped Florence's heart, rotting it from within . . . it infected Giorgio Vasari as well.

What Tommaso found strange was the lack of that same darkness in Lorenzaccio de' Medici. Perhaps the calculated viciousness of the youth, his own innate *wrongness*, rendered him immune to contamination from other sources of evil, the way strong bile burns away other poisons.

Tommaso set his pen to paper once more. He wrote circumspectly about Giorgio, knowing Ascancio would read between the lines and discern what to pass on to Cencio and Paulino. Tommaso also trusted Ascancio to glean and pass along the hidden messages for Michelangelo, who Tommaso dared not write directly.

Tommaso paused again and put his head in his hands. Living in the miasma that enveloped Florence day and night, he missed Michelangelo as he'd miss the sun.

Someone tapped his shoulder. Tommaso turned. The wizened, bright-eyed face of his great-grandmother peered at him, so close that if she'd been a bird she could have pecked him.

"I know that everyone here sings my praises to you," she said, "yet still you keep your distance." She smiled, but her voice was as tart as green apples. "Is this how young gentlemen treat ladies these days? Making women act the supplicant? Perhaps that's the modern custom; therefore, I come to you. It's time you learn from me. I grow no younger every day."

43

"S"he's in the gardens," Sister Teresa Lucrezia told Tommaso when he next arrived at the Murate.

Caterina was picking flowers with Reparata when Tommaso found her. He told her everything Lorenzaccio had said.

"'A deserving Medici prince will rule Florence,'" Tommaso quoted indignantly. "You know he speaks of himself. He doesn't mean to serve you. His ambitions center only on his own person."

A straw hat shaded Caterina's face. Its brim bobbed as she nodded. "I nurtured those ambitions in him myself, in Rome," she said. "With hopes they'd come to full bloom here in Florence."

She held out a rose the color of blood for Tommaso to smell. He inhaled deeply. It smelled like almonds, honey and iron. Caterina dropped the blossom into the basket. Her hair was bound into one long braid, twined through with a violet ribbon. It made her look very young.

"I know too little of the future," she said, her voice pensive. "Will Ippolito come for me, or will I suffer exile and marriage in France? Will those who throw in their lot with mine prosper or suffer? A fog of uncertainty hampers my actions. The one thing I'm certain of is that Cousin Lorenzino will serve Florence but not rule her.

"Let him think what he will, Tommaso. Don't attempt to disabuse him of his aspirations. He can't help but be of use to me.

"Look at this new tax Alessandro means to levy. It's an attempt to turn the citizens against me. By learning of it beforehand, I can make sure the blame doesn't fall on me. If fortune smiles, I'll even turn it to Alessandro's disadvantage." She smiled. Caterina's mood had turned full circle.

Her cat came racing up the path in full pursuit of a butterfly. It launched into the air with as spectacular a leap as any acrobat's. The moment retarded to a miracle of slowness. Multicolored cat spun about multicolored butterfly in a graceful dance that traced arabesques against the sky. Somewhere bells marked the tempo of each arc, with lingering echoing chimes.

Then the cat turned and descended toward the earth, paws down, while the butterfly fluttered up and away, none the worse for its part in the aerial waltz. The cat looked about as if to say, "Where is that flapping thing? Surely I caught it, after such effort."

Tommaso knew the cat's expression for a sham, the pose of a master clown. At the same time he realized the silver chiming was Caterina's and Reparata's pealing laughter.

"It's good to see you happy," Tommaso said. He pointed to the basket of flowers. "And pursuing young girls' pleasures."

"Alas, this is labor, not lighthearted pursuit. We gather these flowers for my perfume-making class."

"What a shame," Tommaso said with a smile. "You deserve time to play."

"Yes, I do," Caterina agreed. She peered at Tommaso. "And so do you. You appear worn. Don't you think so too, Reparata?"

Reparata, who'd gone back to picking roses after the cat's performance, looked over her shoulder at Tommaso. She nodded.

"I am fatigued," Tommaso admitted, "though life was more hectic in Rome: more work in the kitchen, more classes to attend. Perhaps I'm just getting old," he joked, though he knew very well why he felt listless and enervated in Florence. Who wouldn't? The shadow Alessandro cast over all their lives leached away energy and joy.

"Then we both need to play, to become young again," Caterina said. She unbound her braid, drawing out the long ribbon twining through it. Knotting the ribbon's ends together, she formed it into a loop. She slung the loop over her wrists. "Hold your hands out," she commanded Tommaso.

"Cat's cradle? That's a game for toddlers and . . ." Tommaso stopped himself before he said "girls." He filled in the awkward pause with, "I haven't played cat's cradle since I was little. I'm sure I don't remember how."

"I'll help you. It'll return to you quickly," Caterina cajoled. "It's the perfect game for when one is weary."

Tommaso let her push him down till he sat in the grass, between the row of flower beds and next to a stone bench. Caterina sat next to him and flipped the loop onto his wrists.

"You begin with the basic form. I'll make the first pattern, then guide you through a few more until it starts to come back to you," she said.

The cat sauntered up. It batted at the loose rectangle of ribbon formed by Tommaso's outstretched hands. Tommaso laughed and raised the rectangle out of the cat's reach. The cat responded by crawling onto Tommaso's now open, available lap.

"I can't pet you while my hands are otherwise engaged," Tommaso warned the cat.

The cat blinked up at him and curled herself into a ball.

"She, too, needs rest. You can be *her* 'cat's cradle,' in truth," Caterina said. "Stroke her when I have the patterns on my hands, while you're deciding your next move."

Caterina plucked her fingers in and out of the simple loop, drew it away from Tommaso, then stretched it wide. The ribbon formed an angled circle in the middle. Long, triangular rays shot out from it to the pattern's edges.

"The lovely, warm Sun, that makes this garden grow," Caterina said.

Tommaso petted the cat while he studied Caterina's design. The cat purred.

Caterina led Tommaso through the steps of winding his fingers through the angles of her sun. When he transferred the ribbon back to his own hands and drew it apart, it looked like a simple version of a spider's web.

"That's the Weaver," Caterina told him. "An auspicious cradle to make early in the game, since weaving *is* what we do here."

Back and forth they wove and transferred, Caterina leading Tommaso through figure after figure.

The Sun again.

The Sun Clouded Over.

Rain Clouds.

Lightning.

Rain—a pattern with drooping droplet shapes slung between the two long, supporting strands of ribbon.

The next figure placed the cat's cradle back on Tommaso's hands. "The Wind," Caterina said.

A breeze picked up. It ruffled Tommaso's hair. "It doesn't look like the wind," he objected. The picture made by the lines of the ribbon suggested a small, piquant face framed by long, sweeping feathers.

"It's the spirit of the wind." Caterina picked and plucked just a few strands and took the ribbon back. She showed Tommaso the new design. "The Wind As a Woman of Rank."

"Like you," Tommaso smiled.

Caterina nodded. "Now you try," she said.

"I don't know any patterns," Tommaso protested.

"Just play with it. See if anything comes to you. The chances are that any pattern you invent has been done before by someone else and given a name or names. I'll see if I can recognize it. That's part of the game."

Tommaso stared at the ribbon's twined intersections. He hesitated, then stuck a few fingers between them. He looked up at Caterina for some hint. Her face was as remote as a sphinx's. He looked about for Reparata, hoping she could be commandeered into the game in his stead. Reparata was picking flowers several rows away.

Tommaso returned to studying the web before him. The sun, shining on his head, felt too warm. Sweat prickled his forehead. The abstracted face in the pattern suggested something to him. He looped two long shapes around his middle fingers, readjusted the rest, untangled his thumbs and took the new design from Caterina's hands. Now the string face possessed sharp ears. The feathers became whiskers.

"From Wind into Cat." Caterina clapped her hands. "Very good."

She tangled her fingers in the ribbon and next chose A Sky Full of Stars.

From that Tommaso formed Ladder Down from a Star, Up to a Star. The breeze picked up, drying and cooling his forehead. The shifting patterns almost seemed to tell a story.

Two Girls Run Away Up the Ladder, through . . .

A Hole in the Sky.

Tommaso was surprised at how much he enjoyed the game. He

didn't remember its possessing so much nuance the few times he'd played it with Ginevra when they were young.

In his exhausted state his entire focus sank into the lines strung before him. He started to see the abstract logic underlying their structure. If he drew one strand on top of another here, a different one there, it shifted the design into a whole new configuration. He was aware of nothing else, except for at times the strengthening breeze and the cat purring in his lap.

Hills.

Wind over Hills.

Wind Swaying Trees.

The ribbon and its pattern telescoped away from Tommaso, growing simultaneously clearer and smaller. He felt himself floating above it.

Bird Flies on the Wind.

He *was* flying on the wind. He *was* the wind. The cat flew with him. No, the cat still lay curled on his lap; that's why it seemed to fly with him.

Bird Builds Nest (Home)

Bird Protects Nest (Net over Home)

With the Net, Bird Leashes the Hounds of Hell

The ribbon stretched away below him, winding through the garden rows. Its outer lengths encompassed the circumference of the garden. It passed out of sight around the buildings of the convent. Like him, the convent and its grounds also floated, but in a dark, dark sea, rather than up in the sky. Black waves lapped against the ribbon's outer edges. Only Caterina was tethered solidly to the ground. She walked and walked and walked, keeping the framework of the ribbon tightly in place.

Something shook Tommaso gently.

"Tommaso."

It shook him again. "Tommaso, wake up."

He felt the cat being lifted from his lap. He opened his eyes.

Caterina stood over him, holding the cat. "You drowsed off," she said.

Tommaso jumped to his feet, bewildered, his body stupefied by the bone-deep ache daytime napping sometimes leaves in its wake.

"Sleep? I've been asleep? For how long?"

Caterina ran one hand along her coiled braid and smiled. "Long enough for Reparata to rebind my hair."

Tommaso blushed with embarrassment. "Your Grace, I'm so sorry."

Caterina shifted the cat in her arms. "Think nothing of it. You needed to sleep. You were exhausted."

"I might as well have not slept. I don't feel the better for it," Tommaso said ruefully. "My head seems full of thick clouds. You'd think I'd been drinking bad wine."

"That happens sometimes if one falls asleep in the sun," Caterina said. "It will pass. But now I must make ready to attend my perfumery class. We'll escort you to the gate." She put the cat down on the ground.

"I forgot—I brought you some *brigidini* this time." Tommaso belatedly handed her a small covered basket.

Caterina took out one of the wafers as they walked along. Reparata and the cat trailed behind. When Caterina bit into the cookie it crunched sweetly.

"Just like the ones you baked to seduce that fabric merchant all unwitting to our cause, back in Rome. Those were good days," she said wistfully.

She asked after Piera and the rest of Tommaso's family.

"When next you see your mother, tell her to visit me when she can," Caterina said. "I've yet to meet your new baby brother."

She wanted to know how Tommaso's Befanini relatives fared. She remembered them all fondly from the days when she learned something of the culinary arts in their kitchen.

Tommaso told her he'd started an apprenticeship of sorts with Angelina Befanini.

"I began reluctantly," he admitted. "But after only two days of working beside her, I confess myself amazed at her wisdom. She knows how to calm the excitable, energize the listless, heal all sorts of small illnesses—all unbeknownst to those suffering. She simply adds little amounts of this or that to their food or drink." Tommaso shook his head. "In her own way, she's as good a doctor as Ruggiero the Old. I recall my mother doing much the same thing when I was a child, but I never paid attention then."

Caterina took his arm in hers and patted it. "Then this is a fortuitous opportunity for you. How fares your cousin Umberto? I remember well how we all used to play together."

Tommaso laughed. "You wouldn't recognize him, he's grown so tall and thin."

"Umberto? Thin? Impossible!"

They'd reached the outside entrance to the convent.

Caterina patted Tommaso's arm again. "Thank you, my gossip, for playing with me today. You let me relive that happy time in my childhood."

Tommaso bowed. He turned to go. As he stepped out onto the street he remembered something from his nap: the way the black ocean's tide washed up to these very gates. He looked down. Only innocent cobblestones lay beneath his feet.

Later that day Caterina returned to the garden, accompanied only by Gattamelata at her feet and Ginevra resting against her breast. Caterina began to walk again the pattern of protection, meandering from the heart of the garden outward. As she traced it with her footsteps along the outer borders she looked down to where the inky shadows licked, always tasting and testing, trying to find a weakness in the boundaries protecting her.

The small stones Piera and others like Piera had embedded around the Murate years ago still held fast. Caterina's own powers now strengthened the barriers, but she was troubled by how many of Florence's secret resources had gone toward saving her rather than the city.

It went well today. Ginevra's thoughts glowed warm against Caterina's breast. *What Tommaso sees, the Little Kitchen Goddess sees. What She sees, he will see. He begins to move to Her bidding. Look how he comprehended and shifted the components of the cat's cradle.*

Don't you fear for your brother? Caterina asked Ginevra. *My whole life I've chafed at the power denied me. At every juncture attempts are made to turn me into a biddable pawn. Is what we're doing to Tommaso any better?*

A sad smile flavored Ginevra's responding thoughts. *We've exchanged places, you and I. Up to now it's been my duty to chide you on Tommaso's behalf. What has altered?*

I thought by now we'd be embarked on happier times. Caterina's admission was bitter. *I thought by now Ippolito and I would be wed, or nearly so. I thought we'd have passed the times of dangerous actions. That any labors required of Tommaso as the Little Kitchen Goddess's familiar would be joyful, not jeopardizing.* Caterina looked sullenly at the cat at her feet.

When Ginevra's reply came, it was from a distance. *The stars ordained*

Tommaso's binding to the Little Kitchen Goddess before his birth. The pity is in that fact's discovery so late, not in the part you play in his life. Take comfort in this thought: As much as she uses him, the Little Kitchen Goddess protects him. Since your return, how many Florentines have you seen with poison shadows pooling in their eyes? But for the Little Kitchen Goddess, Tommaso might be one of them. And know this. The Little Kitchen Goddess asks nothing of Tommaso that he wouldn't choose to do himself.

Tommaso fell asleep that night dreaming that he lay in Michelangelo's arms. I miss you, he heard himself say over and over, until Michelangelo silenced his mouth with a kiss. Never let me leave you.

It was already too late. He felt himself growing thinner, insubstantial as he was pulled from the room, flying faster and faster away from Michelangelo, sweeping down hallways in a large dim mansion.

He recognized what was happening. He'd become a breeze again, unnaturally blowing through the Salviati palazzo. I'm repeating that dream. The despair he felt at being torn from Michelangelo's arms abated. He knew he'd sweep into the Greek scholar's room and hear once more the plot against Caterina's life, which he'd once more help foil. The same past, the same future.

Then he saw that the dream had changed. He was soaring through a different house—the de' Medici palazzo.

Of course, for that's where I now live. Where I fell asleep. That's where this mirage would start, he assured himself with a dreamer's logic. Just like before, he heard faint voices coming from a room somewhere deeper within the mansion. Yes, it is the same.

As he drew closer, though, the voices didn't clarify into those he remembered. He heard no strong Greek accent, no gruff Roman voice. Tommaso flattened and slid like water under the door.

Lit oil lamps lined the walls. As if they were no more than flat, pigment-formed lanterns painted on some artist's canvas, their flames cast no true light. Darkness seeped through the luxuriously furnished suite.

Lorenzaccio de' Medici perched on the edge of a carved oak bench. The bench stood next to a sideboard lined with wine bottles and decanters. Lorenzaccio was turning and considering those within his reach. "I see not why you covet any woman's attributes," he said. "They could prove antithetical to your nature. Even *The Courtier* states that 'virtue (*la virtù*) is feminine, and vice (*il vizio*) is masculine.'"

Lorenzaccio appeared to address his remarks to a nearby large bed, in which lay a pool of shadow.

To Tommaso's horror, those shadows deepened, became denser, rose up into a shape.

"Trust that I have no interest in virtue, whether belonging to a woman or anyone else, my philosopher." The voice that emerged from the solidifying darkness was Alessandro de' Medici's. "But if virtue precipitates in its wake any sort of power . . . yes, that I covet."

If Tommaso could have screamed, he would have. The sound he made whistled like a draft keening through warped window casements.

The oily black creature turned in his direction, shrank back a little. "What was that?" it said.

Lorenzaccio made his choice and seized a decanter by its neck. "Nothing. Just a night breeze."

The hideous amorphous shape shifted restlessly in the bed. "Nighttime. Time to inspect my city. *My* city." It oozed to and then over the edge of the bed. As it poured it gradually took on the contours, lightness and dimensionality of Duke Alessandro.

Has he always been thus? Tommaso wondered. He searched his memory for all the times he'd encountered Alessandro in the past. A villain, yes, but surely a man. This is a dream, Tommaso reminded himself. Naught but a dream. Then he remembered the first time he saw Alessandro, silhouetted as an inky outline on the kitchen steps, hovering over Caterina.

Lorenzaccio sighed. "Riding out on the town? Again?" Lorenzaccio regretfully placed the decanter back on the sideboard. He seemed no more aware of Alessandro as a monster than he was of Tommaso as a breeze.

Tommaso followed the two rogues. They walked down to the stables and saddled their horses. Tommaso whirled about Lorenzaccio, trying to get his attention. Lorenzaccio just shivered and drew his cloak tightly about him. "It's chilly tonight," he complained to Alessandro.

Alessandro laughed at him. "A hard ride will warm you," he said. He wheeled his mount around, then galloped out through the mansion's gates. Lorenzaccio grimaced and followed.

Tommaso kept pace, gliding above them as they rode through the streets. Alessandro acted like a madman, careening through empty food stalls, racing to trample tipplers lurching their way home. He dismounted once to briefly and brutally couple with a prostitute in an alley. When she demanded payment for the abuse, he cuffed her, saying, "Your compensation is the honor of servicing your Duke."

She spat at him.

He knocked her down, kicked her in the ribs, then rode on.

"So much for women's virtue!" he crowed to Lorenzaccio.

Alessandro seemed to ride randomly, with no rhyme or reason. From Tommaso's high vantage point, however, a pattern started emerging. Street to street, then back along the same roadways,—with his wild peregrinations Alessandro wove a figure that reminded Tommaso of the design Caterina had walked through the Murate gardens. Even as that thought occurred to Tommaso, Alessandro and Lorenzaccio arrived at the Murate's perimeter. They rode back and forth around its boundaries, like spiders spinning restraints around trapped prey. Only the Murate's frontage down to the Arno kept them from encircling it completely.

Without flying into the Murate itself, Tommaso sensed Caterina's presence. He felt her lying on her bed, body stiff, fists clenched, fighting the black tides reaching for her.

Tommaso lingered after Alessandro and Lorenzaccio rode on. He swept down to the sticky, black, spiderweb-like threads left behind by Alessandro. Tommaso bunched himself into a ball of wind, then sprang forth, a miniature but potent gale. Some of the threads frayed. He blew again. They broke. The pattern recoiled, gave way, collapsed in that section. Tommaso glided over to another segment of the pattern, exhaling explosively over and over again.

This is only a dream, Tommaso reminded himself. This is only a dream.

The next morning Umberto couldn't wake Tommaso. His cousin lay like as unmovable as a corpse. Umberto shook him.

"Should we call for last rites?" one of the other apprentices joked.

"No. He still breathes."

"Leave him, then," the other boy said. "There's no need of him. Breakfast in the banquet hall has been delayed till noon. Duke Alessandro hasn't yet risen. He took it in his head to go out riding through the streets in the middle of the night. He came home just before dawn."

44

June, 1532

Piera handed Tommaso a letter one day when he arrived at the Ruggiero kitchen for a visit.

"This came here yesterday, addressed to you," she said. She peered at Tommaso closely. "There are circles under your eyes. Are you ill, or having trouble sleeping?"

Tommaso leaned over the cradle set up near the outer kitchen door so baby Ambrogio could enjoy the honeyed summer air. When he crossed his eyes at his little brother, Ambrogio chuckled with delight. Tommaso smiled. "This one is so different from Luciana," he said.

Piera folded her arms and frowned.

Tommaso sighed. She wasn't going to let him change the subject. "I'm troubled by a surfeit, not a lack of sleep. I dream so often and hard, I vow I find more rest in waking."

"Then I'll make a tea for you tonight that returns peace and pleasure to slumber," Piera promised. "When you go back to the Medici palazzo, tell Grandmother Angelina of your quandary. She'll concoct an even finer cure for you."

Tommaso kissed his mother on the cheek. "Good as she is, that's not possible. The best remedies come from *your* two lovely hands."

Piera rolled her eyes. "We'd such high hopes for you as a cook. Instead you strive to cultivate courtiers' skills."

Tommaso feigned wounded feelings. "What? Can't a young Florentine gentleman offer his own mother honest flattery?"

Piera swung a wooden spoon at him, to the amusement of the scullions nearby. Tommaso ducked and pulled up a stool near the cradle so he could rock it. He opened the letter. Skimming its contents, he started to grin.

Gentile walked in from the storage room, carrying a small cask of walnut oil. "Is the news of good fortune, or do you smile at some fool's misadventures?" he asked.

"Both, I suppose," Tommaso replied. "This letter is from my friend Ascancio in Rome. Among other things, he writes of Benevenuto Cellini's most recent escapades."

At the mention of Cellini, Amado and the scullery maids carried whatever they were working on closer to Tommaso.

"Can you share the tale with us?" Piera asked.

Tommaso looked about him. "Yes, as long as my audience is not of too tender and impressionable years."

"Luciana and Paolo are out playing in the garden," Piera assured him.

"Then I'd be happy to tell the story," Tommaso said.

"Wait! Let me fetch Marchetto before you begin," Francesca said, running from the room.

"You remember how I told you of Cellini's infatuation with a young courtesan? How the girl's mother and brothers spirited her away? And of Cellini's subsequent pathetic behavior?" Tommaso asked when his audience assembled.

Tommaso had also related Cellini's friendship with the necromancer and the necromancer's ensuing predictions, but he'd left out the harrowing episode in the Coliseum.

"Well, Ascancio writes me the conclusion of that tale."

> "Shortly after you left, Tommaso, Signor Benevenuto Cellini became involved in one of those public brawls he's infamous for. Cellini picked up and hurled what he later claimed he thought was just a lump of mud at the fellow he was exchanging insults with, one *Ser* Benedetto. Perhaps his fine, goldsmith's hands aren't as sensitive as he claims—they didn't detect the heavy, sharp rock in the center of the clod. This projectile struck Cellini's adversary in the head. The man fell as though dead.

"It so happened that just then Cellini's old nemesis Pompeo—Pope Clement's personal jeweler—strolled by. Pompeo thought the man laid low was Tobbia, a goldsmith who with Pompeo's connivance had stolen several important papal commissions away from Cellini.

"Pompeo ran post haste to the Pope. He told the Pontiff that Cellini had just murdered Tobbia. Furious, the Pope ordered Cellini to be hanged at once on the very spot where he'd 'murdered' Tobbia.

"Cardinal Ippolito, recently returned to Rome on a visit, sent one of his men to warn Cellini. Cellini for once put discretion before valor and fled. He knew the Pope would eventually find out the truth of the matter. But that would do him, Cellini, no good if he were already hung.

"Cellini traveled through Palombara and toward Naples. Near Naples he chanced upon an inn run by a fellow Florentine. Since the time neared when the necromancer had predicted he'd find his love again, Cellini asked the innkeeper if he knew of two Sicilian courtesans, Beatrice and her daughter Angelica. The innkeeper replied he'd heard of two doxies named just so, but whether they hailed from Sicily he knew not. Their house wasn't far from the inn.

"Cellini sought the place. There he discovered his Angelica, on the last day of the month in which the necromancer predicted he'd find her.

"Courtesan and goldsmith spent a brief time together in bliss, during which period Cellini also wrangled an introduction to the Viceroy of Naples. From this circumstance he gained several commissions from His Excellency the Viceroy.

"Then Cellini received several letters from Cardinal de' Medici, instructing him to return immediately to Rome to reclaim his good name. The

Cardinal had intervened on Cellini's behalf with the Pope. Now was the time for Cellini to take advantage of this truce, since the Cardinal planned on returning to Hungary soon.

"Cellini's courtesan wept and begged him to take her with him. He dickered over the price with her mother, who kept increasing the girl's worth: fifteen ducats; then thirty ducats; also a black-velvet gown for the girl; then a gown for the mother; outlays for Beatrice's roguish sons; and yet *more* money.

"At last Cellini refused. He left, laughing.

"That's what all those months of moping, pining and languishing came to: a turned heel and disinterested laugh. These days he appears quite unbeglamored."

The end of the tale entertained Tommaso's parents and the rest of the Ruggiero kitchen help as much as the beginning of the adventure had entertained the Salviati kitchen staff in Rome.

Later, when his family and the rest of the kitchen were busy serving the Ruggieros supper in the main house, Tommaso sat by the fire and read the rest of the letter. In it there was more valuable information enciphered for Caterina about Ippolito's comings and goings. And this:

"All here who love and miss you send their greetings," Ascancio wrote. "In spite of summer's warmth, life has turned dreary for them. In the absence of the sun, they turn to a lesser light, under which they shall not bloom so well, but will survive."

Tommaso stared, stared and stared again at these words, trying to make out their meaning.

45

Tommaso did as his mother bid him. The next night he asked Angelina Befanini for a soporific recipe.

"We'll make my best tea," she said, pulling jars of herbs from the shelves. "Yarrow, of course." She scooped some into a bowl. "Aniseed. A pinch or so of motherwort. Some fennel. Hops, linden, calendula . . ." She kept adding herbs until Tommaso could no longer keep track of them.

"Wait," he protested. "Let me fetch something to write on."

Angelina put out a hand to stop him. "Pages can be lost." She tapped the side of her temple with an index finger. "Learn to write in the permanent ledger of your head. Don't despair. There's common sense to each herb. You'll learn. Use reason."

"I'll try," said Tommaso. "I know that linden, calendula and hops make one drowse. Yarrow . . . ?"

"To lend sleep some warmth and comfort," Angelina said. She mixed up all the ingredients in the bowl with a wooden spoon.

"And motherwort . . ." just saying the name brought the memory of that herb's flavor to Tommaso's tongue. "I remember my mother making tisanes of it for Ginevra and me when we were little."

Angelina nodded. She put several heaping spoons of the tea mixture into a pot, then poured boiling water over it. "Motherwort sharpens your dreaming, makes it stronger."

"Then isn't it contraindicated for me? I'd prefer less strength and more peace to my dreams."

"You just think you do. Motherwort improves the third eye's ability, makes second sight keener," Angelina told him. "To want less of that is like wishing for blindness.

"The linden, calendula and hops counterbalance motherwort's side effects but not its purpose. Usually I add just one of those three for sound sleep. But in your case, all three together are required to assure restful slumber."

Talk of a third eye and second sight made Tommaso uneasy.

"The aniseed..." Surely that was a safer topic. "It must be good for many things. A general health tonic? I've noticed you add it to almost everything we eat here in the kitchen."

"We didn't use to have to cook that way," Angelina's voice turned suddenly melancholy. "Did you also notice we add no aniseed to dishes intended for the banquet hall?"

In spite of the shift in his great-grandmother's mood, Tommaso was amused. "A cunning form of poisoning by omission?" he guessed. "By denying the Duke and his compatriots subtle nourishment might they, if we add sufficient prayers, fall prey to some mortal illness?"

Angelina fixed him with a sharp eye. "Don't mock me! Aniseed wards off evil spirits. That's why we use so much of it in this kitchen." She poured the tea through a strainer into a big cup, then handed it to Tommaso.

Tommaso smiled sarcastically. "If you truly believe that, then why not feed aniseed to Alessandro in buckets? All Florence could use to have his evil demons driven from him."

Angelina put her hands on her hips and glared at Tommaso. "Drink!" she commanded.

Knowing he'd pushed too far, Tommaso bowed his head and contritely sipped the tea. It tasted both astringent and bitingly aromatic. The hops lent it a meaty, soupish heft.

"If aniseed could drive evil spirits from Alessandro de' Medici, we'd have purged him years ago, when he, Caterina and Ippolito all dwelled under this roof together," Angelina said as she funneled the remainder of the tea mixture into a glass bottle.

"You're an educated young man, Tommaso. You know your

numbers, know how to account. You know one can't subtract something from itself and have anything left. Alessandro doesn't suffer from possession by evil spirits. His flaw is that he *is* an evil spirit. And because he's an evil spirit, we could poison and kill his body. That would be the worse for us, since his venomous essence would remain, spreading even more through the city than it does already."

Tommaso choked on a mouthful of tea. A stinging, alkaline sensation of yarrow and motherwort shot up his nose. He sniffed it back down wetly, coughing.

"Great-grandmother, why do you tell me such things? I was raised an Arista, not a Befanini. Share that sort of knowledge with someone born and raised here, like Umberto. I lack the abilities of a witch or a mage. It would take a..."—he thought for a brief moment—"a Ruggiero to comprehend them."

"Which is precisely why I'm telling *you*," Angelina said. She ground a stopper into the top of the bottle.

Tommaso thought he saw the point she tried to make. "I grew up *at* the Ruggieros, not *with* them, not *taught* by them. Our kitchen there constitutes a separate world. Look at my father. He works for the Ruggieros, respects them for their physicking. But he holds no countenance with their occult labors."

"That matters not. How you're raised, what you're taught—that *can* be important. But in the end it's blood that tells," Angelina said. "Your father's proclivities . . . well, sometimes talent skips a generation. Look at my own son, your grandfather! I wasn't talking about the Ruggiero's ambience influencing you. I meant their blood. Their blood in you."

Tommaso stared at her, stupefied.

She sighed. "I'm not surprised you don't know. I'm sure your father doesn't either, the secret was that well kept. Possibly even Ruggiero the Old is blind to what went on almost under his nose. What do you know of your father's lineage?"

Tommaso flushed. "That he was almost born a lowly country bastard." He repeated the family history Galleoto Arista had told him in Rome.

Angelina threw back her head and laughed till she coughed. "That Galleoto! Always the donkey's rump. I never doubted that he was fooled. He always believed whatever might favor him with an advantage." Angelina wiped tears from the corners of her eyes.

"No 'almost' about it. Your father *was* born a bastard, but not a lowly one. Marcantonio's first wife—that silly country girl—she was so hopelessly smitten with dashing young Marcantonio that she'd have done anything for him. And did. She claimed Gentile as her own child. Her reward was Marcantonio's hand in marriage and his bastard son in her cradle. She lacked the intelligence to understand until too late that she'd never lay claim to Marcantonio's heart. And hardly ever his bed, from what I heard."

"Then who was my father's mother?" Tommaso asked.

"Can't you guess?" Angelina winked at him. "Think back on Galleoto's tale. The clues are all there."

Tommaso couldn't organize his stunned, muddy thoughts around the question.

Angelina finally took pity on him. "Remember, Ruggiero the Old's mother often took her children to the country in those days. That's how Marcantonio first came to travel there—to serve them.

"After the revelation that the young Arista scoundrel had compromised some maiden, the whole Ruggiero family but for Ruggiero the Old and his father rushed back to the countryside for long months. A lingering illness in one of the younger children was their pretext. Once there, the eldest Ruggiero daughter contracted the illness as well. They cloistered her in an outbuilding to keep the contagion from spreading. Or so they told everyone.

"The truth was simpler. They secluded her to hide the fact of her thickening waist. Only two people visited her at that time: her mother and the fellow who brought her all her meals, the fellow who'd impregnated her—Marcantonio.

"Once she gave birth, the family whisked the girl swiftly back to Florence. They married her off as soon as possible to one of Florence's well-off families.

"Marcantonio and his bastard son remained at the farm, banished. Old chef Arista and Madonna Ruggiero put their heads together. They wed off MarcAntonio as well, to the infatuated peasant maid.

"Later, after that sad, disillusioned girl died, Marcantonio married again, a young woman I heard he came to care for deeply, if not with as great a passion as his first true love.

"In the meantime, the elder Ruggiero's heart softened. I'm of the belief that his now-married daughter came to him and pleaded the case of her secret, firstborn child. And maybe he wanted his first grandson near him, bastard or no. Whatever the reason, he permitted your father, now a sturdy young boy, to come to Florence to be raised by his Uncle Ambrogio.

"It wounded Marcantonio to let Gentile go, but he wouldn't stand in the way of his son's future. Perhaps he hoped Gentile's mother might be afforded the opportunity to see her son now and then."

"Did she?" Tommaso asked.

Angelina shrugged. "I know she visited and dined with her parents on occasion. I also know your father helped serve at the table. But I don't believe he ever knew the truth of it. She died some years later in childbirth. I doubt Gentile would be made any happier to know this story now. I only tell you so you won't deny your own potential. There's even more Ruggiero in you than Befanini."

She poured Tommaso another cup of tea. Tommaso drank it, but he doubted he'd derive any benefit from it. His head whirled with too many thoughts, too many questions, to allow for the possibility of slumber that night.

He fell asleep before he could draw the covers up to his chin.

46

In August, Tommaso's family celebrated his birthday. They invited his artist friends, Elissa Pecorino, and all the Befanini cousins, who came in shifts from their work in the de' Medici kitchen, and members of Florence's other culinary families. Ruggiero the Old gave his permission for a fête honoring Tommaso to be held in the garden. The younger Ruggiero children, grown so tall Tommaso didn't recognize them, helped carry out chairs and benches from the main house, under their older brothers Cosimo and Lorenzo's direction.

Gentile hired musicians and even a small fireworks display to be held on the Arno after nightfall. He took great pains to introduce Tommaso to the guest cooks as they arrived, with many asides as to whether this one or that one would make a good choice for the *Duchessina*'s cooking staff.

Tommaso finally begged for a little respite from all the socializing. He helped himself to a goblet of lemon water and looked for a place to rest.

Piera sat on a garden bench, nursing Ambrogio, tapping her toes to the musicians' lively music and watching a number of the guests dancing. Tommaso sat down next to her. Cousin Leonora was dancing with his artist friend Vittorio, Salvatore danced with one of Leonora's nubile daughters, Cousin Umberto danced with Elissa Pecorino. Even laconic Enzio danced with Massolina. Gherardo was trying to coax little Luciana into capering about with him. Luciana fixed Gherardo with a strong look, as though he were mad. Gherardo feigned a broken heart at her refusal. Luciana marched off, clearly undesirous of associating with adults who acted like children.

Tommaso nudged Piera and pointed out the little drama to her. "Poor Gherardo! What hope does he have if even a five-year-old rejects him?"

"He shouldn't feel dejected. Luciana's trothed her heart to another," Piera said. "Wait. You'll see."

A few moments later Luciana made her way around the outskirts of the dancers to where little Paolo was playing a dice game with some other young boys. Luciana poked at Paolo, then hauled him to his feet and dragged him to the edge of the circle. She positioned him carefully, then started dancing around him. Paolo looked vexed at first. Bit by bit, the music, a *lavanderine*, took hold of him. He still stood still, but his feet tapped and shuffled in place. He tried to clap his hands at the proper time. Finally, he started copying Luciana's leaping steps, though he lacked Luciana's grace.

"Oh dear," said Tommaso, laughing. "I don't remember my own terpsichean education. Is that how all men learn to dance?

Piera was laughing too. "Not you, but many, I wager. You always loved dancing and didn't need such persuasion. When you were but half Paolo's size, as soon as a piper struck up a tune you'd commence in jumping and prancing. Gentile used to call you his little redheaded flea."

Salvatore waved for Tommaso to join them.

Tommaso didn't even try to shout above the music. He shook his head and raised his glass to show he was drinking.

Piera looked at him. "You're somewhat discomfited by this party, aren't you?."

Tommaso nodded. His mother knew him too well.

"Why?" Piera asked. "You've attended many celebrations. One thing can be said about cooks: We attend more festivities than any other occupation, except, perhaps, musicians."

Tommaso squirmed. His parents had made so much of this fête, had spent so much on it, he felt guilty that he couldn't abandon himself to its pleasures.

"What you say is true, but it feels strange to attend a party and not be working. Even stranger, to be the sole focus of the celebration. It makes me feel inside out, somehow."

Piera patted his knee. "I know what it is," she said. "You grew unaccustomed to them. How many of your birthdays and saint days passed us by, because they fell during the plague or siege, or you'd left for Rome? Think of *this* occasion as making all of that up to you at once. We missed celebrating those days that marked the sum of your accomplishments each year and how much you'd grown."

Tommaso nodded again, accepting his mother's reasoning.

"But I'm only seventeen today. This particular celebration..." He looked around at the crowd. "It's the kind you'd hold for me in seven or eight years, when I'd be old enough to go into business for myself, or ready to look for a wife."

Piera bowed her head. "Yes. It's that kind of a celebration too. It seems likely when the time for that observance naturally arrives, you'll have flown far away from us. So your father and I decided to seize the opportunity now."

She rose from the bench. "Come. I've a gift for you."

She led him into the kitchen, where she settled a milk-drowsy Ambrogio into his cradle. "Wait here," she told Tommaso.

A few moments later she returned from the family room carrying something folded and dark.

"A mark of your coming of age. No good, sober Florentine gentleman's wardrobe should lack one," she said, handing it to Tommaso.

Tommaso unfolded it. It was a *lucco*, the traditional long, black, hooded men's gown, woven from an exceptionally fine grade of lamb's wool.

"I've never owned such fine clothing before," Tomasso said.

"Hold it up against you and see if it fits," Piera said.

Tommaso shook it out to its full length. "Oh my," he laughed. "So much for sartorial sobriety."

The satin lining inside the hood blazed forth, an eye-scalding blue.

"I thought it would look splendid against your hair," Piera said.

Tommaso rolled up the *lucco's* fabric at its lower hem. The bright lining continued all the way down.

"And this, too, against my ankles?" he teased.

"Wear it when you walk the city's streets," Piera said, ignoring his comment. "Take your place among Florence's men." She took the *lucco* back from him and refolded it.

"For safekeeping," she said. "I'll return it to you tonight. That will be the first time you wear it. Now go and dance."

Tommaso *did* now feel more like dancing. The musicians were playing a traditional men's dance, so he leapt in to join his friends. Later the tunes turned back to couples' jigs. Tommaso didn't know whom to ask. He couldn't bear to confront the faces of the guest cooks' and carvers' daughters. He knew their parents hoped to betroth one of them to him before he departed in Caterina's service. A few of the girls smiled at him, as Alessa Ramerino had in Rome. More looked miserable and afraid.

To marry me will be a curse, Tommaso thought. It might serve their parents well, but these poor maidens know they'd likely suffer permanent exile from Florence and their families.

Rather than cause any of them undue hope or fear, Tommaso bowed to Leonora's young daughter Teodora.

Everyone smiled at the gallantry Tommaso showed a child.

Unlike Luciana's refusal of Gherardo, Teodora curtsied gravely in return and gave Tommaso her hand.

Too young to know the steps to couples' dances, she moved through the footwork as best she could, with a deliberate, gathered grace. "Someday I'll dance better," she told Tommaso, her voice serious but not apologetic.

"Someday you'll be an excellent dancer," Tommaso agreed. "You're learning well right now. But do you enjoy it?"

"Yes," Teodora said solemnly.

"Ah. I wasn't certain. Most people smile when they enjoy themselves. Especially when they're dancing," Tommaso said, teasing her.

Teodora frowned at first, as if he'd rebuked her. Then she favored Tommaso with a shy smile.

Who would have believed gregarious, outrageous Leonora could produce such a restrained, sober child? Tommaso thought, amused.

The musicians halted for dinner. The younger men spread blankets on the ground and on the benches for supping al fresco. Gentile, Amado and Marchetto brought out pans of artichoke frittatas from the kitchen to join the platefuls of *crostini*, stuffed cabbage rolls, braised fava beans and cardoons, and dozens of other dishes.

Much later, when appetites finally flagged, Tommaso endured a number of speeches meant to laud him, inspire him or poke fun of him.

Ruggiero the Old and Madonna Ruggiero even joined the festivities for a while. Ruggiero the Old presented Tommaso with a black-velvet cap. Cosimo Ruggiero then gave him a very small pouch. "To go with the cap," he said.

Tommaso slid out the pouch's contents. Cosimo's gift was an elegant pin, of the sort intended to decorate a cap or hat. This one was made of cast gold, further embellished with gold granulation. It depicted a lion grasping a lily.

"A lion because you were born under Leo's sign," Cosimo said. "The lily represents Florence."

"It's beautiful," Tommaso said, pinning it onto his new cap. "It reminds me of Benevenuto Cellini's heraldic device." He smiled a little ruefully.

"Not entirely a coincidence," Cosimo said. "It's a common device. It symbolizes one who defends or represents Florence."

Tommaso set the cap on his head, posing for the other guests.

He received other gifts as well: a pair of good gloves; some velvet slippers. Gentile gave him a set of new carving knives, their handles impressed with the same design as Cosimo's pin. "To remember that you stand for Florence, no matter where the stars guide you," Gentile said.

Gherardo, Salvatore and Rafaello da Montelupo's old apprentice Zuccone had gone in together to buy Tommaso a sheaf of good drawing paper. "So you'll not forget you're also an artist, and always a member of our company," Salvatore told him.

Vittorio followed right after them with a small, slender wooden case. Tommaso opened it. Inside lay several fine ink brushes wrapped in paper.

"Take good care of them," Vittoriano admonished him. "They came all the way from Venice." He embrace Tommaso, kissing his cheeks. "Have a care with the paper that wraps them," he whispered in Tommaso's ear. "It too traveled far to reach you, from Rome."

Later, when the ink of night spilled downward to the horizon, the party strolled over to the Arno. Tommaso wore his new *lucco* for the first time. His friends demanded that he whirl about frequently, so the azure lining might swirl into view.

As stars started to pinprick the sky, the fireworks artisans launched their fiery compositions from a boat in the middle of the river. The reflecting surface of the water, the banks of the shore, the faces of

Tommaso's friends and family; all were brindled with light—with gold, emerald, violet, ruby and sapphire blue luminescence.

In this small space, for this short time, the opaque threatening shadows fled, banished.

After everyone had gone home and gone to bed, Tommaso sat at the Ruggiero kitchen table. By an oil lamp's light he carefully spread out the paper that wrapped Vittorio's pens. It had been folded in half and then sealed. Tommaso broke the seal, unfolded the paper. Verses in a beloved hand greeted his eye.

> "If chaste love, if supernal pity,
> If one equal fortune between two lovers,
> If bitter fate befalling one becomes the other's
> If one spirit governs two heart's moiety.
>
> "If one soul is made eternal in two bodies, two
>   behests,
> Both rising to heaven with equal wings,
> If Love with a single blow of a golden dart flings,
> Discerns and burns the entrails of two breasts.
>
> "If loving one the other, himself neither
> With one pleasure and one delight, to the same
>   reward
> Which both would reach together with a single
>   breath.
>
> "If thousands and thousands would not make up
>   one hundredth
> of such a knot of love, such faith, such a binding
>   cord
> Only contempt could break it, only scorn it
>   dissever."

The handwriting was Michelangelo's.

47

Early in the fall Duke Alessandro sent orders to the kitchen to pre-pare a great banquet. He had important visitors to entertain and he meant to put on a feast worthy of his ancestors. For the first time in a long while some of the kitchen staff would help present the dishes. Tommaso and Giacomo practiced a clever, two-roast tandem demon-stration of carving skills to serve as both an entremet and the initiation of the roast meats course.

By the evening of the banquet, two long tables had been set up in the dining hall. Alessandro presided at the head of one, Francesco Guic-ciardini at the head of the other. A number of the *Signoria* attended, as did members of several other councils; the *Dodici Buonomini*, the *Sedici Gonfalonieri*, and the Six of Commerce. Notably absent were any members of the dismantled Ten of War, though all of the Eight of Security were present.

Most of the council members—especially if they brought young, pretty wives—endeavored to sit at Gucciardini's table. Giorgio Vasari also sat at Gucciardini's table, at the foot. Giorgio looked unhappy.

At his table, Alessandro hosted his out-of-town guests, most of whom were visiting from Rome. Alessandro's comrades sat at the Duke's table as well, as did many of the invited clergy. Tommaso knew the priests hoped to curry favor with Alessandro, so he'd report favorably on them to the Pope.

A few of the council members escorting their wives had been unable to get themselves seated with Gucciardini. Most of their spouses, however, were older or unattractive. There were a few exceptions. Tommaso recognized one of them, a Soderini daughter married to a Signor Ginori. A pretty woman with attractive manners, she doted, in an unsimpering and dignified manner, on her much older and rather stuffy husband. Alessandro kept breaking off his conversation to stare at her. The expression on his face conveyed to all that he wished she were the next course.

The guest sitting beside Alessandro in the seat of honor also appeared interested in Madonna Ginori, though in a slightly less rude manner. Giorgio Vasari had good reason to look apprehensive and disgruntled. The visiting guest of honor was Benevenuto Cellini.

Tommaso and Great-uncle Giacomo approached to stand between the heads of the tables—Tommaso closer to Gucciardini, Giacomo next to Alessandro. While they made the necessary preparations for their presentation, Tommaso eavesdropped as much as he could on the Duke's and Cellini's conversation.

Alas for Giorgio. Cellini was angling for commissions to design medals and new coins for Alessandro.

When Giacomo and Tommaso were ready, Alessandro's trumpeters blasted forth a few notes to draw everyone's attention. As Tommaso set his eyes fully forward, so that he looked down the length between the two tables, he felt Cellini's eyes and recognition finally fall on him. Tommaso fought a desire to cringe.

At the second round of trumpet roar, Tommaso and Giacomo thrust their forks each into his own roast and hoisted them in unison. The slivers of meat from the two haunches fell at exactly the same moment, gliding down to the serving platters to form the precise same patterns. At the conclusion of the demonstration, Giacomo and Tommaso marched side by side around the tables with the platters held before them, to provide the diners with a closer look at the perfection of their art. Then they separated to serve the meat.

As Tommaso came around on the inner length of Gucciardini's table, heading back up toward its head, Cellini momentarily caught his eye, then turned back to Alessandro.

"Yes, Your Excellency. Valerio Vincentino enjoys the praise of any admirer of stone engraving, including myself. Vincentino is one of the few other artisans employed by His Holiness that I don't object to, his mastery of his art is that excellent.

"But the news from the art circles that all Rome talks of centers around the divine Signor Buonarotti. Not his sculpture or painting this time, but his poetry. He's written a good deal of it of late, some of which has come to public light."

Alessandro made some polite noises. Cellini leapt on these as an invitation to recite. He didn't stand, but his strong, dramatic voice carried well down the tables.

> "If chaste love, if supernal pity,
> "If one equal fortune between two lovers..."

Cellini continued to relate the entire set of verses Tommaso had received on his birthday from Michelangelo.

The blush on Tommaso's face spread from his neck downward, till his entire body felt lightly scorched.

How did this come out? he thought. Then, No one will know the poem is meant for me. This is merely Cellini's cruelty privately visited on me.

"How pretty. The sculptor loves and speaks," commented Lorenzaccio, sitting only several seats away from Alessandro and Cellini. "But is this single effort enough to laud him for literary talents?"

Tommaso was surprised when Cellini, who usually dismissed other men as lesser lights with an easy, uncaring arrogance, cast Lorenzaccio a glare of active dislike.

"Judge for yourself," he said coldly. "Here's another recent effort from Signor Buonarotti's pen."

> "I believed the first day I saw and admired
> so many forms of beauty, unique, without
>   compare,
> That I could fix my eyes like an eagle in the air
> upon the least of the many I desired.
>
> "But then I knew by error was I inspired,
> For he who seeks without wings to follow an
>   angel there

is flinging seeds upon rocks, and words to winds,
and mere intellect to God.
Thus vainly I aspired.

"Hence I approach, my heart cannot support
such infinite beauty which, dazzling, blinds the
    eyes,
Nor from afar assures me or trust instill.

"What will become of me? What guide or escort
might ever shield or solace me against surprise?
If I draw near, you burn me; if I depart you kill."

Tommaso froze where he stood. He recognized Michelangelo's shining love in those words. Words not meant for him, but for someone Michelangelo had not yet conquered.

The tray began to shake in Tommaso's hands. He felt a hoisting fork thrust into his chest, rip his heart out from between his ribs, and turn it, bleeding, for the entertainment of all.

48

Late October

Once the weather turned cold and damp, Caterina met her visitors in one of the Murate's guest salons. Tommaso smiled as he approached her, shaking some errant rain from his hair.

"I see I'm not your only caller," he said as he pulled up a stool. "Will you introduce me to your small companions, who you play with so prettily?"

Caterina scowled and set the doll she held next to several others piled up beside her on the settee. This crowded her cat from its seat. It escaped to jump into Tommaso's lap.

"They're not toys," Caterina said sulkily. "They're meant to model current French fashion. My Uncle Albany sends me at least one a week. I'm supposed to use them to instruct my dressmakers." She held up a small ledger book in which she'd been writing. "I'm making an effort."

She looked at him sadly. In French she asked, *"How are your lessons progressing? I hope you enjoy them better than I do mine."*

Tommaso regretted his jest. He hated to see Caterina losing hope. He still spoke French far more haltingly than she did, but he did his best. *"I confess that I find the instruction a good excuse to flee the kitchen. My tutor is a student of languages at the University. His father worked as a merchant in Paris for a number of years, so he speaks fluently."* Tommaso grinned. *"He's therefore up-to-date on modern French vulgarisms, which I doubt you learn from the good women here."* He dropped his voice. *"Shall I teach you some?"*

That, at last, brought some light to Caterina's eyes. *"By all means,"* she said.

"Why are you so melancholy?" Angelina asked Tommaso that evening as they rolled out dough for pasta dumplings together.

"I worry about the *Duchessina*," said Tommaso. "She's pale, listless, sad all the time. I did my best to raise her spirits, but I fear she's losing all hope for the future and resigning herself to the fate the Pope chose for her." He described the French fashion poppets to his great-grandmother.

Angelina clicked her tongue in disapproval. "Shut indoors with a bunch of dolls. Now wonder she's wan. She should be outdoors, traipsing over hill and dale in the fresh air."

Tommaso smiled, remembering what Great-uncle Giacomo had told him about Angelina's childhood; how she'd roamed through the countryside herself with the wild-game-shop women.

"On that she'd agree with you," he said. "She complained that at this time of year she should be out hunting."

"Did she like the pastries stuffed with wild-boar sausage you made her?" Angelina asked.

"Yes. And Mother visited her earlier in the week, bringing her *cibreo*. That also cheered her."

"What word from abroad?"

Tommaso knew his great-grandmother referred to Ippolito. Even in the safe haven of the kitchen, no one risked mentioning the young cardinal's name.

"Good news, but nothing certain." Tommaso knew Ippolito sent word-of-mouth messages to Caterina by way of Cosimo Ruggiero, the Strozzis, and her cousin Cosimo de' Medici. Ippolito still worked to secure a safe escape route from Florence to Hungary.

"I understand why Caterina despairs." Tommaso sighed. "How can they succeed with all the darkness that surrounds her here? How can one battle shadows?"

"So, you see the shadows?" Angelina's look fixed Tommaso like a snake's gaze fixes a small bird.

Tommaso flushed. He'd never meant to admit his visions to anyone other than Cosimo Ruggiero. It had just slipped out. "Do *you?*" he asked defensively.

"Of course," Angelina said. "And I guessed that you did. But I'm surprised to hear you admit it."

Tommaso's mouth fell open. He stared at his great-grandmother, dumbfounded by the turn the conversation had taken.

"Don't look so amazed," said Angelina. She reached over and lifted Tommaso's chin, closing his mouth. Tommaso felt the powdery dusting of flour left on his jaw by her fingers.

"Do you think our name is Befanini for nothing?" Angelina shook her head and raised her hands in defeat when his jaw dropped open again.

"To answer your question: One doesn't need to battle shadows. Shadows are nothing but shadows." She pointed to her own faint, hearth-cast shadow on the floor, then picked up her skirts and danced on it with a stamping, gingerly, frail jig.

"If you do indeed perceive the same dark shapes that I do, you'd know they're more than that," Tommaso said with asperity.

"True," Angelina agreed. "But they possess many of the attributes of simple, honest shadows. They, too, are substanceless phantasms. They're cast on the surface of our world as mere distorted silhouettes of solid, real entities."

"Evil entities. Devils. Hideous demons." Tommaso shuddered, remembering the creatures erupting throughout the Coliseum in Rome.

"Evil for us, surely. As anyone's foe is, so of course we battle them," said Angelina. "But in their own land?" She shrugged. "They're not evil or even ugly there. After all, do they not strive for their own good, albeit at our expense? Would we, do we, do no less? Can we truly judge them? The bird sees not the cat's beauty."

Anger rose in Tommaso, scalding hot. "Are you becoming mad again?" he hissed in a whisper. "Has proximity to the Duke corrupted your mind? Must I now worry that my own flesh and blood intends to betray Caterina?"

Angelina looked at him with mild eyes. "Just listen to yourself," she said. "You might as well. You're certainly not minding *my* words. Did I not say they were our foes?

"Such rage as yours engenders rash acts. Too often that provides the means by which battles are lost. To fight well, one needs to assess one's enemies as dispassionately as possible. Only if one strives to understand them can one find their strengths and weaknesses."

She patted Tommaso's arm. "I know you speak to me disrespectfully because of fear. You're one of the few with eyes to see that there is, indeed, just cause to feel terror. The darkness draws closer about us. It can fill one with a helpless sense of doom."

Tommaso stared at her. "If you know what I feel, how can you tell me not to despair, when nothing can be done?"

"Nothing can be done?" Angelina laughed. "We're cooks, Tommaso. By our profession, by our very nature, we make the best soldiers, the best mages for this kind of war.

"Our foes are creatures much like ourselves. They only see objects. They gain ground by oozing their dark reflections along and over *things*. Things that they can perceive. There's much that is invisible to them. That which is invisible makes for our strongest weapons."

"Like what?" Tommaso asked, thoroughly confused.

"Like our breath, which keeps us alive." Angelina waved her hands. "Like winds, breezes, anything air can carry: scents, perfumes, the aroma of good cooking. Clear glass, water, white wine. They can perceive items of food, of course, but not the elusiveness that is flavor. Mirrors—which are but reflected clarity—confuse them. Certain colors blind them."

She winked at Tommaso. "What do you think I've been teaching you? If my spices and herbs can keep rot and death itself at bay, imagine what sort of alchemy I can bring to bear in this war."

How could I not dream, after such a day? Tommaso thought as he found himself soaring once again over Florence's dark streets. The cobblestones glimmered—a silvery, wet patchwork under the street's oil lamps. Below him trotted a single, overburdened horse. Its hoofs skittered as it occasionally lost traction on the slick pavement. Its struggles to stay upright drew no sympathy from the two men riding it. They howled with drunken laughter, oblivious to their own danger if their mount fell.

With Tommaso gliding above them, they rode on to the Medici palazzo. A shocked gatekeeper let them in. They half tumbled together off the horse. Staggering arm in arm, they supported each other up and into the mansion, leaving the gatekeeper to shout for a groom to take care of their mount. Tommaso whisked into the mansion after the two sots.

"What think you? Was that not excellent sport?" Alessandro's voice was slurred. He flung his cloak open, splattering water on the marble floor of the inner courtyard. "Shadowfest, shadowfest," he chanted. "The union of God and Goddess. The jest is on them, for I own the shadows. I'll be both God and Goddess, in one."

Tommaso recoiled. Underneath his cape, Alessandro wore women's clothes: a red *gamurra* with gold damask sleeves. A diamond-and-emerald necklace garnished his neck.

"Sport for you, perhaps," Lorenzaccio said, his voice glum. Although perhaps even more inebriated than Alessandro, he took off his cape and folded it neatly, if a little unsteadily. He, too, wore a gown, of mauve-and-violet brocade. It was badly rain-splashed. "I'm short and slight. You're not. You're bearded. I'm not."

Alessandro stroked Lorenzaccio's smooth cheek with one hand. "That's true. You make for the much more fetching wench." He shoved Lorenzaccio against one of the courtyard pillars and kissed him, pressing his body hard against Lorenzaccio's. Lorenzaccio gave way. His eyes looked blank, but when Alessandro pushed away from him and reeled up the stairway, Lorenzaccio stared after him with uncompromising hatred.

Wake up, wake up, Tommaso moaned to himself. This is too horrible. He fled up and past Lorenzaccio, past Alessandro now staggering down the hallway. Alessandro shivered and pulled his cloak back up over his hairy, nearly bare shoulders. "Cursed draft," he muttered. "Philosopher, I'm cold," he shouted back at Lorenzaccio. "Since you're not using it, give me your cape to add to mine."

Tommaso, too, was suddenly cold. He shivered uncontrollably. My feet are freezing. The floor is like ice, he thought.

Lorenzaccio caught up to Alessandro. He'd regained his composure. He handed the folded cape to Alessandro, then froze, his eyes fixed on Tommaso.

Tommaso's mind thought two things in the same instant. He sees me, and I have no shoes.

The two ideas meshed. This isn't a dream, he realized with dread.

He looked down past a broad expense of eye-opening blue to his bare feet. *I'm wearing my lucco. It's inside out.* His thoughts turned sluggishly, as though his brains had been soaking in brine for six months.

He looked back at Lorenzaccio, who continued to gape at him.

Alessandro turned. "What is it? What phantom do you see?" Alessandro looked straight at Tommaso with a blind man's wandering gaze.

Lorenzaccio turned unbelieving eyes on Alessandro. He closed them, then opened them once more. "Nothing. I see only my own drunken stupor."

Tommaso flattened himself against the wall as Lorenzaccio swept past, Alessandro stumbling after.

As Tommaso expected, Lorenzaccio summoned him first thing the next morning. Tommaso found the youth pacing the confines of his room like a caged jackal.

"What were you thinking, wandering about the palazzo at that hour of the night, spying on Duke Alessandro for the *Duchessina*, and in that garb?" he snarled.

"I wasn't thinking anything," Tommaso said stiffly. "Apparently I was somnambulistic. A man doesn't know what he does when he walks in his sleep. You and the Duke surprised me awake."

Lorenzaccio pressed his hand against his forehead. He pinched the furrow between his brows with thumb and index finger. Tommaso doubted the gesture was for affect. Lorenzaccio must be suffering an evil hangover this morning.

"Luckily for you the Duke was drunk to the point of oblivion last night," Lorenzaccio muttered. "He must have been. You glowed there against the wall like a luminescent peacock, like a barefoot patch of sky."

49

In mid-November Tommaso received a letter from Rome, from Ascancio Condivi. He took it outside to read in the Medici herb garden.

"My Dear Gossip,

I'm not one to put pen to paper to write, as you know. Circumstances, however, guide my conscience to inform you of certain matters that have occurred here in Rome.

Benevenuto Cellini recently returned from a trip to Florence. It's evident from his boasting that he spent much of his time there telling tales that weren't his to tell. I'm sure you heard them. I can imagine your suffering. I believe it's better for you to know the truth, and perhaps find some solace in it, than let your heart fall prey to wild imaginings.

Part of what you've heard is true. My master's interest has been captured by another. Let me tell you how it happened, for I was there.

I accompanied my master this summer to a viewing of some new works by Valerio Vincentino. I was glad Master chose to attend. Though nothing can stop him from his work, he'd been downcast and seen almost no one socially since a certain day this last spring, when his heart left him and flew away with you to Florence.

Vincentino's *bottega* was crowded. All of Rome's aristocrats and wealthy merchants vie to own one of his small, exquisite pieces. Master and I were standing together, conversing with some other artists, when we heard behind us someone call out loudly, 'Tommaso! Tommaso! Come join us over here!'

Hearing that particular name, Master's eyes kindled with a glow I hadn't seen in months. He turned his head this way and that, though he had to know that the one he sought wasn't there. He pushed through the crowds. Concerned, I followed behind.

He arrived at the group that called out just as the object of their attention—a young aristocrat by the name of Tommaso Cavalieri—joined them.

The youths were amazed at their luck that the great Maestro Buonarotti should seemingly blunder into their group. They begged to introduce themselves to him. Soon he was fast friends with all of them, though his eyes never left Tommaso Cavalieri. I grudgingly admit this to you, Tommaso: Young Signor Cavalieri is the first young man I've seen who can match you in fairness of face and form.

Since then, Master seeks out this youth whenever he can. I know for a certainty that at least as of this date I write you, their friendship is nothing more than that—friendship.

I know you can't help but feel wounded when you read these words, but let not your generous heart suffer anger. You left. He pined. Can you begrudge a great soul such as his at least some happiness?

I've begged him to write you and explain. He only turns away looking sad and ashamed. So, for the bond we share as Florentines, art apprentices and

friends, I write you in his stead, not wishing you to
be cruelly buffeted by rumor and innuendo.
Your faithful gossip,
Ascancio Condivi"

Tommaso remembered the beautiful children he'd glimpsed in the
Cavalieri kitchen. He put his head in his hands and wept.

50

Great-grandmother Angelina hobbled down the steps to the garden several hours later. She handed Tommaso a steaming cup of tea, then sat down next to him.

"A broken heart, eh?" she said.

"Does your *strega's* art tell you that?" Tommaso asked through numb lips. The cup felt wonderfully warm against his cold palms.

"No. Your red-rimmed eyes. The devastation in your face. Having felt it before myself, I easily recognize the symptoms. As could anyone who's ever loved. Which is almost everyone."

Tommaso bowed his head to the tea, analyzing its complex blend of herbs. "And this. Is it for mending broken hearts?"

Angelina shook her head. "No. For warming. Your *lucco* and that small patch of wintry sun you sit in aren't sufficient to keep you from cold. Especially when you choose to sit so still outside for so long at this time of year, though I'd wager the heat of your anguish overwarmed you at first."

She nudged him. "Drink the tea while it's hot. Use what you've learned from me. See if you can guess its contents."

Angelina was right. First he'd burned with grief. Then the heat dissipated. Cold had crept in until his core felt like a column of ice. He sipped at the tea. It tasted good, spicy.

"Ginger, yarrow, honey," he said.

Angelina nodded. "Yes, those are dominant. And what else?"

As Tommaso's center started to melt, so did his heart. Tears streamed down his face again, blinding him. He couldn't answer his great-grandmother.

She patted his back. When he could look at her again, in her eyes he saw, instead of mere sympathy, a sadness equal to his own.

"This won't be the last time you weep over this," she said softly.

"You truly do know, then." Tommaso's words came in painful gasps. She nodded.

"When you felt like this . . . when did you get over it? How did you get over it?"

Angelina thought for a moment before replying. "Tommaso, I've foreseen a little of your future. You will recover from this someday. When, I can't say for sure. Broken love mends slowly." She sighed. "As for me, I never completely mended. I've mourned a little each day, except for the dim years, when I sat on the stool in the corner."

Tommaso thought back to all the family legends about Angelina: her unmarried status, her son's illegitimacy.

"The man who sired Grandfather Befanini?"

Angelina shook her head. "No, though my liaison was the cause of my lost love. The father of my child—we grew up together in this house, played hoops, sang songs, raced each other in the courtyard. When we were very little, we were as good friends as is possible for the child of a servant and the child of a master to be.

"I grew to maturity. You must remember what a wild maid I was. To my surprise, I fell in love with a good, decent, sober young man, another cook. He was shy. He seemed not to feel a similar affection for me, which wounded my pride. To heal it, I left Florence to travel with my friends among the women who own the wild-game shops.

"On one such journey, I chanced upon my childhood friend at one of the Medici country estates. In later years our relationship had lapsed to that of servant and master. But away from Florence and this mansion, catching each other by surprise, we saw each other in a different light. We became lovers. The affair continued after we'd both returned to Florence.

Master and servant. "Your lover was Lorenzo il Magnífico?" Tommaso asked in amazement.

Angelina laughed. "Oh no! Lorenzo was a sensual, passionate man who many woman found attractive. I didn't. He was too homely for my taste. I've always been drawn to beauty. My lover was Lorenzo's younger brother Giuliano.

"I might have chosen not to become pregnant by him. By then I knew the combination of herbs that block conception. But for many reasons, including an intuition of his early death, I knew I should bear his child.

"I was already pregnant when the young cook I fancied finally declared his love for me. We had such a brief time together." Tears welled in Angelina's eyes now.

"I told him of my condition. At first he was willing to claim the child as his own, but learning that the father was Giuliano de' Medici crushed him. Giuliano was one of the courtliest, bravest, kindest and refined young men in the city. My love felt he couldn't compete against such a fellow, could never feel certain of the constancy of my heart after such an affair. He forgave me and still wished to wed, however.

"I couldn't enter a marriage or raise my son under those conditions, and I felt I'd done nothing that required forgiveness. I refused him. I spent years bearing witness to his defeated spirit. A long time later I arranged an introduction between him and a fine woman I knew. At last he married."

"Who was he?" asked Tommaso, who'd forgotten his own woes for the moment. "Can you tell me?"

Angelina patted his hand. "Why not? You would have known him if he hadn't died before you were born. He was your father Gentile's uncle, Ambrogio Arista."

51

March, 1533

A sauce maker, a baker, someone to organize and dispense table service according to course, a pasta maker, a carver to act as his second... Tommaso looked down at the long list before him. He'd *thought* he knew every position he wanted filled and what it entailed. It seemed so clear when he put pen to paper. Now, however, while he sat at the grand table in the cook's hall, attended to by guild masters, interviewing applicants and their families, sampling the applicants' cooking, the categories had become unsure and slippery.

The problem was that he didn't have a grasp on the inner workings of French kitchens. Or royal kitchens. Or, in particular, French royal kitchens. He'd spoken to many who'd visited France; a few who'd even dined at His Most Christian Majesty François I's table. But not one of them was a cook. From them Tommaso had gathered only two facts.

First, that royal kitchen work was almost certainly structured differently than the way it was structured in large Italian kitchens. Second, that King François traveled incessantly, almost never stopping in one place for more than two weeks. The grand spectacle of Caterina's wedding, now scheduled to take place in Marseilles in the fall, would be one of the few exceptions. Decamping as frequently as François did would make the logistics of preparing food for large numbers of people of refined taste a nightmare.

Gentile reached over Tommaso's shoulder to tap a finger on one of the positions on the list. "Here, where you've written 'baker.' You'll want to break that up into several categories. Add a position for baked sweets—cakes and the like. I recommend someone from your grandmother's family. No one can match the Siennese for desserts. Perhaps young Gabriele Cavallucci. I hear he's among their best, and I know he's adventuresome."

Tommaso looked at his father gratefully. Only Gentile's calm, efficient presence and intimate knowledge of Florence's cooking families was going to allow Tommaso to survive this day.

Gentile patted Tommaso's shoulder. "Put yourself at ease. You're doing well. The guild masters are impressed with your comportment. I'll go bring in the next applicant."

Tommaso tried unsuccessfully not to think of the other, larger secret problem that loomed over these proceedings. These men were applying for jobs cooking for Caterina at the royal French court. If all Tommaso's hopes came true, that would be the one place they'd *not* be cooking.

Caterina would still need cooks, wherever she went. If she someday wed Ippolito she might even need as many cooks as Tommaso had written down on his list. Tommaso wondered how someone like Gabriele the pastry-sweets chef would feel about moving to Hungary rather than France.

What if Caterina successfully fled Florence with Ippolito? Would any of these cooks Tommaso was hiring follow after the renegades if Tommaso sent for them? Would the guild revoke Tommaso's membership, perhaps even his standing in the guild, if they believed he'd misrepresented the terms of employment he was offering today?

Tommaso wanted to put his head in his hands. He sighed. He couldn't let himself enjoy even that small luxury. It would make him look too young, unprofessional.

He compared again his list against the list of applicants.

"Tommaso, may I speak with you?"

Tommaso looked up to find Umberto standing before him. He'd been so engrossed in his problems that he hadn't heard his cousin enter the hall.

Tommaso smiled. "Have you come to help me too? I could use a good, levelheaded Befanini opinion."

"Help you? Yes, in a way," Umberto said, shifting from foot to foot, rolling and unrolling the edge of the cap he held before him like some kind of shield. "Help you *and* help me," he blurted. "Tommaso, take me with you when you leave."

Tommaso looked at his cousin in surprise. "You've never spoken to me of this before."

Umberto looked embarrassed. "I know. I should have. I thought maybe..." He hesitated and chewed his lip.

It was Tommaso's turn to feel embarrassed. *He* should have known, from the first day he returned to Florence, when he and Umberto spoke together of the darkness in the Medici palazzo while he'd unpacked his things in the apprentices' dorm.

"Are you sure, Umberto?" Tommaso lowered his voice. Gentile had entered with a new applicant. They stood waiting at the back of the hall. "I know better than anyone how things stand in the Medici kitchen, but your position there is assured. Who knows what might happen once we depart for other lands? You've never left Tuscany, hardly ever left Florence. I have doubts whether you could be happy elsewhere."

"Let me but try," Umberto said desperately, "for I *know* I can't be happy here, as long as our monstrous Duke holds sway. He's young. He could rule over us for the rest of our lives, and after him his children. Save me from that, Tommaso."

Tommaso smiled wanly. "Then enter your name with the guild masters for a position. At least you won't have to present me a sample of your cooking. I certainly know it well enough already."

52

In June Pope Clement sent word throughout the college of cardinals to be mindful of their schedules. They should expect to begin gathering in Rome in August. He meant to use Caterina's wedding for a show of sacral power unmatched in recent history. This might, in part, ease if not erase the memory of the Sack of Rome. Clement recalled Papal legates from all over Europe, including Ippolito from his official position and unofficial exile in Hungary.

"He wants to keep Ippolito close, where he can watch him," Caterina told Cosimo Ruggiero as they strolled through the Murate's gardens.

Cosimo concurred. "And His Holiness will be particularly alert until Ippolito stands before Him. Clement will send papal informants to watch for him throughout northern Italy."

"Yes, but it's hard to track the movements of a fast-moving band of men on horseback," Caterina said. "I know for a certainty Ippolito is sending a double to make fortuitous appearances along the most logical route from Hungary to Rome. Clement will expect this poseur to detour at some point to rescue me. That's where we can expect papal forces to gather."

"Not all of them," Cosimo cautioned. He drew his dirk, cut a bright red rose, and handed it to her. "Alessandro already posts forces here in Florence on the lookout for Ippolito's arrival." Cosimo looked at Caterina soberly. "Alessandro's resources are more varied and deadly than Clement's."

Caterina nodded. "*I* know that too well, but I fear Ippolito under-estimates the dangers. Because plans for Alessandro's own marriage to the Emperor's bastard daughter draw closer, Ippolito believes Alessandro will now want me conveniently gone rather than dead. The Emperor defeated Clement in Rome and King François in Pavia. With that sort of might as a protective father-in-law, Alessandro now has little reason to fear that France might attempt to annex Florence on my behalf."

She bent her head to smell the rose. "Ippolito lacks the understand-ing you and I share: that political jeopardy is the least of the ways in which Alessandro fears me. The only way for Alessandro to reign here secure in his power is to see both Ippolito and myself dead. Since my return to Florence, Alessandro has contained me, but he's had to expend tremendous energy and resources to do so, and even then I've chipped away at him. He's been forced to remain so focused on me that new powers begin to grow and spread behind his back, out of his control. And he suspects as much."

She clutched the rose stem in her hands until her knuckles whitened. "Ippolito's claims to the Medici legacy are no stronger than Alessandro's, unless coupled with my own as the sole legitimate heir. Without me, Ippolito ceases to seriously threaten Alessandro. Many are the times I've held a knife to my own breast, wondering if my death might secure Ippolito's safety. Alas, every vision that plagues me tells me that just as I'm the element that most endangers Ippolito, so I'm also his only pro-tection."

Cosimo watched with concern and pity as droplets of blood began to ooze between Caterina's clenched fingers.

53

Mid-August, 1533

Yesterday would have tired God himself, Tommaso thought. After a full day of hard work, he'd walked across the river for a late, quiet birthday supper with his family.

"It's a good thing we threw a big celebration for you last year," Gentile said, serving up lamb chops with artichokes. "With half of Tuscany in town to bid the *Duchessina* farewell, we'd have never been able to hold it for you now. The Ruggieros alone are hosting an army's worth of guests."

Gentile put down the serving fork. He looked at Tommaso with sadness and pride. "Would that I could hold back the hours. My heart protests that in only a fortnight you'll leave us to begin your journey to France." He sighed and picked up the serving fork again.

Tommaso and Piera shared a glance. Tommaso would be leaving, but with any luck it would be much sooner, and not for France.

After dinner Tommaso's old art apprentice friends and several of his Befanini cousins showed up, carrying carnival masks.

"Umberto here told us where to find you," Gherardo said, slapping a flinching Umberto on the back. "What better way to turn eighteen? The city is full of pageantry, dancing, wine—and we're just the right age to enjoy it."

Salvatore bowed low to Piera. "Forgive us, Madonna Arista, but like you, we lose Tommaso soon. Give us your permission to steal him away.

We consider it our duty to impress a reveling memory of Florence on his soul."

Gentile looked as though he'd object. Piera put out a hand to silence him.

"These youths asked *me*. I give my consent." She looked at Gentile and smiled. "Have you forgotten your own reckless, happy youth, before you met and married me? Tommaso has had such little chance to be a carefree young man in Florence. This is his last opportunity. We lose nothing by it: He'll always be our son."

Salvatore handed Tommaso a turquoise blue peacock mask. "We saved this one for you, my beautiful friend."

They stayed out far too late, almost until dawn. What Salvatore said was true. Tommaso wanted to gather as much of Florence unto himself as he could that night. He tried to breathe in the lapping essence of the Arno, memorize each gilt-and-ruby dazzle of the fireworks-spangled sky, embed in his bones the feeling of his dancing feet as they launched themselves from Florence's pavement. He'd surely drink Tuscan wine again, but would it taste the same when not drunk beneath a Tuscan moon?

The next morning Tommaso knew he should feel exhausted, but his nerves, humming with excitement, kept him awake and alert.

Only a handful of people other than himself knew the importance of this day. The timing of Ippolito's plan to rescue Caterina seemed to be proving wise after all. Most of those whose safety she feared for had already departed the city, for an impeccable, unassailable reason: to prepare to meet her along her route to France as part of her wedding retinue.

And with so many extra visitors and suppliers arriving every day, Alessandro's guards at the city gates were hard-pressed to discharge their duties well. It wouldn't be easy for a rescue party to slip in and out of Florence, but it would be possible.

Anticipation strung through Tommaso as tightly as an arrow notched to a bowstring, and as ready to release. Caterina hadn't apprised him of the details of the escape. That knowledge was too dangerous. He only knew that his own timetable and avenue of departure required him not to leave too early. His absence would be noticed if he didn't serve at the banquet Alessandro was hosting this night. Nor could he leave too late. Once Caterina escaped, any of her remaining servants and associates would be questioned and tortured.

✳ ✳ ✳

Chaperoned by Reparata, two nuns and two men-at-arms, Caterina left the Murate that afternoon. Her destination was a visit to her cousin, Caterina Cibò. The Murate's facilities had proved inadequate to store the vast array of gowns being sewn for the *Duchessina* and her ladies-in-waiting. The Cibò palazzo had been drafted to serve as wardrobe room until Caterina's entourage left for France. Most of Caterina's fittings took place there. One was scheduled for that day.

A number of nondescript men straggled behind Caterina's little troupe when she left the Murate. They followed her until she entered the Cibò mansion's front gates.

A short while later the two chaperoning nuns and one of the men-at-arms left the palazzo. A few of the trailing agents fell in line behind them. It was common knowledge that the *Duchessina* had passed herself off as a nun in her childhood. It wouldn't be surprising if she tried that ruse again.

The men were disappointed in their suspicions. The nuns returned straight to the Murate. Grumbling at the extra effort they'd made for nothing, the men trudged back to their post of waiting for the *Duchessina* outside the Cibò palazzo.

In her suite at the Murate, Caterina and Reparata stripped off the nuns' habits they wore.

Sister Teresa Lucrezia bustled in. "Leone Strozzi made sure the Duke's men had gone, then he left to let Ippolito know you were on your way," she told them.

"Good. We're almost ready," Reparata said, throwing a coarse, long, brown woolen skirt over Caterina's head. She pulled it down till it settled at Caterina's waist. Caterina was already drawing on the knee-length work smock that went over the skirt. Next followed a scarf wound all around Caterina's head and neck, effectively hiding her hair. A broad cap constituted the last touch. It flopped around her ears and on her forehead.

Caterina helped Reparata into a similar costume. She tied the strings to Reparata's stained apron. "There. I believe we can pass for game-shop women, returning to our store after supplying the Murate's kitchen with good meat."

Sister Teresa Lucrezia still stood in the doorway. "I don't like that

you'll make your way through Florence to the Ponte Vecchio unprotected. I know Leone Strozzi couldn't have remained in his disguise as
your man-at-arms. Couldn't he, too, have pretended to be a laborer, and
escorted you?"

"I'd have preferred that," Caterina concurred. "But we're risking
enough with Reparata and myself leaving like this. It would be too
noticeable for an unaccounted-for fellow to leave from the back of a
convent. If any of Alessandro's men are nearby, they'd wonder what
happened to the *Duchessina*'s man-at-arms who was posted outside. When
Leone went off as he was, in my livery, they'll think he's taking a break
in his duties after escorting the two nuns back here."

"Don't forget we have these as part of our costumes." From a sheath
on her belt Reparata pulled a sharp knife, the kind game-shop owners
were known to brandish.

Sister Teresa Lucrezia threw up her hands. "I've said my say. I'll go
back to the kitchen and make sure the handcart Leonora left us is ready
for you to trundle out."

"Do we have everything?" Caterina asked once the nun left. They
were taking very little with them. Caterina had worn a pouch belt with
some florins, papers and jewels under her undergarments all day. Two
bundles sat on her desk. They carried a single change of clothing for
each of them; the kind of garments that might serve as a craftsman's
daughters' Sunday finery.

"Yes, everything but the cat," Reparata said. "She's hiding somewhere."

Caterina stared at Reparata. "That's not possible," she said. She
looked in Gattamelata's basket. The cat should be curled up in there
already, waiting to leave. She wasn't.

Caterina threw the crumpled blankets from her bed, rummaged
through rumpled piles of clothing in chests. Reparata joined in the
search.

"She's under the bed," Reparata called. Caterina got down on hands
and knees to join her.

Two slitted green eyes glared out at them.

"Here, puss, puss." Reparata thrust her arm under the bed. The cat
hissed like a serpent. Reparata pulled her hand back hastily.

Caterina started to tremble. This couldn't be happening. Everything

Caterina knew and believed started to tumble around her. She must leave. Ippolito awaited her. Time was precious. At any moment Alessandro's ferretlike shadows could stumble onto their plans.

Through the rough cloth of the smock, Caterina clutched at the pendant at her breast. *Ginevra, what is happening? What's possessed the Little Kitchen Goddess?*

Ginevra's answer came from far away. *Listen. You must listen to Her.*

How could she listen? *This is my last chance,* Caterina's thoughts screamed.

"If the cat won't come, the cat won't come," Caterina said with difficulty. Her lips felt swollen, frozen. She seized her bundle.

The cat streaked out from under the bed. Caterina dropped her bundle. She and Reparata grabbed for the cat. It raced around the room like a whirlwind, evading them as they scrambled after it.

"She's gone mad," said Reparata, panting.

Caterina felt time, a torturing weight, pressing against her from all sides. "Leave her," she said. She couldn't breathe. She seized her bundle again and headed for the door.

The cat sprinted ahead of her. It stopped, crouching, in the doorway. Its ears lay flat against its skull. A high-pitched, dangerous keening emerged from the back of its throat. Its eyes could have passed for a demon's.

Caterina took a step to sidle past it. It launched itself at her and clawed it way up the thick, nubby fabric of the work smock. Caterina seized it with both hands before it reached her face. She stared into its eyes, transfixed.

In all her imaginings of what it might be like to see the Little Kitchen Goddess unveiled, what had she thought she'd perceive? A sensuous, mysterious cat's soul? A wraithlike feminine spirit? Caterina saw neither. She saw nothing she expected to see, nothing she recognized: no feminine or feline personality.

Instead, for a dizzy moment Caterina felt as though she teetered on top of a steep cliff. Stretched out below her was a vast, seething tempest. Caterina stepped backward. She understood at last the wind's desperation, its rage.

"It's a trap," she whispered. "Alessandro is waiting to spring a trap."

Reparata dropped the bundle she'd snatched up.

Caterina had turned more pale than ivory. She still clutched the cat, who'd gone limp. Caterina's eyes stared at nothing.

"If this is true, what shall we do?" Reparata asked.

"Let me sit and think," Caterina said, but she didn't move.

Reparata pulled a chair over to her, and gently bent Caterina's wooden form into it.

"Ippolito and his men must be warned." Reparata urgently tried to reach through Caterina's trance. "How can we reach him? Leone Strozzi has already departed."

"Leave me. Let me think," said Caterina. "Go tell Sister Teresa Lucrezia to hide the cart again."

When Reparata left Caterina still sat in the chair with unseeing eyes, holding the cat.

Exhaustion hit Tommaso suddenly and strongly. Today of all days, I must stay awake, be alert, be ready to leave. He cursed himself. What was I thinking, staying up all night? His eyes felt dry, heavy. The lobes of his ears burned. If I can rest on this bench for a moment and close my eyes to moisten them, I'll be all right. I'll feel refreshed, he promised himself. He lowered himself to the bench, then descended well past it, down into wonderful, perfect black velvet.

Something touched his shoulder. He jerked awake. Umberto bent over him. "Tommaso, are you all right?"

"Asleep. I've been asleep." Tommaso sat upright. His hands and face were clammy. "How long have I been asleep?" The question was somehow important.

"About ten minutes," Umberto said. "You walked over to the bench and collapsed."

"Only ten minutes." Tommaso jumped to his feet. "Thank you for waking me. Thank you, Thank you," he called over his shoulder as he ran out of the kitchen.

His legs knew where he flew; he did not. The dream came back to him as he ran through Florence's streets. This is madness, he thought, but that didn't help his mind gain control over his feet. When I arrive, if Ippolito is there, then I'll know the dream is true, he tried to reassure himself.

The entrance to the Ponte Vecchio loomed. Then he was on the bridge, racing down its length. There, before him—Cousin Leonora's stall. Tommaso's feet tripped and slowed to a trot.

Cousin Leonora stood out front at the stand outside the shop, doing business as usual. She'd obviously just received a shipment of game from the country. A brace of pheasants, tied by their legs, half spilled over the edges of a cutting block. Only a huge butcher blade, embedded at its point into the block, kept them from sliding all the way off. Two of Leonora's older daughters alternately pushed and pulled a large hind into the shop itself. Young Teodora teetered on top of a tall stool, hanging several unplucked woodcocks from a hook at the front of the stand. She glanced down, saw Tommaso and smiled.

Nearby was the wagon that had just unloaded the game. A lean, gnarled driver sat on its seat, his back to Tommaso, waiting for two young peasants to clean out the bloodstained straw lining the wagon's bed. The game merchants—possibly the wagon's owner and the hunters—stood paying close attention to the *scudi* Leonora counted out for them. She must be paying them well. With so many visitors crowding into Florence these days and needing to be fed, the game suppliers enjoyed a sellers' market.

I'm an idiot, Tommaso thought. His face burned with embarrassment. Thank heavens no one knows I'm here at a dream's command. I'll pretend I came to buy some supplies for the kitchen, then go. He patted his belt. Yes, his pouch there held a few *scudi*. He'd buy some woodcocks. He turned toward Teodora on her stool and bumped into one of the young peasants, a dark, grimy, bearded fellow.

"Tommaso, what are you doing here? Where's Caterina?" Ippolito's voice muttered out of the dirty face. "Leone Strozzi arrived here saying she was on her way almost an hour ago."

Tommaso stood rooted to the spot in shock as he felt the world shift about him. The dream was true.

"I was looking for you," Tommaso croaked. "I've come to warn you. It's a trap. Alessandro hopes to catch you and Caterina together."

"When did Caterina tell you this?" Ippolito whispered. "How does she know?"

The other peasant youth had come up and was listening. Tommaso at last recognized Cosimo Ruggiero beneath the filthy, bloody clothing. Tommaso felt the blood in his veins turn to ice water. Cosimo shouldn't be here. His father told him not to interfere, the strange thought floated to the surface of his thoughts, as unwanted and unsolicited as a belly-up dead fish. "Trust me that she knows," Tommaso pleaded to Cosimo more than Ippolito. "You know she has ways to reach me."

Cosimo paled beneath the layer of dirt. It made him look gray.

"What's the problem here?" One of the game merchants joined them. It was Piero Strozzi. He'd grown a full, covering beard since Tommaso'd last seen him. His companions were Pier Antonio Pecci and young Cosimo de' Medici. At the sight of the other Cosimo, Tommaso's chill turned to nausea. Not him! some alarm cried within him. We can't afford to lose the king from the board, as well as the queen. Tommaso shook his head. He must be going mad.

"It's a trap," Cosimo Ruggiero said. "Caterina sent word with Tommaso. Ippolito, you must leave *now*."

Tommaso felt shadows closing in on them from somewhere nearby. He looked around frantically. Where was Lorenzaccio, whom Caterina called her good blade? Shouldn't he be here as well, to help her? Tommaso's heart flooded with suspicion. Why wasn't Lorenzaccio there?

Ippolito strode rapidly over to Leonora. "Madonna, someone betrayed us. Alessandro's men are on their way. You've been seen here with us. They'll want to interrogate you. Close your business up quickly."

Leonora turned into the shop and said a few quiet words to her daughters. They finished pulling the hind the rest of the way into the shop and began closing its shutters. Teodora tried to unknot the woodcocks she'd so carefully tied in place.

"Too late," cursed Pier Antonio Pecci. City guards were running toward them up the bridge, from the direction Tommaso had come.

The game-cart driver cracked his whip over the heads of the cart's draft horses. Startled, they back-shuffled, reared, then turned so the cart blocked part of the bridge's passageway. Leonora's older daughters slammed the shop closed from the inside. Tommaso heard a latch fall into place.

"Run!" Cosimo de' Medici shouted.

Past Cosimo's shoulder Tommaso saw a white-faced Teodora crouch on her stool to scramble down. The stool started to tip over. Tommaso lunged forward to catch her, knowing he was too far away and too late. Ippolito turned and caught her as she fell. Still holding Teodora, Ippolito started dodging his way to the opposite end of the bridge, Leonora racing close after him.

"Traitors! Stop them!" the guards shouted. Shopkeepers and customers along the length of the bridge ran in every direction. Tommaso flattened himself against the shop as the first guards drew abreast of him. He was perfectly happy to be mistaken for an ignorant bystander. He'd seen the dark blankness filling the guards' eyes before, in the *Signoria* who'd gathered to spirit Caterina from the Murate so many years ago.

A few guards from the other side of the river began to run toward them from the opposite direction. A passerby stretched out a leg. One of the guards went crashing down. Tommaso caught a glimpse of white teeth flashing in a dark red face. Tommaso skimmed a look over the panicking crowd. If Beroaldo was here, Domenico must lurk close by.

Before Tommaso could locate the Tartar, his gaze fell on another familiar form, coming up behind the nearby guards. It was not, as he'd expected, Lorenzaccio de' Medici. The wrathful, shadow-haunted, scabrous face belonged to Giorgio Vasari. "In the name of Duke Alessandro, stop them! They're kidnapping the *Duchessina!*" Giorgio screamed.

To Tommaso's horror, the guards drew their arquebuses, fell to one knee, and tried to aim around scattering citizens at Ippolito's retreating back. All that could be seen of Teodora, wrapped in Ippolito's protecting arms, was her billowing skirts.

"Can't you see that's not the *Duchessina?*" Tommaso shouted. "She's too young, too little." Then he saw that the guards meant to fire anyway, and realized their orders were to kill Ippolito at any cost, and possibly Caterina as well.

Tommaso seized the butcher knife embedded in the chopping block. Freed, the brace of pheasants slid, softly heavy, against his leg. Tommaso slammed the knife down on the guard nearest him, right at the top of the joint between arm and shoulder. The guard screamed and fell sideways onto the guard next to him. The force of the blow had driven the musket downward. It fired, discharging into the cobblestones lining the bridge's roadway. Punishing chips of stone flew. The guards threw up their arms to shield themselves.

At the opposite end of the bridge, a guard rushed at Ippolito with a sword. Ippolito set Teodora down behind him and pulled a short drover's cudgel from his belt.

That was all Tommaso saw before he felt someone at his own back. He turned just as Giorgio Vasari lunged at him with a dining dirk.

Tommaso contracted his belly and swiveled, trying to become as flat as a ship's sail. He felt the fabric of his surcoat part, then felt swift heat, and blood oozing.

Giorgio pulled back for another strike. Tommaso looked down. The butcher knife was still embedded in the writhing guard's shoulder. He'd never pull it free in time. He'd have to run. He prayed Giorgio didn't know how to throw knives.

Tommaso took a step. Stumbling over the flailing guard, he went down.

Giorgio slid toward him, teeth bared in a grin. He pointed the dirk downward, level with Tommaso's eyes. "I believe you see too much, old friend. Let me relieve you of that affliction."

A callused hand locked on Giorgio's fist, crushing it. Giorgio yelped and dropped the dagger. He looked up at the man blocking him, the old cart driver. Giorgio blanched. So did Tommaso, when he saw who the man was. Then Tommaso watched as a thousand shadows fled from Giorgio's face, leaving him looking bewildered and very young.

"M-M-M-Maestro?" Giorgio stuttered, while Tommaso's heart thrummed. Beloved.

Michelangelo shook his head sadly. "Ah, Giorgio. It's come to this?"

Tommaso pulled his slit surcoat tight about him and pressed his hand to his side. He looked down the length of the bridge. Ippolito, Beroaldo, the two Cosimos, Pier Antonio Pecci, and Piero Strozzi had all vanished. Most of the guards on that end lay knocked to the ground. Leonora stood at the side of the bridge, holding Teodora by the hand. The ambush was over.

"There will be an investigation," Tommaso said.

Michelangelo nodded. "The *Signoria* will find that some overzealous guard commander overreacted to a scurrilous rumor and fired on innocent citizens, who only defended themselves. I'm sure our good Duke will punish the commander severely."

He looked at Tommaso with concern. "How badly are you wounded?"

Tommaso smiled wryly. "I'll live."

"Probably, but I want to see to your injury." Michelangelo grasped Tommaso around his shoulders and pulled him away from the stunned, speechless Giorgio Vasari.

Out of Giorgio's and the guards' earshot Tommaso whispered, "We need to conceal you. Public disclaimer aside, Alessandro will comb the city looking for the conspirators."

Michelangelo nodded in agreement. "I know just the place to hide," he said.

They soon came to a street Tommaso knew well. He pulled back. "Il Tribolino's? You'd come here? Don't you know how he meant to betray us all during the siege?"

"He finally admitted as much to me. Apparently some rowdy, model-throwing young apprentice made him see the error of his ways," Michelangelo said dryly. "Tribolo suffered blind loyalty to the Medicis. He didn't understand then that not every Medici has Florence's good at heart. The lesson came hard for him. Fear not. He bears Duke Alessandro no love." Michelangelo knocked at Il Tribolino's *bottega* alleyway door.

Gherardo opened the door. His jaw nearly hit his chest when he saw who stood there.

"Let us in, then fetch your master," Michelangelo ordered him.

Both Il Tribolino and Elissa Pecorino came running.

Michelangelo already had Tommaso's shirt off and was examining the wound. "It needs dressing," Michelangelo said. His fingers trailed gently over Tommaso's ribs. "I'm sorry I wasn't quicker," he said contritely.

The wound had started to sting. Tommaso managed a crooked smile. "You saved my life. You saved my eyes. I shan't complain."

Michelangelo turned to Il Tribolino. "No one knows Florence the way I do. I can escape tonight, but till then we need a place to hide, and I want to see to Tommaso's wound."

Il Tribolino nodded. "The same place as . . . ?"

Michelangelo grinned. "Yes. That will do nicely. Fetch us a flask of distilled liquor, some clean cloth suitable for bandaging, and two hooded cloaks. As long as we can hide Tommaso's hair we should be able to make our way there undetected."

Il Tribolino brought the cloaks. Elissa Pecorino brought the liquor, bandages, and a small packet. "For healing," she said, handing it to Tommaso.

"Where are we going?" Tommaso asked as he, Michelangelo and Il Tribolino set off down the street.

"Someplace Duke Alessandro will no more think to search than Clement did after the siege," Il Tribolino said.

They seemed to be heading back to the place Tommaso now called home, the Medici palazzo. They stopped just a block shy of it, in the Piazza San Lorenzo.

"The church of San Lorenzo?" Tommaso was even more surprised then when Michelangelo had taken him to Il Tribolino's.

"Under Alessandro's very nose," Michelangelo said with satisfaction. "Think how easy it will be for you to slip back to your work."

They entered the church, drifting down the edge of the aisles, past the church's massive pillars. Near the Medici chapel they knelt in prayer on the diamond-patterned stone tiles. Tommaso's side had stiffened, making it hard for him to kneel. His knees hurt. They felt unusually bony against the cold floor.

Only a few other silent worshipers knelt in prayer, up at the very front, before the main altar. A lone priest was lighting some candles. Michelangelo nudged Il Tribolino.

"Surely you feel great need to make confession. Give us a while, then knock when it's clear again."

Once the priest and Il Tribolino entered the confessional, Michelangelo led Tommaso to a secret panel that opened onto a space behind the Medici chapel.

"Hold the door ajar a moment so I can see while I light this." Michelangelo picked up one of several oil lamps sitting on the dusty floor.

Tommaso closed the door as soon as the lamp took on a glow. Michelangelo then lit three more lamps.

"That should give us sufficient light," he said.

Tommaso picked up one of the lamps to look around the space. There were several stools scattered about, some old conté crayons and charcoal sticks on the floor. He cast the lamp's light upward onto the walls. Charcoal drawings loomed at him out of the gloom. The work was distinctly Michelangelo's.

Michelangelo pulled over two stools. He motioned for Tommaso to sit on one.

"This is where I hid when I had to abandon my secret refuge at the Ruggieros' after the siege," he said, sitting down on the second stool. "I hated leaving you, Tommaso, but I'd put Ruggieros' whole household in danger."

"But this place is so bare," Tommaso protested.

Michelangelo smiled. "Water, food, a cot, a table, a pot to piss in, light, something to draw with, something to draw on. I even enjoyed some company. I had everything I needed, save for your own sweet presence." Michelangelo waved at the near-empty space. "All of those things have since been smuggled back out again."

Michelangelo pointed to one of the charcoal drawings, a study for a resurrection. "Do you like that one? Tribolo helped me with it. He and a few of my other colleagues thought to hide me in this place. They came to visit me here often."

He opened Tommaso's shirt and reexamined the wound. He took out the flask of liquor and the bandages he'd hidden under his cloak. Tommaso's breath was an inward hiss as Michelangelo dabbed some of the liquor onto the wound.

"It's a good thing you can turn and twist like a cat," Michelangelo said, binding the wound. "The cut is shallow and thin. It's only a little more serious than a scratch. Have Cosimo Ruggiero look at it no later than tomorrow, but I wager that unless it becomes infected, you'll hardly have a scar to boast of." He tousled Tommaso's hair. "The first time I met you, you were hurt a hundred times worse."

Tommaso felt his head bend on its own accord into Michelangelo's hand. "Why did you come back to Florence?" he made himself ask.

Michelangelo's hand stilled. Then it dropped to rest on his knee. "I wanted to return to Florence the members of the Medici family my beautiful city deserves. And I wanted to attend other matters I've been too much the coward to..." His words trailed off. He finally looked Tommaso full in the face.

"You're a man now, but young. Your life stretches ahead of you. I'm growing old. How many years of passion are left me? I beg you, Tommaso—free me."

Tommaso's eyes filled with tears.

"Not from loving you," Michelangelo said softly. "How could I ever be free from loving you? If the stars decreed differently and we could be together, in Rome or in Florence, you're all I'd ever want. Even now, after these long months, I swear I've never been unfaithful to you."

"But now you desire another instead of me," Tommaso whispered.

Michelangelo's face was a picture of agony. "Not *instead* of you. I desire you still, Tommaso. If you weren't injured, I'd take you here and now."

"Then you mean you desire another as well as me," Tommaso said.

Michelangelo bowed his head in assent. "When you're leagues away from here, do you want to think of me old, alone and cold in my cot? Isn't my existence lonely enough as it is? If I can hope for a happy life for you, can't your heart be generous enough to wish the same for me?"

Tommaso wanted to shout "No!" He couldn't. It wouldn't be true. He kissed Michelangelo instead. "Good-bye, Beloved."

54

"How could this happen?" Tommaso stormed at his great-grandmother. His temper was not at its best. His side ached from the wound. His heart ached from leaving Michelangelo.

He'd slipped back into the kitchen just before the banquet was served. The only circumstance that improved his mood was knowing bile must be eating away at Alessandro de' Medici's innards after the afternoon's failure, yet the Duke would have to put on a gay, nonchalant face for his guests. Then Tommaso remembered that Ippolito and Caterina had suffered failure that day as well.

Now would be the time to chance upon one of those vile shadows, he thought. For nothing could be more black, more foul, than my disposition at this moment. Even the cats dashed out of his way.

He and Angelina were the last in the kitchen that night. Tommaso was making himself a healing tea with the herb packet Elissa Pecorino had given him.

At last he could bear it no more. "You said we had the means to combat the shades. All these long months of mixing herbs, lighting fumigations, your lessons. It's all come to nothing. Today Alessandro routed Ippolito from Florence, probably for good. It's a miracle Ippolito wasn't killed, and Caterina with him."

"No miracle saved them," Angelina said calmly. "You did. You had a dream, a message sent to you by the efforts of Caterina and two others." She took down some jars and sprinkled a few more herbs into Tom-

maso's tea. "You saved their lives. I would say that's very effective combat."

Tommaso opened his mouth, closed it, opened it again. He finally
sat down without saying anything.

"We will win the war, if that's what you want to call it, in the end,
though we didn't triumph in this particular battle. But neither did our
enemies," Angelina said. "I never promised you the ending you hoped
for Caterina, that she hoped for herself."

Then Angelina sighed. "I confess that I wanted it for her too. Perhaps there was nothing to be done to bring it to pass. The black seeds
were sown long years ago, when Florence was rising toward its glory.
For that we have not an enemy to blame, but, far worse, one of our
own. A traitor."

"A traitor?" Tommaso was mystified. "Who?"

"Lorenzo il Magnífico's mother. Lucrezia Tornabuoni."

"She wasn't a cook," Tommaso protested. To call Lorenzo the
Great's mother a traitor was like spitting on the host during communion,
or cursing the memory of Cosimo Pater Patriae. "Legend has it she was
a fine woman: a wife and mother above reproach; an entrepreneur in her
own right; a poet; a lady of beauty; a devout lady."

"Yes, such a paragon," Angelina said. She put her hands on her hips.
"Don't forget that I knew her. Doesn't it make you wonder how a single
woman could embody so much?"

Tommaso looked at his great-grandmother. He felt totally confused.

Angelina folded her arms and looked smug. "We're not the only
streghe in Florence."

Tommaso was outraged. "How can you say such a thing? Lucrezia
Tornabuoni was renowned for her piety, her dedication to the Church."

Angelina nodded her head. "Exactly the problem. She didn't mind
inheriting her family's talent and using it, but she denied from whence
it came."

After mixing up a different mixture of herbs, Angelina poured some
boiling water over them. "We were the first, we cooks. We discovered
how to cajole plants into revealing their essences for our benefit," she
said, nodding at Tommaso's steaming cup. "We were the ones who first
used fire to transform raw flesh into meat. Ours was the first, the strongest magic.

"But we weren't the only ones. There are clans, like the Ruggieros, who unlock the secrets of the stars. Others pay fealty to the moon. She rewards them in turn. There's magic, too, in how the lines of the earth lie.

"All of us know at least a little of the other's art. Some know much, for nothing in this existence stands apart. The body of knowledge to learn, however, is so vast, the level of skill to be attained so great, that the families naturally fell into one tradition or another, depending on their talents.

"Lucrezia Tornabuoni's family's artistry favored them as leaders: They could intuit which way fate would fall. For centuries they prospered, and Tuscany with them. They were nobles who bore the name of Tornaquinci. At just the right instant in time, they knew when to disavow their aristocratic name and standing, that they might better profit as merchants and guild members.

"With perhaps just the same instinct, Lucrezia changed her alliance to the new religion, the ignorant religion, the intolerant religion. When the time came for her to play her part in maintaining the balance of the world, she turned her back on us all."

Angelina sipped at her tea. "Sadly, it's been her children, and children's children, who've paid the price. It says much that two of her miscreant descendants ended up as popes.

"Years passed before Lucrezia's daughters and granddaughters found their way again. By then it was too late. Weakness, prone to that shadowy infection now plaguing Florence, had taken hold of the bloodline. Caterina's grandfather Piero for example, who through arrogance and incompetence contrived to get the Medici exiled from Florence. Your Grandfather Befanini's corrupt half brother, of course, who now calls himself Pope. Pah!" Angelina spat on the ground.

Tommaso sat very still. "So we're doomed."

Like a dog shaking water from its coat, Angelina shook off her ire and melancholy. "Of course not." She smiled. "Oh, Florence will suffer some deprivation for a while. Caterina is a fine girl: In her I see the best of the old Tornaquinci talent, the Medicis' strength, and more. What she could have brought to this city...ah." Angelina shook her head regretfully, but she still smiled.

She reached over and patted Tommaso's hand. "Our enemies think they've at least exiled us. No. They're the wind that broadcasts far and wide the seeds of our knowledge, our skill, our faith. Look at you,

Tommaso. Why do you think it was so important to me to bear Giuliano de' Medici's child? In the veins of you and your siblings flow the sturdy stock bloodlines of the Aristas and the Medicis, and the talents of the Befanini, the Tornaquinci, the Ruggieros. Go out and grow in the world beyond Tuscany. Change it. Someday the seeds will blow back here. That I promise you."

55

September, 1533

Caterina's wedding retinue left Florence on the first of the month. Besides Tommaso and his cooks and Reparata and the rest of Caterina's staff, her party included Cosimo Ruggiero and his brother Lorenzo, her uncle Fillipo Strozzi, Maria Salviati and Cosimo de' Medici, her cousin Caterina Cibò. The Gondi family and another banker, Réne Birago, and a Gonzaga cousin of Isabella d'Este's met her along the way. A small bevy of artists, intended to act as the visual reporters of the historic event, also accompanied the group. One of the artists was Giorgio Vasari.

They traveled overland north to La Spezia on the coast. In La Spezia's sheltered bay, Caterina's Uncle Albany waited to sail her to France.

Tommaso and Cosimo Ruggiero strolled down to the harbor one afternoon several days after their arrival in La Spezia. Sunshine glared out of a bright, harsh blue sky and bounced off the harbor's still waters.

"Which ships are taking us?" Tommaso asked Cosimo.

Cosimo swept his arm in answer, indicating almost every large vessel crowded into the bay.

Tommaso gasped.

"Albany brought a fleet of twenty-seven. Not all will fill with passengers here. Some are for fetching the papal party later," Cosimo said. He pointed to a long, low vessel. "The royal galley. That will convey Caterina and her immediate entourage—including you."

"What about you?" Tommaso felt afraid. He couldn't believe this was happening: that they were really leaving Florence, Tuscany, Italy, forever. He wanted to be surrounded by familiar faces until he safely woke from this terrible dream.

"I'll be in that one, I believe." Cosimo pointed to a different ship. "I've already predicted fair weather and calm waters, so Caterina doesn't require my constant presence until we arrive in France. Don't worry." Cosimo smiled at Tommaso's stricken expression. "You'll be so busy learning to cook on a ship that you won't miss me or anyone else."

"Ho, Cosimo, over here!"

Cosimo and Tommaso peered over the edge of the dock. Cosimo's brother Lorenzo waved at them from a boat arriving nearby.

"This is the vessel you want," Lorenzo called. "It's assigned to the *Duchessina*'s galley. If you'll help with the next load we can all ride out together."

Tommaso looked at the knotted, burly arms of the men rowing and thought that he and Cosimo were more likely to hinder than help, but he nodded his assent.

In spite of his doubts, the boat's crew was happy to get what help they could. By the time the boat sat low in the water from its load of heavy chests and crates, Tommaso's back was stiff, his clothes sweat-glued to his skin. He was grateful to sit up in the prow of the boat and let the cool air near the water's surface flow over his face.

The galley loomed large as they rowed toward it. Tommaso tried to count the oaring stations. He finally gave up, pointing and asking Lorenzo, "How many?"

"Impressive, isn't it?" Lorenzo laughed. "I had to know too. It takes three hundred rowers to move that ship."

When they arrived, the Ruggiero brothers and Tommaso left the boat crew to unload while they went exploring. Tommaso wanted to go straight to the ship's kitchen. Lorenzo, however, insisted on conducting a tour through the entire ship. "After all, you'll need to know just as much where you'll be serving meals as where you'll be cooking them," he said.

The city of Florence often employed beautiful and ornate galleys for water pageants on the Arno during festivals, but Tommaso had never before seen a galley like this one. Its stateroom, on the top deck, ran from the mainmast to the rudder. Purple awnings covered the stateroom from the elements. The walls of all the individual rooms belowdecks, though cramped and low-ceilinged, were lined with gold cloth.

Lorenzo led them over to the rowers' benches. "Look at this," he said, yanking on the chain anchoring one of the benches to the inner wall of the ship. "It's silver. And the rowers' uniforms are red-and-gold damascened satin. Don't you think we'll cut fine figures all the way to France?"

Cosimo was right. Cooking on a ship kept Tommaso far too busy to miss anyone or anyplace. The ship's cook hired for the voyage occupied a large kitchen designed for preparing very basic hearty fare for the rowers and the rest of the crew. Tommaso, Umberto, and the rest of Caterina's cooking staff manned the smaller but better equipped passengers' kitchen.

Besides the difficulty of maneuvering around each other in cramped quarters, a perpetual concern was making sure all fires used in cooking stayed contained. Tommaso had never before had reason to appreciate the way an oven with its foundation in the earth or a well-constructed flooring didn't swing and sway, threatening to spill its fiery innards. He'd never before appreciated the way one could simply run away from a house that caught on fire. One mistake in his crowded ship's kitchen could send them all floundering, sinking into the sea.

Simple service of a meal proved nightmarish. Although most dining took place at night after they'd stopped in the haven of some bay or harbor, and in the morning before they weighed anchor, the ship at rest rollicked sufficiently to stagger land-loving legs and send trays flying. Tommaso adapted quickly by commandeering several amused, agile-footed sailors for the safe delivery of meals from the kitchen to the diners. There he and Umberto valiantly attempted to transfer food from platters to plates. They were usually successful, which Tommaso credited as much to the deep-sided plates and bowls of the ship's dining service as to their skill.

Happily, Cosimo Ruggiero's prediction for fair weather proved correct. The fleet hugged the coastline as it sailed northward past Genoa, then south and west to Nice, where Caterina and her entourage disembarked. Several days later Albany departed with some of the galleys to retrieve Clement and his retinue at Leghorn, back in Italy.

While they waited for Albany's return, Tommaso and his staff enjoyed little respite from work. The mansion hosting Caterina's entourage lacked sufficient servants and supplies to accommodate its visitors properly. After watching French scullery maids laying out forkless place settings, Tommaso ordered one of Caterina's dinner service sets unpacked. Shopping in Nice's markets allowed him the opportunity to test his French language skills.

When Albany returned with the Pope, many of Caterina's attendants joined the throngs of Nice's citizens at the port to watch the papal party disembark. Tommaso and Umberto went with the Gondi family. Many people in the crowd prayed for a glimpse of the Holy Father. Even more hoped to see some small part of Caterina's fabulous dowry that Clement had brought with him.

Tommaso watched for only one thing. So many cardinals accompanied Clement that the pier they disembarked on filled with a solid stream of red cloaks. It looked as though it flowed with blood. Somewhere among those faces and hats floating above that scarlet current floated Ippolito's face and cardinal's hat. Tommaso hadn't seen him since that terrible day in Florence. At last he caught sight of him. Ippolito's features appeared pale and tense in the bright sunlight.

That night the Duke of Albany officiated over a grand banquet attended by his, Caterina's and Clement's entourages, and Nice's most prominent citizens. Since the French hosted the event, Tommaso and his staff were relieved of cooking duties and helped as servers instead. This gave Tommaso the opportunity to observe the French dining together in large groups. Albany and his men and all the Italians were served properly: Tommaso expected no less, since Albany had spent considerable time in Italy. But the rest of the French...

"They're eating everything with their fingers, just like those boorish servants at that place we're staying at," Umberto whispered, scandalized, as he passed behind Tommaso with a soup tureen.

"Yes," Tommaso murmured back, "but they do it very well." Each diner picked up his meat, bread or vegetables with the thumb and first two fingers in an almost dainty manner.

"But they're wiping their hands on the tablecloths instead of their napkins. I even saw one woman *drink* the water from her finger bowl," Umberto hissed. "And where are their master carvers? I've seen a *guest* at each table forced to cut the meat for his fellow diners."

Tommaso couldn't reply as he moved past Umberto, but found his cousin a little later in the kitchen, sitting in despair on a stool, his head in his hands. "We've been cast adrift among barbarians," Umberto mourned.

"There are reasons for what they do," Tommaso said. "They lack carvers because it's the duty of one of the higher-ranking nobles at each table to serve that function. It's part of the aristocratic education here to learn at least the rudiments of the carver's skill. Don't you find that admirable?"

"But eating with their hands! Wiping their fingers and mouths clean on the tablecloths!" Umberto wailed.

"Take heart," Tommaso said. "We must think of ourselves as ordained to bring enlightenment, in the manner of Saint Paul going out among the Corinthians. Look at the *Duchessina's* Uncle Albany. His table manners are excellent. I'm sure we'll find the royal court itself not unsophisticated. Remember that on this occasion the purpose of eating is only secondary. Think of the whole meal we've served as merely the *primi servizi di credenza*, which often has many dishes properly eaten with the hands. The main course of this banquet is neither food nor manners, but the presentation of the dowry."

The dining over, a procession of papal chamberlains carried in that main course Tommaso spoke of. First came the jewels for Caterina's personal use, each piece presented to her on velvet cushions, then marched for viewing around the banquet hall before finally being delivered to Caterina's sergeant at arms for safekeeping. A hush fell over the diners. Their stomachs might have been filled till their appetites were sated and their taste buds dulled, but their eyes lit as they took in the savorous beauty of a glowing belt of gold garnished in its center with eight great balas rubies and one huge diamond; a pendant set with one each of a large, fine diamond, ruby and emerald; a string of eighty pearls; a rose confection of twenty diamonds; countless rings; and a matched, peerless set of seven of the largest, most extraordinary pearls ever seen in Christendom.

Next came that part of the dowry intended for the French royal house. These were presented to Albany, who would be responsible for them until Clement placed them directly into King François's hands. They included sculptures, paintings, rare maps and books.

The nearly stupefied spectators held a little of themselves back for the final course, the most treasured single item in the entire dowry, whose inclusion and value had only been rumored of after the Pope set foot in Nice.

Even cold Albany's face colored with pleasure when Antonio Gaddi knelt before him and stretched out the dark blue velvet cushion toward him. On it rested a small casket. Panels of pure rock crystal divided its sides and tops. Engraved scenes from the life of Christ had been carved into the crystal by Valerio Vincentino, the cutter of precious stones that Cellini envied so. Silver lined the panels on the inside of the casket so that the scenes stood out in relief, so exquisitely clear and well proportioned that Tommaso could make out each illustrated episode from where he stood behind a table of cardinals.

As Gaddi made his slow way around the hall, he opened the casket, revealing inside the pyx of fine enamel set with rubies. The Host, that humble transfigured portion of the Savior's body, had never before rested on so precious a bed.

"I understand His Holiness paid Vincentino two hundred gold crowns for it," Tommaso heard one cardinal say to another.

No one spoke of Caterina's value.

56

The morning after Tommaso had left Florence with Caterina, Piera woke to find a number of her pebbles missing from her small domain, which had always acted as Florence in miniature. Tommaso's stone was gone. Caterina's stone was gone. And Cosimo Ruggiero's. And others. Piera shook her head and mourned, but it was no less than she'd expected. She reassured herself of the placement of the remaining pebbles.

She looked last in the pantry, under some grain sacks, where she kept her flat, black bowl of a speculum hidden. The bright blue pebble she often found hidden in the bowl was also missing.

This stone often wandered on its own volition—it would return in several months. When it was gone Piera knew its cobalt color warded away any evil it might encounter. All she could do was keep it safe when it was in her jurisdiction and rejoice in its presence.

Whenever it returned to her for safekeeping she rolled it in good Florentine dirt until it was as dusty as she kept her speculum. This hid the true nature of both stone and bowl. With Caterina gone, the soul that belonged to the blue stone was Florence's last chance at salvation.

Piera's thought turned to the tasks she must accomplish to assure that salvation. She went out to her herb garden, carrying some grain to feed her small flock of black French hens. They'd shed two handfuls of ebony feathers. Piera smiled at the good omen. She gathered the feathers and washed them clean with water from the rain barrel.

Later in the day, when everyone else was busy in the kitchen, she returned to the quiet, empty family bedroom. From the bottom of the dower chest she'd begun to fill for her daughter Luciana, she extracted a linen bag and drew out the three ends of the cord wound up within it. She braided the feathers into the cording, whispering a curse over each plume. When she was finished she took the whole ever-lengthening rope of black feathers out of the bag and shook it several times to fluff the feathers. Then she coiled it again and returned it to the bag and the bottom of the chest.

In his *studiolo* Ruggiero the Old straightened the velvet cloth covering the great speculum. He wished it were nightfall already, so he could peer into its depths, as he had all the night before. He wished to be distracted by any kind of busyness. His two oldest sons were gone from him. He closed his eyes tightly especially against the aching gap of Cosimo's absence.

Today I'll sleep, he thought. What else is there for an old man to do?

He needed to sleep, or he'd not have the energy for this night's incantations. The queen was gone, departed for her new part on a different chessboard. Slowly, slowly, the young king must be brought out of hiding and into play.

57

Messengers rode round the clock between Nice and Marseilles, the site of the wedding.

The citizens of Marseilles learned of the splendid banquet and dowry display in Nice.

The citizens of Nice heard of the gradual arrival in Marseilles of the nobles and ladies, chancellors and cardinals of the French royal court.

On October 8 King François, his queen, the two princesses, and the three princes—the Dauphin, Duke Henri the bridegroom, and the youngest son, Charles of Angoulême—reached the village of Aubagne, where they'd remain until the round of festivities preceding the nuptials.

This wedding held as much importance as a war. The Grand Master and Marshal of all France, Anne de Montmorency, had been assigned the responsibility of organizing the event. He supervised the least detail in the same manner in which he planned for battle.

As prescribed by protocol, Caterina and Clement left Nice in different vessels, not that either of them would have wished to travel together. The fleet arrived in Marseilles's harbor on Saturday, October 11. On Sunday, the twelfth, Clement was to cross the harbor. Prince Henri and Charles of Angoulême would greet Him and escort Him on a grand processional through Marseilles to the Cathedral, where Clement would conduct Mass.

At dawn, an excited but white-faced Reparata woke Caterina. "Mistress, I must dress you quickly. There's someone here to see you," she whispered.

Caterina sat up, still dazed from her dreams. The aroma of warm food melded with the briny smell of the harbor. Gattamelata perched on her hindquarters, pawing rhythmically at the cabin door with her front paws—thwip, thwip, thwip, thwip. The red cabochon pendant lying against Caterina's breast warmed, then turned cold, chilling her. Caterina's heart began to pound. She knew who waited for her. She fairly flew into her clothing.

"Let them into the drawing room," she told Reparata. "They mustn't be seen."

People were crowded into the tiny, low-ceilinged cabin that acted as Caterina's reception area.

Madonna Gondi stood near the doorway. Though the light reflecting off the gold cloth lining the walls washed everything in the room with a gilt stain, she was as pale as Reparata.

Tommaso leaned against the doorway to balance the tray of pastries he carried. Tall and slender, his waxen countenance crowned by his flamelike hair, he could have passed for a frozen candle.

Ippolito, Antonio Pecci, Domenico, Beroaldo, and two of the Nubian wrestlers crowded into the middle of the room. For once no broad expanse of ivory teeth grinned across Beroaldo's florid, handsome face. Antonio Pecci's forehead was as wrinkled as a hound's. Domenico stood as still as a statue. Only Ippolito was animated. The galvanic force filling the room emanated from him.

He bowed to Caterina. His eyes sparkled. "Would Her Grace care to stimulate her appetite this morning with a little breakfast?" He turned and took the tray Tommaso carried and presented it to Caterina.

Like his companions, Ippolito wore a simple servant's livery. His hair and beard were as sleek as raven's feathers. His face glowed with laughter and expectation. Caterina knew she'd never seen anything so alive. Her heart ached at his beauty. She wanted to weep.

Ginevra's thoughts spread across her chest as a tight, icy band of steel. *No, no, no, no.*

I would do anything to keep him alive, Caterina thought back fiercely.

"What are you doing here? You're supposed to cross the harbor with Clement this morning," she said, her voice shaking.

"And so I shall," Ippolito replied. "Then when I'm assured that he's assured of my presence, I'll slip back here on a waiting boat manned by my friends here and the Gonzaga. Clement and the French will still believe you're readying yourself for your grand entrance into Marseilles by the time we've sailed halfway back to Genoa. When they realize we've escaped and begin to rally their search parties, we'll be racing across Milan toward Mantua and Isabella d'Este's protection. Before that good woman is compromised we'll be traveling onward to Venice and Hungary."

A long, frozen moment of silence followed the description of Ippolito's plan.

"This is neither Florence nor Rome," Ippolito finally said softly. "No dark shadows hang over us in this place. Here, at last, is our chance."

Caterina blinked rapidly. She felt her face harden. I will not cry. "We must speak of these things alone," she said. She turned to Reparata. "Will you, Madonna Gondi, and Tommaso please take the pastries to my ladies and keep them busy in their cabin? And will you," she addressed Antonio Pecci and the other men, "stand watch outside my door? If anyone comes by, tell them you're an honor guard sent by Cardinal Ippolito to guard my person and my jewels."

Soon only Ippolito, Caterina and Gattamelata remained in the room. Caterina reached up and took Ippolito's face between her hands. His smile was so loving and confident that she, too, became infected with the belief that in a few brief hours they'd be free and together at last. He bent toward her.

The long slow sweetness of his kiss wrapped around every fiber of her being. And in the middle of that kiss she knew that after all they'd been promised, after all they'd promised to each other, this was all they'd ever have. The tears she'd blinked back earlier streamed down her cheeks. Ippolito started to draw away from her. She clung to him. Our lives together last only as long as this kiss. This kiss must last forever.

Then it was over, their lives gone.

Ippolito touched her cheek. "What is this?" He bent to kiss her tears away. Caterina shivered as his lips grazed her skin.

"Ippolito, my love, my greatest desire is to die with you. I only wish that could be so."

"*Die* with me?" He laughed. "My dearest, we will die together only after a long, long life together."

Caterina shook her head. "Do you still doubt my prescient abilities?"

Ippolito became very still. He drew back to look at her. "Is that all you see for us?" he whispered. "Death?"

Caterina's cheeks felt scalded by the heat of her still-flowing tears. She couldn't stop them. "If it were only that, I'd run away with you, joyfully, eager to face eternity in your arms. What a happy, preferable fate to a life without you," she sobbed.

"But what of the others? You know of the lifeless faces I've seen in the glass, but you can't imagine how many. Every faithful heart who just left this room. All our friends in Florence and in Rome. Trapped as he is in the papal entourage, my Uncle Fillipo Strozzi would be the first to be executed. Afterward his children, my cousins, would be hunted to extinction. Mantua, whom Isabella d'Este kept safe from even Cesare Borgia, I witnessed finally fall. The Salviatis, the Ruggieros—all condemned as coconspirators.

"You and I were born to lead. Is it possible to act as traitors, leading Florence itself to destruction? This is exactly what Clement, Alessandro, and the evil that guides them have waited for."

Ippolito sat down heavily on the edge of her bed. "I want to doubt you," he said.

"But you cannot."

He shook his head. "No. Not after what I saw in Florence when I came for you."

He clutched at her hands. "Is this what Fate condemns us to? You exiled to a strange country, reduced to breeding French princes? Me living out my days in a sterile cleric's life? Florence suffering for how many generations under Alessandro and his heirs?"

Caterina gently freed one of her hands and stroked his hair. Standing over him like a mother comforting her son, she felt tired, ancient.

"I've envisioned so many possible futures," she said. "I can't vouchsafe which will come to pass. Only that it will not be one we share. Our paths diverged." She didn't have to say when. They both knew: when he'd failed her in Rome.

"I've dreamed many times of a contingent of prominent Florentines approaching the Emperor with complaints of Alessandro, requesting you as ruler in his stead. It's for that future we both must live, and not indulge ourselves with fantasies of a happy death together."

Ippolito said nothing in reply. Caterina saw his sad acceptance in his eyes. At least I've given him something to believe in. May it only come true. She opened the door. She needed Ippolito to fly away, so she could forget all her hopes and begin blindly rushing toward her future.

"Signor Pecci, please ready my cousin to accompany the Pope across the harbor. There will be no rescue attempt today or any other day. If the Cardinal agrees, I'd like you to return to me this evening. I have brief need of your services."

Ippolito nodded in agreement, his eyes dulled.

Antonio Pecci looked astonished. "But Your Grace, surely this is not the end. Surely..."

Caterina held up her hand, silencing him.

"*Ser* Domenico," she addressed the Tartar, "would you find Cosimo Ruggiero and tell him I wish him to attend me this morning? Tell him to bring his charts and whatever devices of his craft he requires."

Caterina stood in the doorway, watching Ippolito and his companions walk away from her down the corridor, recede away from her and out of her life.

Reparata and Madonna Gondi must have been listening just inside the door of the ladies-in-waiting cabin. They emerged as the echo of Ippolito's last footsteps faded.

"Reparata, if Tommaso is still serving my ladies, tell him I'd like some light repast soon. And inform my ladies that, after I sit in consultation with Cosimo Ruggiero this morning, I intend to spend most of the rest of the day in prayer and contemplation. They should take the opportunity to attend to their preparations for the upcoming festivities."

Cosimo arrived soon. Under one arm he carried a box, under the other several scrolls and books.

"Sit, Cosimo. Relieve yourself of your burdens," Caterina said.

Cosimo sat. He said nothing, waiting for her to speak.

"There's nothing more I can do, no hope for me," Caterina said. "I submit to your father's prophecy. You know I sometimes see distant events in the moment they happen, and that I also possess the ability to glimpse many possible futures. But I lack the power to see the one true future. That is your talent."

Cosimo nodded. "By narrowing the variables with your acceptance, it's now possible for me to extend the horoscope my father cast at your birth."

Caterina sat down opposite Cosimo. "Then begin," she said.

It took a long while. Besides Caterina's chart, Cosimo drew forth a number of already completed diagrams from his bundle of papers. None of these bore identifying names—Cosimo didn't need them. Caterina knew that for him a glimpse of each chart bore a clearer picture of that person than a glimpse of their face. She guessed who some of the charts belonged to: Ippolito, Alessandro, Clement, Henri of France.

Cosimo finally laid down his calculations. "It is done," he said. "Your life will not be easy or secure. For a number of years your greatest triumph will be to just endure. But even during those difficult times you'll enjoy friendship with those in the most exalted positions. You'll know laughter, wit, pleasure. Eventually you'll achieve your rightful place. You'll bear many children. Your sons will sit on the throne of France as kings. You yourself will sit on that throne as queen. You'll love deeply and truly, and set an example as one of the finest wives in Christendom. You will come to be loved in turn. You will know both accomplishment and happiness."

"What of Florence?" Caterina asked. "What of her fate, now that I abandon her?"

Cosimo shook her head. "You haven't abandoned her. You sacrificed yourself for her. Because of that sacrifice she'll suffer under Alessandro for only a scant while longer. Then she'll throw off his rule like a horse a bad rider. A wise, good man of de' Medici blood will take up her reins. I see a day in the future when one of your children's children will return to Florence in triumph to happily wed one of that man's descendants."

"And enjoy the marriage I'm denied," Caterina whispered.

As Caterina had requested, Antonio Pecci returned that evening. Caterina was being fitted in her bedroom for one of the many ornate gowns she'd wear over the next few weeks. Through the door she heard Antonio arrive in the drawing room and regale her ladies with descriptions of the Pope's progress across Marseilles's harbor: How the Holy Father was met by her bridegroom and his younger brother Charles of Angoulême.

How together they genuflected to the Holy Sacrament before Clement set the Host in the tabernacle and placed it on a white horse. How two footmen holding white silk reins led the horse away, a third man marching before them and ringing a golden bell, so the waiting throngs would know to prostrate themselves.

Caterina changed into a simple shift and surcoat and entered her drawing room. Antonio Pecci halted his narrative, smiled, and bowed to her, as did Domenico and Beroaldo, who accompanied him.

"Signor Beroaldo," Caterina addressed the Indian diver. "I know you to be Signor Pecci's equal at bantering. Pray continue to entertain my ladies while I confer with Signor Pecci."

Caterina drew Antonio and Domenico over to a sideboard. "Please, Antonio, do me the honor of pouring me some wine. This business of wearing enough brocade and jewelry to break a donkey's back is thirsty work. My spirit needs refreshing."

Behind them Caterina's ladies were exclaiming at Beroaldo's descriptions of the pomp of the Mass in Marseilles's cathedral.

"How fared my cousin this day?" Caterina said in a low voice.

All of Pecci's frivolous courtier's charm vanished. "Like a dead man walking across a battlefield, searching for his own cut-out heart." Antonio's own eyes were sad, wounded.

Caterina's goblet trembled in her hand. "I did what I did to save him," she said.

Antonio nodded. "Surely Your Grace didn't wish me to attend you this night just to tell me that," he said.

"No," Caterina agreed. "I have a commission for you. It's this: As you love my cousin, once I've been wed to Henri of France, promise me you'll never leave Ippolito's side."

Antonio Pecci looked startled.

"Not even for an hour," Caterina said.

"Is he in danger?" Antonio asked.

"Always," Caterina said. "Until that day when Alessandro de' Medici no longer walks this earth."

She saw the three men out the door herself. A young man was walking away down the narrow ship's corridor, as if he'd just happened to pass by her cabin. It was Giorgio Vasari. Giorgio should have been across the harbor in Marseilles with the other artists, recording the Pope's reception there. Instead, on those brief occasions when Caterina had left her cabin that day, he'd always been skulking somewhere nearby. She'd hoped after the way he'd betrayed her, had betrayed Florence, that day on the Ponte Vecchio, that the shadows might recede from his eyes. They had not.

Hours later, Caterina sat up in her bed, alone except for Gattamelata crouching at her feet and Ginevra's spirit dangling against her breast. She held a mirror in her lap. Her dirk lay on a pillow beside her. The waves in the harbor outside rocked the boat in a slow lullaby of motion. Caterina balanced the mirror against the soft swaying. She placed a moonstone in the mirror's center. "Let this be the white horse upon which the host of my wishes rides," she murmured.

Cosimo Ruggiero had left her to hope that the "wise, good, strong man" fated to save Florence would prove to be Ippolito. Images of Ippolito's possible futures swam swiftly across the mirror's surface, like a school of small, flickering fishes.

In some futures he lived out his life as a venerated Prince of the Church. In a very few he rode triumphant into Florence. In most he died by Alessandro's hand.

Caterina picked up her dirk. With both hands she held it out over the mirror. Her thoughts turned toward a different man. This one lived like a spider in the shadows of Alessandro's mansion. And like a spider he'd been born to ambush, born to kill. The face of Lorenzaccio de' Medici filled the mirror below the moonstone.

"I pray you strike, my good, dark, blade," Caterina whispered. "Strike well. Strike soon."

58

On the next day, October 13, King François and his eldest son, the Dauphin, made their way into Marseilles in a magnificent procession, eclipsing those of the Pope and bridegroom of the day before. Messengers rushed back and forth all day across the harbor. Tommaso heard snippets of description of pomp and splendor. He was too busy to pay attention to them. Tomorrow Caterina would follow the state entry of the queen and princesses of France into the city with a procession of her own.

When the bride made her long way through Marseilles to be presented to her new family and thereafter escorted to her prenuptial lodgings, all of her belongings, her staff, and her staff's belonging were to be transferred to either the French royal family's quarters or her own temporary lodging, according to need.

Umberto mournfully marked several crates with their contents and stacked them for the quartermaster to deliver. "The monstrous gullet of the French court will crush and absorb us, like so many small, tender *crostini*," he said.

Alvise, one of the other Florentine cooks Tommaso had chosen to join his staff, rolled his eyes sarcastically as he packed up a box behind Umberto.

Tommaso had no time to spare for his cousin's melancholy. A French stevedore asked him the way to the sergeant at arms's quarters. Tommaso gave him directions. "That's the eighth French lackey in an hour," he said in exasperation as he wrapped pewter platters in cloth before placing them in a box. "Why do they keep asking me? I'm only a cook. Why don't they harry the chamberlain?"

"Because the chamberlain looks like every other Italian to them," Umberto said. "You're the only man here with bright red hair, and everyone knows you're in the *Duchessina's* confidence. Therefore, you're the one person most likely to know, well, anything and everything. Besides, you speak French better than the rest of us."

Tommaso cursed the lessons Caterina had required him to take. "Then help me find a linen to cover my hair," he begged Umberto.

Umberto laughed and shook his head. He dragged one of his crates out toward the gangplank to be unloaded.

"It pleases me that I've so restored your humor," Tommaso shouted after him. A few moments later he followed, dragging one of his own boxes out to the deck. As he bent over to lift it onto a pile of similar crates waiting to be carried to the docks, someone tapped his shoulder from behind, and asked in French, "Do you know where I could find...?"

Tommaso whirled around in a fury of exasperation, only to find himself facing the Duke of Albany. Behind the Duke were four men-at-arms.

"...my niece?" the Duke finished, taking a startled step away from Tommaso's abrupt motion. "She's nowhere on this ship."

Tommaso snapped his mouth shut on his intended retort, straightened up, then bowed deeply.

"Excuse me, Your Grace." His mouth fumbled, searching for the proper words in French. "You surprised me. I thought you gone officiating at the ceremonies for King François."

"I concluded my duties there. It's more important that I oversee the *Duchessina's* preparations for her entrance into Marseilles tomorrow. She is...?" The Duke arched one eyebrow in cold inquiry, but Tommaso clearly saw the fear in the man's eyes. Of course—Clement would have warned Albany that Caterina might take flight.

"Her Grace and her ladies went ashore to the stables, to assure themselves that their mounts for tomorrow are properly caparisoned," Tommaso said.

Albany's relief was palpable. He turned to go, then turned again. "You shall accompany us *Ser*... Arista, is it not?"

"Why? I don't know where the stables are," Tommaso replied, bewildered.

The Duke drew in a sharp breath, unaccustomed to having a servant refuse him.

"Forgive me, Your Grace," Tommaso said, "but the *Duchessina* specifically assigned me the task of overseeing the transport of her valuable table service and all of her culinary supplies. I can hardly leave my post."

"I'm sure your cooking chores can wait," Albany snapped. He gestured to two of his men-at-arms. They fell in on either side of Tommaso and marched him swiftly off the ship before Umberto's and Alvise's astonished eyes.

At last Tommaso understood. If Caterina wasn't at the stables, if she'd fled, Albany would waste no time. He'd need a servant-accomplice handy to beat the truth out of on the spot.

On the docks a fifth man-at-arms held the reins of six horses. All the men mounted. Tommaso stood terrified, surrounded by stamping hoofs and huge, sweating, skittish bodies.

"Take him with you," Albany ordered the largest man, astride the largest horse. The man reached down and grabbed Tommaso by the wrist. Then Tommaso was lofting into the air behind the man and scrabbling his legs over the horse's impossibly broad haunches. The horse indicated its displeasure by dancing about, making Tommaso's task that much harder. He finally got his legs straddled and arms clutched tightly around the rider's waist.

The man turned his head and laughed. "I thought Italians were all master equestrians."

"Your feet are in stirrups, your hands on reins. Mine are not," Tommaso said sourly.

The man laughed harder. "Be careful not to squeeze all the breath from my lungs, my brave Italian," he said.

Tommaso was about to answer with another sharp retort when Albany's troupe gathered itself in formation and began trotting down a road leading away from the docks. Tommaso's spine, jaw and teeth clattered in time to the horse's jarring trot. With his head jammed up against the rider's broad back, he could see little more than glimpses to either side of laborers and tradesmen scurrying out of the way and wedging themselves against the walls of the buildings lining the street.

After a journey long enough to loosen every bone in his body from its socket, the horsemen rode into a large stable yard. Tommaso was relieved to see several of Caterina's men-at-arms and Cosimo de' Medici standing guard before the stable's broad, open doors. Cosimo stared as Tommaso was marched like a prisoner into the stables.

Caterina and her ladies were inside. Maria Salviati perched on a sidesaddle on a mare while grooms and hostlers bustled about, checking the length and security of all sorts of buckles and straps. Caterina's ladies were calling out laughing suggestions to Maria which she, excellent equestrian that she was, just as laughingly declined. The horse Maria sat astride stood miraculously still in the midst of all this noise.

Considering what he'd just been through, Tommaso wasn't in the mood to admire horseflesh, but that mare had to be the calmest, most tranquil beast he'd ever seen. Or the most lazy and stupid.

"My Uncle Albany, what brings you hence?" Caterina asked pleasantly. Tommaso knew she saw him hemmed in at the back of Albany's guard, but she said nothing to that fact.

Albany bowed. "To be sure all the preparations for tomorrow go smoothly, Milady."

"They go well, as you shall see," Caterina said. Maria Salviati dismounted. She and Caterina's ladies followed as Caterina led Albany and his entourage through the stable. "Thus far I'm satisfied with the equipages for my ladies. And all alterations to their riding gowns are finished."

Albany examined some horse trappings of silver inlaid with gold. "The queen and princesses will enter the city first, before you, in six triumphal coaches. Their thirty ladies will accompany them on horseback. Your ladies' caparisons are more magnificent than theirs." He looked at Caterina with grudging approval. "A wise choice. There's some dissatisfaction throughout the country: In spite of your royal French blood, you're considered both a foreigner and a minor heiress from a mere merchant's family. To begin to disabuse these notions publicly before the wedding can do nothing but improve your position in the court and with the people."

At the end of the line of stalls a hostler groomed a stunningly beautiful, tall, black mare. Spread out nearby on a clean horse blanket was a saddle and set of trappings even more magnificent than that of Caterina's ladies.

"This is my mount and caparisons," Caterina said, stroking the mare's neck.

"*Your* mount?" Albany no longer looked pleased. "I just told you: The women of the royal family ride tomorrow in coaches."

Caterina nodded. "So I've already been informed, by messenger. Restrain your ire, good Uncle."

She next guided them around a corner, toward the back door to the stable.

There a number of stableboys polished the most elegant open carriage Tommaso had ever seen. Its sides gleamed like polished obsidian. Its intricate inlaid decorations of gold and mother-of-pearl featured the *palle* of the Medici coat of arms and Florence's lions and lilies. Black sable velvet, deeper and thicker than forest moss, furnished the interior of the carriage.

"My carriage will follow directly behind me in the procession, indicating that I ride horseback by choice, not necessity," Caterina said.

Albany could think of nothing to say in reply.

"Since I trust I've assuaged your fears, perhaps you can now tell me why my head cook accompanies you," Caterina said. "My instructions to him were to oversee the transfer of all kitchen supplies and implements, and my quite valuable dining service, from the ship to French soil. Tommaso, is the work completed?"

Tommaso bowed. "No, Your Grace, unless the rest of my staff finished in my absence."

Caterina looked back at Albany. "You're so unfamiliar with my countenance that you felt compelled to bring my cook away from his assigned duties to identify me?"

Albany flushed. Tommaso smothered a grin. What Albany thought foresight in forcing his company had turned out to be a rash, poorly thought-out action.

Albany's quick courtier's wit failed him. He couldn't think of an excuse.

"At the end of this month I wed the second son of the King of France," Caterina's voice was as frosty as her gaze. "My retainers have sacrificed homeland and family to follow me. They are never to be treated with anything but courtesy and respect.

"I serve you fair notice that from this day forth I'll brook no interference from you in my affairs. If you lack a household of your own to meddle in, you should petition the king to grant you one. If you ever wish to enjoy my support in court matters, I suggest this is a good time for you to commence currying favor with me."

Several of Caterina's ladies gasped, but Tommaso saw Maria Salviati slowly nod. Albany's men shifted on their feet, looking uncomfortable. Albany stood stiffly erect. Two bright spots pinked his pale cheeks. Finally, he bowed to Caterina.

"How did he come here?" Caterina asked.

Albany blinked in confusion.

"My cook," Caterina said. "How did you convey him hence?"

"On horseback. Sitting up behind one of my men."

The beginnings of a smile crooked the edge of Caterina's lip. "Tommaso is a chef, not an equestrian. He doesn't enjoy being forced to straddle a horse." The small smile left her face. "You will hire him a good litter to carry him back to the ship, out of your own purse."

Caterina turned on her heel, dismissing her Uncle Albany for once and forever.

The Marshal of France, Anne de Montmorency, had organized Marseilles to the efficiency of a field camp in the cause of the political advantage this marriage would garner. The citizens of the city waged battle for their king with the celebratory weaponry of banquets, balls and galas. All menus had been decided months before, all culinary preparations weeks before. For the next fortnight Tommaso and his fellow cooks could do little more than act as extra pairs of hands.

When Caterina made her triumphant procession through Marseilles, Tommaso was jointing a beef carcass. When Albany formally introduced her to her new family, Tommaso was garnishing pastries. Not needed for menu consultations, he hardly saw her at all during the flurry of prenuptial festivities.

The morning of October 28, her wedding day, found Tommaso, Umberto and the others shifting crates about once again, this time preparing to move from the baronial estate that had served as Caterina's temporary home to the royal residence in Marseilles. The preparations didn't take long. They'd hardly unpacked anything other than Caterina's table service in the last two weeks.

"That's all until we're needed to help serve tonight," Tommaso said, as they loaded the last chest onto the wagon under the watchful eyes of one of Caterina's men-at-arms. "There's still time to go to the cathedral."

"Why?" asked Umberto. "It's not as if you could actually get in to see the wedding."

"No, but we could view the procession afterward."

Umberto shrugged. "We face a lifetime of being crushed together at affairs of state with hordes of Frenchman. I prefer to go with the wagon, unpack my belongings at our new abode and rest before this evening. The banquet tonight promises to be the most monstrous event in a month of monstrous events."

Most of the other chefs were of Umberto's mind, but Alvise and Gabriele Cavallucci agreed to go to the Cathedral with Tommaso.

The ceremony wasn't yet over. Throngs pressed together in the plaza for eventual glimpses of the royal family and the nobles who ruled them. November loomed, chilly, only three days away, but the packed mob made such a steamy stew that almost everyone had divested themselves of surcoats or jackets. Tommaso's grasp of French was strained as he tried to decipher the rustling fragments of conversation whirling about his ears like autumn leaves in the wind.

The doors to the Cathedral opened. No wedding guests crowded out: They emerged instead in neat arrayed procession, even the least, most insignificant page dressed in resplendent satins or silks.

A lovely woman, her hair more golden than even Caterina's, accompanied the two royal princesses.

"*La plus belle des savants et la plus savante des belles,*" a man crushed up against Tommaso murmured. *The most beautiful of the wise and the wisest of the beautiful.* "Now there is the only woman fit for our king since beloved Queen Claude died," he said with approval.

Gabriele, pressed into Tommaso's other side, raised his eyebrows in query.

"The famous Madame d'Etampes," Tommaso whispered in Gabriele's ear. "The king's mistress and also governess to the princesses."

People nearby began muttering unflattering comments about foreign women. Tommaso was afraid to look, knowing Caterina must be stepping out onto the plaza to this animosity. But when he raised his head he saw instead another woman, with black hair, dark protuberant eyes, and small, fleshy pursed lips. In spite of the crowds' muttering, she wore the emblems marking her, too, as a member of the royal family.

"She must be Eleanor of Austria, the king's second wife," Tommaso explained *sub votto voce* to Gabriele. "Emperor Carlos's sister, whom François was forced to marry after the defeat at Pavia."

Soon afterward two young men marched down the cathedral steps to cheers from the waiting throngs. The older of the two waved and smiled at the crowd, who responded with joyful shouts of "Long live the Dauphin!" The young man was tall and handsome, clean-shaven, poised. There was nothing false about him—he clearly loved the people he would someday rule as François II.

The youth beside him was just as well built and tall, although obviously younger. He, too, was handsome, but the expression on his face was as grave and closed as his brother's was open. A sparse novice's beard and moustache garnished his chin and mouth. No doubt he wished to seem more the man for the occasion. This was Caterina's new husband; Henri, Duke of Orleans.

Alvise tugged at Tommaso's sleeve. "He hardly seems any older than the *Duchessina*," Alvise muttered.

"He's not," Tommaso said. "He was born but a fortnight before her."

Tommaso danced from foot to foot. Nothing must have gone amiss at the nuptials. The church continued to pour out its dignified, ordered contents of wedding guests, who posed and marched like well-behaved actors. But where was Caterina?

The crowd shared his impatience. When they muttered, "Where's the Italian bride? Bring on the Italian bride and her papal booty," Tommaso knew they thought of her as little more than a mule loaded down with treasures to enrich the national coffers. And they wanted to see the proof of it. They wanted to see her dripping with gems.

Two people stepped out of the dark recesses of the Cathedral into the light. The wind-whipped rustling voices died away to silence. Caterina stood at the top of the stairs, leaning lightly on the arm of the King of France himself.

They descended, one slow step at a time. Tommaso marveled that Caterina could move at all. Her posture was even more erect than usual, supporting the weight of the yards of thick brocade her gown had been engineered from. Clement's gift of the great gold belt with its balas rubies and diamond girded her waist. The bodice of her dress could scarcely be seen under the pendants and brooches of rare gems, including a corsage of ermine filled with pearls and diamonds. Her neckline, however, had been left relatively uncluttered, to set off the necklace of the seven fabulous pigeon egg pearls. She appeared older, taller, as though she'd grown overnight to bear all the weight.

This was the first time Tommaso had seen the King.

François lacked the handsome features of his sons. His nose was enormous and hooked downward. His mouth was inconsequential behind an undistinguished beard. His small eyes were heavy-lidded and upturned at the corners. But those eyes sparkled and the mouth smiled as the King looked down at Caterina. François bent to say something to her which made her laugh.

François was as athletically built as his sons. He carried an aura about him as light and warm as the sun's, which expanded to envelop and include Caterina. Tommaso instantly liked him, and understood why the French people were so devoted to their sovereign.

François reminded him of something his grandfather Befanini had once said in trying to describe Lorenzo il Magnífico to his grandchildren: "Lorenzo the Great was at one and the same time astoundingly homely and impossibly attractive. In his presence you knew you would never witness greater intelligence or charm. One wanted to never leave his side, for that was like stepping from the height of spring directly into winter."

This man could be Lorenzo the Great reborn, Tommaso thought. And from the way François was looking at Caterina, it was evident that no matter how well the French people or her new husband did or did not take to her, this one great man understood her worth, her value. In François she'd found both protector and friend.

59

Tommaso felt sure that the great hall couldn't hold another person. Three long rows of tables almost filled it, barely leaving room enough for all the seated guests, the servers standing one to every three diners behind them, and those like himself, rushing food back and forth from the kitchen.

Whenever he could, back in the kitchen and working alongside the French servants, Tommaso asked about the various guests, since these were the people he'd soon be living among. Then, when he emerged, carrying a filled plate or serving bowl, he tried to match the faces to the names and descriptions.

Clement and King François shared the head of the table that fed the noblemen of France and all the honored male guests, including Fillipo Strozzi, the Duke of Albany, and the Marshal of France, who kept leaping from his place at the table to assure himself of some detail or another.

Clement tried to appear pious and austere, but he basked in François's aura of power and grace with the greedy look of a starving man. The Pope's face was pale and yellowish. He was almost blind in one eye. Tommaso experienced a sudden, startled premonition. *He won't live long. After this is over he'll have outlived his usefulness. Whoever or whatever sustained him all these years will abandon him.*

Clement had propagated one last, cruel act on Caterina. She sat at the head of the table assigned to the clergy. Every French cardinal, and every Italian cardinal not too old or infirm to make the journey from Italy, stretched in two red lines down and away from her. Ippolito was close enough for her to see clearly, but far enough away to prevent them from conversing. Ippolito didn't look at Caterina. Tommaso knew he couldn't.

The table was wide enough for the Dauphin and Caterina's new husband to sit on either side of her at the head. The Dauphin turned to Caterina often, engaging her in discussion, trying to put her at her ease. Henri, however, spoke little to Caterina, although when he did it was with courtesy. The melancholy look on his face had deepened since his departure from the Cathedral.

Sharp as a carving knife, anger stabbed through Tommaso. How dare the young Duke act that way toward Caterina? He'd wed a lovely young woman who was better educated and more intelligent than most of the crowned heads of Europe. He should be doting on her every word with dawning admiration.

Instead he spent most of his time looking down at his hands in his lap, occasionally looking up to glance at the table next to his: the royal ladies' and noblewomen's table.

Madame d'Etampes was instantly recognizable. So was the Queen. François's sister, Marguerite of Navarre, could be no one else *but* François's sister. She shared her brother's strong facial features, only slightly scaled down to more feminine proportions. Well-known in Italy as one of France's leading intelligentsia, the people of France esteemed her even more as King François's greatest advocate, and the heroine who'd rescued her brother when he lay ill and pining unto death as the prisoner of the Emperor in a tower in the Alcazar.

To Tommaso's surprise, it wasn't one of these three women who presided at the head of the ladies' table, but a plain, cold-faced woman.

"That's Diane de Poitiers, widow of the Grand Senechal," a *saucier* had told him back in the kitchen. "When the young princes were re-turned from Madrid after substituting for their father as the Emperor's hostages, Duke Henri was despairing and unruly from the poor treatment he suffered there. His Most Christian Majesty sought the rehabilitation of his second son by assigning La Grande Senechale as his tutor and mentor."

Which would explain her elevated position at her charge's nuptial feast, Tommaso thought. And why he glances at her so frequently.

Tommaso gazed around at the people he already knew, memorizing their faces, assigning them to memory. Maria Salviati sat next to Caterina Cibò at the women's table. Cosimo de' Medici stood behind his mother, acting as her page and server for the occasion. Giorgio Vasari stood pressed against a back wall, scribbling swift portraits of all the notables for later reference. Like the pale ghost of a god, Ippolito de' Medici stared down at the food on his plate. He hadn't eaten a bite.

These are part of Caterina's, and therefore my own, past, Tommaso thought.

Gattamelata rested in an open basket padded with a silk pillow. The basket sat on the floor of what would be Caterina's private quarters after the wedding feast.

In spite of the rigors of the last two months of traveling, Gattamelata felt stronger than she had in many years. But not as strong as she might have been.

Six and a half years before she'd divided much of herself among seven new bodies. It took seven years for her daughter-selves to mature and grow hardy, ready for regathering back into herself. But one of her young, vulnerable selves had been destroyed. Another was crippled to such an extent that it split away from her. And now the shadow creatures drove her into exile two seasons shy of the time of assimilation. But assimilate she did. She had no choice. Her life in fur, flesh and bone was slowly coming to its conclusion.

EPILOGUE

The day Caterina's entourage had crossed over Tuscany's last boundaries, Piera rose earlier than usual. She'd only been able to sleep in fits and starts, knowing the sad task that awaited her in the morning.

As a young girl she'd grown up in the de' Medici palazzo surrounded by glowing, silken tortoiseshell cats. Her mother used them to teach her how to count: "one, two, three, four, five, six, seven and eight; Mother Cat and her daughters, all looking just the same. The kittens came into this world the very month that you were born. That's how we knew you were so special, and why your older sisters spoil you so."

Her mother counted off the cats from thumb to little finger of one hand, then little finger on up on the other hand. This left Piera with two fingers uncounted. Her Grandmother Angelina sidled over and tugged at the leftover index finger. "This finger is nine, for the Maiden, who points the way for us." Then the old woman would tap the last thumb. "This thumb is for ten, for Mother Aradia, who does all the work."

When Piera turned seven, she woke in the middle of one night from a terrifying dream: A wind swept through the Medici palazzo, blowing everything away before it—people, furniture, artwork, her family, every worktable, stool, pot, pan and utensil in the kitchen. She sat alone and weeping before the gale-swept fireplace. Then the wind came back. She fled through the desolate mansion, knowing the wind searched for her. It found her. It picked her up and carried her through room after empty room. She flew, helpless, through the air. At last the wind returned her to the kitchen and dropped her. It began to circle in on itself, tighter and tighter, smaller and smaller, until it vanished. In its place lay a plain round pebble.

She woke up crying in the big family bed, nestled between her sisters. No one woke to comfort her. Her father, mother and sisters lay unnaturally still. Only their warmth and soft breathing told her they were asleep, not dead. Piera's heart throbbed unsteadily.

Still filled with her dream, she clambered over her family and out of bed. She had to see if the rest of the mansion had been swept barren.

She heard noises in the kitchen: not the wind, but the reassuring sounds of people talking quietly. Piera's heart calmed. She tiptoed to the kitchen.

Grandmother Angelina stood next to another woman, who held a single candle. They seemed to be praying over something lying on the floor. A girl of perhaps ten or eleven stood beside them, carrying an empty grain sack.

Piera couldn't make out the amorphous shape at their feet—the woman stood in the way. Then she noticed other similar forms scattered about the kitchen floor. She saw a long, long tail extending out from one of them, and realized that they were the cats—her cats. But that couldn't be. They lay too still, too flat, like boneless skins. She crept over to one of them. It's eyes were open and unseeing. Piera reached out a small, trembling hand to pet it. Its fur still felt silky, but there was no spirit or flesh underneath it responding to her touch.

Piera looked about at all the scraplike forms, then back at the women. She recognized the other lady now: She ran one of the wild-game shops on the Ponte Vecchio. Her name was Madonna Arista. Piera instantly knew what the empty sack was for. Her eyes filled with tears. She threw back her head and began to keen.

A soft hand covered her mouth. "Hush, hush," said the girl with the sack. "It's not what you think. They're not dead. They're just . . . empty."

"That's right," the woman with the candle nodded. "Good, Leonora."

Grandmother Angelina motioned for Piera to come stand beside her. Eyes streaming with tears, Piera walked carefully around the bodies of her small friends.

Grandmother Angelina bent down to Piera. Her rust-and-gray hair brushed Piera's forehead. Her eyes were sad, but she smiled. "Yes, Piera, this is terrible. But it's wonderful too. I'll show you when we're done here. Help us with our prayers for them. It's time you learned the words anyway."

Piera followed the singsong chanting of the two women and Leonora as best she could. When they finished, Leonora opened up the sack and held it out. "Do you want to do it?" she asked Piera. "To say goodbye?"

Piera could hardly see through her tears, but she nodded. She picked up the body. It felt impossible light. She slid it into the sack.

"Count," Angelina whispered. "Count them as we go."

They repeated the prayers over each body. One, two, three, four, five, six, seven.

Piera looked around the kitchen. Mother cat and kittens made eight. Where was the eighth body? She didn't see it anywhere.

"Come with me," said Grandmother Angelina. She led Piera to the pantry and handed her Madonna Arista's candle. "Open the door and tell me what you see inside."

Piera looked inside. The eighth body was coiled up on a grain sack. It moved when the light from her candle fell on it. Piera gasped and jumped back. Behind her Leonora laughed quietly.

The cat extended one front one leg, then the other. It laid back its ears. Its spine rippled in a voluptuous stretch.

"Go closer," Grandmother Angelina told Piera. "Gaze into its eyes."

Piera's hands shook, shivering the candlelight about the pantry's sacks and full shelves. She crouched to set the candle on the floor. The cat looked up at her, its eyes as green as emeralds. In them Piera saw the spirit of each cat she'd just laid to rest in Leonora Arista's sack.

That had been the beginning of her formal apprenticeship in the mysteries of the Little Kitchen Goddess. No words were spoken, but everyone in her family seemed to know.

The cat had many litters of fine kittens afterward, but never tortoiseshells, and never so many, until years later, not long before Luciana's birth.

When Piera was married out of the Befanini kitchen, Grandmother Angelina handed Piera a carrying basket. Inside was Gattamelata. No one in the Befanini kitchen questioned Angelina's wedding gift.

Lately Piera had dreamed the wind again. She doubted herself at first. It was too soon—seven years had not yet passed since the birth of the identical kittens.

When Clement hastened the date of Caterina's wedding, Piera understood why the dreams came so early. The Little Kitchen Goddess would be forced to act when Caterina left.

Now, on this still-dark morning, Piera braced herself for the empty bodies of the three cats in the Ruggiero Kitchen. Grandmother Angelina would deal with the two in the de' Medici palazzo; Elissa Pecorino with the one in her possession.

Piera found one thin carcass before the hearth, as though it had lingered there for one last sensation of the pleasure of warmth. She placed it in a sack. Later in the day Francesca would take the sack to Leonora.

Piera started to cry. She wept not for her small friend's death—she'd come to understand that this was not truly death back when she was seven years old. She wept because all her life she'd lived in the presence of the Little Kitchen Goddess. Now she'd have to live out the rest of her life without Her.

The second body lay under the main worktable. Piera lifted it into the sack to join its lifeless sister.

She couldn't find the body of the third cat anywhere. She heard people beginning to move around in their bedrooms. The scullery maids would arrive at any moment. Piera gave up. She hid the sack in the back of the pantry. Francesca could easily retrieve it from there. Piera wiped her sweating hands against her skirt as she emerged from the pantry.

"Look, Mama, what she caught!"

Piera turned. Luciana stood in the doorway that opened out to the herb garden. In her arms she held a squirming, very alive tortoiseshell cat, its mouth clenched shut on a small, very alive mouse. The cat broke free and jumped to the ground. It landed badly, losing its hold on the mouse. The mouse scurried across the floor. The cat followed after with a lurching, limping run. It was Gattamelata's crippled daughter.

Piera stood speechless. It wasn't possible. Her heart, emptied by loss, filled with joy.

ACKNOWLEDGMENTS

Many thanks are owed to my infinitely patient editor, Beth Meacham, for her guidance, and to Lisa Goldstein and Charles N. Brown for their helpful insights. Thanks also to my agent, Merrillee Heifetz of Writers House, and Karin Schulze and Maja Nickolic for their encouragement. And of course, kudos to Richard, my husband, for his amused grace. A belated thank you to Rachel Holmen, for years ago giving me the wonderful book on cats' cradles that inspired so much of the magic in this book.

FOOD RECIPES

FRITTELLE DI CREMA
(FRIED CUSTARDS)

---

5 eggs	*2 cups milk*
⅓ cup sugar	*fine bread crumbs*
1 cup all-purpose flour	*extra virgin olive oil*
grated zest of one lemon	*1 Tblsp. confectioner's sugar*

Beat the eggs. Add the ⅓ cup sugar and beat well. Gradually add the flour, milk and lemon zest. Beat thoroughly. Pour mixture into a heavy saucepan. Stir *constantly* over *low* heat until mixture simmers and thickens enough to coat a spoon. Pour into a lightly but thoroughly oiled pie plate. Let cool completely. Slice the cold custard into approximately 1" by 2" rectangles. Dredge the rectangles in the bread crumbs to coat evenly.

In a deep, heavy skillet, heat the olive oil to 350° (180°C). A few at a time, slip the custards into the oil. Fry until golden, about three minutes, turning once. With a slotted spoon, remove to drain, then put in a low temperature oven to keep warm as you finish frying the rest of the custards. Sprinkle with the confectioner's sugar.

Author's note: These are very rich and heavy. I strongly recommend serving them with sliced fruit or a light syrup.

PASTICCIO DI RISO E MELE

⅓ cup raisins
1 cup Vin Santo or other
    white dessert wine
4 cups milk
1½ cup Arborio rice
pinch of freshly grated nutmeg

1 tsp. ground cinnamon
6 Tblsp. butter
1 Tblsp. butter
3 eggs, beaten
2 sweet apples
pinch of salt

Soak the raisins in the *Vin Santo* for six hours.

In a heavy saucepan, bring the milk to boil with the pinch of salt. Add the rice, lower the heat and simmer until all the milk is absorbed. Check it frequently, but it should take about a half an hour.

Remove from heat and stir in nutmeg, raisins, cinnamon and four tablespoons of the sugar. After mixture cools completely, stir in the eggs, then pour into a buttered springform pan. Preheat your oven to 350°.

Peel, core and thinly slice the apples. Arrange the apple slices in concentric circles on top of the batter. Sprinkle with remainder of sugar. Place in oven and bake until set, about one hour.

Remove from oven and let cool slightly. Remove pan sides and serve warm.

OYSTERS IN CUMIN SAUCE

1 Tblsp. total, lovage, parsley,
    mint, malabathrum and cumin
    pepper to taste
1 tsp. honey

½ cup vinegar

1 Tblsp. garum
oysters

Grind the herbs and spices in a mortar, using enough cumin so that it's the strongest flavor. Mix with the honey, vinegar, and *garum*. Let stand ½ hour before serving.

Author's note: This is a seafood vinaigrette sauce, meant to be served with cooked oysters. I didn't know where to even begin to find malabathrum, but since the predominant flavor is supposed to be cumin anyway, I didn't worry about it overly much. *Garum* was the ancient Roman's fermented fish sauce. I experimented a little and ended up most pleased with a mixture of soy sauce and Thai fish sauce (*nam pla*). I always like larger portions, so I increased the entire recipe fourfold from this when I made it.

PORK STEW WITH CITRONS

1 lb. pork shoulder
¾ lb. ground meat, formed into small meatballs
1 Tblsp. olive oil
1 Tblsp. garum (substitute a mixture of soy sauce and Thai fish sauce)
2 leeks, chopped
1 bunch fresh coriander, minced

1 tsp. pepper
1 tsp. pepper
1 tsp. total, cumin and rue
2 Tblsp. sapa (use reduced wine)
2 citrons
1 tsp. cornstarch
1 tsp. honey or sugar (optional)

Boil the pork shoulder, cut into cubes and set aside. In a casserole sauté the *garum*, leeks and coriander in the olive oil. Then add the pork shoulder and meatballs. Mix the pepper, herbs and *sapa*, then add to the cooking meat.

Peel the citrons, cut them into quarters, and then boil them for ten minutes in water. Add to the meat and finish cooking. Thicken with a bit of dissolved cornstarch, or bread crumbs. Adjust the acidity with honey or sugar. Sprinkle with more pepper and serve.

Author's note: This is a fairly sour stew. The recipe recommends adding the honey to balance the taste, but I liked it just the way it was.

CAST OF CHARACTERS

*denotes historical personages

Agnolino Gaddi—a friend of Benevenuto Cellini's, who accompanies him on the misadventure in the Coliseum.

Alamanno—a servant in the Cavalieri kitchen.

Albany, Duke of—Caterina de' Medici's French uncle, the eldest brother of her mother, Madeleine de la Tour d'Auvergne.

Alessa Ramerino—eldest daughter of the Salviati kitchen's master baker, Bindo Ramerino.

Alessandro de' Medici—ostensibly Caterina's bastard half brother, but almost surely Pope Clement's illegitimate son.

Alpeno—a guardian spirit.

Alvise—a Florentine cook who joins Tommaso's staff.

Amado—an apprentice in the Ruggiero kitchen.

Ambrogio Arista (the elder)—Tommaso's father Gentile's oldest uncle, once the master carver and cook in the Ruggiero kitchen, responsible for raising and training Gentile.

Ambrogio Arista (the younger)—Tommaso's youngest brother, named after Ambrogio Arista the elder.

Andrea del Sarto—a Florentine painter.

Angelica—a young Sicilian courtesan beloved by Benevenuto Cellini.

Angelina Befanini—Tommaso Arista's great-grandmother.

Anna Maria—(Sister Anna Maria) A nun at the Murate.

Antonio Gondi—a Florentine banker and art patron.

Aquila—a mare given to Michelangelo by Ippolito de' Medici (please note that though this was an actual horse, the name is made up).

Aradia—daughter of the Goddess Diana.

Ardingo Arista—a member of the Roman Arista family. One of Galleoto Arista's grandsons.

Arnolfo—Caterina's falconer.

Ascancio Condivi—an apprentice of Michelangelo's.

Assatore—a childhood friend of Alessandro de' Medici, hired by Alessandro to assassinate Caterina de' Medici.

Averardo Fancelli—the oldest apprentice in the Salviati kitchen.

Balaan—one of the demons invoked in the Coliseum.

Bartolommeo Scappi—a renowned Italian master cook.

Beatrice Arista—Tommaso's younger sister, who died during the plague.

Beatrice the courtesan—a Sicilian prostitute, mother to the prostitute Angelica who was beloved by Benevenuto Cellini.

Belial—one of the demons invoked in the Coliseum.

Belphegor—one of the demons invoked in the Coliseum.

Benedetto—Ser Benedetto; a fellow Cellini quarreled with.

Benedetto Valenti—the Procurator-Fiscal of Rome.

Benevenuto Cellini—a famous, and infamous, goldsmith and sculptor.

Bernardina—a Roman Arista, the daughter of Galleoto.

Beroaldo—a Bengalese diver in Ippolito de' Medici's service.

Bertino—once an apprentice, now a journeyman in Il Tribolino's studio in Florence.

Bindo Ramerino—one of the two head chefs in the Salviati kitchen, in charge of all grain-based and baked foods.

Boadilla Arista—sister to Ambrogio, Galleoto and Marcantonio Arista.

Boccolino—a servant in the Cavalieri kitchen.

Caia Arista—one of Ambrogio, Galleoto and Marcantonio Arista's sisters.

Carlos V—King Charles V, King of Spain and Emperor of the Holy Roman Empire.

Caterina Cibò—a cousin of Caterina de' Medici.

Caterina de' Medici—a great-granddaughter of Lorenzo the Great, and the last direct legitimate heir from his line of the Medici family.

Cencio—a Florentine apprentice of Benevenuto Cellini's.

Cesare Borgia—the infamous Cesare Borgia.

Charles of Angoulême—King François's youngest son.

Chiara—one of Piera Befanini Arista's older sisters.

Chrystosophos—a Greek scholar and a guest of the Salviatis.

Clarice Strozzi—Caterina's aunt; her father's sister.

Claude—Queen of France, King François's first wife.

Clement VII—Pope Clement VII, illegitimate son of Lorenzo the Great's younger brother.

Constanza Sedani—Married to Ambrogio Arista, and mother of Leonora Arista. Owned a wild-game shop on the Ponte Vecchio.

Cornelia Arista—one of Ambrogio, Galleoto and Marcantonio Arista's sisters.

Cosimo Ruggiero—occultist and physician in Caterina de' Medici's service. His father is Ruggiero the Old.

Diane de Poitiers—La Grande Senechale, widow of the Grand Senechal, governess to Henri, Duke of Orleans. One of François's former mistresses.

Diomede Arista—a Roman Arista, one of Galleoto's sons.

Domenico—a Tartar in the service of Ippolito de' Medici.

Eleanor of Austria—Emperor Carlos's sister, King François's second wife.

Elissa Pecorino—the housekeeper at Il Tribolino's *bottega*, also a cousin of Leonora Arista.

Enzio—a Ruggiero man-at-arms, married to Massolina.

Etienne Romard—a French soldier, one of Tavanne's friends.

Fazio—a Salviati man-at-arms, assigned to serve Cosimo Ruggiero.

Felice Guadagni—Benevenuto Cellini's Roman goldsmith partner.

Filigno—one of Benevenuto Cellini's Roman apprentices.

Fillapella Arista—a sister of Ambrogio, Galleoto and Marcantonio Arista.

Fillipo Strozzi—Caterina de' Medici's Italian uncle, married to her Aunt Clarice.

Filomena—a half-Tartar, half-Greek slave girl once owned by the Ruggieros, now freed.

Fistolo—a demon invoked in the Coliseum.

Focolor—a demon invoked in the Coliseum.

Forneus—a demon invoked in the Coliseum.

Francesca Arista Beccacce—one of Leonora Arista's daughters.

*Francesco Ferruci—a Florentine commander and war hero, killed during
   the siege.

*Francesco Guicciardini—the aristocratic expatriate Florentine whom Clem-
   ent sent to govern Florence after the siege.

Franceschetto Arista—a Roman Arista, one of Galleoto's sons.

*François—King François I, the King of France, also referred to as His
   Most Christian Majesty.

*Frisio—a groom hired by Ippolito de' Medici to take care of the mare
   Ippolito gave Michelangelo (the person historical, the name is made
   up).

Gabriele Cavallucci—a Florentine cook who joins Tommaso's staff.

Gaio—a retainer in the papal court, a source of information for Tommaso Arista.

Galleoto Arista—the patriarch of the Roman Aristas and the original master carver and cook in Cavalieri kitchen. One of Tommaso's great-
   uncles.

*Gaspard de Saulx—a French soldier. Also known as Tavannes and Sieur
   de Tavannes.

Gattamelata—Caterina de' Medici's cat, the embodiment of the Little
   Kitchen Goddess.

Gentile Arista—master cook and carver in the Ruggiero kitchen. Tommaso's father.

Gherardo—formerly an apprentice at Il Tribolino's *bottega*, now a journeyman.

Gianmatteo Vitelli—a Florentine textile merchant and a guest at the Salviatis

Giles Gerard—a French soldier, a friend of Tavannes.

Ginevra Arista—the oldest of Tommaso's younger sisters, destroyed by
   the plague and transformed into a red gem.

Giacomo Befanini—master carver in the Medici kitchen. Angelina Befanini's
   brother.

Giorgio Vasari—a former apprentice to the painter Andrea del Sarto, now working under the patronage of Alessandro de' Medici.

Giovanni del Bande Nere—(Giovanni de' Medici) a cousin from the Pierfrancesco branch of the Medicis, married to Maria Salviati and father of Cosimo de' Medici, killed some years earlier during a military engagement.

Giovanni Gaddi—clerk of the Camera.

Gorini, Ser and Madonna—Laudomia Gorini's parents.

Grandfather Befanini—Angelina Befanini's illegitimate son, and Piera Befanini Arista's father.

Grandmother Cavallucci Befanini—Grandfather Befanini's wife.

Grazia—a servant in the Cavalieri kitchen.

Gregorio Magalotti—governor of Rome.

Guarnieri—Benevenuto Cellini's youngest Roman apprentice.

Guglielmo—a servant in the Cavalieri kitchen.

Helena Ridolfi—Sister Helena. A nun at the Murate, and one of Caterina's tutors.

Henri—Duke of Orleans, King François's second son, and Caterina de' Medici's betrothed.

Il Tribolino—Nicolo de Pericoli, a sculptor, also known as Tribolo, Tommaso Arista was once apprenticed to him.

Ilaria Arista—Galleoto Arista's wife, now deceased.

Ippolito de' Medici—the illegitimate son of Caterina de' Medici's youngest great-uncle, Giuliano, made a cardinal by Pope Clement VII to keep him from marrying Caterina.

Isabella d'Este—the Marchessa of Mantua.

Jacopo Salviati—a wealthy Florentine merchant and politician, married to Lorenzo the Great's daughter Lucrezia.

Laudomia Gorini—a scullery maid in the Salviati kitchen, Beloved by Averardo Fancelli.

Leone Strozzi—Caterina de' Medici's cousin, the second son of Clarice and Fillipo Strozzi.

Leonora Arista—the daughter of Ambrogio Arista and Constanza Sedani, owner of a wild-game shop on the Ponte Vecchio.

Lorenzo il Magnifico—Lorenzo the Great, Caterina de' Medici's great-grandfather.

Lorenzo Ruggiero—the second son of Ruggiero the Old.

Lorenzaccio de' Medici—a Medici cousin from the Pierfrancesco line, also known as Lorenzino.

Louis—a French soldier, friend of Tavannes.

Luciana Arista—Gentile and Piera Arista's youngest daughter.

Lucrezia Salviati—Caterina's great-aunt, a daughter of Lorenzo the Great and married to Jacopo Salviati and mother of Maria Salviati.

Lucrezia Tornabuoni de' Medici—Lorenzo the Great's mother.

Ludovico Arista—one of the Roman Aristas, Galleoto's oldest son and Ardingo's father.

Madame d'Etampes—King François's beautiful mistress.

Maddalena—a Befanini cousin of Tommaso Arista's.

Madeleine de la Tour d'Auvergne—Caterina de' Medici's mother.

Madonna Caterina Soderini Ginori—the pretty young wife of Signor Ginori who Alessandro de' Medici becomes attracted to.

Madonna Gondi—Caterina de' Medici's primary lady-in-waiting, married to the banker Antonio Gondi.

Madonna Ramerino—married to Bindo Ramerino.

Madonna Spada—married to Marcus Gavius Spada.

Marchetto Beccacce—Francesca's husband.

Marella—Caterina de' Medici's palfrey.

Marguerite of Navarre—King François's sister. A leading French intellectual.

Maria Salviati—Caterina de' Medici's cousin, the daughter Jacopo and Lucrezia Salviati and mother of Cosimo de' Medici.

Marcus Gavius Apicius—an ancient Roman gourmand and gourmet.

Marcus Gavius Spada—the master carver of the Salviati kitchen, named after Marcus Gavius Apicius.

Massolina—a scullery maid in the Ruggiero kitchen, married to Enzio, the

Ruggiero man-at-arms.
Meana—a guardian spirit.
Michelangelo Buonarotti—famous sculptor and painter, Tommaso's lover.

Nannina—one of Caterina de' Medici's ladies-in-waiting.

Pagolo di Arezzo—a former apprentice of Il Tribolino.
Paolo Beccacce—Francesca Arista Beccace's son.
Paulino—a Florentine apprentice of Benevenuto Cellini's.
Pier Antonio Pecci—Ippolito de' Medici's right-hand man.
Pier Giovanni—Pope Clement's chamberlain.
Piera Befanini Arista—Tommaso Arista's mother.
Piero Strozzi—one of Caterina's cousins, the oldest son of Clarice and Fillipo Strozzi.
Pietro Arista—Tommaso's younger brother, killed by the plague.
Pietro Urbino de Pistoia—Michelangelo's assistant in Rome.
Pompeo—Pope Clement VII's personal jeweler.

Rafaello da Montelupo—a Florentine sculptor.
Rastilli—(Giacomo Rastilli) the Salviatis' physician.
Razanil—a demon invoked in the Coliseum.
Réne Birago—an Italian banker, a friend of the Gondis.
Reparata—one of Caterina de' Medici's Florentine ladies-in-waiting, sibling to Sister Anna Maria, a nun at the Murate.
Rintrah—a demon invoked in the Coliseum.
Ronove—a demon invoked in the Coliseum.
Ruggiero the Old—a respected occultist, physician and mathematician in the employ of the Medici family, also the employer of the Arista family of cooks.

Salvatore—a journeyman artist in Il Tribolino's studio.
Salviati, Cardinal—a Salviati relation and an enemy of Benevenuto Cellini's.

Settrano—a guardian spirit.

Tago—a guardian spirit.
Tana—a spirit of the stars.
*Tasso—a Florentine woodcarver.
*Tavannes—also known as Gaspard de Saulx and Sieur de Tavannes, a French soldier.
Teodora—one of Leonora's daughters.
Teresa Lucrezia—(Sister Teresa Lucrezia) a nun at the Murate, in charge of the kitchens there.
*Tobia—a goldsmith rival of Benevenuto Cellini's.
Tommaso Arista—the young cook destined to become Caterina de' Medici's head chef, the protagonist of this tale.
*Tommaso Cavalieri—a young Roman aristocrat, beloved by Michelangelo.

Umberto—Tommaso Arista's Befanini cousin, who joins his cooking staff.

Valerina—a Salviati household maid.
*Valerio Vincentino—a renowned stone engraver, who carved the rock-crystal case presented to King François by Pope Clement on the occasion of Caterina's wedding.
Vanozza—one of Piera Befanini Arista's older sisters.
*Venier—the Venetian ambassador to Rome.
*Vicenzio Romoli—a friend of Benevenuto Cellini's who accompanied him on the misadventure in the Coliseum.
Vieri—one of the Salviati kitchen apprentices.
Vittoriano—the youngest apprentice in the Salviati kitchen.
Vittorio—once Il Tribolino's journeyman, now a master artist in his own right.

Zuccone—the sculptor Rafaello da Montelupo's assistant.